PENGUIN BOOKS

The Assassin

Clive Cussler is the author or co-author of a great number of international bestsellers, including the famous Dirk Pitt® Adventures, such as *Crescent Dawn*; the NUMA® Files adventures, most recently *Ghost Ship*; the *Oregon* Files, such as *The Silent Sea*; the Isaac Bell historical thrillers, which began with *The Chase*; and the recent Fargo Adventures.

Justin Scott is the author of twenty-six novels, the Ben Abbot detective series, and five modern sea thrillers under the name Paul Garrison. He lives in Connecticut.

Find out more about the world of Clive Cussler by visiting www.clivecussler.co.uk.

Also by Clive Cussler

The Assassin

CLIVE CUSSLER
and JUSTIN SCOTT

PENGUIN BOOKS

PENGUIN BOOKS

UK | USA | Canada | Ireland | Australia
India | New Zealand | South Africa

Penguin Books is part of the Penguin Random House group of companies
whose addresses can be found at global.penguinrandomhouse.com.

First published in the USA by G. P. Putnam's Sons 2015
First published in Great Britain by Michael Joseph 2015
Published in Penguin Books 2015
001

Set in 12.5/14.75 pt Garamond MT Std
Typeset by Jouve (UK), Milton Keynes
Printed in Great Britain by Clays Ltd, St Ives plc

A CIP catalogue record for this book is available from the British Library

A FORMAT ISBN: 978–1–405–93276–9

www.greenpenguin.co.uk

The Assassin

Prologue

Let 'em have it, boys!

1899
Pennsylvania

'Do I hear a train?' asked Spike Hopewell.

'Two trains,' said Bill Matters. The heavy, wet *Huff!* of the Pennsylvania Railroad's 2-8-0 freight locomotives carried for miles in the still night air. 'They're on the main line, not here.'

Spike was nervous. It made him talkative. 'You know what I keep thinking? John D. Rockefeller locked up the oil business before most people were born.'

'To hell with Rockefeller. To hell with Standard Oil.'

Bill Matters had found their Achilles' heel. After thirty years fighting the 'Standard,' thirty years of getting driven into the mud, he was finally going to break their pipe line monopoly.

Tonight. Under a sky white with stars, in a low-lying hayfield in the foothills of the Allegheny Mountains. Wooded slopes ringed the field. Pennsylvania Railroad tracks crossed it, bridging the dip in the hills on a tall timber trestle.

Spike Hopewell was going along with the scheme, against his better judgment. Bill had always been

3

susceptible to raging brainstorms that verged on delirium, and they were getting worse. Besides, when it came to driving independents out of business, John D. Rockefeller had personally invented every trick in the book.

'*Now!*' Bill drew his big old Remington six-cylinder and fired a shot in the air.

Whips cracked. Mules heaved in their harness. Freight wagons full of men and material rumbled across the field and under the train trestle – a framework of braced timbers that carried the elevated tracks above the low ground.

Pipe lines that Matters and Hopewell had already laid stopped just inside the woods at either edge of the field. The west trunk stretched two hundred miles over the Allegheny Mountains to Pennsylvania's oil fields. The east continued one hundred and eighty miles to their seaboard refinery in Constable Hook, New Jersey, where oceangoing tank steamers could load their kerosene. Pumps and breakout tanks were installed every thirty miles, and all that remained to join the two halves was this final connection on land they had purchased, under the railroad.

Spike would not shut up. 'You know what the president of the Penney said? He said, "Imagine the expense I would save on locomotives, Pullman cars and complaints if only I could melt my passengers and pump them liquefied through pipes like you pump oil."'

'I was there,' said Matters. In Philadelphia, at

4

Pennsylvania Railroad headquarters high above the Broad Street Station, asking, hat in hand, to lease a right-of-way. The president, high-toned owner of a Main Line estate, had looked down his Paris-educated nose at the oil field rowdies.

'I envy you gentlemen. I would love to own a pipe line.'

Who wouldn't? Just ask Rockefeller. Shipping crude direct from the well to the refinery beat a train hands down. Instead of laboriously loading and unloading barrels, barges and tank cars, you simply opened a valve. And that was just the beginning. A pipe line was also a storehouse; you could stockpile crude in your pipes and tanks until supply dropped and the price rose. You could lend money like a bank and charge interest on credit backed by the same oil in your pipes that the producer was paying you to deliver. Best of all – or worst of all, depending on your morals – when you owned a pipe line, you set the shipping rate to favor your friends and gouge your enemies. You could even refuse to deliver at any price, a Rockefeller specialty to bust independent refineries; Matters and Hopewell's Constable Hook refinery was sitting idle, dry as a bone, because the Standard declined to pipe them crude.

Spike laughed. 'Remember what I told him? "We'll melt your passengers in our refinery, but it's your job to make 'em solid again."'

The president of the railroad had granted Spike's

joke a thin smile and their lease a death blow: 'You can't pay me enough to let your pipe cross my tracks.'

'Why not?'

'Orders straight from the Eleventh Floor.'

In the year 1899, there was only one 'Eleventh Floor' in the United States of America – Rockefeller's office at Standard Oil's Number 26 Broadway headquarters in New York – and it packed more punch than the White House and Congress combined.

Tonight, Bill Matters was punching back.

Sixty men piled out of the wagons with picks and shovels and tongs and pipe jacks. Working by starlight, they dug a shallow trench across the field and under the trestle. Tong hands wrestled thirty-foot-long eight-inch steel pipes off the wagons, propped them on jacks over the trench, and screwed the lengths together.

The distant train sounds they had heard earlier suddenly grew loud.

Matters saw a glow in the trees and realized, too late, he had misjudged their distance. They were indeed on this branch line, not far away, but steaming slowly, quietly, one from the north, one from the south.

Ditchdiggers and tong men looked up.

Headlamps blazed. The monster H6 Baldwin 2-8-0 locomotives burst from the wooded hills and rumbled onto the trestles.

'Keep working!' shouted Bill Matters. 'We own this land. We got every right! Keep working.'

The ninety-ton engines thundered overhead and

stopped on the trestle, nose to nose, cowcatchers touching, directly above Matters and Hopewell's just-laid pipe. One was hauling a flatcar crammed with railroad cops, the other a wreck train with a hundred-ton crane. The railroad cops shoved the locomotive firemen from their furnaces, threw open the fire doors, and snaked hoses from the locomotive boilers.

A giant mounted the front of the wreck train. The glaring headlamps lit a hard, hot-tempered face and a mammoth chest and belly. Matters recognized Big Pete Straub, a towering Standard Oil strikebreaker, with a company cop star pinned to his vest, a gun on his hip, and a pick handle in his fist.

'Drop your tools!' Straub shouted down at the men in the field.

'Stand your ground!' yelled Matters. 'Back to work.'

'Run!' roared Straub.

'Law's on our side. We got every right!'

'*Let 'em have it, boys!*'

The railroad cops scooped burning coals from the furnaces and whirled opened steam valves. Fire and boiling water rained down on Matters' workmen.

'Stand your ground!'

Burned and scalded, they fled.

Matters intercepted the stampede and waded in with both fists, knocking men down as they tried to get away.

Spike grabbed his arm. 'Ease off, Bill. Let 'em go. They're outgunned.'

Matters smashed a ditchdigger's ribs and knocked another man cold with a single blow. 'Cowards!'

A burning coal sailed down from the starry sky trailing sparks.

It set Matters' coat sleeve on fire. Hot coals fanned his cheek. The stink of singed hair seared his nostrils. He jerked his Remington from his coat, ran straight at the trestle, and climbed the pier.

Spike charged back into the battle zone and grabbed his boot. 'Are you nuts? Where you going?'

'Kill Straub.'

'He's got twenty years on you and fifty armed men. Run!'

Spike Hopewell outweighed Bill Matters. He dragged him off the trestle.

Fire and steam drove them out of range. Bill Matters aimed his horse pistol at Straub. Spike knocked it out of his hand, snatched it from the mud, and tucked it in his coat.

Matters watched with helpless fury. The hundred-ton crane lowered an excavator bucket. Its jutting spike teeth bit into the freshly dug soil like the jaws of *Tyrannosaurus rex*. Steam hissed. The jaws crushed shut. The crane clawed pipes out of the ground and dropped them in a welter of bent and broken metal.

A pair of dim lights bounced slowly across the starlit field. The county sheriff pulled up in a Pittsburgh gasoline runabout. A scared-looking deputy was seated beside him.

Bill Matters and Spike Hopewell demanded protection for their workmen. Matters shouted that they had a legal right to route an independent pipe line under the railroad's right-of-way because they had bought this low-lying farm where the elevated tracks crossed on tall trestles.

'The railroad can't block us! We own this land free and clear.'

Here was their deed.

Matters shook the parchment in the dim glow of the runabout's headlamp.

The sheriff glanced down from his steering tiller. He answered too quickly, like a man who had been ordered to read a copy days ago. 'Says on your deed that the Pennsylvania Railroad leased their right-of-way across this farm.'

'Only for track and trestles.'

'Lease says you mustn't damage their roadbed.'

'We're not hurting their road. We're trenching *between* the trestle piers.'

Matters shoved more paper into the light. See their engineer's report! See their attorney's brief asserting their case! See this court case precedent!

'I'm no lawyer,' said the sheriff, 'but everybody knows that Mr Rockefeller has a mighty big say in how they run the Pennsylvania Railroad.'

'But we own –'

The sheriff laughed. 'What made you think you can fight Standard Oil?'

*

A coal-black Pittsburgh sky mirrored Bill Matters' despair.

'Business is business,' his banker was droning. Mortgaged to the hilt to build a pipe line they could not finish, they had to sell for pennies on the dollar to Standard Oil. 'No one else will make an offer. My advice is to accept theirs and walk away clean.'

'They tricked us into building it for them,' Matters whispered.

'What about the Hook?' asked Spike.

'Constable Hook?' asked the banker. 'Part of the package.'

'It is the most modern refinery in the world,' said Matters.

'There's no deal without the refinery. I believe Standard Oil intends to expand it.'

'It's made to grow. We bought the entire hill and every foot of waterfront.'

'The Standard wants it.'

'At least we won't owe much,' said Spike.

'We planted,' said Matters. 'They'll reap.'

The banker's voice tube whistled. He put it by his ear. He jumped to his feet. 'Mr Comstock is here.'

The door flew open. In strode white-haired Averell Comstock, one of John D. Rockefeller's first partners from back in their Cleveland refinery days. Comstock was a member of the trust's innermost circle, the privileged few that the newspapers called the Standard Oil Gang.

'Excuse us,' he said to the banker.

Without a word, the man scuttled from his office.

'Mr Rockefeller has asked me to invite you gentlemen to join the company.'

'What?' said Spike Hopewell. He looked incredulously at Matters.

Comstock said, 'It is Mr Rockefeller's wish that you start as co-directors of the Pipe Line Committee.'

Matters turned pale with anger. His hands trembled. He clenched them into fists and still they shook. 'Managing the pipe line monopoly we tried to beat? Bankrupting wildcatter drillers? Busting independent refiners out of business?'

The tall, vigorous Comstock returned a steely gaze. 'Standard Oil wastes *nothing*. We make full use of every resource, including — especially including — smart, ambitious, hard-driving oil men. Are you with us?'

'I'd join Satan first,' said Spike Hopewell.

He jammed his hat on his head and barreled out the door. 'Let's go, Bill. We'll start fresh in Kansas. Wildcat the new fields before the octopus wraps its arms around them, too.'

Bill Matters went home to Oil City, Pennsylvania.

His modest three-storey mansion stood on a tree-lined street cheek by jowl with similar stuccoed and shingled houses built by independents like him who had prospered in the early 'oil fever' years before the Standard clamped down. The rolltop desk he used for an office shared the back parlor with his daughters' books and toy theaters.

The paper models of London and New York stage sets that the girls had preferred to dollhouses occupied every flat surface. Rendered in brightly colored miniature, Juliet loved Romeo from her balcony. Hamlet walked the parapet with his father's ghost. Richard III handed the death warrant to murderers.

Nellie and Edna found him there with tears in his eyes. He was cradling the Remington he had bought from a Civil War vet. The 'faithful friend' had won shoot-outs with teamsters who had gathered in mobs at night to smash his first pipe line – a four-miler to Oil Creek – that put their wagons out of business.

The two young women acted as one.

Nellie threw her arms around him and planted a kiss on his cheek. Edna wrested the gun from his hands. He did not resist. He would die himself before he let harm come to either of them. Edna, his adopted stepdaughter, a cub reporter for the *Oil City Derrick* who had just graduated from Allegheny College, was the quiet one. The younger, outgoing Nellie usually did the talking. She did now, cloaking urgency with good-humored teasing.

'Whom do you intend to shoot, Father?' she joshed in a strong voice. 'Do burglars lurk?'

'I came so close,' he muttered. 'So close.'

'You'll do better next time.'

Matters lifted his head from his hands and raised his

gaze to the clear-eyed, slender young women. The half sisters looked nearly alike, having inherited their mother's silky chestnut hair and strong, regular features, but there the similarity ended. One was an open book. One a vault of secrets.

'Do you know what Rockefeller did?' he asked.

'If he drowned in the river, they'd find his body upstream,' said Edna. 'JDR is the master of the unexpected.'

'I wish he would drown in the river,' said Nellie.

'So do I,' said Matters. 'More than ever.' He told them about Rockefeller's invitation to join Standard Oil. 'Head of the Pipe Line Committee, no less.'

Nellie and Edna looked at the pistol that Edna was still holding, then locked eyes. They were terrified he would kill himself. But would giving up his lifelong fight for independence kill him, too? Only more slowly.

'Maybe you should take it,' said Nellie.

'Father is better than that,' said Edna.

His glistening eyes flickered from their faces to the toy theaters and settled on the gun. Edna drew it closer to her body. A queer smile crossed Matters' grim face. 'Maybe I could be better than that.'

'You are,' they chorused. 'You are.'

Their helpless expressions tore him to pieces. 'Go,' he said. 'Leave me. Keep the gun. Ease your silly minds.'

'Are you sure you'll be all right?'

'Give me until morning to get used to getting beat.'

He ushered them out and closed the door. Wild thoughts were racing through his mind. He could not sit still. *Father is better than that?*

He prowled his office. Now and then he paused to peer into the toy theaters. Twice a year he would take the girls on the train to plays in New York. And after the Oil City skating rink was converted to an opera house, they attended every touring company that performed. Shakespeare was their favorite. Romeo loving Juliet. Hamlet promising his father's ghost revenge. Richard III instructing his henchmen. Secret promises. Secret revenge. Secret plots.

Could he bow his head and accept Rockefeller's invitation to join the trust?

Or could he *pretend* to bow his head?

What do you say, Hamlet? Make up your mind. Do you want revenge? Or do you want more? A tenth of Standard Oil's colossal profits would make him one of the richest men in America. So what? How many meals could a man eat? In how many beds could he sleep?

A tenth of the Standard's *power* would crown a king.

What do you say, Richard? How many plots have you laid? What secret mischief?

Even Richard was surprised how blind his enemies were.

Matters calculated the odds by listing his enemy's weaknesses.

The all-powerful monopoly was like a crack team of strong horses. But seen through Bill Matters' clear and bitter eye, those horses were blinkered, hobbled, and hunted: hobbled by fear of change; hunted by government prosecutors and Progressive reformers determined to break their monopoly; blinded by Standard Oil's obsession with secrecy.

Could they be done in like Romeo and Juliet by the confusion of secrets?

The Standard's systemized secrecy, the secret trusts and hidden subsidiaries that shielded the corporation from public scrutiny, bred intrigue. On the occasions he'd been summoned to the Standard's offices, he had never been allowed to see another visitor. Who knew what private deals were struck in the next room?

Richard was the man to beat the Standard, the plotter of 'secret mischiefs.'

But where were his henchmen? Who would help him? Who could he count on? Spike wouldn't be worth a damn. His old partner was a two-fisted brawler, but no conspirator, and too sunny a soul to kill when killing entered the plot. He needed henchmen with hearts of ice.

BOOK ONE
Bullets
Six Years Later, Kansas

No caress was gentler than the assassin's finger on the trigger

I

A tall man in a white suit, with a handsome head of golden hair, an abundant moustache and fierce blue eyes, stepped off an extra-fare limited at Union Depot and hurried forward to collect his Locomobile from the express car. He traded jokes with the railroad freight handlers easing the big red auto down the ramp, lamented Kansas City's loss of first baseman Grady to the St Louis Cardinals, and tipped generously when the job was done.

Could they recommend a fast route to Standard Oil's Sugar Creek refinery?

Following their directions, he drove out of the run-down, saloon-lined station district, when two wagons suddenly boxed him into a narrow street. The men who jumped off were dressed more like prizefighters than teamsters. A broad-shouldered giant swaggered up, and he recognized Big Pete Straub, whom he had seen board the train at St Louis.

Straub flashed a badge.

'Standard Oil Refinery Police. You Isaac Bell?'

Bell stood down from his auto. He was as tall as Straub, well over six feet, but lean as wire rope on a one-hundred-and-seventy-five-pound frame. A head held high and a self-contained gaze signified life at full tide.

Straub guessed his age at around thirty. 'Go back where you came from.'

'Why?' Bell asked nonchalantly.

'There's nothing for you in Kansas. We'll fire any man who talks to you, and they know it.'

Bell said, 'Move your wagon.'

A haymaker punch flew at his face.

He slipped it over his shoulder, stepped in to sink left and right fists deep, and stepped back as quickly. The company cop doubled over.

'*Get him!*' Straub's men charged.

An automatic pistol with a cavernous muzzle filled Bell's hand, sudden as a thunderbolt. 'Move your wagon.'

They sold gasoline in the freight yards. A hardware store supplied spare tubes and tires, a towrope, cans for water, motor oil and extra gasoline, a bedroll, and a lever-action Winchester repeating rifle in a scabbard, which Bell buckled to the empty seat beside him.

He stopped at a butcher to buy a beefsteak to grill on an open fire when he camped for the night, and a slab of ham, coffee beans, and bread for breakfast in the morning. Downtown Kansas City was jammed with trolleys, wagons and carriages and fleets of brand-new steam, electric and gasoline autos. Finally clearing the traffic at the edge of the suburbs, he headed south and west, crossed the state line into Kansas, opened the Locomobile's throttle and exhaust pipe cutouts, and thundered on to the prairie.

2

No caress was gentler, no kiss softer, than the assassin's finger on the trigger.

Machined by a master gunsmith to silken balance, the Savage 99 lever-action rifle would reward such a delicate union of flesh and steel with deadly precision. Pressure as light as a shallow breath would fire the custom-loaded, high-velocity smokeless powder round that waited in the chamber. The telescope sight was the finest Warner & Swasey instrument that money could buy. Spike Hopewell appeared near and large.

Spike was pacing the cornice atop an eighty-foot oil derrick that stood on the edge of a crowd of a hundred rigs operated by independent wildcat drillers. They towered over the remnants of a small hamlet at a remote Kansas crossroads forty miles north of Indian Territory. Since he had struck oil, a horde of newcomers seeking their fortunes had renamed the place Hopewell Field.

Houses, stables, picket fences and headstones in the churchyard were stained brown from spouters that had flung oil to the winds. Crude storage tanks, iron-sided, wood-topped affairs eighty feet wide and twenty high, were filled to the brim. Pipes linked the tanks to a modern refinery where two-hundred-barrel stills sat on brick furnaces in thickets of condensing pipe. Their chimneys lofted columns of smoke into the sky.

A boomtown of shacks and shanties had sprung up next door to feed and entertain the oil workers, who nicknamed it Hope-Hell. They slept in a 'rag town' of tents. Saloons defied the Kansas prohibition laws just as in Wichita and Kansas City. Housed in old boxcars, they were not as likely to be attacked by Carrie Nation swinging her hatchet. Behind the saloons, red brakeman's lanterns advertised brothels.

Railroad tracks skirted the bustling complex. But the nearest town with a passenger station was ten miles away. Investors were selling stock to build an electric trolley.

The refinery reeked of gasoline.

The assassin could smell it seven hundred yards away.

A red Locomobile blazed across the Kansas plain, bright as fire and pluming dust.

Spike Hopewell saw it coming and broke into a broad smile despite his troubles. The auto and the speed fiend driving like a whirlwind were vivid proof that gasoline – once a notorious refining impurity that exploded kerosene lamps in people's faces – was the fuel of the future.

His brand-new refinery was making oceans of the

stuff, boiling sixteen gallons of gasoline off every barrel of Kansas crude. Fifty thousand gallons and just getting started. If only he could ship it to market.

The assassin waited for a breath of wind to clear the smoke.

You could not ignore wind at long range. You had to calculate exactly how much it would deflect a bullet and you had to refine your calculations as impetus slowed and gravity took its toll. But you couldn't shoot what you couldn't see. The old oil man was a murky presence in the telescope sight, obscured by the smoke that rose thick and black from a hundred engine boilers and refinery furnaces.

Hopewell stopped pacing, planted his hands on the railing, and stared intently.

A breeze stirred. The smoke thinned.

His head crystallized in the powerful glass.

Schooled in anatomy, the assassin pictured bone and connecting fibers of tendon and muscle and nerve under his target's skin. The brain stem was an inch wide. To sever it was to drop a man instantly.

Spike Hopewell moved abruptly. He turned toward the ladder that rose from the derrick floor. The assassin switched to binoculars to inspect the intruder in their wider field of vision.

A man in a white suit cleared the top rung and bounded on to the cornice. The assassin recognized the lithe, supple-yet-contained fluid grace that could only belong to another predator – a deadly peer – and every nerve jumped to high alert.

Instinct, logic and horse sense were in perfect agreement. *Shoot the threat first.*

Reckless pride revolted. *No one* – no one! – *interferes with my kill. I shoot who I want, when I want.*

Isaac Bell vaulted from the ladder, landed lightly on the derrick cornice, and introduced himself to Spike Hopewell with an engaging smile and a powerful hand.

'Bell. Van Dorn Detective Agency.'

Spike grinned. 'Detecting incognito in a red Locomobile? Thought you were the fire department.'

Isaac Bell took an instant liking to the vigorous independent, by all reports a man as openhearted as he was combative. With a knowing glance at the source of Spike's troubles – a mammoth gasoline storage tank on the far side of the refinery, eighty feet wide and twenty high – Bell answered with a straight face.

'Having "detected" that you're awash in gasoline, I traded my horse for an auto.'

Hopewell laughed. 'You got me there. Biggest glut since the auto was invented . . . Whatcha doing here, son? What do you want?'

Bell said, 'The government's Corporations Commission is investigating Standard Oil for violating the Sherman Anti-Trust Act.'

'Do tell,' said Hopewell, his manner cooling.

'The commission hired the Van Dorn Agency to gather evidence of the Standard busting up rivals' businesses.'

'What's that got to do with me?'

'Fifty thousand gallons of gasoline you can't ship to market is the sort of evidence I'm looking for.'

'It's sitting there in that tank. Look all you want.'

'Can you tell me how your glut filled it?'

'Nope. And I won't testify either.'

Isaac Bell had expected resistance. Hopewell had a reputation for being tough as a gamecock and scrappy as a one-eyed tom. But the success of the Van Dorn investigation hinged on persuading the independent to talk, both in confidence and in public testimony. Few oil men alive had more experience fighting the monopoly.

Age hadn't slowed him a bit. Instead of cashing in and retiring when he struck enormous oil finds in Kansas, Spike Hopewell had built a modern refinery next to the fields to process crude oil for his fellow independent drillers. Now he was in the fight of his life, laying a tidewater pipe line to ship their gasoline and kerosene to tank steamers at Port Arthur, Texas.

Standard Oil was fighting just as hard to stop him.

'Won't testify? The Standard flooded the courts with lawyers to block your line to the Gulf of Mexico.'

Spike was no slouch in the influence department. 'I'm fighting 'em in the State House. The lawmakers in Topeka know darned well that Kansas producers and

Kansas refineries are dead unless I can ship their product to European markets that Standard Oil don't control.'

'Is that why the railroad untied your siding?'

There were no tank cars on the refinery siding. A forlorn-looking 0-6-0 switch engine had steam up, but it had nowhere to go and nothing to do except shuttle material around the refinery. A quarter mile of grass and sagebrush separated Hopewell's tracks from the main line to Kansas City. The roadbed was graded, and gravel ballast laid, and telegraph wire strung. But the connecting spur for the carloads of material to build the refinery had been uprooted. Switches, rails and crossties were scattered on the ground as if angry giants had kicked it to pieces.

Hopewell said, 'My lawyers just got an injunction ordering the railroad to hook me up again.'

'You won a hollow victory. Standard Oil tied up every railroad tank car in the region. The commission wants to know how.'

'Tell 'em to take it up with the railroad.'

A wintery light grayed the detective's eyes. His smile grew cool. Pussyfooting was getting him nowhere. 'Other Van Dorn operatives are working on the railroad. *My* particular interest is how the Standard is blocking your tidewater pipe line.'

'I told you, son, I ain't testifying.'

'With no pipe line,' Bell shot back, 'and no railroad to transport your products to market, your wells and refinery are worthless. Everything you built here will be forced to the wall.'

'I've been bankrupt before – before you were born, sonny – but this time, I just might have another trick up my sleeve.'

'If you're afraid,' Bell said, 'the Van Dorn Agency will protect you.'

Spike's manner softened slightly. 'I appreciate that, Mr Bell. And I don't doubt you can give an account of yourself.' He nodded down at the Locomobile eighty feet below. 'That you think to pack a towrope to cross open country tells me you're a capable hand.'

'And enough extra parts to build a new one to pull the old one out of a ditch,' Bell smiled back, thinking they were getting somewhere at last.

'But you underestimate Standard Oil. They don't murder the competition.'

'You underestimate the danger.'

'They don't have to kill us. You yourself just said it. They've got lobbyists to trip us up in the legislature and lawyers to crush us in court.'

'Do you know Big Pete Straub?' Bell asked, watching for Hopewell's reaction.

'Pete Straub is employed by Standard Oil's industrial service firm. That's their fancy name for refinery cops, strikebreakers and labour spies. He smashed my pipe line back in Pennsylvania.'

'I bumped into Straub only yesterday in Kansas City.'

The older man shrugged, as if monumentally unconcerned. 'Standard Oil has no monopoly on private cops and strikebreakers. You'll find Big Pete's bulldozing union labor in coal mines, railroads and steel mills. For all you know, he's on his way to Colorado to bust up the miners' union. Heck, Rockefeller owns half the mines out there.'

'He's not in Colorado. He's in Kansas. Last time Straub visited Kansas, independent refiners bucking the Standard turned up dead in Fort Scott and Coffeyville.'

'Accidents,' Spike Hopewell scoffed. 'Reed Riggs fell under a locomotive – drunk, if he held to pattern – and poor Albert Hill was repairing an agitator when he tumbled into a tank.' Hopewell shot Bell a challenging look. 'You know what an agitator is, Mr Detective?'

'The agitator treats crude gasoline distillate with sulfuric acid, washes away the acid with water, neutralizes it with caustic soda, and separates the water.'

Hopewell nodded. 'You've done your homework. In that case, you know that the fumes'll make you light-headed if you're not careful. Albert tended not to be.'

'I'm not one hundred per cent sure both were accidents.'

'I'm sure,' Hopewell fired back.

Bell turned on him suddenly. 'If you're not afraid, why won't you testify?'

28

Hopewell folded his ample arms across his chest. 'Tattling goes against my grain.'

'*Tattling?* Come on, Spike, we're not schoolboys. Your work's at grave risk, everything you built, and maybe even your life.'

'It'll take your commission years, if ever, to change a damned thing,' Spike retorted. 'But folks in Kansas are itching for a fight right now. We'll beat the Standard in the State House – outlaw rebates and guarantee equal shipping rates for all. And if the Standard don't like it, Kansas will build its own refinery – or, better yet,' he added with a loud laugh, 'buy this one from me so I can focus my thoughts on my pipe line.'

Isaac Bell heard a false note in that laugh. Spike Hopewell was not as sure of himself as he boasted.

Could you snipe a man in the neck at seven hundred yards?

Ask the winner of the gold medal for the President's Match of 1902.

Could you even *see* him a third of a mile away?

Read the commendatory letter signed by Theodore Roosevelt in which TR, the hero of San Juan Hill, saluted the sharpshooter who won the President's Match for the Military Rifle Championship of the United States.

Doubt me?

Read about bull's-eyes riddled at a *thousand* yards.

Did President Roosevelt shout *Bully!* the assassin smiled, when the champion took 'French leave'?

But who'd have had the nerve to tell Teddy that the deadliest sniper in the Army deserted his regiment?

'Mr Hopewell,' said Isaac Bell, 'if I can't persuade you to do the right thing by your fellow independents, would you at least answer some questions about one of your former partners?'

'Bill Matters.'

'How did you know I meant Matters? You've had many partners, wildcat drilling partners, pipe line partners, refinery partners.' Bell named three.

Hopewell answered slowly and deliberately as if addressing a backward child. 'The commission that hired your detective agency is investigating Standard Oil. Bill took up with the Standard. He sits to lunch with their executive committee in New York. Lunch – Mr Anti-Trust Corporations Commission Detective – is where they hatch their schemes.'

Bell nodded, encouraging Hopewell to keep talking now that he had gotten him wound up. His investigation so far had been a study in how the giant corporation fired imaginations and spawned fantasies. Standard Oil had been at the top of the heap since before most people were born. It seemed natural that the trust would possess mystical powers.

'Were you surprised?'

'Not when I thought about it. The Standard spots value. Oil, land, machinery, men. They pay for the best. Bill Matters was the best.'

'I meant were you surprised when Bill Matters changed sides?'

Spike Hopewell raised his eyes to look Bell straight in the face. Then he surprised the detective by speaking softly, with emotion. 'You spouted the names of a few of my partners. But Bill and I were different. We started together. We fought men, shoulder to shoulder, and we beat 'em. Teamsters that made grizzlies look gentle. We beat them. We thought so alike, we knew ahead of time what the other was thinking. So when you ask was I surprised Bill went with the Standard, my answer is, I was until I thought it over. You see, Bill was never the same after he lost his boy.'

'I don't understand,' said Bell. 'What boy? I'm told he has daughters.'

'The poor little squirt ran off. Bill never heard from him again.'

'Why did you say "poor little squirt". An unhappy child?'

'No, no, no. Smiley, laughy little fellow I never thought was unhappy. But all of a sudden – *poof* – he was gone. Bill never got over it.'

'When did he leave?'

'Must be seven or eight years ago.'

'Before Bill joined the Standard?'

'Long before. Looking back, I realize that the boy running off broke him. He was never the same. Harder. Hard as adamantine – not that either of us was choirboys. Choirboys don't last in the oil business. But somewhere along the line, Bill got his moral trolley wires crossed and –'

Hopewell stopped abruptly. He stared past Bell at the gasoline storage tank. His jaw worked. He seemed, Bell thought, to be reconsidering.

'But if you want to understand the oil business, Mr Detective, you better understand that Bill Matters was not the first to give in to Standard Oil. Half the men in their New York office were destroyed by Rockefeller before he hired them. John D. Rockefeller, he's the devil you should be after.'

'What if I told you I suspect that one of those newer men like Bill Matters can lead me to him?'

'I'd tell you that no man in his right mind would bite the hand feeding him like he's feeding Bill.'

'Would *you* have switched sides if the Standard asked?'

The oil man drew himself erect and glared at Isaac Bell. 'They did ask. Asked me the same time they asked Bill.'

'Obviously you declined. Did you consider it?'

'I told them to go to blazes.'

Bell asked, 'Can't you see that I'm offering you an opportunity to help send them there?'

He pointed down at the orderly rows of tanks and the belching furnaces, then across the forest of derricks looming over the roofs of what must have been a peaceful town. A gust of wind swept the smoke aside.

Suddenly he could see clear to the farthest of the wooden towers.

'You built your refinery to serve independents. That's where your heart lies. Wouldn't you agree, sir, that you owe it to all independent oil men to testify?'

Hopewell shook his head.

Bell had one card left. He bet the ranch on it. 'How much did the Standard pay for a barrel of crude when you drilled two years ago?'

'A dollar thirty-five a barrel.'

'How much are they paying now? Provided you could deliver it.'

'Seventy cents a barrel.'

'They raised the price artificially high, nearly doubled it, to encourage you to drill. You and your fellow wildcatters did the Standard's exploratory work for them, at your own expense. Thanks to your drilling, they know the extent of the Kansas fields and how they stack up against the Indian Territory and Oklahoma fields. They suckered you, Mr Hopewell.'

'More homework, Mr Bell?' said Spike Hopewell. 'Is that the Van Dorn Detective motto: "Do your homework"?'

'The Van Dorn motto is "We never give up! Never!"'

Hopewell grinned. 'That's my motto, too . . . Well, it's hard to say no to a man who's done his homework. And damned-near impossible to a man who won't give up . . . OK, put 'er there!'

Spike Hopewell thrust a powerful hand into Bell's. 'What do you want to know first?'

Bell stepped closer to take it, saying, 'I'm mighty curious about those tricks up your sleeve.'

Hopewell stumbled backward, clutching his throat.

3

Still gripping the hand that Hopewell had extended, Isaac Bell heard a muted gunshot and realized that the sound was delayed by the time it took a bullet to fly an enormous distance. He pulled Spike down on the cornice's narrow plank floor, behind the partial shelter of the railings. But it was too late to protect him. The oil man was dead. A slug had pierced his throat and torn out the back of his neck.

A second slug passed through the space that Bell's own head had occupied a half a heartbeat earlier. It twanged against the steel crown pulley, ricocheted, and splintered oak. Bell looked for the source. The shot echoed crazily. It seemed to come from the west, where a plain riddled with gullies drained toward a creek. On the far side of the creek, low, wooded hills stretched to the horizon. He spotted a flicker of motion to the north. A figure was climbing down a derrick at an astonishing seven hundred yards' distance.

Isaac Bell plunged three rungs at a time down the ladder.

His Locomobile was parked between the slanting legs of the derrick and the engine house. Still hot, the motor fired on the second spin. He leaped behind the steering wheel and thundered off in the direction the shot had come from, weaving a wild path through the densely packed oil derricks and skidding around drill machinery, pump houses, engines and machine shops. When he burst out of the last row of derricks, he saw a big man on horseback galloping across the open plain that stretched beyond the oil field.

Bell raced after him.

The fleeing rider was well mounted on a strong, big-boned animal of fully seventeen hands. Bell shoved his accelerator to the floorboards and wrenched his steering wheel side to side as he plowed his big auto over rough ground, slewing around hummocks and dodging gullies.

Ahead of the horseman, the grassland ended abruptly at a thick wood. If he got inside the trees, he was free. Bell drove faster. The deep cut of the creek bed separated the grassland from the trees. Bell exulted; he had him trapped.

He yanked open his exhaust bypass for maximum power. Unimpeded by back pressure, the Locomobile's four cylinders roared with all their might.

The horseman galloped straight at the creek and dug his spurs in. The horse gathered its legs and jumped. Its forelegs struck the far bank. Its left rear hoof slipped down the earthen wall of the creek. The right hoof dug into the grass, and the animal scrambled free and galloped for the trees.

Isaac Bell was forced to slam on the Locomobile's

anemic brakes and slide the auto into a sideways drift to stop before it tumbled into the creek. He yanked his Winchester from its scabbard buckled to the passenger seat. The horseman was already inside the woods, partially screened by the thinly scattered outer fringe of trees. Bell saw one chance and opened fire.

He worked the Winchester's ejection lever in a blur of motion. Had a cartridge jammed, the pivoting lever would have snapped in his hands. The heavy rifle boomed repeatedly. The horseman's hat flew in the air. He swayed and started to fall off. A flailing hand gripped his saddle horn and he stayed on his mount. Before Bell could fire again, horse and rider found the shelter deep inside the woods.

Bell heard a loud report behind him. Another gunman? It seemed to come from the oil derricks. It was followed immediately by a metallic clanging noise like a blacksmith's hammer. Then he heard a sharp retort like a blasting cap or a quarter stick of dynamite.

A blinding light flashed from the refinery.

A hollow *Boom!* shook the air. The explosion blew the top off a crude oil tank that stood in the outermost ring of tanks. Shattered planking tufted into the sky. Black smoke pillared. The first explosion, Bell surmised, had ignited the natural gas that rose from the crude oil and collected in the top of the tanks. The gas explosion had set the oil itself to burning.

That it threatened to destroy Spike Hopewell's entire

refinery was evidenced by the sight of gangs of oil workers arriving on the run with shovels and picks to dig a trench between the burning tank and its neighbors. They converged from the derricks and the refinery, the rag town and the saloons. A gang rolled out a cannon on a two-wheeled gun carriage.

A field gun would be a baffling sight had not Bell studied the oil business from top to bottom to prepare for the Corporations Commission investigation. Regular procedure for fighting an oil tank fire was to shoot holes in the tank below the liquid line to drain the oil that fed the fire. Artillery allowed the firefighters to stay outside the lethal range of explosions.

One of the gun carriage wheels slipped into a shallow gully and sunk axle-deep in the wet, spongy ground. Bell raced to help, driving the Locomobile across the prairie ground as fast as the clumped grass would allow. He could see at the base of the roiling smoke column a diamond-bright core of flame growing wider, taller and brighter.

Bell heaved his steering wheel hard left and drove as close as he dared alongside the cannon while keeping his own wheels on firm ground. He threw the towrope he kept coiled around the spare tires. The gun crew tied on to the carriage trail. Bell accelerated the powerful auto and dragged the cannon out of the gully. Plowing ahead slowly enough to let the men guiding it run alongside, he pulled it into a position that gave them a clear shot at the burning tank.

The intense heat was making the crude oil boil and foam into a maelstrom of red flame, white steam and black smoke. Already the heat was too intense for the ditching gang. The men backed away. Suddenly the boiling, foaming oil tank exploded. Tentacles of liquid flame shot into the sky and cascaded to the ground, falling on neighboring tanks.

The firefighters dropped their shovels and ran. They barely escaped. Two more explosions in quick time sent lids flying. Two more tanks gushed geysers of flame that fountained skyward and collapsed on tanks as yet unscathed. An explosion breached the wall of a tank. Oil spilled, tumbling over the ground, across ditches, and splashing against a burning shack, leveling the flimsy wooden structure, and igniting.

The fires spread, gaining speed.

The flames leaped the outer ditch around the refinery. Several buildings erupted into flame, and soon the fire was slithering past the refinery toward the biggest holding tank in Kansas, which Spike Hopewell had built to store his glut of gasoline.

The cannon crew exchanged frightened looks.

'Shoot!' said Isaac Bell. 'On the jump!'

More frightened looks. Most scattered, leaving Bell with three brave men: an independent wildcatter sporting a boss's knee-high riding boots and watch chain, a gray-bearded Civil War vet in a forage cap, and a young farmer in a battered slouch hat.

'Can't shoot gasoline,' said the wildcatter.

'Too volatile,' said the vet. 'It'll blow that tank like a nitro shot. Kill everyone within a mile.'

'But if the cannon doesn't set it off,' said Bell, 'the fire will.'

He thought fast and pointed at the 0-6-0 switch engine idling on the refinery siding. 'Who can run that locomotive?'

'Me,' said the bearded old soldier.

'Steam it to this end of the siding close as you can to the tank.'

Bell pointed at a giant spool of drilling cable. The other two understood his plan immediately. Terrified expressions on their smoke-grimed faces said they didn't like it.

'It's our only chance,' said Bell.

The spool was six feet high. They extracted the loose end of the cable from the coil, put their shoulders to the spool, and commenced rolling it to uncoil the cable. Men watching saw what they were up to and came to help.

A rigger ran up with a monkey wrench and a sack of cable clamps, nuts and bolts. 'You boys must be loco,' he shouted over the roar of fire. 'Guess I'll join the crowd.' He bent the loose end of the cable into a loop, clamped it together and dragged it toward the locomotive, while Isaac Bell and the others dragged their end to the gasoline tank.

Tanks were burning behind them and to either side. Columns of smoke rose from the incinerated crude, swirling like tornadoes. They climbed swiftly, joined high overhead, and turned the sky black.

Pursued by the fire, Bell and his helpers pulled the cable to the foot of the gasoline tank. It was as high as a three-storey house. A ladder led up its iron side. Bell slung the loop over his shoulder and climbed. The men below pushed the stiff cable up, trying to relieve him of some of the weight. He was breathing hard when he reached the top and swung on to the wooden roof. The farmer followed close behind carrying a crowbar and an axe.

'Can you run get me that monkey wrench?'

'What are you going to do?'

'Chop a hole in the roof,' said Bell, swinging the axe with all his might. 'Run,' he said again. 'In case I throw sparks.'

The fires were advancing quickly. Another oil tank exploded and thick burning crude flew through the air. With very little time to pierce the roof, he thanked his lucky stars for the Northwest timber case when he'd masqueraded as a lumberjack. Tar, wood chips and splinters flew.

He chopped open a hole at the edge of the roof, just inside the iron wall. The fumes that suddenly vented were almost overwhelming. His head spun. The farmer came up the ladder again, gasping for wind. He passed Bell the monkey wrench.

'What's it for?'

'Anchor,' said Bell, fastening the wrench's jaws firmly around the cable. 'Run while you can.'

He shoved the wrench and the cable loop through the hole and wedged it tightly with the crowbar and the axe. Then he signaled the Civil War vet, dropped down the ladder as fast as he could, and ran toward him.

A space of about two football fields separated the gasoline tank from the switch engine, which backed away, drawing the slack out of the drilling cable. When it was tight at a long, shallow angle between the top of the tank and the siding, Bell swung aboard the engine. 'I'll take her.'

'Welcome to it.'

Bell put his hands on the throttle and quadrant, admitted steam to the cylinders, and backed away smoothly. 'Nice and easy, now.'

'Fine touch,' said the vet. 'Where'd you learn it?'

Bell eyed the cable, which was tightening like a bowstring. 'Borrowed a locomotive when I was in college.'

The drilling cable was strong enough to do the job. And the switch engine had the power. But would his makeshift anchor hold fast to the tank's iron wall?

More steam. Bell peered through the smoke. Was the wall bulging or was that wishful thinking?

'Where'd you take the locomotive?'

'Miss Porter's.'

'Girls' school?'

'Young ladies.'

A little more steam. It looked like a bulge.

Suddenly the cable flew high in the air.

'The wire busted!' yelled the vet.

42

'No,' said Bell, 'the wall.'

A section of the tank's iron wall, a panel six feet wide, popped a row of rivets, peeled open like a sardine can, and bent toward the ground. Gasoline cascaded.

Isaac Bell held his breath.

One of two things would happen now and it was even money which.

With luck, the escaping gasoline would drown the sparks struck by clashing metal.

But if it didn't – if the river pushed volatile gas fumes ahead of it – the sparks would detonate the fumes and blow the refinery, the oil field, the hamlet of wooden houses, the boomtown's shacks and the rag town's tents to the other side of Kingdom Come.

4

A fifty-thousand-gallon river of gasoline surged through the hole Isaac Bell had ripped in the tank and spilled on to the ground. It flooded down the shallow slope that surrounded the tank and spread in a billowing torrent of rapids and whirlpools.

'Run!' said Bell and led the way.

That they were still alive meant he had prevented a catastrophic explosion. But there was no stopping the fire – not with globs of burning crude oil from the exploding oil tanks falling like brimstone. At least, he hoped, people had a chance to escape.

The gasoline ignited within seconds. It burned fiercely, tumbling great rollers of flame across the prairie. The rollers poured into the gullies and filled them with fingers of fire that raced toward the distant creek and set it ablaze.

Herding men ahead of it, plucking the fallen to their feet, Bell spotted Hopewell's headquarters. It was a house he had converted into an office. What must have been its garden was now bracketed by a refinery furnace and a storage tank. Telegraph wires ran from it along the uprooted rail spur to the main line.

Bell pushed in the front door.

'Can you wire Washington?'

The telegrapher gaped at the cliff of flame engulfing the tank next door and jumped out the window. Isaac Bell took over the key and rattled out a message to Van Dorn headquarters as fast as he could send Morse code:

DISPATCH INVESTIGATORS HOPEWELL
FIELD MURDER ARSON
ON THE –

The key went dead under his hand.

He looked out the window. The telegraph poles that joined the Hopewell Field to the Western Union system along the main rail line were burning. The wires had melted. The last word never made it, but every detective in the Van Dorn outfit knew that urgent wires from Isaac Bell ended JUMP!

Valuable men arrived the next day on fast mail trains.

The volatile gasoline and kerosene had burned off in the intervening twenty-four hours, but the fires still rampaged, feeding relentlessly on the heavy crude oil. Bell brought the first arrivals up to date on what little he had discovered while they were en route and marched them through the destruction.

'I'm pretty much it for witnesses. Everyone was busy working before the explosion and running like the devil after. As for motive, the independents blame Standard Oil for the shooting and burning.'

'Anyone offering proof of a connection?'

'I ran into Big Pete Straub in Kansas City, and there are rumors "someone" saw him yesterday in Fort Scott. The man whose hair I parted with my Winchester fit the "big" part, but I never saw his face.'

The tall detective was hollow-cheeked and hoarse, having not slept since the killing and the fire. His eyes glittered an angry blue in a face black with soot. Quick thinking and decisive action had saved lives. No one had died after Spike Hopewell. But the fire would bankrupt Spike's friends, the independents.

Damage ranged over both the field and the refinery. The heat had been so intense that it melted the stationary engines that powered the drills and twisted steel pipes. Wooden derricks and pump houses had burned to ash. Wells were ruined, with their casing falling into the bores. Of one hundred wells being drilled or already pumping, only a handful had survived with both derrick and pump house intact.

Van Dorn explosives expert Wally Kisley, who dressed like a traveling salesman in a three-piece checkerboard suit, gave a connoisseur's whistle of appreciation. 'You just can't beat a refinery fire for utter mayhem.'

Redheaded Archie Abbott, a socially prominent New Yorker, a master of disguise, and Bell's best friend, was not at all appreciative and in a foul mood. 'I was impersonating a London-based jewel fence in Chicago and was one bloody *inch* from nailing Laurence Rosania when the Boss pulled me off the case.'

'This is a thousand times more important,' said Bell, 'than a gentleman safe cracker robbing Chicago tycoons' wives and mistresses. That Mr Van Dorn pulled you off the case ought to give you a clue how crucial the Corporations Commission's contract is to the agency.'

'We've got to catch Rosania before he accidentally blows someone's house up along with his safe.'

'I let old Hopewell down,' Bell cut him off coldly. 'I will not rest until his killer hangs.'

'You weren't on a bodyguard job,' said Archie.

Bell stepped closer with a glacial stare.

Wally Kisley, their elder by many years, reckoned that Archie Abbott was stretching the limits of a friendship that had started in a collegiate boxing ring. He signaled Archie to shut his trap before it turned into a rematch and spoke before the fool made it worse.

'Ready when you are, Isaac.'

Bell said, 'First question: Did the same criminals do the shooting and set the fires?

'Archie, I want witnesses. Someone must have seen the sniper either climb up that derrick or climb down. Carrying a rifle, maybe disguised as a tool. Someone must have seen his damned horse.

'Wally, I want you to look for any sort of delayed detonation: clockworks or a slow fuse. It's likely a team of men attacked, though a timing device would allow one man to first prime an explosive, then pick up his rifle. But crack marksmen are specialists. Would such a sniper also know how to rig a timing device?'

'Any oil driller or refinery hand can turn firebug,' said Wally. 'It's the nature of refineries to explode. Lightning bolts blow them up regularly.'

'I paced the distance from the derrick where I saw the killer to where Spike was shot. Nearly seven hundred yards. How many common arsonists could shoot so accurately at extreme range? Such marksmanship would take a top-notch sniper, not the sort to dirty his hands and risk capture setting fires. Snipers prefer to operate far removed.'

'A delayed detonator can be far removed,' said Archie. 'Time instead of distance.'

'Witnesses,' said Bell. 'Find witnesses.'

Kisley interrupted whatever answer Archie was about to utter. 'Fire's cooling down. Isaac, can you point me toward the first tank to catch fire?'

Isaac Bell traced the rapid *click-click-click* of a typewriter to a wall tent pitched beside the burned-out ruins of Hope-Hell. It stood next to a buckboard wagon. The mule was out of its traces, grazing on a patch of grass that had escaped the fire. He rapped his knuckles on the tent pole.

'E. M. Hock?'

The typewriter kept going.

Bell ducked his head to pass through the canvas flaps and was astonished to see a woman hunched over the portable machine. She was typing in such a deep state of concentration that he doubted she had any idea he was five feet behind her. She had silky chestnut hair cut so short that Bell could see the graceful line of the nape of her neck. A pale shirtwaist with a high neck snugged close to her long, elegant back.

The tent contained a folding cot with a bedroll, a Kodak developing machine on the card table behind her, and a stack of typing paper. A straw hat was perched on the bedroll as if tossed there as she rushed to the typewriter. Bell read the top sheet of paper:

SPECIAL TO THE OIL CITY DERRICK.
NEW YORK PAPERS PLEASE COPY

Hopewell Field,
Kansas

A mysterious fire swept the Hopewell tract of buildings, tanks, stills and derricks, devastated the hamlet of Kent, and destroyed the shack-and-canvas boomtown that serviced the fields. The average loss equals $3,000 a well. Most were ruined by tubing dropping into them. Fewer than six of one hundred wells survive with derricks and pump houses standing. The independents are wiped out. Only those drillers who were backed, secretly, by subsidiaries of Standard Oil can afford to rebuild their ruined engines, burned derricks and melted pipe.

Bell asked, 'How many wildcatters were backed by Standard Oil?'

'Put that down,' she called over her shoulder. 'It's not ready to be read.'

'I'm looking for E. M. Hock.'

'She's busy,' said the woman and kept typing.

'I sometimes suspected that the mysterious E. M. Hock was a she.'

'What aroused your suspicion?'

'A higher than usual degree of horse sense in her reporting and a distinct shortage of bombast. What's the E. M. stand for?'

'Edna Matters.'

'Why keep it secret?'

'To derail expectations. Who are you?'

'Isaac Bell. Van Dorn Detective Agency.'

She turned around, looked him over with severe gray-green eyes softened only slightly by the boyish cut of her hair. 'Are you the private detective who just happened to be with Mr Hopewell when he was shot?'

Her ears, thought Bell, were exquisite, and he was struck forcibly by how attractive a woman could be with the shortest hair he had ever seen.

'We're investigating for the Corporations Commission.'

'Do you know anything about oil?'

'I'm an expert.'

A dark eyebrow rose skeptically. 'Expert? How? Did you work in the oil fields?'

'No, Miss Matters.'

'Did you study chemical engineering?'

'No.'

'Then how'd you become an expert?'

'I read your articles.'

She turned away, poised her fingers over the typewriter keys, and stared at the sheet of paper in the machine. She banged away at the keys. A smile quirked the corner of her mouth and she stopped typing.

'OK, we have something in common, Mr Bell: Private detectives flatter their subjects as shamelessly as newspaper reporters to make them talk.'

'I sincerely meant to compliment E. M. Hock's *History of the Under- and Heavy-handed Oil Monopoly*. You're a wonderful wordsmith, and you seem to be in command of your facts.'

'Thank you.'

'Besides, I would not bore a beautiful woman by flattering her good looks, which she must hear every day.'

'Mr Bell, do me the courtesy of leaving my "womanliness" out of this conversation.'

That would be like discussing the nature of daylight without mentioning the sun – a concept Isaac Bell kept to himself in the interest of garnering evidence from a savvy newspaper reporter sent to cover the fire.

'Are you by any chance related to Bill Matters?'

'He's my father.'

'Would that explain your sympathy for the independents?'

'Sympathy. Not bias. I believe that the independent

business man gives American enterprise spine. Independents are brave, bravery is the foundation of innovation, innovation breeds success. That said,' she added with a thin smile, 'I have no doubt that the vast majority of independents given half the chance would be as hard-nosed as Mr Rockefeller.'

'That distinction shines through the articles,' said Bell.

'You do seem to want something from me, sir.'

Isaac Bell grinned. 'I look forward to discussing that "something" when I'm finished investigating murder, arson and corporate lawbreaking. In the meantime, may I ask, do I understand correctly that your father was in partnership with Spike Hopewell before he joined Standard Oil?'

'Until six years ago. Is that what you were discussing with Mr Hopewell when he was shot?'

'Did they part on good terms?'

'Didn't Mr Hopewell tell you that he was angry with Father for joining up with Standard Oil?'

Bell recalled Hopewell's emotional telling of Matters' son, this woman's brother, running away, and said, 'He did not. In fact, he spoke with some sympathy. How did they part?'

'Mr Hopewell called Father a traitor. Father called Mr Hopewell a stuck-in-the-mud fool. Mr Hopewell asked Father was there anything lower than a Standard Oil magnate, except he pronounced the word as "maggot".'

She cast Bell a smile. 'Witnesses swore the first punches were thrown simultaneously.'

Bell asked, 'Have they spoken since?'

'Of course. Six years is too long for old friends to hold a grudge, and, besides, they both flourished – Mr Hopewell wildcatting in Kansas and Father managing the Standard's pipe lines.'

'How will he take the news of Hopewell's death?'

'He will take it hard. Very hard.'

Isaac Bell asked, 'Would I find your father in New York, at 26 Broadway?'

'When he's not traveling.'

Something thumped the canvas roof. Edna Matters looked up. A delighted smile made her even more beautiful, Bell thought. She brushed past him and out the tent flaps. He followed. A thick Manila hemp rope hung down from the sky. Three hundred feet over his head, a wicker basket suspended under a yellow gas balloon was dragging the rope, which hopped and skipped across the ground.

Edna ran after the dragline.

A canvas sack like a bank's money bag slid down it and landed at her feet.

She waved it to the person looking down from the basket and hurried back to the tent, where she opened the bag and removed a sturdy buff-colored envelope. Inside was a tin cylinder of the type that contained Kodak roll film.

'Is that camera film?'

'My sister snapped an aerial photograph of the devastation.'

'Your sister?'

'Half sister. My real father died when I was a baby. My mother married my stepfather and they had Nellie.'

She stepped inside the tent and emerged with binoculars. 'I got the impression you like beautiful women, Mr Bell. Have a look.'

Bell focused on chestnut hair cut as short as Edna Matters', a brilliant smile, and exuberant eyebrows. Edna's fine features seemed magnified in Nellie's face.

'If you find her appealing, Mr Bell, I recommend you leave her beauty and womanliness out of your conversational repertoire.'

'Why?'

'Read.'

The yellow balloon had drifted on the light wind. Now that it was no longer directly overhead, Bell could read huge black letters on its side:

VOTES FOR WOMEN

'A suffragette?'

'A suffra*gist*,' Edna Matters corrected him.

'What's the distinction?'

'A suffra*gette* tries to convert *men* to the cause of enfranchisement.'

'I heard Amanda Faire at Madison Square Garden,'

said Bell, recalling a statuesque redhead who had enthralled her mostly male audience.

'The fair Amanda is a shining example of a suffragette. A suffra*gist* converts women. You'll get further with Nellie if you understand that women will gain the right to vote when *all women* agree that enfranchisement is a simple matter of justice.'

'What about the men?'

'If they want their meals cooked, shirts ironed and beds warmed, they will have no choice but to go along. Or so Nellie believes . . . And by the way, you'll get nowhere if you ever mention Amanda Faire in her company.'

'Rivals?'

'Fire and ice.'

Archie Abbott hurried up, shielding his eyes to inspect the balloon. 'Get ready for a speech if that's Nellie Matters.'

'Do you know her?'

'I heard her in Illinois last fall at a county fair. Two hundred feet in the air, she delivered a William Jennings Bryan stem-winder that had the ladies eyeing their husbands like candidates for a mass hanging.'

'This is her sister,' said Bell, 'E. M. Hock . . . May I present my good friend Archibald Angell Abbott IV?'

The redheaded, blue-blooded Archie whisked his bowler off his head and beamed a smile famous in New York for quickening the heartbeats of New York heiresses and their social climbing mothers and arousing the suspicions of their newly wealthy fathers. 'A pleasure, Miss Hock. And may I say that rumors I have heard among journalists that you are a woman are borne out splendidly.'

Bell could not help but compare the chilly response when he uttered a similar compliment to the warm smile Archie received from Edna.

'How'd you happen to get here so quickly?' Archie asked her. 'The fire is still smoldering.'

'I was passing by on my way back from Indian Territory.'

Archie stared at the buckboard. 'In that?'

'Reporting on "oil fever" takes me places the trains don't visit.'

'I salute your enterprise and your bravery. Speaking of oil fever, Isaac – I'm sure you've heard this already, Miss Hock – the wildcatters are blaming Standard Oil for the fire.'

'Did you interview any witnesses who presented evidence to support their contention?' asked Bell.

'Mostly, like you said, they heard that somebody saw Straub, somewhere – that's Big Pete Straub, Miss Hock, a Standard –'

'Mr Straub was just promoted to refinery police superintendent,' Edna interrupted.

'Which means he travels anywhere he pleases,' said Bell. 'Go on, Archie.'

'I did find one guy who claimed to see Mr Straub renting a horse in Fort Scott.'

'Did he see the horse?'

'Said it was tall as a Clydesdale.'

'The one I saw was a mighty lean Clydesdale. Are your witnesses suggesting Standard Oil's motive for setting the fire?'

'One school of rumor says Standard Oil wants to shut down Kansas production to raise the price of oil by limiting the product reaching market.'

Bell looked to see Edna's reaction. She said, 'The Standard is still heavily invested in the Pennsylvania and Indiana fields. They're somewhat depleted, so the oil is more expensive to pump. The Standard will lose money if they don't keep the price up.'

'What else, Archie?'

'Another rumor, a doozy, claims that Standard Oil is laying pipe lines straight through Kansas to tap richer fields in Oklahoma. After they connect those fields to their interstate pipe line, they'll bypass Kansas oil completely and shut down Kansas production. Then when the producers are forced to the wall, the Standard will buy their leases cheap and lock the oil in the ground for the future. *Their* future.'

Bell looked again to Edna Matters.

The newspaperwoman laughed. 'When you grow up with a father in the oil business, you learn that rumors about Standard Oil are always true. And JDR hears them first.'

'What about this one?' asked Bell.

'The Kansas part fits their pattern. Indian Territory

and Oklahoma appear rich in new strikes. But the Standard's pattern does not include shooting people and setting fires.'

'Exactly what Spike Hopewell told me.'

Edna Matters said, 'Clearly, Mr Hopewell was murdered. But there's no evidence of the cause of the fire.'

'Yet,' said Bell. He conceded that the only crime that he knew for sure had occurred was the sniper killing of Spike Hopewell. If anyone could determine the cause of the fire, it was Detective Wally Kisley. But to get the best work out of Wally, he had to stay out of his way until he asked for a hand.

Archie asked, 'How does John D. Rockefeller hear the rumors first?'

'When two men shake hands, JDR knows the terms of their deal before they report to their front offices.'

'How?' asked Bell.

'He pays spies to keep him ahead of every detail in business and politics. Refiners, distributors, drillers, railroad men, politicians. He calls them correspondents.'

'Does he pay newspaper reporters?'

Edna Matters Hock smiled at the tall detective. 'He's been known to ask reporters.'

'What do they say?'

'I can't report on other reporters. There are confidences involved. Among friends.'

'Do you have any personal experience in what

reporters say?' Archie asked, his most eligible bachelor in New York smile working overtime.

Edna smiled back. 'Personally? I quoted my father's old partner, poor Mr Hopewell.'

'What did Hopewell say?'

'Why don't you ask Mr Bell? He was the last to speak with him.'

Bell said, 'He told Rockefeller to go to blazes.'

'Actually,' Edna corrected, 'he was paraphrasing. What he originally said, at least according to my father, was, "I'd join Satan first."'

'How did Rockefeller respond to *your* preference for Satan?'

'I haven't a clue. JDR does not ask in person. He sends people who ask for him.'

'He's a famous negotiator. Did they come back with a counteroffer?'

Edna Matters answered Bell seriously. 'They asked me to reconsider. So I did. JDR never gives interviews. I said, All right, I'll fill you in on some things I learn if, in return, Mr Rockefeller will sit down with me and my questions for a full day interview.'

'What happened?'

'I never heard back.'

'But it's interesting,' said Bell. 'That he doesn't seem to hold your writing against your father. I understand he is a member of the inner circle.'

'My father is a valuable man, and JDR appreciates valuable men.'

'Even valuable men whose daughters are a thorn in his side? He can't love your articles. You've exposed all sorts of behavior, both underhanded and outright illegal.'

Edna asked, 'Doesn't his willingness not to hold me against my father speak rather highly of Mr Rockefeller?'

Wally Kisley hurried up, grease-smudged and reeking of smoke. He tipped his derby to Edna. 'Isaac, when you have a moment . . .'

Bell said, 'Be right there. Come along, Archie.'

They followed Wally toward the tank that had exploded first.

'Extraordinary!' said Archie. 'A journalist who doesn't reek of booze and cigars.'

'Hands off,' said Bell. 'I saw her first.'

'If I weren't almost engaged to a couple of ladies due to inherit steel mills, I would give you a run for your money.'

Bell said, 'Keep in mind the sooner we arrest the marksman who shot Spike Hopewell, the sooner you can go back to catching your jewel thief.'

'What does that have to do with Miss E. M. Hock?'

'It means go find witnesses. I'll deal with Wally.'

Archie made a beeline for the caboose saloon. Bell caught up with Wally Kisley at a heap of ash and warped metal where the crude storage tank had folded up like a crumpled paper bag.

Wally said, 'It blew when you were down by the creek, right?'

Bell pointed. 'Past that bend.'

'By any chance did you hear a second shot fired?'

'Not down there.'

'How about behind you? Back at the oil field.'

'I heard something. I don't know if it was a shot.'

'Could it have been?'

'It could have been. There was a heck of a racket all at once. Why?'

'I found this,' said Wally. He was holding an oddly shaped, rounded piece of cast iron by a square bracket attached to the top. 'Careful, it's still hot. Take my glove.' He passed Bell his left glove and Bell held the metal in it.

'Heavy.'

He examined it closely. It was six inches high. On one side, the entire surface was pocked with minute indentations, as if a blacksmith had peened it with a hammer. 'It's shaped like an upside-down duck.'

'I thought the same thing, at first.'

Bell upended it and held it with the bracket under it. 'It *is* a duck.'

'Shaped like a duck.'

'You know what this is?' said Bell.

'You tell me.'

Bell had apprenticed under Wally and his ofttimes partner, Mack Fulton, years ago, and one of the many things he had learned from the veteran investigators was not to voice an opinion until a second brain had an opportunity to observe without being influenced by the first.

'It's a knockdown target. A shooting gallery duck.'

Wally nodded. 'That bracket attaches to the target rail. The duck hinges down when a bullet hits it.'

'Where'd you find it?'

'Thirty feet from the first tank that blew.'

'What do you think?'

'The racket you heard right before the explosion could have included a rifle shot, a bullet smashing into this duck, and a blasting cap.'

'So while I was chasing the sniper on the horse, another marksman detonated the explosive that ignited the fire.'

'That's my read. He shot the duck, which jarred a blasting cap.'

'Or,' said Bell, 'the man I chased led me on a wild-goose chase while the real assassin stayed put to set the fire.'

'High marks for a sense of humor,' said Wally Kisley. 'Using a shooting gallery duck for a target.'

'I'm not laughing,' said Isaac Bell. 'But I will give them high marks for the nerve it took to set up the duck, the cap and the dynamite right under everyone's noses. I wonder why nobody noticed.'

'Oil fever. Too busy getting rich.'

5

Midnight was warmed by a slight breeze as a crescent moon inched toward the west. The assassin sat on a large barrel that had been cut into a chair in front of the switching office of the railroad freight yard. The interior was dark and empty since no trains were due to leave or arrive until late the next morning.

The assassin lit a Ramón Allones Havana cigar and retrieved from a coat pocket a leather pouch that contained a gold medal, a fifty-dollar bill, and a letter on heavy stock. The touch of wind dissipated an attempt at blowing a self-satisfied smoke ring.

The medal was as heavy as a double eagle gold piece. And the center was fashioned like a target, with concentric rings and a single dot in the precise center of the bull's-eye. It hung from a red ribbon that was attached to a gold bar pin engraved 'Rifle Sharpshooter'.

The fifty-dollar treasury note would have been just another bill of paper money except when you turned it over you saw that the president had signed the back – as if, the assassin often thought, the busy president had suddenly shouted, 'Wait! Bring that back. I'll sign it for that fine young soldier.'

It had to be Roosevelt's signature because it matched

his signature on the commendation letter that the president had typed, as he was known to do with personal letters, on White House letterhead. The assassin read it by the light of a globe above the switching office door for perhaps the hundredth time:

THE WHITE HOUSE

Washington
October 1, 1902

I have just been informed that you have won the President's Match for the military championship of the United States of America. I wish to congratulate you in person . . .

The assassin skipped some folderol about honoring the regiment and the value of volunteer soldiers – as if their eyes had sighted the targets and their fingers caressed the trigger. Fat chance. Then came the best part.

I congratulate you and your possession of the qualities of perseverance and determination –

A sound of footsteps on gravel interrupted all thought. Quickly, everything went back into the leather pouch and was returned to the coat pocket.

'Why here?' Bill Matters grunted. 'We could have met in the comfort of my private car.'

'Too ostentatious,' said the assassin. 'I have always preferred a life of simplicity.' Before Matters could reply, the assassin motioned to another barrel chair with the cigar. 'I admit they'd be more comfortable with seat cushions.'

Even in the dark Matters showed his anger. 'Why in blazes – why in the face of all good sense – did you shoot Hopewell when the detective was with him?'

The assassin made no apology and offered no regret but retorted loftily, 'To paraphrase the corrupt Tammany Haller Senator Plunkitt, I saw my shot and I took it.'

Bill Matters felt his heart pounding with rage. 'All my kowtowing to those sanctimonious sons of bitches and you blithely undermine my whole scheme.'

'I got away clean. The detective never came close to me.'

'You brought a squad of Van Dorns to the state.'

'We're done in this state.'

'We're done when I say we're done.'

Matters was deeply troubled. His killer, who was vital to his plan, operated in a world and a frame of mind beyond his control, much less his understanding: efficient as a well-oiled machine, with gun in hand, but possessed off the killing field by a reckless faith that nothing could ever go wrong, that fortune would never turn nor consequences catch up.

'I'm surprised by your disappointment.' There was a pause to exhale a cloud of cigar smoke. 'I naturally thought you would celebrate your old friend's departure.'

'Van Dorn detectives have a saying: "We never give up!"'

To Matters' disgust, this drew another, even colder response. 'Never? I have a saying, too: "Never get too close to me." If he does, I will kill him.' The assassin flicked an ash from the cigar. 'Who's next?'

'There's a fellow giving me trouble in Texas.'

'Who?'

'C. C. Gustafson.'

'Ah!'

The killer nodded in vigorous agreement, admiring Bill Matters' cunning. C. C. Gustafson was not merely a newspaper publisher and a thorn in Matters' side but a vocal foe of Standard Oil and a firebrand instigator beloved by the reformers hell-bent on driving the trust out of Texas.

Matters said, 'With a crackerjack Van Dorn private detective on the case – thanks to you – we've got to throw off suspicion.'

Nothing in the murderer's expression indicated the minutest acceptance of blame. In fact, it looked as if the murder of Spike Hopewell under the nose of a Van Dorn had been completely forgotten while Matters' inclusive 'we' had kindled delight.

'May I offer you a fine cigar?'

Matters simply shook his head no.

'Brilliant! Public outrage expects the worst of Standard Oil. They'll blame Gustafson's killing on the bogeyman everyone loves to hate.'

'Can you do it?'

'Can I do it?' The assassin accepted the assignment with a dramatic flourish: 'You may consider Mr C. C. Gustafson's presses stopped.'

Matters did not doubt they'd be stopped. A bullet through the head would take care of that. But what bothered him the most was how near was his private assassin to flying out of control.

6

Isaac Bell went looking for the coroner in Independence, the Montgomery County seat, not far from the Indian Territory border. The courthouse clerk directed him to the coroner's undertaking parlor. A plumber repairing the refrigerating plant told Bell to try the jailhouse. Dr McGrade was visiting the jailer in his apartment above the cells. They were drinking whiskey in tea cups and invited Bell to join them.

Like most Kansans Bell had met, Dr McGrade was fully aware of the Corporations Commission investigation and hugely in favor of any action that reined in Standard Oil. Bell explained his connection.

'Glad to help you, Detective, but I'm not sure how. Didn't the Bourbon County coroner conduct the autopsy on Mr Hopewell?'

'I've already spoken with him. I'm curious about the death of Albert Hill.'

'The refinery fellow,' Dr McGrade told the jailer, 'who drowned in the still.'

The jailer sipped and nodded. 'Down in Coffeyville.'

Bell asked, 'When you examined Mr Hill's body, did you see any signs of bullet wounds?'

'Bullet wounds? You must be joking.'

'I am not joking. Did you see any bullet wounds?'

'Why don't you read my report from the inquest?'

'I already have, at the courthouse.'

'Well, heck, then you know Mr Hill tumbled into a still of boiling oil. By the time someone noticed and fished him out, about all that was left was his skeleton and belt buckle. The rest of him dissolved . . .' He paused for a broad wink. 'Now, this wasn't in my report: His belt buckle looked fine.'

'How about his bones? Were any broken?'

'Fractured femur. Long knitted. Must have busted his leg when he was a kid.'

'No holes in his skull?'

'Just the ones God put there for us all to see and hear and breathe and eat and whatnot.'

'And no damage to the vertebrae in his neck?'

'That I can't say for sure.'

'Why not?'

'I don't understand what this has to do with the Corporations Commission . . .'

Bell saw no reason not to take the coroner and the jailer into his confidence. If the word got around, someone might come to him with more information about Albert Hill. He said, 'Seeing as how Mr Hopewell was shot while I was discussing the commission investigation with him, I am interested in running down the truth about the deaths of other independent oil men.'

'OK, I get your point.'

'Why can't you say for sure whether the vertebrae in Mr Hill's neck suffered damage?'

'I didn't find all of them. The discs and cartilage between them must have dissolved and the bones scattered.'

'That wasn't in your report.'

'It did not seem pertinent to the cause of death.'

'Did that happen to the vertebrae in his spine?'

'What do you mean?'

'Did his thoracic and lumbar vertebrae separate and "scatter" the way you're assuming his cervical vertebrae did?'

The doctor fell silent. Then he said, 'Now that you ask, no. The spine was intact. As was most of the neck.'

'Most?'

'Two vertebrae were attached to the skull. Four were still connected to the spine – the thoracic vertebrae.'

'How many cervical vertebrae are there in the human skeleton? Seven?'

'Seven.'

'So we're missing only one.'

The doctor nodded. 'One. Down in the bottom of the still. Dissolved by now, of course. Distilled into fuel oil, or kerosene or gasoline, even lubricants.'

'But . . .'

'But what, Mr Bell?'

'Doesn't it make you curious?'

'About what?'

'You say two cervical vertebrae were still attached to

70

the skull. So the missing vertebra would be cervical number three, wouldn't it?'

'Three it was.'

'Wouldn't you love to get a gander at cervical two and cervical four?'

'Not really.'

'I would.'

'Why?'

'Let's assume that instead of the disc cartilage dissolving, something knocked cervical three clean out of Mr Hill's vertebral column.'

'Like what?' asked the coroner, then answered his own question. '. . . Like a bullet.'

'You're right,' said Isaac Bell. 'It could have been a bullet . . . Aren't you tempted to have a look?'

'The man's already buried in the ground.'

Bell said, 'I'd still be tempted to have a look.'

'I'm strictly against disinterring bodies. It's just a mess of a job.'

'But this poor fellow was just a heap of bones.'

Dr McGrade nodded. 'That's true. Those bones looked polished like he'd passed a hundred years ago.'

'Good point,' said Bell. 'Why don't we have a look?'

'I can lend you shovels,' said the jailer.

The coroner at Fort Scott, a railroad town where several lines converged, was a powerfully built young doctor with a chip on his shoulder.

Isaac Bell asked, 'Did you see any bullet wounds?'

'Of course not.'

'Why do you say "of course not"?'

'Read my testimony to the coroner's jury.'

'I have read it.'

'Then you know that Reed Riggs was mangled beyond recognition after falling off a railroad platform under a locomotive.'

'Yes. But –'

'But what?'

'Nothing in your written report indicates that you did any more than write down what the railroad police told you – that Mr Riggs fell under the locomotive that rolled over him.'

'What are you implying?'

'I am not implying,' said Isaac Bell, 'I am saying forthrightly and clearly – to your face, Doctor – that you did not examine Mr Riggs' body.'

'It was a mutilated heap of flesh and bone. He fell under a locomotive. What do you expect?'

'I expect a public official who is paid to determine the cause of a citizen's death to look beyond the obvious.'

'Now, listen to me, Mr Private Detective.'

'No, Doctor, you listen to me! I want you to look at that body again.'

'It's been buried two weeks.'

'Dig it up!'

The coroner rose to his feet. He was nearly as tall as Isaac Bell and forty pounds heavier. 'I'll give you fair warning, mister, get lost while you still can. I paid my way through medical school with money I won in the prize ring.'

Isaac shrugged out of his coat and removed his hat. 'As we have no gloves, I presume you'll accommodate me with bare knuckles?'

'What did you do to your hand?' asked Archie Abbott.

'Cut it shaving,' said Bell. 'What do you think of that water tank?'

They were pacing Fort Scott's St Louis–San Francisco Railway station platform where refiner Reed Riggs had fallen to his death. 'Possible,' said Archie, imagining a rifle shot from the top of a tank in the Frisco train yard to where they stood on the platform. 'I also like that signal tower. In fact, I like it better. Good angle from the roof.'

'Except how did he climb up there without the dispatchers noticing?'

'Climbed up in the dark while a train rumbled by.'

'How'd he get down?'

'Waited for night.'

'But what if he missed his shot and someone noticed him? He would be trapped with no escape.'

'You're sure that Riggs was shot?'

'No,' said Bell, 'not positive. There's definitely a hole in his skull. In a piece of the temporal bone, which wasn't shattered. But it could have been pierced by something other than a bullet. Banged against a rail-road spike or a chunk of gravel.'

'What did the coroner think?'

'He was inclined to agree with my assessment.'

Bell and Archie took the train down to Coffeyville, a booming refinery town just above the Kansas–Indian Territory border. They located Albert Hill's refinery and the tank in which Hill had died while repairing the agitator.

They looked for sight lines. They climbed to the roof of the boiler house, four hundred yards' distance, then to the roof of the barrel house. Both offered uninterrupted shots at the tank. The barrel house had its own freight siding to receive the lumber trains that delivered wood for the staves.

'Rides in and out,' said Archie.

'I'd go for the boiler house,' said Bell. 'They'd never hear a shot over the roar of the furnaces.'

'If there was a shot.'

'I told you,' said Bell. 'Albert Hill's number two cervical vertebra appeared to have been nicked.'

Archie said, 'Based on how he killed Spike Hopewell, the assassin is capable of hitting both Hill and Riggs. But he's one lucky assassin that no one saw him. Or coolly deliberate in choosing his moment.'

Isaac Bell disagreed. 'That may be true of Albert Hill. But when Riggs was shot, the timing was dictated by the approach of the locomotive. In both cases, the shots were fired by a marksman as calculating and accurate as the killer who shot Spike Hopewell.'

'If there were shots fired at all,' said Archie, and Wally Kisley agreed, saying, 'There could have been shots, and shots would explain how the victims happened to fall, but they could have just as easily fallen as Spike Hopewell suggested to Isaac: one drunk, one overcome by fumes.'

Bell said, 'I have Grady Forrer looking into their backgrounds.' Forrer was head of Van Dorn Research.

Isaac Bell went looking for Edna Matters Hock and found her loading her tent on to her buckboard. He gave her a hand. 'Where you headed?'

'Pittsburgh.'

'In a wagon?'

'Pittsburgh, Kansas.'

'I was going to ask could you print me that aerial photograph your sister snapped, but you've packed your Kodak machine . . .'

'Actually, I made an extra. I thought you'd ask to see it.'

She had it in an envelope. She handed it to Bell. 'Oh, there's a second photograph that Nellie took before the fire. So you have a before the fire and an after.'

'She flew over before?'

'By coincidence. She was hoping to address a convention in Fort Scott, but the wind changed and the balloon drifted over here. I hope the pictures help.'

Bell thanked her warmly. 'Speaking of coincidence,' he told her, 'my father served as an intelligence officer in the Civil War and he tried to take balloon daguerreotypes of Confederate fortifications.'

'I've never seen an aerial of the Civil War.'

'He said that the swaying motion blurred the pictures. When the wind settled down, a rebel shot the camera out of his hands.'

'Quite a different war story.'

'Actually,' Bell smiled, 'he rarely talked about the war. The very few times he did, he told a humorous tale, like the balloon.'

'I really must go.'

He helped her on to the wagon. 'It was a pleasure meeting you. I hope to see you again.'

Edna Matters Hock gave him a long look with her gray-green eyes. 'I would like that, Mr Bell. Let us hope it happens.'

'Where are you going next?'

'After Pittsburgh, I'm not sure.'

'If I were to wire the paper sometime, perhaps they could put us in touch.'

'I'll tell them to,' she said.

They shook hands. 'Oh, please say good-bye to Mr Abbott.'

Bell promised he would. Edna spoke to the mule and it trotted off.

Bell took the photographs to Wally Kisley. Wally gave a low whistle.

'Fascinating. I've never had a look like this before.'

The photograph Nellie Matters had snapped after the fire looked like raindrops on a mud puddle. All that was left of the storage tanks were circular pockmarks in the ground. The brick furnaces of the refinery stood like ruined castles. The steel pots were warped, staved in, or completely flattened. The remains of the derricks looked like bones scattered by wild animals.

The picture she had taken before the fire was shrouded in smoke, but Spike's refinery still looked almost as orderly as an architect's blueprint. What stood out was the logic of Hopewell's design to efficiently move the crude oil through the process of brewing gasoline.

'Now you see, Isaac, they couldn't have picked a better tank to blow. Look at this.'

'But their target was the gasoline tank. Why didn't they blow it first off?'

'Couldn't get to it. Out in the open like it was, in plain sight, there's no way to lay the explosives and set up the target duck. But look here. They could not have chosen a tank better positioned for the first explosion to start things rolling. Someone knows his business.'

Ice-eyed Mack Fulton, an expert on safecrackers, arrived from New York dressed in funereal black. He had news for Archie Abbott. 'Jewel thief the New York cops are calling the Fifth Avenue Flier sounds a lot to me like your Laurence Rosania, in that he's got an eye for top quality and beauty.'

That caught Archie's interest because Rosania was known to leave ugly pieces behind regardless of value. They compared notes. Like the discriminating Rosania, Mack's Fifth Avenue Flier robbed safes on mansions' upper floors.

'New York cops think he's scaling walls, but I'm wondering if he's talking his way upstairs, romancing the ladies and charming the gents, like your guy.'

'How'd he get there so fast?' asked Archie. A recent robbery in New York had taken place less than a day after a Rosania-sounding job in Chicago.

'Twentieth Century Limited?'

'If he's pulled off half the jobs we think, he can afford it.'

'He gets to play the New York and Chicago fences off each other, too. Bargain up the price. That reminds me, Isaac. I brought you a note from Grady Forrer.'

Bell tore open the envelope from Research.

But to his disappointment, Forrer had not discovered any special connections between Spike Hopewell, Albert Hill and Reed Riggs – no mutual partners, no known feuds. All they had in common was being independent oil men. Even if all of them were shot, the shootings were not related on a personal level.

'OK,' said Bell. 'The only fact I know for sure is that Spike Hopewell was shot. Two questions, gents. By whom? And why?'

Archie said, 'Hopewell had an enemy who hated

him enough to kill him and just happened to be a crack shot at seven hundred yards.'

'Or,' said Mack Fulton, 'Hopewell had an enemy who hated him enough to hire someone to kill him who happened to be a crack shot at seven hundred yards.'

'Or,' said Wally Kisley, 'Hopewell had an enemy who hated him enough to hire a professional assassin to kill him whose weapon of choice was a rifle with an effective range of over seven hundred yards.'

Bell said, 'I'm betting on Wally's professional.'

'That's because a professional makes it more likely that your other two victims were actually shot. But, oh boy, Isaac, you're talking about amazing shooting.'

'For the moment, let's agree they were shot. Who's the mastermind?'

'All three independent oil men were battling Standard Oil.'

'Was Hopewell a Congregationalist by any chance?' Wally Kisley asked. He grinned at Mack Fulton. The joke-cracking partners were known in the Van Dorn Agency as 'Weber & Fields,' for the vaudeville comedians.

'Presbyterian.'

'Too bad,' said Wally. 'We could have arrested Rockefeller if he was.'

The newspapers were full of stories about a Congregationalist Convocation in Boston that had turned down a million-dollar donation by John D. Rockefeller because Rockefeller's money was 'tainted.'

'That money sure is tainted,' chorused Wally and Mack. ' 'Tain't yours! 'Tain't mine!'

'Listen close,' said Bell, grinning. 'The last words Hopewell said to me were that he had what he called tricks up his sleeve to build his tidewater pipe line. Wally and Mack, talk to everyone in Kansas who knew him. Find out his plan.'

'You got it, Isaac.'

'Archie? Run down Big Pete Straub. Find out where he was when Spike was shot. Find out if maybe I winged him with my Winchester. But watch yourself.'

'Thank you, Mother. But I think I can handle him.'

'That's your call,' Bell shot back firmly, 'if he's alone. But if he's running with a bunch, get ahold of Wally and Mack before you brace him. I'll be back soon as I can.'

'Where you going, Isaac?'

'Washington, D.C.'

'But you don't have anything to report.'

'I'm not going to report.'

'Then what are you going for?'

'To shake up the Boss.'

7

By 1905 the Van Dorn Detective Agency spanned the continent, with field offices in major cities and many towns. It maintained national headquarters at the Palmer House in Chicago, where Joseph Van Dorn had founded the fast-growing outfit. But Van Dorn himself – gambling that a private detective agency with a national reach could profit by contracting its services to a federal government ill-equipped to hunt modern criminals across state lines – spent more and more time in his Washington, D.C., field office.

It was at the new and unabashedly lavish Willard Hotel, two blocks from the White House, and Isaac Bell noted that it had grown by several more rooms since his last visit. He credited the Boss's warming friendship with President Roosevelt, his industrious courting of the powers who ruled the Justice Department and the US Navy, his honest name, his colorful reputation, broadcast in Sunday supplement features, and his Irish charm.

Van Dorn's private office was a sumptuous walnut-paneled inner sanctum designed to make bankers, industrialists, senators and cabinet secretaries feel at home. It was equipped like the nerve center of a great railroad, with numerous telephones, voice tubes, an electric intercom, a self-winding stock ticker, and a telegraph key for the agency's private wire. Windows on two sides offered a preview of clients and informants arriving on Pennsylvania Avenue or 14th Street, and it had a spy hole for sizing up prospects in the reception room.

The Boss was a large, solid man in his forties with a friendly smile that could turn cold in a flash. He was bald, his skull a shiny, high dome, his cheeks and chin thick with red whiskers. Bristly brows, red as his beard and sideburns, shaded his eyes. Only when he opened them wide to stare a man full in the face did he reveal enormous intelligence and colossal determination. He could be mistaken for a well-off business man. Criminals who made that mistake, and they were legion, were marched off in handcuffs.

Van Dorn glanced up at Isaac Bell with genuine affection.

He was leaning over the mouthpiece of one of the three candlestick telephones on his desk, with one meaty fist pressing the earpiece to his ear. The other gripped a voice tube into which he issued a terse request. He replaced the voice tube stopper, roared orders into the telephone, banged the earpiece back on its hook, snatched up another telephone and purred, 'Senator Stevens, I cannot recall such hospitality as was extended by you and Mrs Stevens this past weekend . . .'

A secretary, in vest, bow tie and shoulder-holstered,

double-action Colt, hurried in, placed a typewritten letter on the desk, exchanged cylinders in the DeVeau Dictaphone, and hurried out with the full one.

' . . . Thank you, Senator. I hope you can join me for lunch at the Cosmos Club . . . Oh, yes, I belong. I can assure you that no one was more surprised than I when they tapped me to join. Who knows what the membership committee was thinking . . . I look forward to seeing you next week.'

He returned the earpiece to its hook and signed the letter on his desk.

'Good to see you, Isaac.'

'Good morning, sir. You're looking prosperous.'

'Busy as a one-armed paperhanger. What brings you back from Kansas?'

'What may sound, at first, like a strange request.'

'I'll judge what is strange. What do you want?'

'I want you to inveigle John D. Rockefeller into hiring the agency to arrest the marksman who murdered Spike Hopewell.'

Van Dorn sat back and regarded the tall detective speculatively.

'That *is* strange . . . even by your standards. Why would Rockefeller do that? He knows we're investigating him for the Corporations Commission.'

'I brought you the latest newspapers from Topeka and Kansas City.'

Bell spread the *Kansas Watchman*, the *Kansas City Journal*, and the *Kansas City Star* on Van Dorn's desk and showed him the headlines about the murder of Spike Hopewell. Then he opened them to the editorials.

Van Dorn read quickly. 'They're howling for Rockefeller's hide. They're practically claiming that Rockefeller pulled the trigger. Do they know something about the president of Standard Oil that we don't?'

'Rockefeller did not shoot anyone, of course. But the killing is making him look even worse than the people of Kansas thought he was. And since Standard Oil locked up their pipe lines and their tank cars – and they were already mad as hornets about crude dropping to seventy cents a barrel and kerosene jumping to seventeen cents a gallon – they equate him with the devil.'

Van Dorn looked dubious. 'You're suggesting that if we catch the killer at Rockefeller's behest, it will improve his reputation.'

'According to E. M. Hock, he has a slew of publicists on his payroll to improve his reputation. Being blamed for murder can't be making their job any easier.'

'It's a thought,' Van Dorn said cautiously. 'I'll mull it over.'

Bell knew from experience that Van Dorn's mulling could take a long time. He immediately said, 'We, too, would come out smelling like roses.'

'How so?'

'Mr Rockefeller's fellow magnates and tycoons watch his every move like hungry wolves. They will note the good work the Van Dorns do for him and remember us the next time they need a detective agency. As will your friends at the Justice Department. And the Navy. Even the Treasury Department – if I recall correctly, Senator Stevens chairs the Committee on Finance.'

'True,' Van Dorn nodded. 'All true. I'll see what I can do. I'll have to think on which wires to try and pull.'

'I have an idea for a different approach,' Bell said.

Van Dorn's high brow beetled. 'I'm belatedly gaining the impression that you came here loaded for bear.'

'Rockefeller pays so-called correspondents to spy for him. You can bet he's got plenty in Congress, and probably even some deep inside the Corporations Commission. In addition, he is able to "listen in" on telegrams carried on his pipe lines' private wires.'

'I am aware that Rockefeller understands the power of information more than any other business man in the country. The War Department and the Secret Service could take lessons from his book. What's your "different approach"?'

'What if we were to cause the word to drift back to him that people are convinced the assassin works for Standard Oil?'

'How?'

'We could have people pass rumors to his correspondents. We could even insert false messages on the private lines.'

'All that to give Rockefeller the impression that the public believes that Standard Oil hired an assassin?'

'At which point we ask for the job of catching the assassin. And while we're hunting him, we will also be in a position to collect evidence for the commission from *inside* the Standard.'

'Like a Trojan horse?' asked the Boss.

Isaac Bell smiled. 'I could not put it better myself.'

Big Pete Straub was not easily impressed. His sheer size awed most men. They crossed the street when they saw him crowd a sidewalk, backed up when he entered a room, ran when he reached for a pick handle. He was accustomed to their fear and it made him scornful. What set him apart from saloon brawlers, and raised him high above their ranks, was his ability to distinguish those few men of unusual power or ability that he should not frighten. He knew how to say yes, sir, to a man who could help him and sound like he meant it.

The little guy with the rifle was one of those. He seemed rich. Or rich enough. He paid generously, ten times what Pete earned from the Standard's industrial service firm. In gold, the minute the job was done. He spoke rarely and never loudly – one whispered word instead of two – and never if a gesture would do. He was as alert as a wolf, intensely aware of what was going on around him. He was patient; he could sit all day waiting for a shot. And when things flew apart, he never lost his nerve.

But what made the assassin so special to the hulking Standard Oil thug was that he was something to watch.

In his hands, the sleek, hammerless Savage 99 looked deadly as a rattlesnake. There were times, Big Pete thought, you could not tell where his fingers stopped and the blue steel began. He wore gloves, black gloves, tight as a second skin, with a tiny patch cut out where his finger touched the trigger. He wore a hat with a slightly abbreviated brim, which Straub was sure he had had specially made so it would shade the eyepiece of the telescope but not get in his way. He wore a dark scarf, like a cowboy bandanna, around his throat that covered his neck and his chin.

And could the guy shoot! He could kill people Straub couldn't even see. Sure, he had a telescope, but it was more than the powerful glass, more like something out of a magic show. When his bullet left the gun, it traveled sure as a flier on the rails, a certain connection between his trigger finger and his target's head.

The assassin gestured for Big Pete to fire first. His eyes were empty, his rifle steady.

This was the first time Big Pete had fired alongside the marksman. In the past he had covered the escape route to throw off pursuit, if there was any, and draw fire as he had when the Van Dorns chased him in Hopewell, Kansas. But here in Southeast Texas, in the boomtown of Humble, they were crouching side by side on a flat roof behind the false front of a tall saloon. Planning step-by-step as always, the assassin had chosen shooting holes in the curlicue-carved top of the ornate front.

Straub's job was to fire first to break a window. His hands were steady, but he could feel his palms getting wet. He was a decent shot. The bolt action Springfield '03 was a good weapon. And his target was fully two feet square.

C. C. Gustafson – editor of the *Humble Clarion*, who'd been making a career of criticizing Standard Oil practices in Texas and provoking the legislature to expel the trust from the state – was standing behind the window setting type.

Big Pete aimed at the blood-red dot of his bow tie.

'Don't try to hit him,' whispered the assassin.

'I know,' said Straub. 'Just break the glass.' How had the assassin known where he was aiming? The guy missed nothing. Straub shifted the rifle and sighted dead center in the window. He heard the assassin take a shallow breath and hold it.

'Now!'

Big Pete squeezed his trigger.

The Springfield boomed.

Glass flew.

The editor looked up, wasted a half breath staring, then tried to dive behind the press.

The assassin's Savage gave a sharp crack. The editor tumbled backward. Then, to Straub's surprise, the assassin fired again. Next second, they were running, crouched, across the roof, then down the ladder to the alley behind the saloon.

'Good shot!' Straub exulted.

'Missed,' said the assassin, the voice emotionless.

A man stepped around the corner. He had unbuttoned his fly as if about to urinate on the wall. Squinting around for the source of the gunshots, he saw two men running toward him with rifles.

'Kill him,' said the assassin.

Straub broke his neck.

The assassin gestured.

Straub slung the body over his shoulder and they ran, following the escape route they had rehearsed. After they had put distance between them and the saloon, the assassin gestured to drop the dead man beside a rain barrel on top of Straub's Springfield.

Grady Forrer of Van Dorn Research sent Isaac Bell a telegram to alert him to a shooting in far-off Texas that might possibly pertain to his investigation. Bell had known Forrer since Joseph Van Dorn had hired him to establish the Research Department and trusted his judgment. He immediately wired Texas Walt Hatfield, the formidable Van Dorn detective – a former Ranger, raised by the Comanche – who operated as a one-man field office for the biggest state in the Union.

REPORT EDITOR SHOOTING HUMBLE OIL?

8

Bill Matters read and reread a dozen newspaper reports about a transatlantic cable John D. Rockefeller had sent from Cannes, France, to his Fifth Avenue Baptist Church Sunday school class. The New York and Cleveland papers had published the cable back in January when he was abroad, and it had been printed and reprinted through the spring as paper after paper used the great man's wisdom to inspire the devout and fill space.

'Delightful breezes. I enjoy watching the fishermen with their nets on the beach, and gazing upon the sun rising over the beautiful Mediterranean Sea. The days pass pleasantly and profitably.'

It was an open secret at Standard Oil headquarters that publicists scheming to furbish up Rockefeller's reputation planted stories in the newspapers. But Matters suspected there was much more to this cable than polishing the public image of a greedy tycoon into a glowing example of the pleasant old age everyone looked forward to. A deep feeling gnawed his gut that Rockefeller had transmitted coded messages to his elderly partners about a secret deal he was negotiating overseas under the cloak of a retiree traveling around Europe.

Whatever the pirate was up to, Matters wanted in on it.

Matters himself was no stranger to coded messages. He communicated with his assassin with cryptic instructions in the want ads of daily newspapers. He felt so strongly that this cable was big – something huge, the sort of deal the supposedly retired president had time to pursue thanks to underlings like him taking over day-to-day operations – that he decided to risk consulting a clandestine partner he had cultivated among his fellow managers.

Old Clyde Lapham, an early Standard Oil partner, was losing his grip to dementia. When the others realized he was no longer striking a high batting average, they had begun excluding him from private deals. Lapham knew, or sensed enough of what was happening to accept, warily, the kindness and respect that the much-younger, vigorous Matters pretended to offer.

Lapham said he suspected a secret deal, too, when Matters broached the subject. Stung that he had not been invited to partake, he translated the basics of the message over a supper Matters invited him to at Mcdonald's Oyster House up by Bleecker on the Bowery, where no one would recognize them. Matters ordered wine to loosen him up. Lapham's vague eyes kept locking on the empty littleneck clamshells as if they held some secret. He had a thin voice.

'"Delightful breezes" means big changes are under way,' he reported matter-of-factly. '"I enjoy watching the fishermen with their nets on the beach" means that Mr Rockefeller is spying on competitors.'

But the old man was baffled by 'gazing upon the sun rising over the beautiful Mediterranean Sea.' Pawing purposefully across the table, he picked up an empty clamshell and examined it closely.

'Sir Marcus Samuel's father got his start selling these.'

'Selling what?'

'Seashells. Old Marcus Senior imported oriental seashells, sold them to people decorating their houses. Where did you think Junior got the money to invent his goddamned oil tankers?'

Sir Marcus Samuel, who had pioneered a fleet of bulk-oil-carrying steamers, commanded their powerful English competitor, Shell Transport and Trading. The richest distributor of refined oil, in cans packed in wooden cases, to India and China, Samuel had run circles around the mighty Standard for more than a decade and had recently increased his sales force by forming the Asiatic Petroleum Company with the Royal Dutch Company.

Matters regained Lapham's attention, with some effort, and coaxed him to concentrate on 'The days pass pleasantly and profitably.'

Lapham finally said that he believed that 'The days pass pleasantly and profitably' meant that Rockefeller was laying groundwork for his next move. He picked up another shell.

'What move?' Matters asked.

Lapham shrugged. 'The sun rising over the beautiful Mediterranean Sea rises in the east.'

Of course! The rich Baku oil fields on the Caspian Sea that pumped half the world's oil were in the east. Chaos threatened Baku. January's Bloody Sunday massacre at the Russian czar's Winter Palace in St Petersburg had inflamed revolutionary unrest and Muslim–Christian hatred simultaneously. Civil war threatened the oil fields.

In that instant, Bill Matters had to restrain himself from lunging across the table to kiss Lapham's wrinkled hand. The looney old man had done him a huge favor and ripped the scales from his eyes. He had been thinking too small. Way too small. He suddenly saw the world as Rockefeller did.

That it was definitely code galvanized Matters. He made an educated guess based in part on the six years he'd been circling the rim of the inner circle of the Standard Oil Gang and based in part on a perceptive analysis by the assassin who speculated that Rockefeller sensed an opportunity to break the stranglehold that his overseas enemies – the Nobel and Rothschild families and Sir Marcus Samuel – had on Russian oil.

How could Rockefeller not be tempted by the spoils? Fighting and destruction in Baku would shut down half the world supply and the price of oil would double or triple to two, to three, to four dollars a barrel, prices that hadn't been seen in decades. American oil men would cheer. But John D. Rockefeller was no ordinary oil man.

Wouldn't he imagine much-richer spoils than a temporary jump in price? Wouldn't he see the chaos of civil war as an opportunity to displace the Rothschilds, overthrow the Nobels, sink Shell, and own it all?

Bill Matters knew in his gut that this was the chance he had been working for. Something this big would never come again. Whatever Rockefeller was scheming in the east, Matters had to make himself part of it.

His success thus far, since joining the Standard – his growing wealth and power within the corporation, though still not in the inner circle – proved he had been right to bank on the secrecy that pervaded the trust. Secrets had given him room to operate, as had the madcap distraction of everyone from Rockefeller on down who were busy getting richer.

Business was roaring. New markets were enormous: fuel for ships and power plants, gasoline to feed the automobile boom. But supply, too, was growing; vast new oil fields in Kansas, Oklahoma, Texas, Mexico and California surpassed the old Pennsylvania, Ohio and Indiana fields. It was becoming impossible for the Standard to control production to keep prices high. Competing producers – Gulf Oil and the Texas Company – were springing to life even as the monopoly came under increasing fire from Progressive reformers determined to break up the trust. Rockefeller himself was distracted by the government prosecution and equally by his attempts to repair his reputation by becoming a philanthropist.

The pressure was on the old president to do something.

Thus the Baku push.

Bill Matters approached white-haired Averell Comstock, a charter member of the 'gang' who often profited from private deals. 'I have a scheme for a joint adventure.'

'What sort of scheme?'

'A private partnership with you and Mr Rockefeller to persuade the Russian government to let Standard Oil build new, modern refineries and refurbish the old ones owned by Rothschild and Nobel.'

Comstock was immediately suspicious.

'Where did you get that idea, Bill? It's as if you read our minds.'

Matters felt his spirits soar. He had guessed right about a lot of things.

He answered modestly, 'I'm an old wildcat driller. Good at guessing. Besides, I recall that in '03 Mr Rockefeller considered roping in St Petersburg banks to buy Baku oil fields.'

'Are you sure you haven't been eavesdropping on telephone calls?'

'Quite sure, Mr Comstock.' According to Clyde Lapham, this was not the first time Rockefeller had set sights on the Caucasus. Back in '98, Standard Oil sent geologists to survey for commercial oil reserves in Azerbaijan.

'Or tapping wires?'

'I wouldn't know how to begin to tap wires,' Matters lied.

'What else have you "guessed"?'

Matters took his best shot. 'What if I were to propose to you a plan to beat Sir Marcus Samuel at shipping case oil to Asia?'

Comstock glared. So-called case oil was kerosene shipped in gallon tins packed in wooden boxes. The Asian market was enormous. Chinese and Indians burned the oil in their lamps and used the wood and tin to build their huts, shingle their roofs, make cooking pots and pitchers. Sir Marcus Samuel, the all-powerful English distributor of case oil to India and China, had visited these offices in great secrecy in 1901 to negotiate some sort of partnership. Matters was gambling that Rockefeller and Comstock wished their talks had panned out.

'Mr Rockefeller prefers knowing to guessing,' said Comstock.

Bill Matters stood his ground. 'I am not *guessing*.'

Comstock was scornful. 'Let me remind you that Standard Oil has not managed to beat Samuel in fifteen years. The conniving Englishman parlayed preferential treatment from the Suez Canal into the biggest tank steamer fleet to Asia.'

'I *know* how to beat Samuel,' Bill Matters shot back.

'How?'

'Bypass the Suez Canal.'

'Bypass the *Suez*?' Comstock turned more scornful. 'Have you any idea how long it takes a tank ship to steam around Africa? Why do you suppose they dug a canal?'

'Bypass the Transcaucasus Railroad, too,' Matters shot back. 'And Batum. And the Black Sea. And the Dardanelles, Constantinople, and the Mediterranean.'

'Poppycock! How the devil could we ship kerosene to India and China?'

'Build a pipe line from Baku to the Persian Gulf.'

'A pipe line? . . .' Comstock's face was a mask. But his eyes grew busy. 'Too ambitious. Persia is mountainous and bedeviled by warlords and revolutionaries.'

'No more ambitious than our pipe lines across Pennsylvania's mountains to the Atlantic seaboard,' Matters answered, choosing his words carefully. His hated rivals had never built an inch of pipe line themselves, but stolen his.

Comstock shook his head. 'Great Britain will fight a Russian link to the Gulf every inch of the way.'

'Don't you think Standard Oil should fight back for half the oil in the world and all the markets of Asia?'

Comstock's face remained a mask. Eventually, he closed his hands in a double fist and gazed at Matters over his interlocked knuckles. 'Were Mr Rockefeller to approve a pipe line, he might invite you to join as a junior partner in the enterprise.'

Averell Comstock would of course be a *full* partner.

Matters had braced himself to pretend humble acquiescence and he said, 'I would be deeply honored.'

In fact, he was thrilled – not for a junior partnership but for the access he would gain to the president. Comstock may have his doubts, but he also sensed that the pipe line was a bold idea that Rockefeller would seize upon. In which case, Comstock feared the idea would get to the president from someone else unless he moved quickly.

Matters reminded himself not to get cocky. Older Standard Oil directors, who jealously guarded their power, were the smartest in American industry. There were wise men among them who might intuit Matters' plot, might guess that for Bill Matters the pipe line was only the beginning.

As the assassin had proclaimed after shooting Spike Hopewell, those who get too close will be killed.

Bill Matters summoned the assassin to his private rail car.

'Word's come from Texas that C. C. Gustafson did not die.'

'I'm not surprised. He was quick as lightning. I struck him twice, but neither shot felt right.'

'What happened?'

'Fate intervened,' the assassin said blithely, but, unable to abide a deep sense of failure, added in a voice suddenly dark, 'I am mortified . . . I promise you that such a failure will never again occur. Never.'

'Don't worry about Gustafson. The effect of the attack is the same as if he had died. They'll blame Standard Oil.'

The assassin's spirits continued to fall. 'I have promised myself on my mother's grave that I will never miss again. Never.'

Matters said, 'I need something new from you. Something quite different.'

The assassin leaned closer, intrigued. 'How different?'

'Some old ones must die.'

'Comstock?'

'Yes. He's bringing my pipe line scheme to Rockefeller. After he does, I need him out of my way.'

'And old Lapham?'

'No, not Lapham.'

'God knows what Clyde Lapham remembers,' the assassin warned darkly. 'But whatever he does remember will be too much.'

'Not yet! I need Lapham.'

'OK. Only Comstock. For the moment. What is different?'

'His death must appear to be natural. No sniping. No suspicion of murder.'

'Miles ahead of you,' the assassin crowed – spirits soaring as suddenly high as a skyrocket – and whipped out of a vest pocket a red vial.

From Humble, Texas, Walt Hatfield wired Isaac Bell at the Washington field office.

C. C. GUSTAFSON VEXED STANDARD
WINGED NOT DEAD YET
SHERIFF'S SUSPECT DEAD

Isaac Bell raced to Central Station. The Washington & Southwestern Limited was fully booked, but a pass given him by a prep school classmate's railroad president father got Bell into a seat reserved for friends of the company. Everyone, the conductor told him, seemed to be going to Texas.

In the smoker, he drank a Manhattan cocktail that was exactly the color of Edna Matters' fine, wispy hair. And from what he had glimpsed of Nellie, hers too. He ordered another and raised the glass to salute Thomas Jefferson's Monticello, which the train passed by in the dying daylight. He ate a grilled rockfish in the dining car, and slept in a Pullman Palace sleeper that the Limited picked up in Danville, Virginia.

Twenty-seven hours later, a Van Dorn apprentice from the New Orleans field office ran into Union Terminal with another wire from Texas Walt.

SHERIFF'S DEAD SUSPECT CLEARED
C. C. GUSTAFSON AWAKE

Isaac Bell swung aboard the westbound Sunset Express.

BOOK TWO
Poison
Texas

A swath of buckshot wide as two men

9

'Hummbuuulll, Texas!' bawled the conductor. 'Humble, Texas! Next stop, Humble, Texas!'

Isaac Bell was first at the vestibule door, ahead of a crowd of excited speculators jostling behind him. The still-speeding train leaned into a hard bend in the tracks, and he glimpsed something that made him open the corridor window to lean out in the humid heat. He saw hundreds of oil derricks surrounded by giant crude storage tanks. A sprawling boomtown of fresh-built barracks, boardinghouses, hotels, saloons and a 'ragtown' section of tents crowded both sides of the main line tracks. The sidings and railyards were black with rows of tank cars.

But what had caught the Van Dorn detective's eye was floating in the smoke-stained sky above the town – Nellie Matters' yellow balloon with the block lettering on the bulge of the gas envelope that read VOTES FOR WOMEN. Where had she come from? Bell wondered. More to the point, had her beautiful sister Edna come with her?

The ground shook suddenly at the very moment the Sunset Express pulled into the makeshift station with clanging bell and hissing air brakes. The tracks trembled and the Pullman cars rattled and everyone on the train ran to the windows. A fountain of oil spewed from the top of a derrick. The fountain rapidly thickened. Thundering out of the earth, the eruption blew the derrick to splinters and projected skyward nearly as high as Nellie Matters' balloon.

Bell gave the roaring spouter and its greasy brown spray a wide berth, judging the wind by the direction Nellie's balloon was tugging the rope that tethered it above the fairground. Most of that dusty field had been turned into a 'ragtown' taken up by tents. In the small open space that remained, fifty women in white summer dresses were waving EQUAL SUFFRAGE LEAGUES OF HOUSTON AND HUMBLE banners at Nellie's balloon.

Bell hurried past the fairground and cut down Main Street and into the Toppling Derrick, the boomtown's biggest saloon. Waiting as promised at the bar was Texas Walt Hatfield, a tall, wiry, sun-blasted man with twin Colt six-shooters holstered in low-slung gun belts and a broad-brimmed J. B. Stetson hat. Beside him stood a feisty-looking gent with his arm in a sling and his neck swathed in bandages. His face wore the pallor of recent shock, but his eyes were bright.

'Howdy, Isaac,' said Hatfield, shaking hands as casually as if they had last worked together yesterday instead of a year ago. 'This here's Mr C. C. Gustafson.'

'Craig Gustafson,' said the publisher, thrusting out his good hand.

'Isaac Bell. Congratulations on being alive.'

C. C. Gustafson proved to be as philosophical on the subject of getting shot as any Bell had met. 'My little newspaper is just a fly nipping at the hide of Standard Oil. Fact is, I'm flattered they bothered to swat me.'

Bell asked, 'Do we have reason to believe that's who shot you?'

'I don't know for sure this is true, but I have a vague memory forming in my mind that I was told that a Standard Oil Refinery Police chief arrived on the train the day before. That would have been Tuesday. I got shot on Wednesday.'

'Can you recall any local enemies here in town you might have provoked?'

'I haven't stolen any horses and I haven't burned any churches, and I can also eliminate angry husbands, since I don't run around on my wife.'

Isaac Bell glanced at the barbed-wire-lean, hawk-nosed Texas Walt for confirmation.

The normally laconic former Ranger surprised him by drawling the longest sentence Bell had ever heard him speak: 'Ah had the pleasure of meeting Janet Sue – that is to say, *Mrs* C. C. Gustafson – at the hospital, and Ah can report that there ain't a man in Texas who would entertain notions of running around on such a lady.'

'I *have* irritated Standard Oil for years,' said Gustafson, 'and currently can claim some part of the effort in the Texas State House to ban the monopolistic vultures from doing business in our state.'

Bell asked, 'What do you remember of the shooting?'

'Not a heck of a lot, as I was just telling Walt. It's coming back, but slow.'

'Mr Gustafson only woke up yesterday morning,' Hatfield told Bell.

'I'm surprised they let you out of the hospital so soon.'

'My wife has a theory that hospitals kill people, being full of sick people with infections. She marched me home the second I could walk.'

Bell turned to Hatfield. 'Who's the dead suspect the sheriff cleared?'

'Found facedown on top of a Springfield '03 with his neck busted.'

'As if he fell while running to escape?'

'Until friends remarked that he was near blind without his glasses, which had got busted that morning in a poker table dispute.'

'Did you manage a look at the rifle?'

Hatfield said, 'The sheriff cooperated. The rifle smelled recently fired. Four rounds still in the magazine, which holds five.'

'Telescope?'

'Nope.'

'Maybe that's why the assassin missed.' Bell turned back to the newspaper publisher.

'Can you tell me what you remember?'

'The window broke. I was setting type for my

editorial by the light of the window. All at once, the glass shattered.'

'What happened next?'

'I'm afraid my answer is not going to help you, Detective Bell. What happened next was I woke up in a strange bed with my wife holding a cool cloth to my brow. Looked around. Walt was standing nearby with his hands on his guns as if to discourage additional potshots.'

Bell asked, 'Would you feel up to visiting your newspaper?'

'I was heading there when Walt suggested we have a snort, and then you walked in.'

They walked the long way to the *Humble Clarion*, taking back streets and alleys to skirt the mob collected around the gusher. The riggers were struggling to cap the new well, while ditchdiggers excavated a catch basin to contain the oil that was raining down like a monsoon. The train had gone. Most of the men aboard it had stayed.

The *Clarion* occupied the first floor of a corner building. C. C. Gustafson led them into the composing room where he set type. 'It was that window,' he said. 'My wife replaced the glass, and finished setting the editorial for me. After picking up all the type that went flying.'

Bell looked for bullet holes in the walls. He remarked that the office had been freshly painted.

'Janet Sue cleaned up the mess soon as the sheriff was done looking things over.'

'Did Mrs Gustafson happen to mention how many bullet holes she plastered before painting?'

'She told me three.'

Bell looked to Hatfield. 'How many rounds had been fired from the Springfield the sheriff found?'

'One.'

Isaac Bell stood in the window. It fronted on the side street. Across the street was a frame building under construction. Carpenters building the platform were hammering floorboards on to ground-floor joists. The otherwise-open lot allowed a long view over low-lying neighbors to the tall false front that topped the two-storey Toppling Derrick saloon on the far side of Main Street three blocks away.

Averell Comstock walked at a remarkably brisk pace for a man his age thanks, he was quick to boast, to a regimen he had started when he first came to New York twenty years ago. He walked every midmorning from the office at 26 Broadway to the East River, where he could order oysters shucked fresh off the boat. He ignored the ketchup and crackers, preferring the briny taste of the bivalves unadulterated, and leaving room for coffee and cake from a food stall on Fulton Street, where he had fallen half in love with a middle-aged widow who had a hard face softened by beautiful blue eyes.

She stirred in the sugar for him. Just this week she had begun to insist on refilling his cup at no charge, stirring in more sugar with a pretty smile. What would she think, Comstock wondered, if she learned that the old man in the ancient coat was ten thousand times richer than any customer she had ever served?

'How are you feeling?' she asked.

'A little under the weather.' For several days he had felt not quite himself.

'I thought you looked pale. I hope you've not been eating oysters. They say there's typhoid fever.'

'I eat only those from Staten Island,' he said. 'It's the Jamaica Bay oysters that carry the typhoid.'

'Well, I hope you feel better.'

'Well enough to walk down here,' he said. 'That's all I ask.'

He drained the second cup and hurried off. 'Back to the salt mines. See you tomorrow.'

Mrs McCloud put another sugar bowl on the counter and hid the one from which she had sweetened the old man's coffee.

'Make sure you wash the spoon.'

Mrs McCloud looked up. The man in the old-fashioned frock coat and fancy trilby hat was back, furtive and cold-eyed as a steerer who sends clients to a shyster lawyer.

'What's in it?' she asked.

'What do you care?'

She glanced up Fulton for another glimpse of the tall old man's top hat bobbing slowly through the crowd that thronged the sidewalk. A street car blocked her view. 'I couldn't care less.'

Heading back to the office, Averell Comstock was surprised when he had to stop and rest halfway there, pale and trembling.

Isaac Bell and Texas Walt Hatfield looked for the assassin's shooting spot on the roof behind the Toppling Derrick saloon's false front. They agreed that the sight lines were there, an easy shot three hundred yards to the *Clarion*'s side window. With the roar of drinkers below celebrating new riches, it was doubtful anyone in the saloon would hear a shot, much less do anything about it. No other building looked down on the roof, ensuring privacy and time to draw a bead and wait.

Bell walked the perimeter. The roof sloped slightly to allow rainwater to spill off into a gutter. He saw a golden glint in the gutter, knelt down, pulled from the grit and hardened sediment that lined the wooden trough an empty cartridge shell.

'A wildcat,' said Bell, showing it to Hatfield. A standard factory-made Savage .303 brass case had been reshaped to accommodate customized powder and bullet loads for greater range and impact.

'Man's loading his own,' said Hatfield.

'I'd expect that for his accuracy,' said Bell. A great marksman, which the assassin surely was, would use the so-called wildcat in conjunction with a finely machined chamber and a custom-made barrel. 'But I'm surprised he didn't scoop it up before he ran. It's a heck of a telltale.'

'Maybe he knew he missed,' said Hatfield. 'Got rattled.'

'Maybe . . . Odd, though. The .303 is made for the Savage 99.'

'Fine weapon. Though a mite light.'

'I wonder why he uses such a light gun. That 1903 Springfield would be more accurate.'

'But heavier.'

'His kill in Kansas was nearly seven hundred yards.'

'A man looks like a flyspeck at that range.'

'That's why I assumed a Springfield.'

'Do you suppose he's a little feller?' Hatfield wondered.

'Too small to hold a more accurate heavy gun? Might explain why he has to improve the Savage cartridge. Probably smithed his rifle to a farewell, too.' Bell pocketed the cartridge. 'OK. Let's see where he went.'

Hatfield had been raised by Comanche Indians and was an expert tracker. Prowling the tar roof, he spotted a minute imprint of the corner of a boot-heel, and found it repeated several yards into an alley. Step-by-step, mark by barely decipherable mark, in crusted mud, oil-soaked earth and dried manure, they followed the sniper's escape route down alleys and over a railroad track and into a stable's corral, where they lost the trail in hoofprints.

'Mounted up here and rode off.'

The stable hands were *vaqueros* too old and lame to quit their jobs to get rich in the oil fields. Walt Hatfield addressed them in Spanish and translated for Bell. Two men had left quickly on horses they had boarded in the stable and had ordered saddled up an hour earlier.

'*Two* men?'

'One big, one little.'

'Were they carrying rifles?'

'No guns.'

Humble's hotels were jam-packed, and the rooming houses were stifling, but Texas Walt had rustled up clean rooms above a stable. They sluiced off the dust of the long, hot day in horse troughs and headed back to the Toppling Derrick where, earlier, Bell had tipped generously to guarantee a table for supper.

They passed the fairground on the way. The suffragist rally had dispersed, and a crowd of the oil field hands camping there was carousing under tarpaulins that sheltered a board-on-barrels saloon. Off to one side, Bell spotted a familiar-looking wall tent pitched beside a buckboard wagon. A black iron pot was suspended over a cook fire.

'Walt, you may be dining alone.'

Drawing near the tent, he heard her typewriter clattering. He knocked on the post. She kept typing like a Gatling gun. But the canvas flew open and out stepped a slim young woman with short, wispy chestnut hair, bright eyes, and a brighter smile. Her voice rang.

'If you're not Isaac Bell, my sister's famed descriptive powers have deserted her.'

She thrust out her hand.

'Nellie Matters. I've been looking forward to meeting you.'

Bell swept his hat off his head, took her delicate fingers in his, and stepped close. When he had seen Nellie through binoculars, he had thought of her features as less fine than her sister's. But with only inches between them, her resemblance to Edna was stronger. She had the same gray-green eyes, the same silken hair, the same beautiful nose. All that seemed magnified were her expressive eyebrows and fuller lips.

'I was hoping you would return to earth,' he said.

'Only briefly.'

The typing stopped. Edna called, 'Invite him to supper.'

'Does he like varmint stew?'

'It's not varmint stew. It's jackrabbit.'

'I love jackrabbit,' said Bell. 'One of you must be quite a shot.'

Nellie laughed. 'Not exactly. Edna blasted them with her .410. We'll be cracking teeth on buckshot.'

Edna emerged from the tent, and Bell's first thought was that Nellie was gorgeous, an utterly beautiful woman, but there was something about Edna – her stillness and her steady gaze – that blocked the breath in his throat.

She said, 'We'll chew carefully. How are you, Mr Bell?'

'Happy to see you. What brings you to Humble?'

'Same thing that brought you, I'd imagine. C. C. Gustafson.'

'Are you reporting for the *Derrick*?'

She did not answer directly, saying instead that C. C. Gustafson was a good friend and an important source for her research.

Nellie asked whether he was investigating the shooting.

'Mr Gustafson doesn't remember much.'

Edna said, 'His memory is returning. He told me that the day before he was shot he had heard that Big Pete Straub arrived on the train.'

Nellie laughed. 'Mr Bell, you really ought to hire my sister to assist in your investigation.'

Bell kept to himself that Gustafson had already told him that and said, 'I reckon Edna's too busy – and far too expensive – but what a nice coincidence you find yourselves here together.'

'We often travel together,' said Nellie. 'Particularly to places like this where a woman's better off not alone.' A nod indicated the tarpaulin saloon, where the men were getting loud. 'Two women are somewhat more formidable than one girl on her own, don't you think?'

'Just ask those jackrabbits.'

'Will you stay to supper?'

'Let me run and find some wine.'

'In Humble? Good luck.'

Bell grinned. 'What do you prefer with jackrabbit?'

Edna grinned. 'A chilled Riesling, wouldn't you say, Nellie?'

Nellie tossed Isaac Bell a second challenge. 'On a hot night with a jackrabbit and a handsome gentleman, I'm in a mood for champagne!'

'I'll be right back,' said Bell.

'Where are you going?' they chorused after him. 'Houston?'

'New Orleans!' Bell called over his shoulder and kept going.

'Don't be late.'

Bell went straight to the Toppling Derrick and asked Walt Hatfield, 'Which did you say was the highest-class sporting house in town?'

'Things didn't work out with the lady reporter?'

'I asked you a question.'

'Easy does it, old son. Just joshin' you. The French Quarter was the one I mentioned. Around the corner and over a couple of streets.'

Bell found the French Quarter's kitchen door down an alley and slipped the cook two twenty-dollar gold pieces. He returned to Edna's tent with a whiskey keg under his arm. The barrelhead had been removed. The sisters peered in.

'Ice? Where did you get ice?'

Bell said, 'Forgive me, Edna, but Riesling proved impossible. Will you settle for a Chablis?'

Edna said, 'I am devastated. But I'll settle for Chablis. Just this once.'

'What about me?' Nellie cried. 'Where's my champagne?'

'Moët & Chandon?'

'Are you serious?'

Bell pulled dripping bottles from the ice.

Nellie said, 'Edna, one of us should grab this fellow before he gets away. You are quite the provider, Mr Bell.'

'Here's my suggestion,' said Bell. 'First we share champagne and save the Chablis for the jackrabbit.'

'But we have no champagne glasses.'

'Tin cups will do,' said Edna.

'No need,' called a familiar voice, and around the tent strode Archie Abbott with four champagne flutes in his hand.

'Where in *blazes* did you come from?' asked Bell.

'Train from Houston,' said Archie, smiling at the ladies. 'In the nick of time. Saw you lugging a barrel of ice, put two and two together, and quickly got glasses. Miss Hock, lovely to see you again. And you, Miss Matters, of course, are the famous flying orator.'

He bowed over Nellie's hand. 'What a treat to observe you without getting a crick in my neck.'

'Will you join us for supper, Mr Abbott?'

Bell said, 'Don't you have an appointment with a witness, Mr Abbott?'

'Not on an empty stomach.'

'That would be too cruel,' said Nellie. 'You must let him have a bite first, Mr Bell.'

'Rabbit first,' said Edna. 'Witness later.'

The champagne lasted until night was falling and it was nearly dark.

'If you boys will open the Chablis, Nellie and I will ladle out the rabbit.'

The sisters gathered around the fire. Bell got to work on the wine bottle.

'Two lovelies!' Archie said in a low voice. 'Count 'em, two. Beautiful, intelligent, charming, accomplished, and single. An abundance of riches.'

'Hands off,' said Bell. 'I haven't made my mind up yet.'

'Fear not, *Ma-ma* is vetting prospective fiancées.'

The Abbotts of New York had lost their money back in the Panic of '93. Archie was supposedly on a hunt to replenish the treasury, but Bell doubted it would happen. He was more likely to fall in love, and money would be the last thing on his mind.

'Funny,' said Archie, 'how they keep turning up wherever you're investigating.'

'Intelligent,' said Bell. 'As you said.'

'Come and get it!' cried Nellie.

'Don't mind if we do,' bawled a loud voice at the edge of the firelight.

Six or seven drunk cowhands and oil workers had wandered over from the board-on-barrels saloon.

'You mean the food or the gals?' yelled a rangy rigger.

'Both!' howled a cowboy.

Isaac Bell and Archie Abbott stood up.

'Good evening, gentlemen,' said Archie. 'Go away.'

'Make me.'

Archie took a lightning step forward and threw an even faster left hook. The rigger tumbled backward into his friends. When they pounced at Archie, Bell was ready with a hard right that dropped the cowboy and a left cross for a burly roustabout.

The four drunks still standing were quickly joined by four more.

The two detectives stood shoulder to shoulder. Archie muttered, 'Any more and I'm pulling a gun.'

'Too many folks around for gunplay,' said Bell.

'Bloody hell, you're right about that.'

Nellie Matters laughed. 'Go away! Our hearts are spoken for.'

If Nellie's joke was designed to defang the mob, thought Bell, it had the opposite effect. She seemed oblivious to the danger. But Edna, Bell noticed, was coolly eyeing the tent flaps behind which was propped her shotgun.

He said, 'Let's take 'em, Archie.'

Archie said, 'You're on.'

The trick was to prevent being mobbed by a concerted rush.

The Van Dorns used their long reach and prize ring footwork to keep them at bay, darting in, dropping three more men with powerhouse punches, and backing lightly away. It looked as if five or six still standing were reconsidering their future when an enormous oil hand easily as big as Big Pete Straub lumbered up.

'Who wants it first?'

'Start with me,' said Isaac Bell, flashing forward, faking a left jab, and throwing a roundhouse right that flung the oil hand flat on his back. But as hard as he hit the ground, it seemed to have no effect. The giant shook his head like a dray horse annoyed by a fly, sprang to his feet, and charged. Bell took his measure, spotted his fists rise, which exposed his solar plexus, and lined up a straight left that would take advantage of the momentum.

Suddenly the man clutched his chest.

He lurched at Bell as if shoved from behind by a mighty force. The burst of unnatural speed caught Bell unaware. Before the tall detective could throw a punch or sidestep the charge, the giant slammed into him.

Three hundred pounds' deadweight drove Isaac Bell to the ground.

Hot liquid splashed his face.

Rabbit stew, he thought in a crazy tenth of a second ended by a rifle shot. He heard a second shot. Lead whistled. A muzzle flash lit the night, and the sniper's third shot clanged off Edna's cook pot.

'Down!' he yelled.

Archie swept Nellie and Edna off their feet. Bell levered out from under the giant. The man did not try to hold him but flopped over with his chest spouting a fountain of heart blood that glittered in the firelight.

The dying brawler had jumped into the path of a bullet meant for Bell.

10

'Take off your shoe,' said the assassin.

Big Pete Straub glared down the rifle barrel aimed at his head and weighed his chances of wrapping his mitts around the neck of this man who had played him for a sucker. Not good.

Slowly, he unlaced his boot, biding his time, gathering his enormous frame for an overwhelming rush, figuring to take a bullet or even two before he crushed the life out of him.

'And your sock.'

Straub tugged off a dirty sock and reached for his other boot. Bare feet? Why?

'Leave it on. One's enough.'

'What in –'

'Put your hands behind your back. Lay down on them. All your weight. Close your eyes. Tight! Squeeze 'em tight!'

'Is this because I missed? I would have hit Bell if you let me use my own gun.'

'I knew you would miss.'

'Then why –'

'Open your mouth.'

'What –'

The assassin shoved the rifle between Big Pete's teeth and touched the muzzle to the roof of his mouth. Big Pete felt it tickle the sensitive membrane.

'Ah don't envy Humble's sheriff,' drawled Texas Walt Hatfield.

Texas Walt and Archie Abbott and Isaac Bell were wolfing down the Toppling Derrick's blue plate special breakfast of fried fatback and eggs.

'Ah mean every time the man turns around, someone's shot, and whoever does the shooting gets clean away. Dumb luck last night, only one dead with all that lead flying, and thankfully none of the ladies. Good luck for you, though, Isaac.'

'Look out!'

A flicker of motion in the corner of Isaac Bell's eye exploded into a rock shattering the window. Bell shoved Archie. The rock missed Abbott's aristocratic nose by a half inch and broke the coffee cup Texas Walt was lifting to his lips.

The drunk who had thrown the rock – a middle-aged, unshaven cowhand in tattered shirt and bibless overalls, and one boot peeling off its sole – stood swaying in the middle of Main Street. His truculent expression froze in astonishment when three tall Van Dorn detectives boiled out the swinging doors with guns drawn. Isaac Bell covered the sidewalk to their left with his automatic pistol. Archie Abbott guarded their right with a city slicker's snub-nosed revolver in one hand and a blackjack in the other.

Texas Walt stalked into the street and leveled two long-barrel Smith & Wessons at the rock thrower's face. His voice was cold, his eyes colder. 'You want to explain why you ruined my breakfast?'

The drunk trembled. 'Looks like I bit off more than I can chew.'

'What in Sam Hill are you talking about?'

'Did you read the note?'

'Note? What note?'

'This note,' said Isaac Bell, who had picked up the rock on his way out the door. He slid a throwing knife from his boot, cut the twine that tied a sheet of paper around the rock, spread the paper, and read it.

'Who gave you this?'

'Feller with five bucks.'

'What did he look like?'

'Big.'

'Beard? Mustache?'

'Nope.'

'What color hair?'

'Yeller.'

Texas Walt interrupted to ask, 'Do you want me to shoot him, Isaac?'

'Hold on a minute. When did the fellow give this note?'

'Couple of hours ago, I guess.'

'Why'd you wait to throw it?'

'Thought I'd have a snort first.'

'Got any money left?'

'Nope.'

'Here. Get yourself something to eat.' Bell shoved a gold piece in his dirty palm and went back to breakfast. Archie and Walt followed.

'Why'd you give that sorry fool money?' asked Walt.

'He did us a big favor.'

'Favor? Spilled coffee all over my best shirt.'

'The hostlers at the stable saw "two men". Remember?'

'What two men?' asked Archie.

'Mounted up and rode off after they shot Gustafson,' said Hatfield. 'What favor, Isaac?'

'When his rock broke the window, I realized why there were two men. One fired first to break the window to give the sniper a clear shot at Mr Gustafson.'

'He missed anyhow. Twice.'

'Only because Mr Gustafson has lightning-fast reflexes. Most men would have stood gaping at the window. But it repeats a pattern.'

'What pattern?'

'Big Pete—type assistance. In Kansas he used him to throw off the scent. Here he used him to clear his shot. I'll lay even money he used him, too, when he shot Albert Hill in Coffeyville and Riggs at Fort Scott.'

'What does the note say?' asked Archie.

Isaac Bell read it aloud: '"You'll find me at the I-Bar-O. Come and get me if you're man enough."'

'Someone's been reading too many dime novels,'

said Texas Walt. 'Why's he announcing ahead of time he's going to bushwhack us?'

'Theatrical,' Bell agreed.

'Bad theater,' said Archie.

Bell spoke with the saloonkeeper who told him that the I-Bar-O ranch was north of Humble on a bend of the San Jacinto River. 'That's the old Owens place. Don't know who you'll find living there. Heard they pulled up stakes.'

'We're getting set up for a wild-goose chase,' said Hatfield. 'Long ride on a hot day.'

Bell said, 'Get horses, saddlebags and Winchesters. Pick me up at Mike's Hardware.'

Twenty minutes later Archie and Walt trotted their horses up to the gleaming-new, three-storey brick Mike's Wholesale and Retail Hardware Company leading a big sorrel for Bell. Bell handed them slingshots from a gunnysack and swung into the saddle.

'You been chewing locoweed, Isaac? If it ain't a wild-goose chase, the man has a rifle. So does his sidekick.'

Bell reached deeper in his sack and tossed them boxed matches and half sticks of dynamite with short fuses. 'In case they're barricaded.'

Winchesters in their scabbards, TNT in their saddlebags, the Van Dorn detectives headed out at a quick trot. They rode six or seven miles, perspiring in the thick, humid heat, passing several cattle outfits that had gone bust. There was a shortage of cowhands in

East Texas, Walt explained. Young men flocked to the oil fields.

The I-Bar-O appeared to be another of the abandoned ranches.

No smoke rose from the cookhouse, and the paddocks were empty.

The Van Dorns spread out, dismounted, and approached cautiously, guns drawn, eyes raking windows, doorways and rooftops. The main house, a low-slung single-storey affair, was deserted. So was the cookhouse – stove cold, larder draped in spiderwebs, flypaper crusted with dried-up insects. The only animals left in the barns were hungry cats.

They converged on the bunkhouse, a flimsy building with an oft-patched roof, a few small windows and a narrow veranda. Archie forged ahead on to the veranda and reached for the door.

'Wait.'

Isaac Bell pointed at a clot of mud on the veranda steps and motioned Archie from the door. The redhead pressed his back to the wall and peered in the nearest window. 'Man on the floor. Can't quite see. He's got a rifle beside him, but he's not holding it . . . In fact, if he's not dead, he sure isn't moving.'

Archie reached again for the door.

'Don't!' chorused Bell and Walt. Neither questioned Archie's courage, but his judgment was not seasoned to their liking. He had come late to the detective line – personally recruited by Bell, on the first case

that Mr Van Dorn had allowed him to form his own squad. As Mr Van Dorn put it more than once, 'It's a miracle how a Protestant New York blue blood can get his Irish up as fast as Archibald Angell Abbott IV.'

'It's OK,' said Archie. 'He's alone and he's dead.'

Walt Hatfield cocked both his pistols. 'Archie, if you touch that doorknob, I'll shoot you.'

'Shoot me?'

'To prevent you from killing yourself. Stand aside and let Isaac show you how we do it in Texas.'

Isaac Bell gestured Walt to take cover, bounded on to and across the veranda, shouldered Archie aside, jammed his spine to the wall, and rammed his rifle backward to smash the door open with the butt.

The blast it triggered shook the earth.

11

A swath of buckshot wide as two men screeched through the doorway and splintered both sides of the jamb. Isaac Bell hurled himself into the bunkhouse before the assassin could reload.

Cavernous ten-gauge shotgun barrels stared him rock steady in the face. He dived sideways, hit the floor with a crash, and rolled into a crouch before he realized that the shotgun was lashed tightly to a post.

Ears ringing, Bell lowered his Winchester and looked around.

A horseshoe dangled from a rafter. It was swinging on a string that looped over several nails and down to the shotgun's triggers. Opening the door had bumped the horseshoe off a nail. Its weight had fetched up the slack in the string and jerked the triggers, firing both barrels simultaneously.

Big Pete Straub lay on his back on the bunkhouse floor. His right foot was bare. Flies were darting in and out of a ragged three-inch hole in the top of his head. With one shoe off and one shoe on, the refinery police chief had killed himself by putting his rifle barrel in his mouth and pushing the trigger with his toe.

'So much for your assistance pattern, Isaac,' said Hatfield. 'The man went out alone with a bang.'

'Almost took us with him,' said Archie.

'About that "almost", Archie?' said Hatfield, cocking an eyebrow that demanded an answer.

'Thank you, Walt. Thank you, Isaac.'

'You can thank us by remembering that criminals do the damnedest things.'

Bell was already kneeling by Straub's gun. 'Savage 99.'

Hatfield snapped a spent shell off the floor. 'Another wildcat.'

The sleek, hammerless Savage felt remarkably light in Bell's hands. He noticed an extension on the fore end of the chamber, as if a quarter-inch piece of metal had been added to it. A metal slide under the wooden end released it, revealing the underside of the barrel. A square stud projected from it. The wood had a corresponding hole. Bell fitted the wood to the barrel, held the chamber in the other hand, and twisted firmly. The barrel, which he expected to be compression-screwed into the chamber, rotated an easy quarter turn and pulled loose. He was suddenly holding two separate parts, each barely twenty inches long, short enough to conceal in a satchel, a sample case, or an innocent-looking carpetbag.

'Walt, did you ever see a breakdown Savage 99?'

'Ah don't believe the company makes one.'

129

'Someone made this one with an interrupted screw.'

Bell put it back together by inserting the barrel into the chamber and turning a quarter turn. A metal slide underneath fit into a corresponding slot, locking the barrel in place. Thanks to the interrupted threads – an invention that had made possible the quick-sealing cannon breech – the rifle could be broken down or reassembled in two seconds.

But the question remained why such a light weapon for a man as big as Straub?

'No telescope.'

'Holes tapped for mounting one?' asked Walt.

Bell inspected the top of the frame. 'Mounting holes tapped . . . You should have seen his shot in Kansas. Archie saw it.'

'Better part of a half a mile,' said Archie.

Walt said, 'Mr Straub must have had hawk eyes.'

The Springfield '03 that the sheriff had found under the dead man in a Humble alley was fed ammunition by a removable straight magazine. The Savage had a rotary magazine. The indicator on the side of the chamber read '4.' Bell extracted one of the rounds. Instead of factory-made round noses, the bottleneck cartridges had been specially loaded with pointed, aerodynamic 'spitzer' bullets.

Something about the weapon felt wrong to Bell. He unscrewed the barrel again, rethreaded it in a second, slid the wooden fore end back in place, locking the entire assembly. Then he carried the gun outside. The sorrel had wandered close. He tied its reins to the veranda railing in case shots spooked the animal, took a bead on a fence post a quarter mile away, and fired until the magazine was empty.

He rode the horse to the target and rode back.

'Hit anything?' Walt asked.

'Dead center twice, grazed it twice. It's a good gun . . . But it's hard to believe it's the gun that killed Spike Hopewell.'

'Unless,' Hatfield grinned, 'Mr Straub was a better shot.'

'Doubt it.'

Archie said, 'But we found a custom-made Savage shell.'

Texas Walt said, 'Listen close, Archie. Isaac did not say that Spike Hopewell wasn't killed by a Savage 99. All he's saying is he don't reckon this particular Savage 99 did the deed.'

'Telegram, Mr Bell.'

Bell tipped the boy two bits and read the urgent wire he had been hoping for. Joseph Van Dorn had outdone himself in his constant effort to minimize expenses by reducing his message to a single word:

NOW

Bell told Archie Abbott to follow him when he was done helping Hatfield and sprinted to the station. He barely made the Sunset Express to New Orleans, where he transferred to the New York Limited.

He settled into a writing desk in the club car and was composing a report from his notebook when women's voices chorused like music in his ear: 'Fancy meeting you here, Mr Bell.'

Edna and Nellie Matters were headed to Washington, where Nellie was to address a suffragist delegation petitioning Congress. Her balloon was folded up in the express car. When the sisters said they were sleeping in upper and lower Pullman berths, Bell gave them his stateroom.

Edna protested. Nellie thanked him warmly. 'How can we repay you?'

'Join me this evening in the dining car.'

At dinner, Nellie entertained him, and the surrounding tables, with tales of runaway balloons. Edna, who had clearly heard it all before, listened politely as Nellie rattled on. 'Sideways, the wind blows you into trees and telegraph wires. Low on gas, you fall from the sky. Emergency! Quick! Emergency gas! –'

'Excuse me, young lady,' a clergyman interrupted from the table across the aisle. 'I could not help but overhear. Where do you find emergency gas when you're already flying in the air?'

'I have special steel containers installed in my basket,' Nellie answered. 'Lots of balloons do. It's very handy having extra hydrogen.'

'They must be heavy.'

'They beat falling,' she dismissed him and turned her green eyes back on Bell. 'Where was I? Oh, yes. Too quick, too much emergency gas, you soar too high and suffocate. The air gets so thin, you run out of oxygen . . .'

Over the Neapolitan ice cream dessert, Bell echoed Archie's earlier comment. 'Strange how the three of us keep turning up together where crimes have occurred.'

Edna replied, 'I'm beginning to suspect you, Mr Bell.'

Nellie laughed. 'I suspected him from the start.'

'May I ask you something?'

Nellie grinned at Edna. 'Doesn't he look suddenly serious?'

'Like a detective,' said Edna. 'Go on, we shouldn't be teasing you.'

'At least until he's paid the dinner check,' said Nellie. 'Actually, you really do look solemn. What is it?'

'Spike Hopewell told me that your brother ran off and you never heard from him. Is that true?'

Their mood changed in an instant. Nellie looked away. Edna nodded. 'Yes. Actually, he was a Yale man, like you.'

'Really? What class?'

'You were probably several years ahead of him.'

'He didn't go back after his freshman year,' said Nellie.

'Perhaps you knew him?' said Edna.

'I don't recall anyone named Matters.'

'His name was Billy Hock.'

'Billy Hock?' Bell looked at her curiously.

'Yes,' said Edna. 'He was my older brother.'

'And my older half brother,' said Nellie.

Isaac Bell said, 'I never made the connection.'

'We did,' said Edna. 'Or we wondered. Do you remember now?'

Bell nodded, recalling a slender, eager-to-please youngster, more a boy than a man. 'Well, yes, I knew him, slightly . . .'

Billy Hock had big, bright gray-green eyes as bright as Edna's and Nellie's. 'He enrolled as a freshman my senior year. He was very young, youngest of the boys entering.'

'Fifteen. He was small. Undersized.'

Nellie said, 'He tried out for crew. He would have made a perfect coxswain, being so light. But he was terrified of water. He always had a phobia about it.'

'The crew rowers ragged him mercilessly,' said Edna.

Bell nodded.

'Until some upperclassman stepped in and put a stop to it.'

'Yes.'

'We wondered how.'

'He could not abide bullies,' said Bell.

'One boy against a team?' asked Nellie.

'He trained at boxing.'

Edna directed her level gaze into Bell's eyes.

'When I watched you and Archie boxing those men,

I suddenly wondered was it you who stood up for our brother. Wasn't it?'

'I hadn't realized the connection until this very moment. The different name. We didn't discuss our families at college – unless our people were related – you must remember when you went off to college how we were all so glad to be away from home at that age.'

Both women nodded.

'So Billy Hock was the brother who ran away? Strange . . . I wondered at school how he would fare. When did he go?'

'That same summer, right after his freshman year,' said Edna.

'He was adventurous,' said Nellie. 'Just like me – always running around and trying new things.'

'We never heard from him again,' said Edna.

Nellie said, 'Sometimes I blame myself. I became a kind of model for him, even though I was younger. He saw me running around – one second I was entranced by balloons, then I was trying to be an actress, then I ran off to be an acrobat in the circus – remember, Edna?'

'I remember Father laughing when the ringmaster walked you home.'

'On a white horse! He said I was too young. I said, "OK, take me home on a white horse!" . . . And he did . . . I gave Billy courage. I only hope it didn't push him toward the Army.'

'No, it didn't,' Edna said, laying a reassuring hand on her sister's arm. 'If anything, it gave him courage to go away to Yale. Father,' she explained, turning to Bell, 'so wanted Billy to attend Yale because many "Oil Princes" went to college there – Comstock's son, Lapham's son, Atkinson's nephews.'

'Billy and I talked about joining the Army. The Spanish war was brewing – the papers were full of it – and boys were signing up.' Bell had tried, caught up in the excitement, but his father, a Civil War veteran, had intervened forcefully, arguing with unassailable logic that there were better causes to die for than 'a war started by newspapers to sell newspapers.'

Edna said, 'We *guess* that Billy enlisted under an assumed name. Lied about his age. We *fear* he was lost either in the swamps of Cuba or the Philippine jungle. We never heard. If he did join, he must have changed his name and lied about his family.'

'But we don't really know what happened,' said Nellie. 'Except that it nearly destroyed our poor father.'

'You cut it close,' said Joseph Van Dorn.

Isaac Bell lifted his gold watch from his pocket, sprang the lid, and let Van Dorn read the dial. Then he shook his head at the latest addition to the Boss's Willard Hotel office, a modern, glass-cased table clock from Paris. 'Your O'Keenan electric, imported at untold expense, is running fifty-seven seconds fast.'

'Sit down,' said Van Dorn. 'He's in my private waiting room. But brace yourself. The poor devil lost all his hair to some disease.'

'*Alopecia totalis.*'

'Even his eyebrows and mustache. I had a look through the peephole. He's smooth as a cue ball.'

'Don't worry,' said Bell, 'it's not catching . . . Now, sir, we need a plan.'

They spoke for two minutes, Van Dorn dubious, Bell prepared with persuasive answers. When the tall detective had prevailed, the Boss murmured into a voice tube and his visitor was ushered in from the private entrance.

12

'Mr Rockefeller.'

The retired president of the Standard Oil Corporation was a tall, sixty-six-year-old, two-hundred-pound man. He had piercing eyes that burned in an enormous hairless head, an icily quiet manner, and a powerful presence that reminded Isaac Bell of the long-reigning heavyweight champion Jim Jeffries.

John D. Rockefeller shook hands with Joseph Van Dorn and nodded to Bell when Van Dorn introduced him as 'my top investigator.' He refused a chair and got straight to the point.

'An assassin is discrediting Standard Oil by attacking enemies of the trust. The public, inclined to believe the worst, gossips that Standard Oil is behind the attacks.'

'It's the price for hitting the big time,' Van Dorn said sympathetically. 'You get blamed for everything.'

'This outcry against us is wrong. The public cannot seem to understand that we are not monsters. We are merely efficient – enormously more efficient than our competitors. Oil is not the biggest business in America. Coal is bigger. Railroads are bigger. Steel is bigger. Yet, we own coal. We control railroads. We own steel. Why? Not because we're monsters, but because *they* are chaotic, embroiled in murderous rivalry, each conducting his own business independently of the other and in sharp competition. *We* cooperate.'

Van Dorn glanced at Bell. Bell had been the Boss's personal apprentice when he started at the agency straight out of college and Van Dorn had taught him the trade on Chicago's West Side – as dangerous a city ward as could be found anywhere in the country. Like Apache braves who had stalked game and hunted enemies side by side since boyhood, they could communicate with signs known only to them.

'You sound pretty sure of yourself,' said Van Dorn, uncharacteristically blunt.

John D. Rockefeller fixed him with his cold gaze. 'The next time someone tells you that Standard Oil is an octopus, Mr Van Dorn, you may tell them for me that the "octopus" keeps his books straight, his inventory in order, his bank accounts positive, and pays his debts when due. He is not hoodwinked by alluring prospects. He keeps his powder dry. The octopus is organized and disciplined and the rest of them . . . they are not.'

'If the octopus is ready to get down to brass tacks,' said Van Dorn, 'let's take up the business of this meeting.'

'I intend to hire the Van Dorn Detective Agency to catch the assassin and end the slander.'

'You're too late,' said Isaac Bell. 'The man committed suicide in Humble, Texas.'

'I have rarely heard anything so ridiculous,' said Rockefeller. 'You have your facts wrong.'

'Not unless you know something that we don't about Standard Oil policeman Big Pete Straub,' said Bell.

'I do,' Rockefeller said blandly.

'We are all ears,' said Van Dorn.

'Mr Straub suffered a medical condition the doctors call foot drop. His nerves were damaged by an injury he sustained in the course of a labor dispute. The damage, which was irreparable, caused paralysis of the flexor muscles.'

'Right foot or left?' asked Bell.

'Mr Straub could not move the toes of his right foot. Had he desired to trigger a rifle with his toe, he would have bared his other foot.'

Van Dorn scowled as if embarrassed his detective was found lacking.

Isaac Bell almost smiled. He felt oddly relieved. That light Savage rifle in that big man's hands did not feel right. And their attempt to penetrate Standard Oil had just paid off in a totally unexpected bonus.

'Did your refinery police detectives tell you this?' asked Van Dorn.

'Straub's superiors reported the condition when they read the accounts in the newspapers. Do you see how perfectly silly that verdict of suicide is?'

'Thank you, Mr Rockefeller, I do,' said Isaac Bell. 'He was murdered. The killing was made to look like suicide. Mr Straub was not the assassin.'

Bell spoke coolly, but his head was spinning with questions. The lightweight gun. How to explain such extraordinary accuracy? A circus or Wild West Show performer, hardly likely. He was grasping at straws. The assassin could be an ordinary-size man with a penchant for the Savage 99 and the means and knowledge to have the factory weapon smithed to such a degree, it was custom-made. Like the weapon he had left with Straub's body.

Rockefeller said, 'Van Dorn, I want you to stop wasting your time with the investigation in Washington and put your firm's full effort into catching the assassin.'

Isaac Bell and Joseph Van Dorn knew that Bell's ploy to infiltrate Standard Oil had hooked their man. Now the job was to reel in the cagey president.

Van Dorn said, 'You have your own private detective force. Why don't you put them to work?'

'They're not the men for this job. I want the best and I'll pay for it.'

Bell and Van Dorn exchanged what appeared to be puzzled glances. 'But we are already investigating *you* for the Corporations Commission,' Van Dorn protested. 'As I'm sure you know.'

Rockefeller said, 'You will recall my instructions that I enter your offices, unaccompanied, by a private entrance.'

Joseph Van Dorn's grand roman nose wrinkled as if he smelled something unpleasant.

'Mr Rockefeller, what does your method of arrival have to do with anything?'

'We do not have to inform the Corporations Commission that you're working for me.'

Joseph Dorn's mouth tightened. His nostrils flared. His cheeks turned red as his whiskers as he ceased to draw breath. His voice took on a low, steely note that left no doubt that were Rockefeller a younger man, he would drag him down the Willard Hotel's grand staircase by the scruff of his neck and throw him out the door on to Pennsylvania Avenue.

'I have given my word to my client, the commission. My word is my bond. A sacred oath.'

'This is more urgent,' said Rockefeller.

Van Dorn started to retort.

Isaac Bell interrupted. 'We should concentrate on the assassin. He is the clear and immediate danger.'

'No,' said Van Dorn. 'The agency is honor-bound to do both.'

'I agree with Mr Rockefeller,' Bell said staunchly. 'This killer will murder again. Hanging a murderer is far more important – and more honorable – than parsing the intentions of the Sherman Anti-Trust Act, which the Supreme Court will probably overturn anyway.'

Van Dorn clenched his fists. 'If you feel so strongly that the intentions of a shilly-shallying Congress and a vacillating court are more important than my agency's honor, you are free to resign your position and join Mr Rockefeller.'

Rockefeller turned on his heel and headed for the door. 'I'll be at my estate in Westchester, New York, Mr Bell, where you can call on me.'

The assassin entered the Washington Monument carrying a carpetbag and joined a group of men and women waiting for the elevator to take them to the top of the memorial shaft. They returned the bright smile and hearty hello expected of fellow out-of-town visitors and made room when the car arrived. Piloted by a self-important operator, who seemed to take pleasure in opening and closing the door at a glacial pace, it climbed five hundred feet in twelve slow minutes, a heart-pounding eternity of grating cables, wheels and rails made even longer by the endless din of tourist chatter and the sudden exclamations as they spotted among the memorial stones that decorated the interior walls lumps of rock from their own states. It gets easier every day to be a snob, thought the assassin.

The door opened at last to the smell of turpentine and paint.

The so-called Lincoln Memorial was nothing more than a mud patch, and Clyde Lapham was having a hard time concentrating on the do-gooder's speech. His eye kept wandering toward an exposed tree root that reminded him of a snake slithering up an Allegheny riverbank. The old man remembered the snake so vividly from his boyhood that he could smell the water and hear the flies buzzing around his head. He swore he saw its fast tongue exploring the air with expectant flickers.

'"The Great Emancipator,"' the do-gooder droned in his ear. '"Savior of the Union" . . . Fitting to rise opposite the monument to our first president, don't you think, sir?'

'That snake . . .'

'Beg your pardon, Mr Lapham?'

'You see that snake . . .' Lapham's voice trailed off as he lost interest in whether the do-gooder raising money to build the Lincoln Memorial could see the snake. *He* could see the snake.

The do-gooder pointed at the Washington Monument. It was taller than a New York City skyscraper. Unlike New York skyscrapers, it stood alone. Far, far away. And far behind it, the dome of the Capitol rose into the sky like . . . like . . . he didn't care what it was like. But here, in the mud, the snake.

He tried to remember why he was here instead of back in New York. The do-gooder wanted money from the Standard, and the boys at Number 26 had given him the job of riding the train down to Washington to reckon if it was the kind of thing Mr Rockefeller would want to write a check to. Or so they said. Lapham had his suspicions. They just wanted him out of the office so they could cut him out of another private deal.

'How much money are you begging for?'

'Begging? May I quote Mr Rockefeller himself on the subject of philanthropy? "I am proud," he said, "of my ability to beg money for the good of mankind."'

'How much would this thing cost?'

'Well, sir, if Congress won't act, it's up to patriotic men of means like yourself and Mr Rockefeller. As Mr Rockefeller has undertaken to support many fine causes in his retirement –'

'Retirement?' Clyde Lapham snorted. 'Rockefeller retired? You must be kidding . . .' His voice trailed off. He had just remembered they weren't ever supposed to say that. He corrected himself. 'Retirement. You're right. He's retiring. Retired. Retired. Goddamned-sure retired.'

The do-gooder, a churchman, recoiled at the sound of an oath.

'How much will this thing cost?' Lapham repeated.

'Well . . .' The do-gooder rubbed his hands. 'Wouldn't that depend, sir – Mr Lapham – on the size of the monument?'

'Big as that one?' Lapham asked, pointing at the five-hundred-and-fifty-five-foot, four-sided obelisk erected to the memory of George Washington. He stared at it. His eye fixed on a barely visible square hole near the top. As the tree root reminded him of the snake, that square hole made him think of a wagon riding up the sheer wall of the pillar. He could even see the horses pulling it in the patterns of the marble building blocks.

'What's that up there?'

'The monument?' asked the minister, who was beginning to realize that old Lapham was confused, to put it mildly. Too confused to contribute to his private Lincoln Memorial fund? Or confused in a way that might embrace the fund with open arms.

'Let us remember that magnificent edifice owes its existence to the private effort of the Washington Monument Society when good men like the good men of the Standard raised the funds that Congress failed to provide.'

'That square thing near the top . . . What the devil is that?'

'Oh, that's one of the windows.'

'Windows?'

'People looking out that window will see the Lincoln Memorial right down here.'

'They better have good eyes,' said Lapham. He had lost sight of the wagon, but he could see a clear shot straight from that window to where he stood. 'That's the best part of a mile.'

'When Americans climb the stairs to honor President Washington, they will rush back down them to visit the Standard's gift memorializing President Lincoln.'

'Damned fools should take the elevator.'

The assassin detached from the clot of tourists when the elevator door opened and they were shunted past a canvas curtain toward the observation windows that faced east, south and north. The assassin slipped behind the curtain and put the carpetbag beneath the window that faced west. Stout metal bars had been installed in the window to stop suicides from launching themselves from it. They were set deep in the masonry six inches apart.

The window looked over the Mall, a grass-covered flat land that stretched almost to the Potomac River. At the far end, just before the river, was a stretch of raw mud where a Brooklyn minister – inspired by a previous generation's Brooklyn Abolitionists – was attempting to collect contributions to build a memorial to Abraham Lincoln.

It was a thankless task that the Lincoln Memorial Association had been trying with no success since 1867. His target today, Clyde Lapham, could pay for the entire thing, being a charter member of the Standard Oil Gang. If he could only remember where he had left his checkbook.

Clyde Lapham forgot the snake in the mud and forgot the wagon on top of the Washington Monument. He was mesmerized now by the tip of the obelisk, a shiny point that was a different color than the marble. The marble was turning darker as it was silhouetted against the setting sun. But the tip glowed with an unearthly light.

The do-gooder churchman was rattling on again.

Lapham interrupted.

'Explain why the tip of the Washington Monument is a different color than the bottom?'

'It is made of aluminum,' said the churchman.

'Are you building something similar for President Lincoln?'

I've snagged a live one, thought the minister. *If I can only land him.*

'We have no design yet, sir. Congress fails to fund the memorial, so the money has not been allocated to pay for any proposed designs, and won't be until private citizens step up and take charge.'

A closed carriage pulled up nearby. Two men stepped out and walked toward them. One carried a physician's medical bag. He addressed Lapham, speaking slowly and loudly, 'Good afternoon, Mr Lapham. How are we feeling today?'

'Who the devil are you?'

To the minister's astonishment, they seized Clyde Lapham by his arms and marched him forcefully toward the carriage.

The minister hurried after them. 'You there! Stop. What are you doing?'

'I'm his doctor. It is time for him to come home.'

The minister was not about to let this opportunity be marched away. 'Now, hold on!'

The doctor turned abruptly and blocked the minister's path while his companion walked Lapham out of earshot. 'You are disturbing my patient.'

'He's not ill.'

The doctor pulled a pistol from his bag. He pointed it in the minister's face. 'Turn around. Walk away.'

'Where are you taking –'

The doctor cocked the pistol. The minister turned around and walked away, head swimming, until the carriage clattered off.

The assassin had demanded double canvas curtains to shield the monument's west window just in case some tourist got nosy. Sure enough, through the curtains came a querulous demand: 'What's going on in there?'

'It's a painter,' answered one of the Army privates responsible for guiding visitors. 'He's making pictures of the view.'

'Why's he walled in?'

'So no one bothers him.'

'What if I want to see out that window?'

'Come back another day, sir.'

'See here! I'm from Virginia. I came especially to view Virginia from this great height.'

The assassin waited.

A new voice, the smooth-talking sergeant in charge of the detail who had been tipped lavishly: 'I invite you, sir, to view Maryland and the District of Columbia today and return next week to devote your full attention to Virginia. It will be my personal pleasure to issue you a free pass to the elevator.'

The assassin took a well-lubricated cast-iron screw jack from the carpetbag and inserted it sideways in the window, holding the base against one bar and the load pad against the other and rotating the lever arm that turned the lifting screw. The jack was powerful enough to raise the corner of a barn. Employed sideways, it spread the vertical bars as if they were made of macaroni.

Clyde Lapham's captors timed their arrival at the Washington Monument to coincide with the elevator's final ascent of the day. The man with the physician's bag stepped ahead to speak privately with the soldier at the door, palming a gold piece into his hand as he explained, 'The old gent has been asking all day to come up and now that we're here he's a little apprehensive. I wonder if we could just scoot him aboard quickly. My resident will distract him until we get to the top . . . Who is he? Wealthy donor to my hospital, just as generous a man as you'll ever meet. A titan of industry, in his day . . .'

The private's nose wrinkled at the smell of chloroform on the doctor's frock coat. The rich old guy was reeling on his feet. The resident was holding tight.

'Don't worry, he won't cause any trouble. He's just nervous – it will mean so much to him.'

The private ushered them into the elevator and whispered to the other tourists not to trouble the old man.

They let the others off first and, when no one saw, they stepped behind the canvas.

The assassin pointed at the window. One of the bars had snapped. The other was bent. There was plenty of room between them. Lapham's eyes were rolling in his head. 'What's that stink?'

'Chloroform.'

'Thought so. What are we doing here?'

'Flying,' said the assassin. At his signal, the two men lifted Lapham off his feet and threw him headfirst out the window.

Startled by the wind rushing past his head, Clyde Lapham soon found his attention fixed placidly on the granite blocks racing by like a long gray train of railroad cars. He had always liked trains.

In the passenger hall of the Baltimore & Ohio Depot, the public telephone operator signaled a successful long-distance connection to New York.

The assassin closed the door of the soundproofed booth.

'I have accomplished the mission.'

'Mission?' asked Bill Matters. 'This is a weak line. I can't hear you.'

'I have accomplished the mission.'

'What mission?'

'When the New York papers get the news, they'll flood the streets with extras.'

Even through a weak connection, Matters heard the overblown exuberance that could mean trouble. 'What news?'

'Clyde Lapham leaped to his death from the Washington Monument.'

'*What?*'

'As you requested, his death will seem innocent.'

'No.'

'The poor man was deranged. He jumped from the top of the Washington Monument.'

'*No!*'

'You could tell that he planned it a long time. He brought a barn jack to force open the bars wide enough to slip through. He arranged for the window to be blocked off from public view. He anticipated every detail. Apparently, an artist was painting views for the Army – the Army runs the monument, you know. Dementia is a strange affliction, isn't it? That a man could be simultaneously so confused and so precise.'

'*No! No! No!*'

'What's wrong?'

Bill Matters raged. He clamored he still had use for Lapham. He had not ordered him killed. He was so angry that he shouted things he could not mean. '*Are you insane?*'

The assassin hooked the earpiece back on the telephone, paid the clerk at the operator's desk, and strolled out of the station and up New Jersey Avenue until the incident was forgotten.

13

Isaac Bell walked across E Street, peering into shop-windows, and turned down 7th, where he propped a boot on a horse trough and mimed tying a nonexistent shoelace. Then he continued along Pennsylvania Avenue, skirted the Capitol, and turned down New Jersey. Ahead stood the Baltimore & Ohio Depot.

The clock tower was ringing his train.

He collected a ticket he had reserved for the Royal Blue passenger flier to New York. The clerk warned that it was leaving in five minutes. Bell hurried across the station hall, only to pull up short when an ancient beggar in rags, a torn slouch hat, and white beard deeply frosted with age shuffled into his path and extended a filthy hand.

Bell fumbled in his pocket, searching for a coin.

'Rockefeller's detectives are still on your tail,' the beggar muttered.

'Skinny gent in a frock coat,' said Bell without looking back. 'He took over from a tall, wide fellow on 7th Street. Any more?'

Joseph Van Dorn scratched his powder-whitened beard and pretended to extract a louse. 'They put a man on the train dressed as a priest. Good luck, Isaac. You're almost in.'

'Did the boys manage to follow Mr Rockefeller?'

Van Dorn's proud grin nearly undid his disguise.

'Right up to the back door of the Persian embassy.'

'Persia?' Edna called Rockefeller the master of the unexpected. She had that right. 'What does he want with Persia?'

'Play your cards right and you'll be in a position to find out.'

Bell dropped a coin in Van Dorn's hand. 'Here you go, old-timer. Do your friends a favour, spend it at a bathhouse.'

He showed his ticket and headed out on the platform, hurried the length of the blue-and-gold train, peering through the gleaming leaded-glass windows, and boarded the Royal Blue's first car. Then he worked his way swiftly through the cars. The locomotive, a rocket-fast, high-wheeled Atlantic 4-4-2, whistled the double ahead signal.

Four cars back, he spotted the Standard Oil detective dressed like a priest. He clamped a powerful hand around his dog collar. The locomotive huffed steam, gently for a smooth start, and the drivers began turning. Bell lifted the priest out of his seat by the scruff of his neck. Passengers stared. Bell marched him off the train.

'Tell Mr Rockefeller he's wasting his money and my time shadowing me with amateurs.'

'What are you talking about?' the detective blustered. 'How dare you assault a man of the cloth.'

The train was rolling, the side of a coach brushing

Bell's shoulder. 'Tell the thin man in the frock coat and his fat friend in the derby next time they follow me, I'll punch both their noses.'

Bell ran to catch up with the Royal Blue.

'And that goes double for the clergy.'

Voices were raised when Isaac Bell walked into the club car looking for a well-earned cocktail. The loudest belonged to a red-faced United States senator in a dark sack suit, a florid necktie of the type President Roosevelt was making popular, and a hawser-thick gold watch chain draped across his ample belly. He was hectoring the only woman in the car, Nellie Matters, who was wearing a white shirt, a broad belt around her slim waist, a straight skirt to her ankles, and a plain straw hat adorned with a red ribbon.

Bell ordered a Manhattan and asked the perspiring bartender, 'What is going on?'

'The suffragette started it.'

'Suffra*gist*,' Bell corrected. 'Seems to be enjoying herself.' Her eyes were bright, and she had dots of high color in her cheeks. Bell thought he had never seen her quite so pretty before.

'They were debating enfranchisement, hammer and tongs, before we even got rolling.' The bartender filled his glass. 'We don't often see a lady in the club car, it being a bastion, shall we say, of "manliness".'

'The gents appear willing to make an exception for a looker.'

'But the senator prefers an audience to a looker.'

'Yet another reason not to trust a man who enters politics,' said Isaac Bell.

The senator loosed a blast of indignation. 'I read in the newspapers, Miss Matters, you intended to fly your balloon over the Capitol and drop *torpedoes* on the Congress! *And would have dropped them if the wind had not blown your balloon the other way!*'

'I made a terrible mistake,' said Nellie Matters, her clear voice carrying the length of the car.

'Mistake?'

'I forgot to read the weather report. A balloonist must always keep track of which way the wind blows.'

'Good lord, woman, you *admit* you intended to bomb Congress?'

'Nonsense!' Nellie's eyes flashed. She tossed her head, and every man in the club car leaned in to hear her answer. 'I would never harm a soul – not even a senator.' She turned and opened her arms wide as if to take everyone in the car into her confidence. 'My only purpose in soaring over the Congress was to expose the members for the idiots they are.'

That drew chuckles and catcalls.

Isaac Bell raised his voice in a strong baritone: 'How could flying your balloon over senators and congressmen do that?'

Nellie flashed him a smile that said Hello, Mr Bell, thanks for setting up my next line: 'My balloon soars on gas or hot air. I had no fear of running out of either in their vicinity.'

The car erupted in laughter. Business men pounded their palms pink. Salesmen slapped their thighs. From every direction, dyed-in-the-wool anti-woman-voters vied to buy her a glass of wine.

'No thank you! I don't drink.' She cast Bell a glance that clearly said: Except, of course, when dining on jackrabbit in Texas. 'But, gentlemen, in lieu of your glasses of wine, I will accept contributions to the New Woman's Flyover.'

'New Woman's Flyover?'

'What's that?'

'The New Woman's Flyover is a stunt when a fleet of red, white and blue balloons full of suffragists take to the sky to boom an amendment to the Constitution enfranchising women voters.'

'Never heard of it.'

'I just thought it up! And you gentlemen are going to make the first contributions, aren't you?'

'Open your carpetbag, Miss Matters,' Isaac Bell called. 'I'll pass the hat.'

He whipped his hat off his head, deftly palmed the derringer holstered within, and walked the length of the club car like a deacon until it was brimful with contributions. Nellie opened her carpetbag wide. Bell poured the money in.

Nellie called, 'Thank you, gentlemen! Every suffragist

in the nation will thank you, and your wives will welcome you home warmly.'

'Another coincidental meeting?' Bell asked. 'But no crime this time. At least none yet.'

'It's no coincidence.'

'Then how do we happen to be on the same train?'

'I asked the clerk at the Willard Hotel for your forwarding address. The Yale Club of New York City.'

'Were you planning a trip to New York?'

'I decided to visit my father.'

'Spur-of-the-moment?'

'Whenever I like,' she smiled back.

Bell said, 'I would like to meet your father.'

'How should I introduce you?' Nellie asked. 'Father will not cotton to a private detective investigating his corporation.'

'I'm not on the commission case anymore.'

'Why not?'

'It's a long story,' said Bell.

'We have time for a long story. It's six hours to New York.'

'Let's just say it won't be an official visit,' Isaac Bell lied.

Only part a lie. The chance to observe Spike Hopewell's former partner in his own home would be absolutely official, but it would not require much pretense to act the part of a man who desired to visit Bill Matters' daughter. Either daughter.

'Why don't you introduce me as a gentleman caller?'

'Father won't believe you. He knows I am not the sort of woman who sits at home waiting for gentleman callers.'

'Then tell him I'm a man hoping for a ride in your balloon.'

'You can ride in my balloon anytime you'll make a speech for women's votes.'

'Actually, I rode in a balloon once, in the circus. Is that where you discovered balloons? In the circus?'

'I prefer theaters to circuses. They're more fantastical.'

'I don't agree. I ran away to a circus when I was a boy.'

'You must tell me about the circus sometime.'

'How about now?'

'Spur-of-the-moment?'

'Whatever you like.'

'I would like to eat dinner,' said Nellie Matters. 'I'm hungry, and it's my turn to take you.'

At Central Station, the twelve-year-old boys peddling the *Washington Post* Late Extra Edition were shrill as a flock of jays.

'Tourist falls from Washington Monument.'

'Extra! Extra! Tourist falls!'

Archie Abbott tossed pennies for the paper and ran to the horse cabs. Mr Van Dorn had sent a wire care of the Danville, Virginia, stationmaster ordering him to report the instant his train pulled into Washington.

Top hands like Isaac Bell took direct summons from the Boss for granted, but this was his first one ever.

'Willard Hotel. Fast as you can.'

Upon arrival, he dashed up the stairs into the Van Dorn offices.

'The Boss wired my train at Danville. Said to come right over.'

The front desk man spoke calmly into a voice tube. A blasé apprentice walked Archie into Joseph Van Dorn's office. With his coat off and his sleeves rolled up his bulging forearms, Van Dorn, Archie thought, looked less the company proprietor than a prosperous bricklayer.

'Abbott, you're a Princeton man.'

'Yes, sir.'

'I've got something right up your alley.'

'How can I help, sir?'

Van Dorn nodded at the extra edition that Archie had tucked under his arm. 'The "tourist" who fell from the memorial shaft was not a tourist, and I don't believe he fell. The papers don't have it yet, but it was Clyde Lapham.'

'Standard Oil?'

'Rumor has it, he jumped. If he did, I want to know why. If he didn't jump, I want to know who helped him out the window.'

'May I ask, sir, what makes you think he didn't jump?'

'Our investigation has established that not one of

the Standard Oil Gang has a guilty bone in his body. On the remote chance that one was ever stricken with remorse, it wouldn't be Clyde Lapham. He had no doubt that making money was his divine right. Something's fishy. That's where you come in.'

'Yes, sir,' Archie said, wondering what it had to do with being a Princeton graduate.

'They won't let our men near the monument. Were it a Navy facility, I would have no trouble gaining access. But I am not so well connected with the Army, and I've run head-on into a snob of a Colonel Dan Egan, who looks down on private detectives as not worthy of his exalted friendship. Do you get my drift?'

Archie was suddenly on firm ground, with intimate knowledge of the fine distinctions of the social order. 'Yes, sir. Army officers are more likely to be ill-bred and have chips on their shoulders than their Navy counterparts.'

'This particular officer is carrying a chip bigger than a redwood. Fortunately, I've learned he has a son attending Princeton. I'm betting he'll be mightily impressed by the fact that you matriculated, as well as by your manner, which is less that of a private detective than a privileged layabout. Not that I'm suggesting you lie about, necessarily, but I suspect you can act the part.'

'I'll rehearse,' Archie said drily.

'You don't have time,' Van Dorn shot back. 'Colonel Egan is at the monument right now, in the middle of the night, leading what the Army optimistically calls an inquiry. Get over there and sweet-talk your way in before they trample the evidence and insert words in the mouths of witnesses.'

Archie doubted he'd make much headway walking up to a full colonel and saying he went to Princeton. He ventured, 'This might require more than "sweet talking", Mr Van Dorn.'

The Boss stared, his eyes suddenly hard. 'The agency pays you handsomely to do "more than sweet talking."'

'I'll do my best.'

'See that you do.'

14

Joseph Van Dorn was still at his desk when Archie reported back, shortly before midnight.

'Suicide or murder?'

'It's more complicated than you might expect, Mr Van Dorn.'

The glower Van Dorn leveled at him reminded Archie Abbott of an encounter on safari with an East African rhinoceros. 'Let me decide what I expect. In a word, "suicide" or "murder"?'

'In a word,' said Archie, 'the Army was "hood-winked".'

Joseph Van Dorn, so wintery a moment earlier, broke into a delighted smile – as Archie knew he would. Beaming at his old US Marine Corps NCO sword, which hung from his coat tree, the Boss asked, 'What did the Army fall for this time?'

Isaac Bell doubted there was room in Nellie Matters' exciting life for a boyfriend. She was great company at dinner in the Royal's beautiful dining car, entertaining him, and eavesdroppers at nearby tables, with tales of her suffragist travels, balloon mishaps, and rivalries with suffra*gettes* – 'the dread Amanda Faire' – while spinning like cotton candy her newly invented New Woman's Flyover. By the time they got off the train in Jersey City, the suffragist's publicity stunt details were in place. All that remained was to raise the money for a hundred balloons, a prospect she thought not at all daunting.

But on the railroad ferry across the Hudson to New York City, Bell sensed a sudden shift toward the romantic. He credited the beautiful lights of the downtown skyscrapers and the chill wind they braved on deck. He wrapped his arm around her shoulder and Nellie huddled close. Just as the boat landed, she curled deeper in his arm. 'I don't usually meet men I like. I don't mean to say that I *dislike* men. But I just don't find most of them that likeable. Do you know what I mean?'

'No,' said Isaac Bell. 'What is it you don't find likeable?'

'Is that a detective trait to always ask questions?'

'Yes.'

'You're as bad as my sister the reporter.'

A hansom cab whisked them across town. She held his hand, and, all too soon, the cab pulled up to the Matters town house in Gramercy Park, a quiet oasis of a neighborhood that predated the Civil War. Just across the narrow park was one of Archie Abbott's clubs, The Players. The cab clattered off. Bell walked Nellie to the front door. The house was made of brick with gleaming black shutters.

'What a handsome house.'

'We moved up in the world with the Standard,' Nellie replied as she slipped a key in the door. She whirled around suddenly and faced him. 'Come back tomorrow evening to meet Father.'

'As aspiring balloonist or gentleman caller?'

Nellie Matters gave Isaac Bell her biggest smile. 'Both.'

She disappeared behind the door.

He lingered on the sidewalk. He had to admit that he was more than a little dazzled by the vibrant and witty young woman.

Suddenly he was alert, seeing movement from the corner of his eye. A slight figure, a woman in a cloak, materialized from the shadows of Gramercy Park. Lamplight crossed her face.

'Edna?' he asked, caught off base by how happy he was to see her.

'I was just coming home,' she answered. 'I didn't want to interrupt you and Nellie.'

She seemed upset.

'Are you all right?'

Edna Matters paused to consider her answer. 'Not entirely. I mean, I'm in a bit of a quandary.'

'Good or bad?'

'If I knew, it wouldn't be a quandary, would it?'

'Tell me what it is,' said Bell. 'I'm a fair hand, sometimes, at sorting good from bad. Come on, we'll take a walk.'

The hour was late and the well-dressed couple might

have drawn the attention of thieves who would attempt to separate them from their money. That is until a closer inspection revealed a gent light on his feet and cold of eye. They walked until the lights grew brighter on Broadway, its sidewalks crowded with people bustling in and out of hotels, restaurants and vaudeville theaters.

'I grew up with oil derricks,' Edna said suddenly. 'Pipe lines and breakout tanks. And a father beaten repeatedly by the Standard.'

'Is that how you came to write the *History of Under-handed*?'

'Do you think I had a choice?'

'I don't know,' said Bell. 'Nellie didn't respond to your father's losses by becoming a reporter.'

'Wouldn't you say that pursuing justice for women is the other side of the same coin?'

'How?'

'Of trying to make things right.'

'No,' said Bell. 'Enfranchisement is a cause, a worthy cause. Writing the truth is more like a calling. So maybe you're right. Maybe you had no choice.'

'You're not making this easier.'

'I'm sorry, but I don't know what your quandary is. Not making what easier?'

She fell silent again. Bell tried to re-engage her. 'What about Nellie? Did she take your father's losses as hard as you did?'

Edna thought a moment. 'Nellie loves him as fiercely

as I do. But she wasn't around for as much of it. She's traveled ever since she put her teens and pinafores behind her. Here today, gone tomorrow.'

'Maybe she was trying to get away from them.'

'I don't know. She's always on the road – and at home wherever she alights.'

'You travel, too.'

'Like a hermit crab. I carry my home with me. No matter where I land at the end of the day, I'm at my typewriter. I thought it was time to stop writing, my crusade over.'

'Is there a purpose to stop your writing?'

'I thought I was ready to stop. But the new oil strikes make it a new story. And now the unrest in Baku threatens shortages that could upend the petroleum industry all over the world. Imagine what must be going through Mr Rockefeller's mind at a moment like this.'

'What is in Baku for him?'

'Half the world's oil. And a well-established route to the customers. If they burn the Baku fields, who will supply the Russians' and the Nobels' and the Rothschilds' markets? *JDR*, that's who, even if it's true he retired, which I never believed . . . Listen to me! I'm too obsessed with JDR to stop reporting on him. Just when I think I'm done, I learn something new.'

'Like what?'

'I've heard rumors – speculation, really – that Rockefeller uses his publicists to communicate secretly with his partners. They plant a story. It gets printed and reprinted in every paper in the world, and those who know his code get his message . . . Boy!'

She gave two pennies to a passing newsboy hawking the early-morning edition of the *Sun* and scanned the paper in the blazing window of a lobster palace. 'Here! I've traced this one back to last January. It's supposedly a letter he wrote to his Sunday school class from his vacation to France. "Delightful breezes. I enjoy watching the fishermen with their nets on the beach, and gazing upon the sun rising over the beautiful Mediterranean Sea. The days pass pleasantly and profitably."'

Bell said, 'It sounds perfectly ordinary. So ordinary, you wonder why the papers print it.'

'Any pronouncement the richest man in America makes is automatically news. They change details to keep it up to date. After he returned from Europe they added the introductory "I recall, when I was in France", et cetera. Recently they added "the sun rising". I'm sure it's a message. Maybe it doesn't matter – except it might, and I can't stop writing about him . . .' She leafed through the paper. 'Here's another I've been following in the social sections. I cannot for the life of me figure it out, but it has to be code.' She read, '"Monmouth County Hounds, Lakewood. First Drag Hunt of the season. John D. Rockefeller in his automobile was in line at the start, but soon dropped out." And this, supposedly about him playing golf. "Standard Oil President Rockefeller was gleeful over his foursome victory.

168

Dominated the links with long sweeping drives –"
Why are you staring at me, Mr Bell?'

'You should see your face. You're on fire. Congratulations!'

'For what?''

'An excellent decision not to retire.'

Suddenly a ragged chorus of young voices piped, 'Extra! Extra!'

Gangs of newsboys galloped out of the *Times* building. They scattered up and down Broadway and Seventh Avenue, waving extra editions and shouting the story.

'Rich old man jumps off Washington Monument.'

Bell bought a paper. He and Edna leaned over the headline

TYCOON SUICIDE

STANDARD OIL MAGNATE LEAPS TO

DEATH FROM WASHINGTON MONUMENT

and raced down the column and on to the second page.

'Why do you think he did it?' asked Bell. 'Guilt?'

Edna Matters shook her head. 'Clyde Lapham would have to look up "guilt" in the dictionary to get even a murky idea of its meaning.'

'Maybe he felt the government closing in,' said Bell, knowing the Van Dorn investigation had yet to turn up enough evidence to please a prosecutor.

'If he jumped,' said Edna, 'because he felt the

government breathing down his neck, then his last living thought must have been: I should have taken Rockefeller with me.' She cupped Bell's cheek in her hand. 'Isaac, I must go home. I have to look into this . . . I bet you do, too.'

At the Yale Club on 44th Street, where Isaac Bell lodged when in New York, Matthew, the night hall porter, ushered him inside.

'Mr Forrer telephoned ahead and asked that I slip him in privately by the service door. I put him in the lounge.'

Bell bounded up the stairs.

The Main Lounge, a high-ceilinged room of couches and armchairs, was deserted at this late hour but for the chief of Van Dorn Research, who occupied most of a couch. Forrer wore wire-rimmed spectacles, as befit his station as a scholar. Scholarly he was, but a very large man, as tall as Bell and twice as wide. Bell had seen him disperse rioters by strolling among them.

'The Boss and I have been burning up the wires. All hell's broken loose on the Corporations Commission case.'

'I just read the Lapham story. Do we know for sure he killed himself?'

'No. All we know is what Archie Abbott learned when he wormed his way into the official investigation. Mr Van Dorn was impressed, which he isn't always with Archie.'

'What did Archie learn?'

'Someone – if not Lapham, then presumably our assassin – pulled an elaborate fast one on the Army, who operate the monument. So elaborate that it can only be characterized as baroque.'

'"Baroque"? What do you mean, baroque? Complicated?'

'More than complicated. Bizarre. Whimsical as an elaborate prank, except a man died. It's hard to imagine they pulled it off. Harder to reckon why they went to such trouble to kill one old man.'

'How could he fit out the window?' asked Bell. 'They barred them up after that lunatic Anti-Saloon Leaguer tried to jump with a banner.'

'The bars were forced open with a barn jack.'

'It takes time to crank a barn jack. Why didn't anyone stop him?'

'No one saw. The window on the west had been cordoned off from the observation area with canvas drapes to ensure the privacy of an artist painting the view.'

'Where was the artist?'

'No one is exactly sure they ever saw the artist. He left behind his paint box and his easel but no painting. According to Archie, it's not clear he did more than set up his easel. And before you ask his name, it was very likely a false name.'

'What was it?'

'This is where things turn complicated. I'll get to his name in a moment.'

'I've had a very long day, Grady. What is going on?'

'I don't know. Other than to say that the Army – or at least the US Army colonel in command of the Washington Monument, whom Archie interviewed – gave the artist permission to paint the view privately behind canvas curtains because permission was requested as a personal favor by a famous Army sharpshooter.'

15

'He won the President's Medal in 1902.'

Isaac Bell sank in his armchair to ponder that. 'In other words, he's the best.'

'The most accurate marksman in 1902.'

'They shoot up to a thousand yards,' said Bell. 'What's his name?'

'Private Billy Jones.'

'People who are legitimately named Jones and Smith should be issued special identifying cards to prove they didn't make it up.'

'Private Billy "Jones" deserted the First Regiment of Newark, New Jersey National Guard, shortly after he won his medal.'

'Why did the Army give permission to paint in the monument? Why didn't they just arrest him?'

'He didn't ask the entire Army. He asked the idiot colonel in command of the monument. Mailed him a letter. The damned fool had not heard the news that their champion sharpshooter deserted. It happened three years ago and it's likely the Army covered it up, being embarrassed.'

'Not to mention terrified to tell TR,' said Bell.

A smile lit Forrer's solemn expression. 'Grim thought, Isaac. Teddy is not a president that a career officer would want to disappoint.'

'So no one saw the bars jacked open behind the canvas erected for an artist no one saw. Therefore, no one saw whether old Lapham jumped or was thrown.'

'Two men brought him there. Doctors.'

'Then we'll start with the doctors.'

'Unfortunately, no.'

'Now what?' asked Bell.

'The Army hasn't informed the police yet, so the news reporters don't know, but Archie's friend the half-wit colonel admitted the doctors vanished, and no one knows if they really were doctors or merely carrying medical bags.'

'Further suggesting it was murder,' said Bell.

Forrer repeated a saying Bell had heard from him often: 'The job of the chief of Van Dorn Research is to sort fact from assumption.'

'You are provoking me toward sarcasm, Grady. If it wasn't murder, then the men pretending to be doctors who delivered Lapham to the top of the monument carried a barn jack in their medical bag and left it with Lapham, who used it to jack open the bars so he could jump out the window.'

'Seen that way, it does suggest murder,' Forrer admitted.

'But like you just said, why go to so much trouble to kill one old guy? You could pop him on the head and say he fell off his chair . . . In fact, it's less complicated than showy.'

'Did our assassin use the name of a famous sharp-shooter, gambling that the colonel didn't know he was a deserter?'

'Or is our assassin the deserter himself? He's proven himself a champion marksman.' Bell shook his head. 'It doesn't make sense. Why would he draw such attention to himself if he's been safely disappeared for three years?'

It struck Isaac Bell that the assassin's remarkable shooting was merely a means. He had been thinking about him as a sniper. Now he had to think about him as a murderer who would use various means to kill.

'You were going to tell me the supposed artist's name.'

Forrer nodded. 'At this point, it moves into the realm of the bizarre. The artist called himself Isaac Bell.'

'*What?*'

'He knows you're working up the case, Isaac.'

Isaac Bell stood out of his chair and stalked through the empty lounge to the tall windows that overlooked West 44th Street. A thin smile formed on his lips.

'He's calling you out!' said Forrer, who had grown up in the Deep South where calling a man out meant parking yourself on his front lawn with a gun in your hand until he came out shooting.

'Sounds that way.' Bell stared down at 44th Street. Carriages and motor limousines were returning for the night to the many stables and garages on the block.

Suddenly he stared unseeing out the window. 'At last.'

'At last what?' Forrer asked.

'At last he's made a mistake.'

'Thinking he can take you?'

'That, too.'

The tall detective turned abruptly and crossed the big room in several strides, his face alight with energy. 'We're finally getting something. Let's find out who this champion really is.'

Forrer climbed out of his chair and rose to his full height. 'I'll go back to the office.' He kept a camp bed there, and Bell knew that after a short nap he would dive into his files. Assistants and apprentices arriving for work early would find their boss deep in newspapers and magazines and telegrams from the agency's private wires.

Bell walked him down to the front door.

'There's something else I want you to look into.'

'What's that?'

'Edna Matters has an interesting theory.' He told him Edna's theory about John D. Rockefeller's newspaper code.

Forrer was intrigued by the idea of far-flung Rockefeller operatives reading the newspapers for his instructions. 'Not to mention those hundreds of "correspondents" spying for Standard Oil around the world, reading the papers and realizing what he wants information on.'

'Can you crack it?'

'It isn't only *what* he says,' Forrer explained, 'but *when* he says it. He's referring to things they already know, telling them, now we wait, now we get ready, now we move.'

'Check your files back to January when Rockefeller was in Cannes.'

'I'll start earlier.'

'The phrase about watching children digging in the sand appears only in recent weeks.'

'I'll pay particular attention to it. What do you want me to tell Mr Van Dorn?'

'Tell him the assassin is not quite as professional as he thinks he is.'

'He's going to ask me what you mean. I'd like to have an answer ready.'

'Tell him the assassin is a show-off.'

'What do you suppose he'll make of that?'

'He'll make of it what he taught me: Show-offs trip themselves up when they forget to watch where they're going.'

'And where are *you* going, Isaac?'

'Westchester.'

'To see the great man?'

'To see what makes him tick ... Here's another thought for Mr Van Dorn. If our assassin is willing to throw people out of windows instead of shooting them, then he's even less predictable than a professional sniper.'

They shook hands.

'Wait a minute! Do we know why Clyde Lapham was in Washington?'

Forrer said, 'I assume –'

'I thought the Research Department never assumes.'

'I'll get right on it . . . Hey, where are you going?'

Isaac Bell was striding into the street, waving a fistful of money at a chauffeur about to garage an Acme Opera Limousine. 'Grady!' he called over his shoulder. 'Do me a favor and send wires in my name to Nellie Matters and John D. Rockefeller. Apologize for breaking tomorrow's appointments and ask would it be convenient to reschedule for the day after.'

'Now where are you going?'

'Back to Washington.'

'It's the middle of the night.'

'I'll make the Congressional Express.' He paid the yawning chauffeur to speed him to the railroad ferry at 42nd Street.

The 1 a.m. express was fully booked. Even his railroad pass couldn't get him a berth. He whipped out his Van Dorn badge and sprinted to the fortified express car at the head of the train. There would be no berth with crisp sheets there, either, nor even a comfortable chair. But the express messenger, responsible for jewels, gold, bearer bonds and banknotes, was glad to have the company of another armed guard. Bell waited until the train was safely rolling at sixty miles an hour, then made his bed on canvas sacks stuffed with a hundred thousand in National Bank notes. He awakened to stand watch, pistol drawn, at station stops in Philadelphia, Wilmington and Baltimore.

'Greek fire saved Constantinople from the Arab navies, Mrs McCloud.'

The widow who owned the coffee stand on Fulton Street was tied to a kitchen chair with a gag in her mouth. Bill Matters watched from the doorway.

The assassin, who was perched on the rim of the bathtub that shared the tiny space with the chair, a table and a cookstove, loosened the gag and asked, 'Who else did you tell?'

The woman was brave. 'Wouldn't you like to know.'

'Oh, I will know . . . Greek fire burned on water. In fact, it continues to burn even when you splash water on it. Which the invading Arabs discovered when it incinerated their ships. It was made by a secret formula as closely guarded as the workings of the Standard Oil Company. The recipe is long lost. But every guess of its ingredients includes naphtha.'

The assassin held up a gallon tin of naphtha, a familiar solvent sold in hardware stores, and punched holes in the top with a pocketknife.

'You'll find naphtha in the Bible, Mrs McCloud, a word to describe burning liquid. It's mentioned in the Old Testament. The name meant "purification". Assyrians dipped their arrows in naphtha to shoot fire at their enemies.'

'You think you scare me?'

The assassin tightened the gag.

'Today in our modern, gentler age, we use naphtha to clean clothes and dissolve grease and paint. But since the auto became popular, it is especially important to give gasoline its kick. Have you ever seen gasoline catch fire? Imagine the leaps of flame that naphtha produces. Who, Mrs McCloud? Who else did you tell that I gave you the powder that you fed to the old man?'

She shook her head. She was watching the tin, but there was still more contempt than fear in her eyes.

The assassin upended the tin and poured the naphtha on her head, soaking her hair and her shabby housedress, then loosened the gag and asked again in the same quiet, persistent voice, 'Who else did you tell that I gave you powder to put in Mr Comstock's coffee?'

The assassin signaled that it was now Matters' turn. Steeling himself to act, Matters scraped a kitchen match on the cookstove's grate. Flame flared in a burst of pungent smoke.

'Who else?'

'No one. I swear it.'

'No one but the messenger you sent to blackmail me,' said Matters.

'I didn't tell him everything. Just enough to scare you to make you pay.'

'You did that all right.'

'Where is he?' she asked, eyes locked on the flame.

'Who? Your blackmail messenger? He died. After he

180

told us where to find you.' Matters turned to the assassin, who was watching intently. 'She believes me, and now I believe her.'

Mrs McCloud's entire body sagged with despair, and she whispered, 'My son.'

'Ask her,' said the assassin, 'how she traced me to you.'

Bill Matters said to Mrs McCloud, 'You heard the question. What made you think I was the one to blackmail?'

The widow suddenly looked twenty years older and had tears in her eyes. She whispered, 'My son followed the old man to his office. He saw you together. He saw you meet every day in a tearoom. Like you had secrets away from the office.'

'Your son was a good guesser.' To the assassin he said, 'I believe her. Do you?'

The assassin stepped closer and stared into Mrs McCloud's eyes.

'Say it again: No one else.'

'No one else. I swear it.'

'Do you believe her?' Matters asked again.

'I told you, I believe her.'

'All right.'

'But,' said the assassin, 'she will never leave you in peace until she dies.'

Bill Matters pondered in silence. Suddenly he heard his own voice babbling foolishness. 'What could she say? Who would believe her?'

The assassin said, 'They will dig Comstock up and administer the Marsh test. What do you suppose they will find in his remains?'

Matters shook his head, though he knew of course.

'*Poudre de succession!* That is French, you poor man, for "inheritance powder", which is a euphemism for "arsenic". In other words, they will hang you for poisoning Averell Comstock.'

'I won't tell a soul,' said Mrs McCloud. 'I promise.'

Bill Matters kept shaking his head. He could not abide the woman's fear. Mary McCloud's scornful contempt had underscored the deadly threat of blackmail. But her fear pried open his heart. He did not doubt that most men were his enemies. But not women. Twice widowed, father of daughters given to him by women he loved, he heard himself whisper a coward's confession.

'I don't know if I can do this.'

'That's what you have me for,' said the assassin.

16

When Isaac Bell got back from Washington, D.C., he borrowed a Stanley Steamer from a good friend of Archie Abbott, a well-off New Yorker who, as Archie put it, 'passed his days in a quiet, blameless, clubable way.' He drove north of Manhattan into Westchester, passing through Spuyten Duyvil, Yonkers and Dobbs Ferry. The road, paved with concrete in some sections, asphalted in others, graveled here and there, and along a few stretches still dirt, passed country clubs, prosperous farms, and taverns catering to automobilists from the city. He arrived in North Tarrytown in a traffic jam of farm wagons, gasoline trucks and autos all packed with workmen.

It was Election Day, the town constable explained. The wagons, trucks and autos were ferrying three hundred of John D. Rockefeller's estate gardeners, masons, road builders, laborers and house servants to the North Tarrytown polls to vote for Rockefeller's choices of trustees.

'Will he win?' Bell asked.

'He always does,' said the constable, who surely owed his job to the incumbents. 'But, this year, the butcher is waging a mighty campaign.'

He pointed Bell in the direction of the Rockefeller

estate. Soon the bustle of the town was forgotten, dwarfed by vast building improvements – grading new roads, damming rivers, digging lakes, erecting stables and guesthouses, and laying out a golf course – that appeared to absorb the surrounding farms and entire villages. Rounding a blind bend, he saw an old tavern that stood alone in the sea of mud. A sign on the roof named it

SLEEPY HOLLOW ROADHOUSE

A hand-painted addition stated

NOT FOR SALE

NOT EVEN TO YOU, MR PRESIDENT

Bell swerved off the road and stopped in front with a strong hunch that the proprietor of the Sleepy Hollow Roadhouse would be more than willing to tell him a thing or two about Rockefeller's local activities. He ordered a glass of beer and got an earful.

'Retired, the man is lethal,' said the very angry tavern owner. 'If the nation thinks that Standard Oil is an octopus, they should see him operate in Pocantico Hills – where, just so you know, my family logged and fished, and farmed those fields across the road, for two hundred years before that sanctimonious pirate pulled up stakes in Cleveland to foist himself on New York and, by extension, our small hamlet.'

Mine host paused for breath. Isaac Bell asked, 'What makes him sanctimonious?'

'He's a teetotaler. It galls the heck out of him that I'm selling drinks right outside his front gate. He put my competitor out of business by buying up every house in the hamlet that supplied his customers. But he can't do that to me because my customers drive their autos up from the city like you.'

'So it's a standoff.'

'As much as one man can stand off against an octopus. Who knows which way he'll come at me next.'

'Is he here often?'

'Too often. Here all the time, now that he's built his own golf course.'

'How big is the estate?' said Bell.

'Three thousand acres and counting. The man can drive for days on his own roads and never use the same one twice.'

Isaac Bell found the gates open and unmanned. The driveway swept through dense forest, open hayfield, and mowed lawns as green as any he had seen in England. Bridle paths, and carriage roads of crushed slate, crisscrossed the drive and disappeared under shade trees. Clearings at bends in the driveway offered sudden, startling vistas of the Hudson River.

He passed stables and a coach barn, guest cottages, gardens, both sunken and walled, a teahouse, and a conservatory under construction, its graceful framework awaiting glass. A powerhouse was hidden behind a stone outcropping with its chimney disguised by a clump of tall cedars. The drive climbed a gentle slope to a plateau that looked out on the river and circled a large mansion in the early stage of construction. Masons swarmed on scaffolds, buttressing deep cellar holes with stonework.

Bell was wondering in which of the older or newly built smaller buildings Rockefeller actually lived when he noticed below the plateau a canyon-like cut through a stone hill. He drove into it along a flat roadbed. Drill marks in the vine-tangled stone sides, ballast crunching under his tires, and chunks of coal glittering in the sun indicated it was an old railroad cut abandoned decades earlier. He emerged on the far side of the hill beside a cluster of weathered cow barns that appeared to be the remnants of a dairy farm subsumed by the estate.

Sturdy poles carried strands of telegraph, telephone and electric wire into the biggest barn. Isaac Bell parked the Steamer and pressed a button at the door. A buzzer sounded inside.

John D. Rockefeller himself opened the door. He was dressed as he had been when Bell saw him last in Joseph Van Dorn's office, in elegantly tailored broadcloth, winged collar and four-in-hand necktie, a silk handkerchief in his breast pocket and gold cuff links. His eyes were bleak.

'What exactly happened to Clyde Lapham?'

'You can answer that better than I,' said Bell.

'What do you mean?'

'Tell me why you sent Clyde Lapham to Washington.'

'What makes you think I did?'

'I know you did. I want you to tell me why.'

'How could you possibly know that I sent Clyde Lapham to Washington?'

'Van Dorn detectives make friends with local cops.'

'I thought you resigned your position.'

'Word of my resignation hasn't reached my friends in the Washington police. Why did you send Clyde Lapham to Washington?'

'To give the poor man something to do.'

'Poor man?'

'Clyde Lapham was the brightest, widest-awake, most progressive business man. But he was beginning to go down the hill. It finally became apparent that he had had his day because he was losing his mind to dementia.'

'Why did you send him?'

'You apparently know already. Why this charade?'

'I don't know if I can trust you, sir. I want to hear it from you.'

The old man didn't like hearing that, and Bell half expected to be escorted off the property. Instead, Rockefeller said, 'I asked Clyde Lapham to discuss a contribution of money to a minister who is raising funds to build a monument to President Abraham Lincoln.'

'Thank you,' said Bell. For a moment, he debated asking why Rockefeller paid a secret visit to the Persian embassy, but that would definitely get him thrown out on his ear. He had learned nothing more of it on his quick return to Washington and had left Archie Abbott in charge of probing his friends in the State Department.

'To answer your question,' Bell said, 'Clyde Lapham was murdered.'

Rockefeller's expression did not change, but his shoulders sagged perceptibly. He stepped back, indicating Bell should enter, and without a word led the way through a foyer into a high-ceilinged drawing loft. Draftsmen in vests and shirtsleeves were bent over drawing boards, working in the pure glow of north-facing skylights. Bell saw building plans and landscape designs taking shape. Finished blueprints were spread on worktables, where civil engineers and architects were guiding foremen through the intricacies of upcoming work. Rockefeller paused at a table where a draftsman was drawing the steel frame for a stone bridge, traced a line with his finger, and politely ordered a correction.

He continued down a hallway of shut doors. Not visible until they had rounded a corner was a door with frosted glass in the upper panel. Bell followed him through it and saw instantly that the supposedly retired president of Standard Oil was leading a double life at Pocantico Hills, actively managing vast improvements of his new estate while continuing to command his industrial enterprise.

The frosted-glass door opened on a business office as modern as any on Wall Street, staffed by secretaries and bookkeepers, and equipped with private telegraph, overseas cable, telephone lines and ticker tape machines. Rockefeller led Bell through the din into his private office, closed the door and stood behind his desk.

'That you're here,' he said, 'tells me you've come to do what I asked: stop the assassin and end the slander of Standard Oil.'

Bell said, 'I will concentrate on the assassin and leave the slander to you.'

'How do you know that Clyde Lapham was murdered?'

Bell related the events at the Washington Monument step-by-step.

'Byzantine,' said Rockefeller. 'In your experience, have you ever seen a murder as elaborately conceived?'

'Three murders,' said Bell.

'*Three?*' Rockefeller blinked.

'And an attempted murder. And an elaborate act of arson.'

'What are you talking about?'

'As "byzantine", to use your word, as the killing of Clyde Lapham was, it was merely an exaggerated version of his earlier crimes.' He described for Rockefeller the deaths of the independent Kansas refiners Reed Riggs and Albert Hill, the elaborate and highly effective duck-target explosion and burning of Spike Hopewell's refinery, the attempt to shotgun him, Texas Walt and Archie Abbott. Finally, he reminded Rockefeller of the faked suicide of Big Pete Straub. 'By those lights, sniping Hopewell and C. C. Gustafson are his only "normal" crimes.'

'What motivates such complication?'

'I don't know yet,' said Isaac Bell. 'The effect of the straightforward killings is the slander you want to stop, the blaming of Standard Oil. The killings that were masked as accidents don't appear to fall into that category. Perhaps those people were killed for other reasons.'

A secretary knocked and entered and murmured in Rockefeller's ear. Rockefeller picked up a telephone, listened, then put the phone down, shaking his head. He sat silent awhile, then said to Bell, 'My father used to read aloud to us. He liked the Fireside Poets. Do you know them?'

'My grandfather read them,' said Bell. 'Longfellow, Whittier, Lowell.'

'Lowell was Father's favorite . . .' He shook his head again. 'I've just learned that Averell Comstock, one of my oldest partners, is dying . . . "O Death, thou ever roaming shark . . ."'

Rockefeller looked at Bell, his fathomless eyes suddenly bright with pain.

Bell completed the stanza for him – '" . . . Ingulf me in eternal dark!"' – wondering whether the old man remembered it was from a humorous poem about a perch with a toothache who was hoodwinked by a lobster.

'Averell became a warm, close, personal friend of mine in the course of business. I will miss him.'

'I'm sorry,' said Bell. 'Had he been ill?'

'Briefly. The price of getting old, Mr Bell. My partners are dying right and left. Most were older than I . . . They go so quickly. One week ago, Comstock was full of vim and push.'

He stood up, laid a big hand on the telephone, and stared across the desk as if the room had no walls and he could see all the way to New York City.

'When poor Lapham began losing his mind, there was time to get used to the idea that he would go. But Averell was a titan. I figured him for another twenty years.'

He's afraid of dying, thought Bell and suddenly felt sympathy for the old man. But he could not ignore the opportunity to investigate from even deeper inside the heart of Standard Oil.

'Are you afraid the assassin will strike at *you*?'

'Most people hate me,' Rockefeller replied matter-of-factly. 'The chances are, he hates me, too.'

'He strikes me as professional, without emotion.' True of his shooting, thought Bell. True of his deep-laid groundwork. *Not* true of his impulse to show off.

'Then he's paid by someone who hates me,' said Rockefeller.

'A trigger finger that won't shake with personal hatred makes him all the more dangerous.'

Rockefeller changed the subject abruptly. 'Can I assume that having broken with the Van Dorn Agency, you are free to travel on short notice?'

'Where?' asked Bell.

'Wherever I say.'

Isaac Bell threw down a bold challenge calculated to impress the oil titan. If it worked, the lordly Rockefeller might open up to him as he would to an equal rather than a lowly detective.

'Where "children dig in the sand"?'

Rockefeller returned a fathomless stare. Bell gazed back noncommittally, as he would in the highest-stakes poker game – neither averting his eyes nor staring – while Rockefeller reassessed him. He said nothing, though the silence between them stretched and stretched. The old man spoke at last.

'You appear to have studied my habits.'

'As would an assassin.'

'I may go abroad.'

'Baku?' said Bell.

Violence flared in the hooded eyes. 'You know too much, Mr Bell. Are you a spy?'

'I am imagining how an assassin stalks a man of many secrets – a victim like you. Baku is obvious: The newspapers are full of Russia's troubles, and E. M. Hock's *History of the Oil Monopoly* catalogs the territories in Europe and Asia that you've lost to Rothschild and the Nobels and Sir Marcus Samuel.'

'Are you a spy?' Rockefeller repeated. But he was,

Bell guessed, assessing him carefully, and he strove to answer in a manner that would instill confidence and project the picture of a valuable man, seasoned in his craft, alert, observant, and deadly when challenged. A man John D. Rockefeller could trust to guard his life.

'I don't have to be a spy to know that "the sun rising over the beautiful Mediterranean" rises in the east — Russian oil in Baku and the Chinese and Indian refined oil markets you're determined to dominate. If I *were* a spy, I would know the secret meaning of "children digging in the sand". I don't. But the assassin has had more time to investigate and probably does know all about children digging in the sand. Would you feel safer if I accompany you as your bodyguard?'

'Name your salary.'

'I won't work on salary. I've decided to start my own detective agency,' said Bell, embellishing the lie he had concocted with Joseph Van Dorn.

'I applaud your initiative,' said Rockefeller. 'We'll send you a contract.'

Isaac Bell drew a slim envelope from his coat. 'I brought my own.'

'Presumptuous of you.'

'Not at all. I am modeling my business on yours.'

'I am an old man and beyond the influence of flattery. But I do wonder how you would compare a gumshoe to an oil man?'

'E. M. Hock wrote that you achieved your great success in the oil business by being ruthlessly efficient. I heard with my own ears your boast of efficiency to Mr Van Dorn. In order to be the best "gumshoe" in the private detective business, I had better be efficient.'

Rockefeller replied without a hint of expression, and Bell could not for the life of him tell if the man had a sense of humor. 'You'll know you're efficient, Detective Bell, when they call you a monster.'

Bell said, 'I will make the travel arrangements.'

'I have a man who handles them.'

'Not on this trip. I will decide the safest route.'

Rockefeller nodded agreement. 'Of course, none of this is to be repeated. I want no one to know I have business in Baku. We must travel in the utmost secrecy.'

'That will make my job a lot easier,' said Bell. 'When do you want to arrive?'

At Grand Central Station, which was being simultaneously demolished and expanded into an electrified Grand Central Terminal, the sidings reserved for private railcars offered connections to city telephone systems.

'I need another rifle,' said the assassin.

'Another 99?' asked the gunsmith.

'Have you anything better?'

'I always make you the best.'

'Then more of the best! A 99 it is.'

'With telescope?'

'Only the mounting. But I want different bullets.'

'Is there a problem with my loads?'

Picturing the gunsmith's fussy hands and the desperate-to-please eyes of a genius who didn't believe he was a genius, the assassin reassured him, 'Your loads are wonderfully consistent. I trust my life with them. But I've been thinking, have you ever made a bullet that explodes?'

'A dumdum bullet?'

'No. Not a hollow-point. A bullet that *detonates* on impact.'

'Like an artillery shell?'

'Precisely. A miniature artillery shell.'

'It's hard to imagine stuffing an impact fuse and explosive into such a small projectile.'

'But you have a *wonderful* imagination.'

'I am intrigued,' said the gunsmith. 'You are as stimulating as ever.'

17

Back from Pocantico Hills, Isaac Bell wired Joseph Van Dorn in agency cipher:

BAKU VIA CLEVELAND.

And with very little time to set the murder and Corporations Commission investigations in productive motion before he was stuck incommunicado on the high seas, he fired off three more telegrams.

To Detective Archie Abbott in Washington:

WHY PERSIA? ON THE JUMP.

To Detective Wally Kisley and Detective Mack Fulton still in Kansas:

HOPEWELL TRICKS UP SLEEVE? ON THE JUMP.

To Detective Aloysius 'Wish' Clarke, who was about to receive the plummiest assignment of his checkered career:

COME NEW YORK. ON THE JUMP.

Bell himself went to the Sage Gun Company on West 43rd Street.

He walked in carrying a carpetbag and shook hands with Dave McCoart, a hard-muscled gunsmith with long, thin fingers and a ruddy Irish complexion.

'I was just thinking about you,' McCoart greeted him. 'Are you familiar with the FN outfit in Belgium?'

'*Fabrique Nationale*. Firearms manufacturer in the Liège district.'

'Mr Browning gave FN a contract to manufacture a 9mm variant of a new design. I am told it's a beautiful pistol. I'm thinking I can modify it with a chamber bushing to fire an American .380 caliber cartridge. It would be considerably lighter than that brick in your shoulder holster.'

'I like my gun's stopping power. It's served me well.'

'What the Number 2 lacks in stopping power – and you are right to be concerned – will be made up with outstanding accuracy.'

'How outstanding?'

'Compared to your Colt? Like a rifle.'

'OK, make me one. Now, I have a question. Have you ever seen a breakdown model of a Savage 99?'

'No.'

'Could you convert a factory piece to a breakdown?'

'I could.'

'How many gunsmiths could do such a conversion?'

McCoart grinned. 'That depends on whether the

accuracy of the weapon is high on your list of expectations.'

'At the top.'

'Then I would shop very carefully to get the right man. Look for one who has a top-notch machine shop and several pints of artist in his bloodstream.'

'How many such men do *you* know?'

'With a top-notch machine shop?'

'Or access to one.'

'. . . A few, I suppose.'

'How many more would be out there that you don't know personally?'

'Around the country? Quite a few.'

'How many would be known to gunsmiths who you know?'

'There are cities where the best congregate. They settle near where they learned the craft and can turn to each other to make specialty items. Around the Winchester works in New Haven, Connecticut, or Savage's factory upstate in Utica. Springfield in Spring-field, Massachusetts. Remington in Bridgeport, Colt in Hartford. Do you mind me asking what the rifle is used for?'

'I was about to warn you. It's being used for murder.'

'Reckoned as much.'

'So ask carefully. You don't want to get on the wrong side of this guy.'

McCoart asked, 'Do you suppose the smith knows what his customer is up to?'

It was a good question, and Bell thought on it before he answered. 'The smith could believe his customer is a target shooter.'

Dave McCoart shot a hole in that theory. 'He wouldn't think it long if the guy weren't actively competing. He would want to know how his gun did.'

Bell opened his carpetbag. 'What do you think of this one?'

McCoart weighed the parts in his big hands, examined them in the light, then screwed them together. 'Nice. Very, very nice work. The barrel and chamber lock like they're welded.'

'Recognize it?'

'No. Other than it narrows the field considerably. There aren't that many smiths of this caliber. Like I said, an artist. Did you shoot it?'

'I hit a fence post at a quarter mile twice and winged it twice.'

'Could have been the wind. Could have been the loads. Could have been knocked around since it was last sighted in. Would you like me to bench-sight it?'

'And load me some cartridges.'

'Where's the telescope?'

'It wasn't on it.'

'Why do you suppose he left such a beautiful piece behind?'

'To throw me off the scent.'

'Saving money on the telescope. Good ones don't come cheap.'

'Or,' said Bell, seeing another way to backtrack the assassin, 'maybe the telescope is even rarer than the gun.'

'What are your prospects, Mr Bell?' Bill Matters asked bluntly when Isaac Bell called at Matters' Gramercy Park town house.

Bell reckoned he should not be surprised by how young, vigorous and tough Edna and Nellie's father was. 'Hard as adamantine,' Spike Hopewell had dubbed him. 'Choirboys don't last in the oil business.'

Still, he had expected a smoother company man version of Spike Hopewell. Instead, he found a man fifteen years younger than Spike. He had a hard mouth, and harder eyes, and seemed inordinately protective of his accomplished, independent daughters.

'Father,' said Nellie before Bell could answer, 'Mr Bell just walked in the door,' and Edna, who had descended the stairs with Nellie and was now seated beside her on a green silk-covered settee that highlighted the color of their eyes, said, 'This role of vigilant father, Father, does not become you.'

Matters did not smile. Nor would he be derailed. 'I want to know what his prospects are if he's calling on my daughters. That's why you're here, isn't it?'

Edna started to protest.

Bell interrupted.

'Thank you, ladies. I will speak for myself. To answer your question, sir, I enjoyed steady advancement in the Van Dorn Detective Agency. Now I'm striking out on my own. I intend to start my own firm, and I will work hard to make a go of it.'

'How much will you earn?'

'Sufficient for my needs.'

'Sufficient to support a family?'

'Pregnancy,' said Nellie, 'has not come under discussion. Yet.'

Matters glowered.

Edna said, 'I believe that Mr Bell is a Boston Bell, Father. The bankers. He does not need to "marry well".'

'American States Bank? Is that true, Bell?'

Bell looked from Edna to Nellie and addressed his answer to their father's questions to both of them. 'I would rather marry happily than "well".'

Bill Matters barked a laugh that did nothing to soften his eyes. 'Hear! Hear! Well said! OK, you won't be a detective for long. Take over the bank when your old man retires.'

'I will remain a detective,' said Bell. He did not elaborate upon the deep contestation with his father on that issue, nor that his grandfather had interceded with a legacy that made him financially independent. Neither was Matters' business, beautiful daughters notwithstanding.

'Have it your way. Sit down. Girls, let's give Mr Bell something to drink.'

Matters' butler appeared in the doorway. The man wore a tailcoat and white gloves, and his face was remarkably smooth, but Bell pegged his stance and light-footed gait as that of an ex-prizefighter who had retired before he lost a match.

'What is it, Rivers?'

'Telephone, sir.'

Matters hurried off without a word. Edna rose. 'I'll leave you two to it.'

'Where are you going?' asked Nellie.

'Mr Bell is calling on you, not me.'

'Don't be absurd. He's calling on both of us. Aren't you?'

Isaac Bell said, 'Considering we've dined together, traveled together, been set upon by drunks and shot at together, I feel less like a caller than an old friend catching up.'

'Do you want me to stay?' asked Edna.

'Of course,' Bell and Nellie chorused.

Edna was still hesitating when Bill Matters returned to the drawing room, his face set in a grave mask.

'What is it?' asked Edna, resuming her seat.

'Old Comstock died.'

'Another bites the dust,' said Nellie. 'That's two in a week.'

'You won't mourn him, will you?' asked Edna.

'I won't speak ill of the dead,' said Bill Matters. 'But you know I won't miss his badgering.' To Isaac Bell he explained, 'Averell Comstock treated me like some sort of interloper. He made it hard to do business, and hard to advance in the firm.'

'What did he die of?'

'God knows. Even a simple cold will kill at his age . . . The upshot is, Mr Bell, we'll be seeing a lot of each other in weeks to come.'

'How is that, sir?'

'That was Mr Rockefeller on the telephone. With Comstock gone, the president has asked me to accompany him in his travels. He mentioned you will be his bodyguard.'

'You poor things,' said Nellie. 'I would rather die than be stuck all summer in Cleveland. The heat! The humidity! The neighbors!'

'Mr Rockefeller summers at his estate in Cleveland,' Edna explained to Bell.

Matters gave Bell a significant look. 'I suspect we'll create the *impression* he's in Cleveland than range farther afield. Wouldn't you say, Mr Bell?'

'I cannot say, sir,' Bell replied stiffly. 'As his bodyguard, if Mr Rockefeller confided our destination, it would be indiscreet, not to mention reckless, to repeat to anyone where we are going.'

The First Regiment of Newark was billeted in a sturdy National Guard armory, four stories of slab-sided brick walls, relieved only slightly by rounded turrets, and crowned with a parapet. The sentries guarding the arched Jay Street portal remembered Billy Jones warmly but expressed bafflement when Isaac Bell asked why the champion marksman had deserted right after winning the President's Medal.

'Happy guys don't take French leave,' the corporal put it.

'Big fellow?' Bell asked.

'Skinny little guy,' said the private.

'Any guess where he lit out to?'

'No. No one figured him for lighting out. Kept to himself except for one pal, Nate Wildwood.'

'Is Nate around?' asked Bell.

'Nate got killed,' said the private.

'In the Spanish war?'

'Never made it to the war,' the corporal answered. 'Poor Nate fell under a train. Before Billy lit out.'

'Really? Tell me something. How short was Billy?'

'I don't know. Maybe five-three?'

'Little guy,' said the private. 'Short.'

'What color was his hair?'

'Brown.'

'What color were his eyes?'

'Green.'

'Not really green,' said the corporal. 'Gray-green.'

The private reconsidered. 'Yeah, you could say gray-green. They got kind of dead colored, sometimes.'

'Dead?' scoffed the corporal. 'What do you mean dead?'

'I mean *dead*. I was next to him on the firing line more than once. When he started shooting, his eyes looked dead.' The young soldier turned to Bell and explained earnestly, 'What I mean is, after I saw that, I never wondered how Billy Jones could be such a great shot. It was like he could stop every thought in his brain when he pulled the trigger.'

The private reflected for a long moment. 'It was like nothing else mattered. Like he didn't care about nothing. Except the target.'

Isaac Bell took the train back to the ferry. Before he got on the boat, he sent another wire to Archie Abbott.

MAKE ARMY FRIENDS.
TRACE DESERTER BILLY JONES.
SLIGHT BUILD, 5'3".
BROWN HAIR, GRAY-GREEN EYES.

18

When Walter L. Hawley, chief political reporter of the *Evening Sun,* spotted Isaac Bell striding to his desk, he stopped typing to clasp the detective's hand hello.

'You're looking prosperous.'

'You're looking ink-stained.'

'How's the big guy?' Hawley and Joseph Van Dorn had met back in the early '90s when the reporter covered police headquarters and Van Dorn had chased a Chicago arsonist to New York.

'Fired me,' said Bell. 'Or I quit, depending on who shot first.'

'Welcome to Newspaper Row. Multitudes who have failed in all attempts at every occupation turn to journalism to find a stopgap between mediocrity and professional begging.'

'Actually, I did come to discuss a job.'

Hawley looked alarmed.

'Easy does it,' said Bell, 'not for me. What do you make of the situation in Russia?'

'It resembles the bedlam of unchecked human emotion. My beat is City Hall, so maybe I'm not qualified to predict a gloomy future for the czar. But they've had a bad year and it's only June.'

'It could blow the Baku oil business to Kingdom Come.'

Hawley said, 'I won't ask a private detective, assuming you are still one, what that has to do with you. But I will ask, what does that have to do with me? When I need oil, I get it from John D. Rockefeller.'

'E. M. Hock would jump at a freelance assignment to report on the threat to the oil industry in Baku.'

'Are you serious?'

'Absolutely.'

'Wonderful! ... Except, I've always thought the rumors were true. She's a woman, isn't she?'

'Very much so.'

Hawley shook his head. 'I'll tell you, Isaac, I would jump at a chance to hire such a good writer. So would my publisher. He'd approve in a flash. But we would be strongly hesitant to send a woman among heathens. Russians and Moslems, and I believe they've even got some Persians, they're next door, aren't they?'

Bell said, 'When I met Edna Matters in Kansas, she had just driven up from Indian Territory in a buckboard wagon. Her sister was her traveling companion. I imagine Nellie Matters would go along to Russia.'

'Nellie Matters? The Insufferable Suffragette?'

'I find Nellie Matters anything but insufferable.'

'I don't mean to disparage the lady,' the newspaperman said hastily. 'Certainly lovely to look at, and a fiery orator. She'll really make her mark with that New Woman's Flyover.'

'What do you say?' asked Bell. 'Will you hire E. M. Hock?'

'But now you're suggesting sending *two women* among the heathens. If something happened to them in wherever that godforsaken place is – the Caspian Sea? – Joe Pulitzer and Bill Hearst and Preston Whiteway would yellow-journal us into our graves. They would incite *mobs* to tear us limb from limb. Newsies who tried to sell the *Sun* would be hung from lampposts.'

'I'll arrange for the best private detective in the business to stand watch over them.'

'That could get expensive.'

'I'll pay for the detective, you pay Miss Matters' fee.'

'Sounds like you have a wealthy client, Isaac, if you're not working for Van Dorn anymore.'

'I will pay for the detective,' Bell repeated.

Hawley said, 'That's right. You're rich. I forgot. OK. It's a deal! And thanks, Isaac. If she'll take the job, she'll set a new standard for our overpaid hacks.'

They shook on it. Bell said, 'But don't tell her – or anyone – that I have anything to do with this. *No one!*'

Walter Hawley winked. 'Mind me asking which sister you're sweet on?'

Isaac Bell delivered the grin that a married man expected from a bachelor.

'Let's just say that with this arrangement, I can keep my eye on both of them.'

*

Archie Abbott came through with a wire to the Yale Club. His friends in the State Department reported strong rumors that the Shah of Persia was negotiating a monster loan from the Russian czar. Archie speculated that maybe such a loan would explain Rockefeller's clandestine visit to the Persian embassy.

Maybe.

Bell had packed and was just leaving the club to walk to Grand Central, intending to board the train well ahead of Rockefeller, when the day hall porter said, 'There's a street urchin asking for you.'

'Where?'

'He snuck in through the kitchen.'

'Did he say what he wanted?'

'He claims he's a probationary Van Dorn apprentice. I figured if he were, he'd know you don't work there anymore.'

Bell hurried downstairs to the kitchen. A boy who looked like a cleaned-up, dressed-up street rat was standing quietly in a corner. Scarcely into his teens, his eyes alert, his manner so diffident, he was almost invisible.

'What's your name, son?'

'Tobin, sir. Eddie Tobin.'

'Who do you apprentice under?'

'Mr Warren.'

Of course. The Van Dorn street gang expert. If Eddie Tobin was good enough for Harry Warren, he was good enough for Bell.

'How old are you?'

'Not old enough to apprentice. I'm only probationary.'

'I asked how old?' Bell growled.

'Fifteen.'

'*How* old?'

'Fourteen.'

'When I was fourteen, I ran away to the circus. Did Mr Warren send you?'

'Mr Forrer. Mr Warren said it was OK.'

'What do you have there?'

The kid had an envelope of newspaper clippings. Bell had read the top one already:

Averell Comstock, director of Standard Oil, and at one time president of the corporation, died after a brief illness. Comstock was one of the big oil capitalists of the country who laid the foundations for the Standard Oil Company alongside John D. Rockefeller, Clyde Lapham, and Henry M. Flagler. He served, too, as a director of the Western Union Telegraph Company, the Pennsylvania Railroad, and the Pittsburgh National Bank. His wealth was estimated at between $75,000,000 and $100,000,000.

The second clipping reported that Averell Comstock had left ten thousand dollars to a Mrs Mary McCloud who had a coffee stand that the oil magnate had frequented on Fulton Street.

The last clipping reported that a Mrs Mary McCloud had died in a tenement fire in Chatham Square.

Forrer had typed a note.

Same Mrs McCloud. Tenement short walk from Fulton.

'Come with me, Tobin.' John D. Rockefeller's train
was leaving in three hours. If Bell didn't have enough
time, the kid could follow up and wait for reinforcements.
'Yes, sir, Mr Bell!'
They raced downtown on the Elevated.

Before descending to the street, Bell scanned the
squalid neighborhood from the vantage of the Chatham
Square El station. Walt Hawley and the *Evening Sun* and
most of the big New York dailies occupied the clean,
modern Newspaper Row section of Park Row less than
a half mile downtown. This was the upper section of
Park Row, a slum that had been a slum for most of the
city's long history.

He spotted a burned-out tenement and led Tobin
down the stairs, three at a bound.

Sawhorses blocked the sidewalk. The buildings that
flanked it had burned, too. Rain had fallen since, and
the odor of wet charred wood hung heavily in the air.
Settlement House workers were helping families who
lost their homes load bedclothes and furniture that had
survived the fire.

'Maybe this will help,' said Bell. He pressed two
twenty-dollar gold pieces, two months' sweatshop earn-
ings, into the hands of the startled woman in charge.

'God bless you, sir.'

'Did anyone here know Mrs McCloud?' he asked.

None did, but one said she thought Mrs McCloud had worked on Fulton Street. Bell and Tobin hurried downtown and across Fulton toward the East River. At the waterfront, carts and temporary stalls had set up business selling refreshments.

'I hope those aren't Jamaica Bay oysters,' said Tobin.

'Why's that?'

'Jamaica Bay's polluted with the typhoid.'

'We're looking for coffee stands,' said Bell. They found a row of them selling coffee and cake and pastries. One space was empty. Bell paid for coffee and cake for the apprentice. The kid tore into it hungrily but paid close attention as Bell questioned the woman who poured.

'Where is Mrs McCloud?'

'Gone.'

'When did she leave?'

'She didn't leave. She died. She was killed in a fire.'

'That is terrible,' said Bell. 'Did you know her well?'

'Not as well as Mrs Campbell. The shop on the other side. *Kate!*' she called across the empty stand. 'Gentleman here is asking about Mrs McCloud.'

Bell crossed over and ordered a slab of pound cake. 'Mrs Campbell? I'm Jethro Smith. I just heard. I had no idea. I didn't know her well, but I stop by when I'm downtown. What happened?'

'Poor Mrs McCloud. Widowed young. All she had

was her boy and he died. Now this. Are you a newspaperman?'

'No, ma'am. I'm in the insurance line. Why do you ask?'

'Newspapermen came around. They said that Mary inherited *ten thousand dollars*. And never knew it! Died without knowing it.'

'Did you say her son died, too?' Bell asked.

'Drowned in the river.'

'When?'

'The same time as the fire – not that anybody was surprised. Anthony ran with the Five Points Gang. I pray she never knew he drowned.'

'Let us hope,' said Bell. 'Ten thousand! That is a lot of money. Who left her the ten thousand?'

'An old man. He used to come every day. I teased her. He was sweet on her. Every day like clockwork. First he'd eat his oysters on the pier, then he'd come round the corner and drink Mary's coffee. I used to say don't give him so much sugar in his coffee. You'll kill his appetite. He won't order cake. I guess I was wrong about that. Ten thousand!'

Bell checked his watch, motioned to Tobin, and passed him the cake. 'I have to catch a train. Have a look-see at whichever oyster stand the old man frequented.'

'Yes, Mr Bell. Is there anything special you want me to look for?'

Bell paused for a moment. It was a smart question

from a kid just starting out. No wonder Harry Warren had tapped him. Tobin just might be a natural.

'Start with where that stand gets its oysters. Let's make sure Mr Comstock didn't die of that Jamaica Bay typhus you mentioned. Soon as you sort that out, report to Mr Forrer. Then tell Mr Warren I asked would he give you a hand to look into a Five Pointer named Anthony McCloud drowning in the East River.'

BOOK THREE

Gas

June–September 1905
The Black City

Bell has the Maxim gun and they have not

19

'Thank you for seeing me off,' John D. Rockefeller told the New York reporters who mobbed the Lake Shore Limited platform at Grand Central. 'I'd expect you'd have more profitable ways to pass your time, but it is very kind of you.'

He wore an old man's overcoat and held tight to the burly Bill Matters' arm while Isaac Bell stood guard just out of camera range. 'What will I do in Cleveland? Warm these old bones and try my hand knocking golf balls.'

The Cleveland newspapers sent reporters to meet his train at Union Depot, and posted more reporters at the front gate of Forest Hill, Rockefeller's summer residence on the edge of town. A week later, the newspapermen returned when the city's Italian Boys Band came to serenade him. Rockefeller gave them a show, seizing a baton to conduct 'The Star-Spangled Banner.' It would be his last public appearance until October.

That night Isaac Bell slipped him and Matters into a private car coupled to the New York Central's eastbound Lake Shore Limited. Ten hours later, the train was divided at Albany. Some cars continued east to Boston, most headed south to New York City. Bill

Matters joined the New York section to board the four-funnel German ocean liner SS *Kaiser Wilhelm der Grosse*. Isaac Bell and John D. Rockefeller continued on the eastbound section.

Waiting with steam up in Boston Harbor was the three-hundred-foot *Sandra*, a handsome yacht with a lofty raked stack and the lines of a greyhound that Rockefeller had borrowed when Bell pointed out that the newspapers ensured there were no secrets on an ocean liner. Judge James Congdon had lent *Sandra* in a flash, leaving Bell to speculate whether the legendary Wall Street potentate, a founder of US Steel, was in on Rockefeller's deal. Whatever the deal was. So far, Bell had made no progress in getting Rockefeller to confide in his bodyguard.

Sandra's triple-expansion engines drove them across the Atlantic Ocean in twelve days. They landed at Cherbourg and rode in a private car coupled to the boat train to Paris. A French actress whom Bell had known in San Francisco recruited her favorite theatrical costumer and wigmaker from the Comédie-Française. They called on John D. Rockefeller in the privacy of his hotel.

Bell booked train tickets to Constantinople. Then he visited a director of the Compagnie Internationale des Wagons-Lits, whose wife's sapphire necklace Van Dorn detectives had ransomed from the thief Rosania when she visited Chicago. The grateful director of the sleeping car company gave Bell a copy of the passenger manifest. Bell showed it to Rockefeller to ensure that the oil magnate would not bump into fellow tycoons on the Express d'Orient.

The tawny yellow all-stateroom train offered its pampered customers the unique benefit of not being rousted from their beds for passport checks at the border crossings as they steamed through Munich, Strasbourg, Vienna and Budapest. Sixty-four hours after leaving Paris, they awakened to the balmy air and dazzling sunshine of Constantinople, a vast and ancient cosmopolitan city of mosques and minarets, a sprawling bazaar, mangy dogs, and a bustling harbor on a deep blue sea.

A mail steamer carried them up the Bosporus Strait and four hundred miles across the Black Sea to Batum, the world's biggest oil port, where the snow-covered Caucasus Mountains loomed over the harbor, and the six-hundred-mile pipe line from Baku terminated.

Dozens of steam tankers rode at anchor, queuing to load at the kerosene docks. But the city's streets were deserted and buildings shuttered.

'Muslims and Christians are shooting each other,' Bill Matters reported when he met them at the steamer in a Rolls-Royce. 'It's a *pogromy*, Tatars attacking Armenians.'

'Where do the Russians stand?' asked Bell.

'The cops and Army turn a blind eye.'

They drove five miles out of the city to Manziadjani. The American vice consul, a prosperous and well-connected ship broker whom Rockefeller had arranged to meet, had his country place there. Shots were fired from the woods as they pulled in through the front gate. Bell had his pistol out and was opening his carpetbag when Vice Consul Abrams staggered up to the car with blood pouring from his mouth.

They rushed him to a nearby Russian Army fort, where he died within moments of arriving. Isaac Bell raced Rockefeller and Matters back to Batum and onto the train to Baku. At Tiflis, the capital of Georgia, halfway to the Caspian Sea, there were reports of riots. A bomb exploded outside the station. Bell kept his party on the train and they slept the night sitting up on hard benches.

Next morning, the authorities dithered. It was midday before the train pulled out, preceded by a pilot engine, in case wreckers taking advantage of the collapse of law and order had mined the tracks to rob the passengers. They steamed slowly across an endless, ever-more-desolate dry valley between snowy mountains to the north and indistinct highlands to the south.

An hour before nightfall, still fifty miles from Baku, the pilot engine hit a mine.

The explosion blew it off the rails and into a ravine, taking with it the riflemen guarding the train. Horsemen in black cloaks gathered on a ridge that loomed above the tracks.

Isaac Bell opened his carpetbag and joined the Savage 99's barrel to its chamber with a practised twist. Another explosion blocked the rails behind them, and a wild-eyed conductor ran through the car yelling, 'Wreckers!'

They attacked, galloping down the slope, brandishing long guns and sabers.

'Get Mr Rockefeller under cover,' Bell told Matters. 'Fort him up with those bags.'

Matters obeyed instantly, helping Rockefeller to the floor, pulling luggage down from the racks. The old man remained calm and watchful and seemed to have the horse sense to trust the job to the man he had chosen to protect him. If C. C. Gustafson was the most philosophical man on the subject of getting shot, John D. Rockefeller took the cake as the calmest man without a gun that Isaac Bell had ever seen in a gunfight.

Bell counted ten expert riders on agile ponies. Without a telescope on the rifle, he'd be wasting ammunition if he opened up any farther than four hundred yards. But four hundred yards would give him only forty seconds to stop them before they reached the stranded train. He glanced about the car. Some of the men had pulled revolvers. Bill Matters unlimbered an ancient Civil War Remington. Bell's was the only rifle.

20

'When will you shoot?' John D. Rockefeller called to Isaac Bell.

'When I can hit them.'

He chose a large boulder on the hillside as his quarter-mile marker. The lead horseman steered his mount directly at it. As he raised his whip to make the animal jump, Bell pressed the Savage to his shoulder. The whip descended. The animal gathered its haunches and left the ground. Isaac Bell waited for the rider's chest to cross the iron sight and curled his finger gently around the trigger.

Dave McCoart had loaded a box of wildcats for him and Bell decided he owed the gunsmith a box of Havana cigars. The train wrecker slid off his horse almost as smoothly as if he had chosen to dismount. His foot jammed in a stirrup. The panicked animal veered sharply, dragging its dead rider across the line of charge. Two train wreckers crashed into them and went down in a tangle of hoofs.

Bell levered in a fresh shell.

He fixed a bead on a rider who was whirling a carbine over his head like a sword. Again the perfectly balanced trigger kept the weapon dead steady as Bell fired and another wrecker fell off his horse. But they had closed within two hundred yards. Bell's next target was an easy hit, and they were so near for his next that he could have dropped his man with a rock.

'Shoot!' he roared at the men gaping out the windows.

They jerked the triggers of their revolvers, hitting nothing. Through that hail of wild fire, the horsemen charged. The Savage's magazine indicator read one shot left. Bell fired at a man so close, he could see the hairs of his beard.

That shot and the volume of pistol fire broke the charge. Twenty yards from the train, the survivors turned their horses and drove them back up the ridge. Bell reloaded, shouting to the others, 'Keep shooting before they change their minds.'

He sent two slugs whistling over their heads and they kept going, lashing their horses. The revolver-toting passengers stopped shooting or ran out of ammunition. The beginnings of a ragged cheer died on their lips as each and every man considered how close he had come to annihilation. Silence finally descended in the hot, dusty railcar.

Isaac Bell helped John D. Rockefeller to his feet.

'Now what?' asked the Standard Oil magnate.

'We wait for a wreck train to repair the tracks.'

'They're coming back,' a passenger shouted.

Men clutched their revolvers. But this time the thunder of hoofbeats was only a roving police patrol of

Cossacks armed with bolt-action rifles and *shashka* sabers.

Bell broke down the Savage.

'Nice shooting,' said Matters. 'Where'd you get the rifle?'

Bell hid it in his carpetbag. 'What rifle?'

If he owed Dave McCoart a box of cigars for his bullets, he should in all fairness send one to the assassin for his gun. Lacking a name and address, Bell would wait until he installed him in his cell in death row.

Isaac Bell led a much-jauntier John D. Rockefeller off the train at Baku Station than the geezer in the overcoat who had boarded the Lake Shore Limited to Cleveland. His actress friend's Comédie-Française costumers had camouflaged the magnate's famous features with a silver-gray wig to cover his bald head and matching eyebrows fastened with spirit gum to replace those he had lost to alopecia. Tinted spectacles shaded his piercing gaze. A white flannel 'ice cream' suit, a straw panama, and a gold-headed walking stick bedecked a gracefully aging dandy visiting a southern Russian city in the summer.

He even cracked a joke.

'Process servers from the Corporations Commission won't know me from Adam.'

With Bell at his side, he strode through the station, the picture of an adventurous American who might be a tourist or a wealthy missionary. Though, in fact, they had made him a diplomat. Rockefeller's Washington 'correspondents' had provided unassailable documents for a fictitious Special US Envoy for Commercial Affairs to Russia and Persia – the Honorable Joseph D. Stone.

On Bell's orders, Bill Matters had left the train earlier at a suburban station. Matters was traveling under his own name as the representative of the American refinery builder Purest Incorporated of New Jersey – which happened to be one of Standard Oil's secret subsidiaries. His letters of introduction to the mayor of Baku, the prefect, the governor, and the city's leading oil men stated that his mission was to persuade the Russian government to let Purest build new, modern refineries and replace the old ones owned by Rothschild and Nobel. A seemingly chance meeting with Special Envoy Joseph D. Stone would lead to Matters and Stone discovering that their business interests coincided.

Isaac Bell, too, traveled under his own name. Bogus papers established the tall detective as Special Envoy Stone's private secretary and bodyguard who had been granted extended leave from the United States Secret Service.

Compared to Tiflis and Batum, the much-bigger city of Baku seemed peaceful and less tense, exhibiting few outward signs of last winter's murderous riots. Baku was also quite clearly the thriving capital of an oil-rich region that pumped half the entire world's petroleum. The lavish railroad station, bustling with crowds of people speaking Farsi, Russian and Armenian, was the equal of any in Paris or London.

Outside the station, women wore veils, cart horses plodded under tall Russian yokes, and the ruins of a centuries-old Persian citadel loomed on a hill. But swift modern trolleys glided on broad cobblestone avenues. The stonework, mansard roofs, towers, cupolas and porte cocheres of Baku City Hall and the Embassy Row buildings were typical of a great metropolis. The ostentatious private palaces built by the oil kings spoke of vast fortunes made as suddenly as they were on Wall Street – and were no less gaudy than those lining Fifth Avenue.

An hour of buying drinks and eavesdropping in the Hotel de l'Europe's bars and lobby confirmed Bell's decision to base Rockefeller's envoy disguise on the information Archie had turned up in Washington. The rumor repeated most anxiously said that the Shah of Persia had secretly borrowed fifteen million rubles from Czar Nicholas. That the loan might gain Russia's Navy entrée to the Persian Gulf had Great Britain and the United States riled to the core.

John D. Rockefeller was thrilled. Beaming, he confided to Bell in one of the unguarded moments he had begun to offer up since his costuming in Paris, 'Not one man in a hundred will keep his eye on the ball.'

He did not seem at all surprised by the rumors of the czar's moneylending, and Isaac Bell concluded that he had probably known about the loan right down to the last ruble long before they left New York for Cleveland.

21

The assassin's first and strongest inclination had been to masquerade as a Cossack. The pageantry and sheer spectacle of the savage warriors appealed, and there was great advantage to be had playing the role of a character who frightened ordinary folk. But Cossacks were so closely related by blood and clan that they knew one another, and all knew their place from a hundred traditions of tribal hierarchy.

To act the part of an aristocrat was almost as tempting. The privileged *gratin* of Russian society spoke French, which the assassin could understand, and were kowtowed to by everyone, especially soldiers and police. But aristocrats, too, were divided by impenetrable layers of rank. Who knew what superior you would accidentally insult?

Luckily, there was one sort that every Russian feared.

The lowliest peasant, the noblest aristocrat, the angry Tatar, the despised Armenian, the arrogant soldier, the brutal cop, the corrupt bureaucrat, all were terrified by the Okhrana, the czar's secret police.

Plainclothes agents' disguises ranged from the rubbernecking tourist to the city laborer. The assassin had observed that, however disguised, secret agents often betrayed themselves with a superior attitude. Lording it over people was no way for the czar's spies to catch revolutionaries. That was their loss. But from the assassin's point of view, pulling rank was a foolproof way to scare Russians into backing down and leaving you alone.

The riots, and the dread of worse impending, gave the disguise even sharper teeth. The government had put the Baku region in a state of *chrezvychainaia okhrana*, or 'extraordinary security'. People dreading merciless sentences of prison and exile without a trial were doubly in terror of the Okhrana.

Head high and gaze contemptuous, brandishing a master rigger's toolbox, the assassin brushed past the guards at the Nobel refinery gate. They were watching for armed Tatars, and not inclined to tangle with a plainclothes secret policeman masquerading in brand-new, too-clean overalls.

The derricks in the Baku fields were fireproofed with metal and Gypsolite sheathing and more densely positioned than in Kansas – stacked more like the crowded Los Angeles fields along Sunset Boulevard, with the accompanying smoke, fumes, stench and noise. In all other aspects, they resembled those the assassin had studied. Steam engines powered the drill machinery, ladders ran up the sides, cables turned over crown pulleys, and the tops of the derricks were surrounded with parapet work platforms that made an ideal shooting perch.

The workmen tending the engines and the pumps looked away, hoping not to make eye contact that could lead to questions. Even the drillers deepening the wells with bit and casing – a much-tougher lot of men – averted their faces. The way was clear to choose an untended derrick that offered a clear field of fire yet was remote enough to allow an unimpeded escape.

The assassin found the right derrick along the shore of Baku Bay, which sheltered tank steamers, barges and tugboats from the Caspian Sea. Its parapet commanded a perspective of the Baku road and the gate where traffic entered the refinery. The smoke made it hard to see, but wind gusts off the water stirred it sporadically, much as the Kansas wind had at Hopewell Field.

Safely ensconced high in the air with a panoramic field of fire, all that remained was to assemble the Savage, adjust the telescope, insert the clip, and wait for the so-called Special Envoy Joseph D. Stone, Standard Oil directing head Bill Matters, and supposed former Van Dorn detective Isaac Bell.

After months of instigating murder in the streets and homes set afire and property looted in hopes of distracting angry citizens from contemplating revolution – hopes largely realized – it dawned on the czar's government that the European investors demanding stability were right to be alarmed. The Tatar *pogromy* against the Armenians was about to destroy Russia's most valuable industry. So when Purest Incorporated executive Bill Matters and Special Commercial Envoy Stone drove to the Nobel refinery in Black Town, the Baku region prefect and the governor insisted on providing a powerful escort.

Cossack outriders in brilliant red uniforms crowned by tall sheepskin *papakhi* formed a cordon around their auto – a Cleveland-built, 24-horsepower Peerless Tonneau car – which caused Isaac Bell to elevate every nerve end to its highest state.

Surrounded by saber-wielding horsemen, the car's rate of speed was limited to a brisk trot. At the same time, the glittering Cossacks pinpointed the exact location of the Peerless – itself a visual extravaganza of red enamel and polished brass – for a revolutionary with a pistol or a sniper drawing a bead.

Bell was not particularly concerned about a revolutionary getting past the Cossacks, and even if one managed to, the scuffle would give him plenty of time to blow the attacker's head off with his Colt automatic. A sniper was a grimmer story, and Bell watched anxiously for a glint of smoke-darkened sunlight on a distant rifle. He could be stationed on a roof or in an attic window, at any height that presented a line of fire above the tall horsemen.

They moved out of the hotel and embassy districts, past Armenian neighborhoods of shuttered houses, and through slums where the Tatars, distinguished by their blue tunics, darker skin and round faces, stared sullenly. The Cossacks' faces hardened, their tension betrayed by stiffened backs and darting eyes.

Bell had befriended the chauffeur, Josef, a Georgian with a tall pompadour of wavy black hair and the furtive flicker in his coal-dark eyes of a police spy assigned to eavesdrop on the Americans. Josef explained in halting English that the Cossacks had new orders to stop the *pogromy*, to which they had been turning an officially sanctioned blind eye. Now they were the Tatars' enemy. 'Tatar shoot Cossack,' the Georgian flung cheerfully over his shoulder to Bell in the backseat. 'Cossack shoot Tatar. Make peace.'

Bell glanced at Rockefeller beside him. The old man was looking everywhere with big eyes. 'What splendid horses!' He seemed happy, almost joyful. Bell speculated that he was delighted that his Special Envoy disguise allowed him for the first time in decades to move about in public. Tatars were glowering at his police escort, not at the 'most hated man in America.'

Whereas Bill Matters sat rigidly in the front seat next to the chauffeur, uncomfortable as he always appeared to be in Rockefeller's presence. He did not appear nervous, although he was hardly at ease.

Bell was not quite sure what to make of him. As brusque and tough as he had found Edna and Nellie Matters' father on first meeting, he had not seen real indications of the 'hard as adamantine' that Spike Hopewell had characterized. Granted, the man had kept a cool head during the train attack. He was clearly accustomed to command. And it seemed that the former independent had effected a successful transition to what Rockefeller referred to as a 'valuable executive.' But regardless of the high level of Standard Oil director or head of department the president had permitted him to rise to, Bell did not believe that Bill Matters had yet become 'one of the boys' who ran the secretive trust.

The smoke grew thicker in the suburbs, the sky blacker.

They headed southeast toward the Bibi-Eibat oil field and Black Town refineries.

The slow-moving auto and clattering horses crept into an enormous field of refinery tanks. Beyond the tanks were countless refining pots, each with a squat chimney belching smoke. A sharpshooter could crouch on the climbing rungs on one of the chimneys, though he would be taking a big risk of being seen. The more likely sniping position, like the roost that the assassin had climbed up to in Kansas, would be in the virtual skyscraper city of a thousand oil derricks that marched in close-packed ranks to the edge of the Caspian Sea.

A Tatar plumber working on the roof of one of the refinery tanks dropped a monkey wrench. The tool banged resoundingly against the metal side. The noise startled a horse. It reared so suddenly that its rider nearly slid off his saddle. For a moment, there was consternation, angry shouts and milling horses. The chauffeur had to slam on his brakes. The Peerless stopped abruptly, jostling Matters against the windshield, the chauffeur into his wheel, and Rockefeller half off his seat until caught and held firmly in place by Isaac Bell.

In that same instant, Bell heard the crack of a high-velocity rifle slug split the air inches from the back of his seat. He grabbed Rockefeller's arm to drag him down out of the line of fire. A second bullet struck the tall detective like a bolt of lightning.

22

The impact of the high-velocity slug threw Isaac Bell against the side door, breaking its latch. It flew open. He tumbled out of the Peerless, ricocheted off the running board, and sprawled on the oil-soaked road. Still gripping Rockefeller's arm, he found himself vaguely aware that he somehow landed underneath the two-hundred-pound magnate. A bullet shattered the windshield. Bills Matters and the chauffeur jumped for their lives.

Bell heard his own voice. He sounded as if he were calling to John D. Rockefeller from a passing train. 'Are you OK?'

The old man straightened his wig.

'My, my! Mr Bell, your coat is drenched in blood.'

From Bell's neck to his elbow, his white suit jacket was soaked ruby red.

His shoulder felt on fire.

The shooting had stopped. Now the danger was the steel-shod hoofs of the panicked horses plunging and rearing as their riders looked everywhere at once for the source of the gunfire.

Again his voice drifted from a distance. 'We better stand up, Mr Stone. Before we get trampled.'

He struggled to his feet, used his working arm to help Rockefeller to his, then found himself holding on to the old man to keep his balance.

'There!' Bell shouted, pointing at the derricks, the likeliest place the assassin fired from.

The Cossacks drew swords and galloped in the opposite direction.

A Tatar work gang was caught in their path. The Cossacks began slashing and shooting indiscriminately. The Moslems fled from the horses, leaving behind crumpled dead and squirming wounded and some hastily discarded sidearms.

Isaac Bell was surprised to see John D. Rockefeller standing over him, staring down with a concerned expression. 'Mr Bell, you've fallen down again. You are wounded.'

Bell started to stand again.

Rockefeller admonished him with an imperious gesture. 'Right there! As I have been saying, you are wounded.' He raised his voice. 'A doctor! Fetch a doctor!'

It finally struck Isaac Bell that it was not a good idea to stand and he lay back and let his mind fix on his memory of the shooting. He was sure it was the assassin. He was also fairly sure that the bullet had been aimed at him, not at Rockefeller. The car stopping suddenly had thrown off the first shot. That was the one he heard crackle over the seat back. He had taken the second. A terrible thought pierced his whirling thoughts.

Was he drawing fire at the man he was supposed to protect?

Bell motioned to Bill Matters, one of the faces hovering over him.

'Get Mr R – Envoy Stone – under cover. I'll catch up.'

'You OK, Bell?'

Bell took inventory. Bloody as he was, there were no arteries spurting or he'd have bled to death by now. He tried to move his arm. That made his shoulder hurt worse. But he could move it. No bones fractured. The whirling in his head and a general air of confusion he blamed on the shock of impact from a high-velocity bullet.

'Tip-top,' he said. 'Get Envoy Stone under cover! Now!'

Matters knelt to speak privately. 'He says he won't leave you here.'

'Tell him I said to get under cover before he gets killed and I lose my only client. Explain to him that I don't know what's going on and I can't help him at this moment.'

They were still shouting for a doctor.

One appeared, a sturdy, barrel-chested young man in a threadbare coat, who knelt beside him, opened his bag, and took out a pair of scissors. He cut away Bell's blood-soaked coat and shirtsleeves, exposing a ragged tear through the flesh of his upper biceps. He reached for a bottle of carbolic acid and muttered something in Russian.

'What?' asked Bell.

'Is hurting. But important.'

'Beats infection,' Bell agreed. He braced for the fiery disinfectant. For a long moment, the sky turned dark. Afterwards the doctor bandaged the wound, then took a hypodermic needle from its nest in a box padded with red velvet.

'What's in that?' asked Bell.

'Morphine. You are feeling nothing.'

'Save it for the next guy – What are those Cossacks shouting?'

'What?'

'Doctor, you speak English.'

'I study at Edinburgh.'

'I will pay you twenty rubles a day to be my translator. What are those Cossacks shouting?'

The doctor's eyes widened. On January's Bloody Sunday, the workers gunned down at the Winter Palace had been demanding their pay be raised to a daily salary of one ruble.

'What is your name?' asked Bell.

'Alexey Irineivoich Virovets.'

'Dr Virovets, what are those Cossacks shouting?'

'They are recognizing the captured guns as being looted from armory.'

Bell levered himself on to his good elbow. He saw pistols heaped on a horse blanket but no sharpshooter's weapons.

'Now what's he saying?' A Cossack officer was

reporting loudly to a civilian dressed in top hat and frock coat. Bell pegged him for the governor's representative or an Okhrana operative.

'He blames the attack on revolutionaries,' said Virovets.

'Help me up. We're going for a walk.'

'I am not recommending –'

'Your objection is noted.'

Twenty minutes later, with his arm in a sling, the sturdy Dr Virovets at his side, and anxious oil company officials trailing them, Isaac Bell walked beside the Caspian surf breaking at the feet of the derricks until he found one that had been abandoned. As much as he wanted to climb to its parapet, he doubted he could with one working arm and a spinning head.

The doctor climbed for him and reported back that he could see the Cossacks still clustered where the bullets had rained down on the Peerless. Bell was not surprised. Forging ahead before the others trampled the beach, he had spotted a single set of footprints in the sand that had approached the ladder from one direction and left in another.

But it was puzzling. The derrick was less than five hundred yards from where the auto had been. How could the assassin have missed twice? The sudden stop could explain the first bullet going awry. But why hadn't the second or third hit him in the head? Or the assassin's favorite target, the neck?

23

Isaac Bell woke up stiff and sore the next morning to a slew of cipher cablegrams from New York. The first was from Grady Forrer, who continued to substitute as directing head of the case in his absence.

FIVE POINTERS BLAME GOPHERS

Bell took that to mean that Van Dorn detectives had discovered that Anthony McCloud's fellow Five Points gangsters did not believe he had fallen drunk into the East River but had been murdered. They naturally blamed their rivals the Gopher Gang. But whoever had killed him, and whatever the motive, it was a heck of a coincidence it happened the day of the fire that killed his mother.

Bell cabled back

INFORM NEW YORK CORONER

entertaining a slim hope that the city's medical examiner could be persuaded to dig up Averell Comstock's body to investigate for a cause of death other than old age.

A cable that read

HOPEWELL OFTEN NEW YORK

told Bell that Wally Kisley and Mack Fulton were grasping at straws about Spike Hopewell's 'tricks up his sleeve' inference. Any independent trying to build a refinery and pipe line would have to travel regularly to New York City to romance his Wall Street bankers.

But the information that Forrer passed along from Dave McCoart resonated with hope of a breakthrough on the gunsmith front – clues that Joseph Van Dorn believed could lead them to the craftsman who smithed the assassin's deadly weapon.

THREE POSSIBLES.
TWO HARTFORD.
ONE BRIDGEPORT.
BOSS AUTHORIZED DETECTIVES.

Archie Abbott, on the other hand, still had nothing to report about sharpshooter Billy Jones.

ARMY UNFRIENDLY.
PURSUING FRIENDSHIP BRIGADIER
GENERAL DAUGHTER.
IS SUPREME SACRIFICE
AUTHORIZED?

Bell had just written in encipher on the cablegram blank

AUTHORIZED ON THE JUMP

when Doctor Virovets arrived to change his bandage. The wound was clean, with no sign of infection, but they agreed on another dose of carbolic acid to be on the safe side. For distraction, Bell asked about the variety of languages he heard spoken in the streets. 'Tatar,' the doctor explained, 'Georgian and Russian.'

'May I borrow your stethoscope?' Bell asked as the doctor was leaving.

John D. Rockefeller walked in carrying a tray of milk and *pryaniki*, the Russian spice cookies of which Bell had grown fond.

'I'm surprised to see you dressed, Mr Bell. I presumed I would venture out alone today.'

'I could use the fresh air.'

A Renault limousine was waiting with its curtains drawn. At Bell's insistence, the Cossacks had been replaced by plainclothes police detectives on foot. Some trotted alongside, huffing and puffing, as they pulled on to the avenue. Others rode behind them in an identical Renault, Bell having convinced the cops that similar limousines would confuse a sniper.

He and Rockefeller sat in near darkness behind the curtains. Bell watched the streets through a split in the cloth, wondering whether a sense of shared danger might incline the reticent Rockefeller to open up further to him. He tested the waters with a joke.

'I guess we can't blame the assassin for slandering Standard Oil if he shoots at the president.'

'He wasn't shooting at me,' said Rockefeller. 'He was shooting at you.'

'Are you sure about that?'

'You are the one with his arm in a sling, not I.'

'Isn't it possible he hit me when he missed you?'

'The first report you filed when you came to work for me stated that he has missed his shot on rare occasions. And never by much. He was shooting at you.'

'Sounds like you no longer need a bodyguard.'

'Don't worry, your job is not at risk. Baku is teeming with angry people primed to kill for every imaginable reason. I'm glad to have you with us.'

'Are you free to tell me who we are calling on?'

'In confidence. Please bear in mind this is not to be repeated. We are meeting a representative of the Shah of Persia.'

'Has Mr Matters gone ahead?'

'Mr Matters has other business.'

'May I ask – ?'

Rockefeller's eyes cut through the dimly lit passenger cabin like locomotive headlamps. 'You have many questions today, Mr Bell.'

'Getting shot makes me curious about what to expect next. I was about to ask whether you are meeting this representative as Commercial Envoy Stone or as the president of Standard Oil.'

'I am the *retired* president,' Rockefeller shot back.

'I keep forgetting,' said Bell.

That drew a stony silence. But minutes later, Rockefeller dropped his voice to a half whisper and confided, 'I cannot answer your question, because I have not yet decided. I keep hearing a proverb in Baku. Perhaps you've heard it, too. "In Persia no man believes another."'

'They love insults,' said Bell. 'Armenians are sharpers; Georgians are drunkards; Tatars simultaneously violent, unintelligent, and kindly; Germans dull, Cossacks vicious, Russians petty. All agree that Persians are liars. Which shouldn't come as a surprise after centuries of tyranny and misgovernment.'

Rockefeller favored Bell's observation with a thin smile and the further confidence that the detective was angling for. 'I don't know yet whether I am dealing with liars. All I know is that I will begin as Envoy Stone. Whether I become Mr Rockefeller will depend upon how much noise they make and how much dust they throw in the air.'

The Renault stopped at a side entrance to the Astoria, one of the lavish new hotels near City Hall. They slipped in quietly, skirted the lobby, guided by a hotel functionary, to a service elevator that took them to a penthouse kitchen. A Persian secretary greeted Rockefeller in flawless English. 'It is my pleasure to report,

sir, that no one has marked your arrival. We are prepared for the private meeting you requested.'

'*You* requested the meeting,' Rockefeller corrected
him, politely but firmly. 'I requested privacy.'

'Then we are both happy, sir.' The Persian was slim
and lithe as a cat, and as graceful, with large eyes in a
narrow face.

Rockefeller turned to Bell. 'Wait here.'

'I have to inspect the room where you are going,'
said Bell.

'It is perfectly safe,' said the secretary.

'I still want to see it,' said Bell.

'It is all right,' said Rockefeller, 'I trust our hosts.'

Bell said, 'If I cannot see where you are going, I must
insist that I wait directly outside. At the door in the
next room.'

'Insist?' The secretary's eyebrows arched above a
mocking smile.

Bell ignored him. To Rockefeller he said, 'By the
terms of our contract, our agreement is voided if, in my
opinion, you place me in a position that I cannot
protect you. Under those conditions, the severance
fee is calculated on the time it will take me to return
to New York. The purpose of that clause is to make
you think twice about straying too far from my
protection.'

'I recall,' said Rockefeller. He addressed the secretary, 'Take us to the room where we are to meet. Mr
Bell will wait outside the door.'

They put him in the foyer, which was exactly where Isaac Bell wanted to be. He waited until he was alone, closed the outer door, pulled a rubber stop from his pocket, and wedged it under the door. Then he untangled the stethoscope he had borrowed from Dr Alexey Irineivoich Virovets, inserted the ear tubes, and pressed the chest piece against the thinnest of the wooden panels.

The secretary was acting as translator for a Persian of very high rank, guessing by the secretary's obsequious manner of speaking to him. Bell heard a round of elaborate greetings. Then Rockefeller got down to business.

'Tell His Excellency that I have a gift for the shah waiting in my hotel stables.'

This was translated and the answer translated back. 'The shah is a great lover of horses.'

'Tell him that this gift for the shah has many horses.'

The translation back was a puzzled 'How many horses?'

Rockefeller, clearly enjoying himself, said, 'Tell him many, many, bright red and shiny brass.'

'Motors?'

'The finest autos that Cleveland builds,' answered Rockefeller. 'They'll ride circles around Rolls-Royce. Now, tell him, let's get down to brass tacks – that expression means "business", young fellow. Tell him the pipe line will cost the shah not one penny. I will pay for every foot of pipe from Rasht to the Persian Gulf.

And I will build the tanker piers and a breakwater to protect the harbor.'

The answer in Persian was long, and it took the translator a long time to craft a halting, vague reply.

'By the terms . . . of certain . . . understandings . . . In the name of the most merciful and compassionate God, His Majesty the shah . . . prefers . . . to secure, please God, the agreement of certain . . . neighbors.'

Isaac Bell gleaned from Rockefeller's blunt reply that his 'correspondents' had laid a lot of groundwork to get to this meeting with a personage who had the shah's ear. The old man did not sound one bit surprised. Nor did he hesitate.

'Tell him to tell the shah that I am prepared to pay off the neighbor's loan.'

After translation, there was a long silence. Finally, the Persian spoke. The secretary translated, 'How much of it?'

'Every ruble.'

On their way out, they had emerged from the service elevator and were halfway along the edge of the lobby when Isaac Bell suddenly shouldered Rockefeller toward a corridor that entered from the side.

'What is it?' asked Rockefeller, resisting with his full weight. Pain shot through Bell's wound.

'Keep walking. Turn your face toward me.'

Bell steered him down the corridor and into the first shop, a florist filled with giant sprays of out-of-season tulips and elaborate concoctions of roses. Before the door had closed behind them, he heard familiar ringing laughter.

'Good lord. They make Pittsburgh look positively genteel.'

Bell pressed against the window for a sharply angled view of the lobby.

'What is it?' Rockefeller demanded.

'Two ladies who will not be fooled by Special Envoy Stone.'

John D. Rockefeller was enraged, but he had held off saying anything until they were back at their own hotel where Bill Matters could be called on the carpet.

'That newspaperwoman is here,' he railed. 'Your daughter. What is she doing in Baku?'

Bill Matters was genuinely apologetic. He looked completely baffled. 'I had no idea either of my daughters was coming to Baku.'

'She is the author of *The History of the Under- and Heavy-handed Oil Monopoly.*'

'Yes, I know, sir, but –'

Rockefeller whirled on Isaac Bell. 'Mr Bell, did you know that she was coming here?'

'The first I knew,' Bell lied, 'was when we saw her at the Astoria.'

'Find out what she knows. No one must learn I'm here.'

'Let me do that,' said Matters. 'Please. She's my daughter. She'll confide in me.'

Rockefeller looked at Bell, demanding his opinion.

Bell said, 'E. M. Hock has no reason to confide in me. I will call on her, of course, as we've become friends. And her sister. But no, I'm not the one to question her. Better for Mr Matters to do it.'

Half the vast, dimly lit, high-ceilinged vault that housed the Hotel de l'Europe's stables remained a house barn and carriage house. Half had been converted into a modern auto and limousine garage with gasoline pumps and mechanics bays.

Bell went there with Alexey Irineivoich Virovets in the event he needed a translator. He found the shot-up Peerless, with its windshield not yet repaired. They had parked it out of the way, at the back. Hidden behind it were two large wooden shipping crates covered in canvas. Bell lifted the cloth and looked under it. In the crates were two identical red Peerless autos, just as Rockefeller had told the Persians.

Virovets translated the writing on various shipping stickers pasted to the crates. The autos had been originally sent to Moscow, then south on freight trains to Baku. It was strange, Bell thought, when he discussed the details of the trip with Bill Matters, the Pipe Line Committee director had never mentioned the autos. Had Matters thought them unrelated to a bodyguard's concerns for Rockefeller's safety? Or did he not know about them? It seemed, Bell thought, odd for Rockefeller to keep the autos secret from a colleague. But for whatever reason they were hidden, it was clear again that Rockefeller had planned this trip far ahead.

'Well, Father, here we are all three having tea as if we're off to the theater in New York.'

'I'm very surprised to see you.'

'How could you be?' asked Nellie. 'Edna writes about the oil business.'

Edna was quietly watching their father and letting Nellie do the talking.

Their father said, 'I didn't think that the *Oil City Derrick* had the means to send a reporter to Baku.'

Nellie said, 'Cleveland would be more their limit. Edna is writing for . . . May I tell him, Edna?'

'It's hardly a secret.'

'The *New York Sun*! What do you think of *that*, Father? Your daughter is writing for one of the finest newspapers in the country.'

'The *Sun* is no friend of Standard Oil.'

'Fortunately for Standard Oil,' said Edna, 'Standard Oil does not depend on the kindness of friends.'

'And furthermore,' said Nellie, all excited with color high in her cheeks, 'Baku could be the biggest thing to hit the oil business since Spindletop.'

'In an opposite way,' Edna interrupted drily. 'Cutting production in half instead of spouting gushers.'

'I don't know if the situation is that bad,' Matters said automatically. 'The authorities seem back in control.'

'Really?' asked Edna. 'There's a rumor making the rounds that shots were fired at some American business men.'

Bill Matters shrugged. 'An isolated incident.'

'Apparently,' said Edna, 'the Cossacks reacted by slaughtering refinery workers. And now the rest are up in arms.'

Matters shrugged again. 'It's Russia. My impression is the authorities have strict control of the situation.'

'And what are *you* doing here, Father? Last we heard, you were in Cleveland. I just mailed you a postcard there. Had I known, I could have handed it to you and saved a stamp.'

'Mr Rockefeller sent me to rustle up some refinery business – and don't print that.'

'Not without verification,' Edna said.

Nellie laughed so loudly that people glanced from nearby tables. 'Father, you should see your face. You know darned well she won't print that. Certain things are sacred.'

'Father is sacred,' said Edna with a wink that warmed Bill Matters' heart.

He sat back with a happy smile on his face. They had bought his story.

'It's like old times,' he said.

The girls exchanged a glance. 'Whatever do you

mean?' asked Nellie, and Edna asked, 'What are you smiling about, Father?'

'Like going to New York to see a play back when you were in pigtails.'

'"Pigtails"?' echoed Nellie in mock horror. 'Whenever you took us to the theater, we dressed like perfect little ladies.'

'Even after we ceased to be,' said Edna.

'All I'm saying is, it makes me very happy.'

'Who was that man with E. M. Hock and Nellie Matters?' John D. Rockefeller asked Isaac Bell. 'I saw him at the Astoria, and lurking here in the lobby when they came for tea with their father.'

'He is their bodyguard.'

'He looks the part, I suppose. But are you sure?'

'I know him well,' said Bell. 'Aloysius Clarke. He was a Van Dorn detective.'

'A Van Dorn? What is a Van Dorn doing here?'

'Not anymore. Mr Van Dorn let him go.'

'For what?'

'Drinking.'

'Drinking? I'd have thought that was not uncommon among detectives.'

'Mr Van Dorn gave him several chances.'

'Who does he work for now?'

'I'd imagine he's gone freelance. I'll speak with him, find out what's up.'

Rockefeller asked, 'What is that smile on your face,

Mr Bell? There's something going on here I don't understand.'

'I was glad to see him. Wish Clarke is a valuable man. I just may ask him to join forces.'

'Right there! Not while he serves E. M. Hock!'

'Of course not. In the future, after we're all safely back home.'

24

'My daughter is reporting for the *New York Sun*!' Bill Matters exulted to John D. Rockefeller. 'It's a big feather in her cap. A wonderful step up!'

'Does she know I am in Baku?'

'Absolutely not!'

'What makes you so sure? How do you know she didn't follow me here?'

'They sent her to cover the riots.'

'There aren't any riots.'

'That could change in a flash, Mr Rockefeller. You can feel it in the streets. And my daughter told me that the officials she's interviewed sound deeply worried . . . Now, sir, I know that you can't abide the *Sun*. Neither can I, but –'

Rockefeller stopped him with a gesture. 'Right there! The *Sun* is nonsense. Newspapers are all nonsense. The less they know is all that's important to me.'

'She doesn't know you're here.'

Rockefeller stared. 'All right. I will have to take your word for it.'

'It's not only my word, Mr Rockefeller. It is my judgment. And I guarantee you, sir, if she had told me that she knew you were here, I would inform you immediately.'

Rockefeller shook his head and whispered, 'She would never tell you.'

'I beg your pardon?'

'All right! I'm sending you to Moscow.'

'Moscow?' Matters was stunned. How could he work on the Persian pipe line from Moscow? 'Why?'

'We need those refinery contracts. You have done all you can with the local officials. Now you must convince Moscow that the Standard's thoroughgoing, able administration will do much better for Russia's oil business than these old, good-for-nothing, rusted-out refineries. And if you can't find the right officials in Moscow, you'll go on to St Petersburg.'

'But what about the pipe line?'

'First the refineries.'

Isaac Bell met Aloysius Clarke on the Baku waterfront. The oily, smoky air had been cleared by a sharp wind blowing across the bay from the Caspian. Lights were visible for miles along the great crescent harbor, and Bell saw stars in the sky for the first time since he had arrived in Baku.

Bell thought his old partner looked pretty good, all things considered. He was a big, powerful man who carried his extra weight well. His face was getting fleshy from drink, his mouth had a softness associated with indulgence, and his nose had taken on the rosy hue beloved by painters portraying lushes, but his eyes were still hard and sharp. It was difficult to tell what he was thinking, or if he was thinking at all, unless you caught an unguarded glimpse of his eyes, which was not likely. Besides, Bell told himself, a private detective mistaken for a drunkard bought the extra seconds required to get his foot in a door.

Wish wrapped his tongue around the English language with a self-taught reader's love. 'Best job I can remember. Sumptuous feasts and the finest wines shared nightly with a pair of lookers. And Joe Van Dorn pays the piper . . . How bad's that arm?'

'Healing fast,' said Bell. He flicked open his coat to reveal a Colt Bisley single-action revolver where he usually holstered his automatic, and Wish nodded. Since Bell could not yet rely on the strength in his hand to work the slide to load a round into his automatic's chamber, the special target pistol version of the Colt .45 was an accurate, hard-hitting substitute.

'How'd you get your paws on a Bisley?'

'You can buy *anything* in Baku.'

A sudden gust buffeted the sidewalk. Wish said, 'I read somewhere that "Baku" is Persian for "windbeaten".'

They walked until they found a saloon that catered to sea captains who could afford decent food and genuine whiskey. They ate and drank and got comfortable reminiscing. Finally, Bell asked, 'What do you think of the lookers?'

Wish had been his partner on tough cases. The two detectives trusted each other as only men could who had been stabbed in each other's company and shot in each other's company. Having solved every crime they tackled, they trusted each other's instincts. Each was the other's best devil's advocate – roles they could bat back and forth like competition tennis players.

'Edna is a very serious young lady,' said Wish. 'Angrier than you would think, at first, about the way Rockefeller's ridden roughshod over her father. Nellie's a show-off. She'd make a great actress. Or a politician. She'll make a heck of a splash if she can pull off her New Woman's Flyover stunt.'

He gave Bell an inquiring glance. 'Which one did you fall for?'

'Haven't made up my mind.'

Wish chuckled. 'That sounds very much like both.'

'It *is* confusing,' Bell admitted. 'There is something about Edna . . . But, then, there is something about Nellie . . .'

'What?'

'Edna's deep as the ocean. Nellie dazzles like a kaleidoscope.'

'I don't see either making a wife anytime soon.'

'I'm not rushing.'

A gust of wind stronger than the others shook the building. Sand blown across the bay rattled the window-panes like hail.

'Let's get to the real question,' said Wish. 'Who's the assassin shooting for?'

Bell said, 'You know how they call Standard Oil the octopus?'

'Aptly,' said Wish.

'I'm thinking our mastermind is more like a shark. Hanging around this monster-size octopus, thinking if he can just sink his teeth into one or two arms, he'll have himself the meal of a lifetime. He's shifting the blame for his crimes to the Standard. If he can pull it off, he reckons to pick up some pieces. If it really goes his way, he figures he'll control the second-biggest trust in oil.'

Wish nodded. 'I'd call that basis for a mighty strong hunch.'

'He could be inside the company or an outsider, an oil man, or a railroad man, or in coal or steel. Even a corporation lawyer.'

'A valuable man,' said Wish, 'a man on his way up . . . Say, where are you going? Have another.'

Bell had stood up and was reaching for money. 'My "boss", Mr Rockefeller, is waiting for me to confirm that Detective Aloysius Clarke is no longer a Van Dorn but a freelance bodyguard for Nellie Matters and E. M. Hock, who are traveling together for safety. And that Detective Clarke gave no hint to me that either knows that Mr Rockefeller is in Baku.'

'Rockefeller? Never heard of him,' grinned Wish. He glanced at the bottle they were sharing. His gaze shifted to Bell's arm in his sling. 'Hold on,' he said, 'I'll walk you back.'

'Stay there. I'm OK.'

'In the event you get in a gunfight of such duration

that you have to reload, I would never forgive myself if I didn't give your one hand a hand.'

Outside, the sharp north wind that had cleared the sky of smoke earlier was blowing a gale. The stars had disappeared again, obscured now by the sand that the harsh gusts were sucking into the air. The harbor lights were barely visible. A caustic blast rattled pebbles against walls.

'Look there!'

A graceful three-masted, gaff-rigged schooner struggled alongside an oil berth, sails furled, decks rippling with dark figures crowding to get off. The moment it landed, gangs of Tatars armed with rifles jumped on to the pier and ran toward the city.

Wish Clarke said, 'If the city blows?'

'We evacuate.'

The sand-swirled sky over the oil fields across the bay was abruptly aglow.

Within the city itself, small-arms fire crackled.

They hurried up Vokzalnaya toward the railroad station. The gunfire got louder, pistol and rifle shots punctuated all of a sudden by the heavier churning of Army machine guns. Looking back, Bell saw the sky over the bay getting redder. A glow ahead marked mansions set afire in the Armenian district.

They broke into a run toward the hotel district.

'We'll grab the ladies at your place,' said Bell, 'then Mr R. at mine.'

'Then what? Land or sea?'

'Whichever we can get to,' said Isaac Bell.

25

Isaac Bell telephoned John D. Rockefeller from the Astoria Hotel's lobby.

'Pack one bag and wear your warmest coat. We're running for it.'

'Is this logical?'

'Imperative,' said Bell.

'I have to send cables.'

'Quickly.'

Upstairs, he and Wish found Edna Matters with a carpetbag and her typewriter already at the door, and a large-scale map of the lands bordering the Caspian and Black Seas spread out on her bed.

'Where's Nellie?'

'On the roof.'

'What's she doing on the roof?' asked Wish.

'It's the nearest thing to a balloon,' said Edna. 'She's checking the lay of the land.'

'Go get her, Wish.'

Bell turned to Edna's map, which he had already been reviewing in his mind. The train to Tiflis and Batum and a Black Sea steamer would whisk them to Constantinople in four days. But it was too easy to stop a train where outlaws were the only law.

Edna traced the Caspian Sea route north to Astrakhan and up the Volga River. 'Tsaritsyn steamers connect with the Moscow train.'

Bell said, 'I don't fancy getting trapped in the middle of a Russian revolution, if that's what's brewing.'

'No one I've interviewed knows what will happen next,' said Edna.

'Least of all, the Russians.'

'Poor Father. I'm worried sick about him banished to Moscow.'

Bell went to the window and looked down at the street. A trolley had stopped on its tracks. People lugging bags streamed off it and hurried toward the railroad station. He craned his head to try to see the station, but the angle was wrong. The sky looked red. Shadows leaped, thrown by muzzle flashes. Guns crackled and people ran in every direction. For whatever reason Rockefeller had sent Matters to Moscow, he was better off than they were at the moment.

Nellie burst into the room, color high, eyes bright.

Wish Clarke was right behind her, his expression grim. 'Big gunfight on Millionnaya and a riot at the train station,' he reported. 'Nellie spotted a way across Vokzalnaya if we want the harbor.'

'We want it,' said Bell. 'Let's go.'

The Hotel de l'Europe was guarded by nervous plain-clothes police. Europeans paced the lobby shouting at frightened staff. The hotel pianist began playing a Schubert serenade as if, Isaac Bell thought fleetingly, he hoped to help the world right itself. Bell ran to get his carpetbag. Rockefeller's suite, adjoining his room, was empty. Bell searched it and ran back down to the lobby. Wish was standing on the stairs, where he could watch the doors. Edna and Nellie stood behind him. Both women were eerily calm.

'Did you see Rockefeller?'

'No.'

'There!' said Edna.

The oil magnate was exiting the hotel manager's office. He looked like he was headed to a garden party in his dandy's costume, but Edna had seen through the wig disguise in a flash. Bell saw her beautiful face harden. Her lips were pressed tightly, dots of color flushed on her cheekbones, and her eyes settled on Rockefeller with an intensity stoked by hatred.

He glanced at Nellie. Every trace of the big smile usually ready on her lips had extinguished like a burning coal plunged in cold water. The color of her eyes, like Edna's, shed every soft vestige of green and turned gray as ash.

Wish muttered, as they plunged across the crowded lobby to intercept Rockefeller, 'Are you still sure you want to run together? The young ladies are primed to claw his eyes out.'

'Not my first choice,' said Bell. 'But it's our only choice.'

Rockefeller saw them hurrying toward him and said, 'There you are. I was just paying our hotel bill.'

'Bill?' echoed Wish. 'The town's blowing up.'

'I pay my debts.'

The manager ran from his office and put the lie to that.

'Envoy Stone! If they reply to your cables, where shall I forward the answers?'

'New York.'

'Envoy Stone!' Isaac Bell said with the ice of cold steel in his voice. 'We're going – now. Stick close.'

The situation on Vokzalnaya deteriorated radically before they were halfway to the harbor. Here, too, the trolley had stopped. Suddenly Tatars were running up the middle of the street shooting pistols at well-dressed Armenians huddled in groups.

Russian Army soldiers wheeled up a Maxim gun on a heavy Sokolov mount. As the machine gunners propped it on its legs, the Tatars fled around the corner. The Armenians ran toward the station, mothers dragging children, young men and women helping their elders.

Pistol fire rained down on the Russian soldiers from above. The gunners tilted the water-jacketed barrel upward. The Maxim churned, and a stream of slugs blasted second-storey windows.

From one of those windows flew a baseball-size sphere with a glittering tail of a burning fuse. Still in the air, it exploded with a flash and a sharp bang, and the street and sidewalks were suddenly littered with bodies. Wounded were reeling away when a second bomb exploded prematurely still inside the window. No one remained alive in the circle of the two explosions, not the Tatars, Armenians, or the Russian gun crew sprawled around the Maxim.

Isaac Bell and Aloysius Clarke charged straight at it. A Maxim gun and a thousand .303 rounds in trained hands would be their ticket aboard any ship running from the harbor. Wish heaved one hundred and forty pounds of Maxim and Sokolov mount over his shoulder. Bell scooped up four canvas ammunition belts in his good arm and looped them around his neck.

'Go!'

They staggered toward the harbor, closely trailed by Nellie and Edna and Rockefeller. At the foot of Vokzalnaya, a mob of people was storming the passenger steamer pier fighting to get up the gangway of the one remaining ship. Ships that had already fled were far across the bay, lights fading in the sand haze as they steamed for the safety of the open sea.

'Mr Bell!' cried Rockefeller. 'Is that the Nobel lubricating oil refinery afire?'

The Standard Oil president's eyes locked on the sight of a huge fire miles up the coast at Black Town. From the white-hot heart of it, flames leaped a thousand feet into the air.

'Looks like it,' said Bell, who was scanning the

finger piers for a likely ship. They had toured that Russian refinery yesterday. Rockefeller was scheming to buy it, but the Moscow-based branch of the Nobel dynamite family had no intention of selling. Now the prize had gone up in smoke.

'Tramp freighter,' said Wish, swinging his shoulder to point the Maxim up the waterfront toward a steamer so old it still had masts. 'They won't be fighting to get on that one.'

Bell saw that the tramp was billowing smoke from its single stack. 'He's raising steam.'

They herded their charges toward it. But as they got close they saw Wish had been wrong. Crowds converging on its pier had forced their way onboard. Overloaded, the ship was heeling at a dangerous angle.

'Wait, there's one coming in.'

A small ship showing no lights slipped out of the dark. It looked like salvation. Then they saw the Tatars. They were crowded on deck, as they had been on the schooner that landed earlier, a packed mass of angry men bristling with weapons.

'Where's Mr Rockefeller?'

The old man had disappeared.

'He was with us a second ago.'

Bell hurried along a row of shuttered storefronts, businesses that catered to the steamship passengers, past postcard shops, a fruitier, a milliner, souvenirs, Kodak cameras, and shoved through the door of a telegraph office. A frightened telegrapher had his coat and hat on and was eyeing the door as he pounded his key.

'I'll be right there, Mr Bell,' Rockefeller said without looking up. 'I am sending an important cable.'

'We agreed our lives were more important. Let's go.' Bell took his arm. Rockefeller tried to shrug him off. The tall detective squeezed hard and exploded angrily, 'What the devil is more important than the lives of two women depending on us?'

'Nobel's lubricating oil factory is destroyed. The low specific gravity of Baku crude makes Russian lubricating oil the best in the world, so the Nobels had a nice melon to cut all these years. The best we've got is refined at the Winfield plant in Humble, Texas. Not as good as the Russian lubricating oil, but a lot better than no lubricating oil.'

Clearly, thought Bell, John D. Rockefeller could keep his head when all others were losing theirs. Juggling two balls in the air – the Baku refineries and the Persian pipe line – suddenly he tossed up a third, seizing his chance to profit by the fires. But as Spike Hopewell had said about his old partner Bill Matters, somewhere along the line he had gotten his moral trolley wires crossed.

Isaac Bell shook the magnate like a terrier. 'You are risking our lives to cable New York to buy the Winfield refinery?'

'Russia will never get that market back from me.'

'Done, sir,' said the telegrapher, jumping from the key.

Wish and the Matters sisters pushed in the door as the telegrapher ran out, and Rockefeller shut his mouth like a bear trap. Wish dropped the heavy Maxim on the telegraph counter and the women put down their bags. Though still calm, they looked frightened, a tribute, thought Bell, to their common sense.

Wish coolly shifted the gun muzzle toward the door and drew his revolver.

'Isaac, old son. We need a plan.'

'First,' said Bell, addressing Rockefeller, 'get this straight. I am running this like a military operation. There is one leader. Me. Wish is second-in-command. Whatever we say, goes. Is that clear, Mr Rockefeller? No more dashing off on your own. You'll get us all killed.'

'OK,' said the richest man in America. 'I accept your terms. But not before we resolve another question.' He leveled a long finger at Edna. 'I will not allow this woman newspaperman to report my business like public news.'

Edna Matters answered in a voice as cold as it was determined.

'John D. Rockefeller controls half the oil in the world. He is trapped in the burning city of Baku, which produces the other half. That is extraordinary news. This "woman newspaperman" reports the news.'

'I have news for both of you,' said Isaac Bell.

26

'Our only hope of getting out of this city alive is to pull together. I am not *asking* you to team up. I am laying down rules. The first rule is, Mr Rockefeller is not here.'

'Not here?' Edna looked at him, eyes wide and angry. 'What do you mean, not here?'

'You can report on anything that happens, provided we survive. But not his presence.'

'I cannot agree to that.'

'You must. To make it out of here alive, we have to pull together.'

'How will you stop me?'

'I will ask for your word.'

'And if I don't give you my word?'

'Looters are robbing shops,' Isaac Bell answered without the trace of a smile. 'I will join them. I will steal a Persian carpet and roll you up in it. I will unroll you when I have delivered you safely back to Newspaper Row.'

'How Cleopatric!' said Nellie.

To Bell's immense relief, her joke made Edna smile. She looked at the others who were watching closely. 'OK! If Mr Rockefeller promises not to slow us down stopping to cable orders to his head office, I promise not to write about him.'

'Done,' said Rockefeller.

'But when he breaks that promise – which he surely will – he must tell me the contents of the cable.' She extended her hand to Rockefeller. 'I give you my word. Is it a deal?'

'You're a good negotiator, young lady. It's a deal.'

She turned to Isaac Bell. 'You, sir, will find some way to make this up to me.'

'It's a deal.'

A bullet ricocheted off a lamppost and smashed a window.

'The question remains,' said Wish Clarke, 'how are we getting out of here if we can't take a ship or a train?'

'We can drive by auto back to Batum,' Rockefeller ventured. 'Then a Black Sea steamer to Constantinople.'

'What auto?' asked Bell, intending to get Rockefeller to reveal how the Peerlesses he had hidden in the hotel stables served his scheme.

'My Peerless Tonneau car.'

'Impossible. Batum is six hundred miles over hard country.'

'Tiflis is halfway to Batum, and trains are safer in Georgia.'

Bell shook his head emphatically. 'We can barely all squeeze in the car, much less stow the gasoline, oil, food, water, tools and spares for crossing open country.'

'And let us not forget Mr Maxim,' said Wish, patting the weapon he had propped on the telegrapher's desk, 'without whom no one in their right mind would venture on the so-called roads to Tiflis.'

'We would need three autos as sturdy as a Peerless,' said Bell.

'We have three,' said Rockefeller.

'Three?'

'I had three Peerless Tonneau cars shipped ahead.'

'Why?'

Rockefeller hesitated before he answered, 'Gifts.'

'For whom?' Bell pressed.

Rockefeller clamped his mouth shut.

Bell said, 'Mr Rockefeller, Miss Matters agreed not to reveal your business. *You*, in turn, agreed – fairly and squarely and aboveboard, sir – that we're all in this together.'

Rockefeller's jaw worked. His piercing eyes, rarely readable, turned opaque.

Gunfire roared, and it did the trick.

'Very well! The English presented the Shah of Persia with gifts of autos. I would outdo their gifts with solid, Cleveland-built American autos. Show him who needs Rolls-Royce? Who needs England? Who needs Russia?'

Isaac Bell exchanged a fast grin with Edna Matters and another with Nellie: yet another reminder that John D. Rockefeller heard the rumors first. The secretive magnate had planned far ahead for his journey toward 'the sun rising over the beautiful Mediterranean Sea' where 'The days pass pleasantly and profitably.'

'Where are they?'

'In our hotel stables.'

'Let's see if they're not on fire yet.'

At a fast pace in tight single file, they headed back to the Baku Hotel.

Bell led, with the ammunition belts draped around his neck and his Bisley in his good hand. He put Rockefeller between Edna and Nellie so the fit young women could keep an eye on the much-older man. Wish marched rear guard, with his Maxim gun over his shoulder and a single-action Colt Army revolver in his fist.

The many who might have wished them harm gave them a wide berth, perhaps unaware that the Maxim, ordinarily manned by a crew of four, would be a cumbersome handful for two, or were afraid to test how cumbersome. The hotel was not on fire, the Tatars having concentrated their fury on the nearby neighborhood of the Armenians, whose burning mansions were lighting the night sky.

Bell led his people past the hotel and down the driveway to the stables. The watchmen, who were gripping old Russian Army rifles, recognized him and 'Envoy Stone'. Bell tipped them lavishly and closed the barn doors. It was not much quieter. Despite thick stone walls and the surrounding buildings, they could still hear the shooting in the streets, while, inside, nervous horses were banging in their stalls.

Equally nervous chauffeurs watched the new arrivals warily. A few were tinkering with limousine motors. Most were slumped behind their steering wheels with hopeless expressions as if dreading orders to drive to their employers' mansions and brave the mobs.

Bell looked for Josef, the English-speaking chauffeur who had driven the Peerless and who could be valuable as a relief driver, mechanic and translator. When he didn't see him, he asked the other chauffeurs if he was around.

'No, sir.'

'No, sir.'

They muttered among themselves. One man who spoke a little English whispered, 'Revolutionary.'

'Josef?'

'Maybe revolutionary. Maybe police.'

'Police?'

The chauffeur shook his head. 'Agent.'

'Provocateur?'

'Informer.'

That Josef was a police spy, Bell had guessed. But a revolutionary, too? On the verge of hiring this man as driver and translator, Bell changed his mind and decided to trust no one. Better to go it alone.

The bullet-smashed windshield of the Peerless attacked at the Black Town refinery had not been replaced. The missing glass offered a clear field of fire, and Wish Clarke got busy mounting the Maxim gun on the Peerless's backseat.

The other two autos were as Bell had seen them last, still in wooden crates.

'Hammers and bars,' said Bell, wrenching boards loose with his hand.

Edna Matters returned with a blacksmith's hammer. John D. Rockefeller found a crowbar. Nellie Matters pried boards loose skillfully with it, saying to Bell, 'Don't look surprised. Who do you think fixes balloons in the air?'

Rockefeller swung the hammer like a man who had grown up chopping wood on a farm.

Edna said, 'I can't fix anything. What shall I do?'

Bell sent her in search of gasoline and oil and cans to carry it in. He gave her money to buy any cans and tools the chauffeurs would sell her. She came back with cans and tools and several maps.

As the packing crates fell away, Bell was glad to see the autos were equipped with straight-side tires on detachable rims. Stony, wagon-rutted roads and camel tracks guaranteed many punctures. Up-to-date straight-side tires were easily removed from the wheel, reducing the holdup for patching them from an hour to a few minutes.

Edna Matters had gathered cans to hold one hundred and fifty gallons of gasoline and oil. Bell sent her, accompanied by Rockefeller and Nellie, across the stable yard to the hotel kitchen to buy tinned food and bottled water. He checked that the cars' crankcases were filled with oil and poured gasoline into their tanks.

Wish Clarke mounted the Maxim, fed in a fresh ammunition belt, filled its barrel-cooling sleeve with horse trough water. After he cleared his line of fire by removing the empty windshield frame, he gave Bell a hand cranking the Peerlesses' motors. One of the new ones started easily. The other was balky, but eventually Bell coaxed it alive. The car Wish had commandeered for the Maxim gun coughed and smoked. They unscrewed the spark plugs, cleaned the electrodes, and filed them to sharper points.

Outside, bursts of gunfire grew loud. A woman screamed. The chauffeurs stared fearfully at the doors. A man wept. From the hotel came the sound of the pianist still playing.

By one o'clock in the morning, they had all three Peerlesses fueled and oiled and provisions stowed. Bell spread a map on the hood of the lead car to show everyone their route from the Caspian Sea to the Black Sea. They were heading west across Transcaucasia, between Russia's Greater Caucasus mountain range to the north and Persia's Lesser Caucasus range to the south.

Their sixty-mile slot of river valleys between the mountains comprised the restive regions of Azerbaijan, Armenia and Georgia, 'where,' the tall detective said, 'they are actively trying to kill each other. First

273

stop, Shemaha. About seventy-five miles. Any luck, we'll make it before nightfall tomorrow.

'Wish leads with the Maxim. I'll cover the rear. Mr Rockefeller, you drive the middle one.'

'I don't know how to drive,' said Rockefeller.

'You don't?'

'I've only recently arranged to buy an auto. It will be delivered with a man to drive it.'

'I know how to drive,' said Nellie.

'You do?' asked Edna. 'When did you learn?'

'In California. A bunch of us realized that suffragists ought to know how to get themselves around. I must say, it's a lot easier than your buckboard, not to mention my balloon.'

Bell was dubious, to say the least, but had no choice and could only hope she wasn't exaggerating her auto prowess. They needed all three cars to carry supplies and had to have a replacement if they lost one to a breakdown that he and Wish could not repair.

'Nellie drives the middle car,' he said. 'Edna sits in front, Mr Rockefeller in back. Wish, do you have something to lend Mr Rockefeller?'

Wish Clarke pulled a pocket pistol from inside his coat and gave it to Rockefeller. The old man checked that it was loaded.

Bell had already removed his derringer from his hat when no one was looking. He handed the two-shot pistol to Edna. 'Ever shoot a derringer?'

'Father taught us.'

Bell was already wishing that they had Bill Matters with them, carrying the big Remington he had on the train. Thank the Lord for the Maxim. And thanks, too, for the assassin's Savage in his carpetbag on the floor beside the steering wheel.

'What about me?' asked Nellie. 'Don't I get a gun?'

'You'll have your hands full driving – Now listen, everyone. We will stay very close. No headlamps except for Wish. If you have any trouble with the auto, or something happens the others can't see, honk on your horn.'

'Isaac?'

'What, Edna?'

'Wouldn't it be better if Mr Rockefeller sat up front with Nellie and I sat in Wish's car with the Maxim gun?'

'Do you know how to fire a Maxim gun?'

'I saw Mr Rockefeller's refinery police use them to frighten labor strikers. Anyone considering ambushing us will think twice if they see the gun manned – they won't know I'm a woman.'

She had a point, thought Bell, though he didn't love it. Both women had caps pulled over their short hair and had changed into trousers when it was decided to run for it. But a bushwhacker just might shoot her from a distance to disable the Maxim. And yet she was right that a manned machine gun would look a lot more intimidating, which would forestall a lot of trouble before it started.

'Wish, what do you say? Do you want her on your gun?'

Wish didn't love it either, Bell could see. Nonetheless, he said, 'I'm afraid Edna's right.'

They shifted positions. Edna gave Bell's derringer to Nellie and climbed in the back of the lead Peerless. 'Try not to blow my head off,' Wish called over his shoulder.

'Duck if you hear me shooting.'

John D. Rockefeller climbed into the front of the middle car.

Nellie Matters said, 'This should be interesting.'

'What do you mean?'

'Sitting side by side with the devil incarnate.'

'You don't seem that bad to me,' said Rockefeller.

It was the kind of joke that Nellie Matters loved, and Bell expected her to let loose one of her big laughs, but all Rockefeller got was an angry glare. He looked at her sister, hunched over the Maxim behind him, and saw that Edna, too, had not even cracked a smile.

'Looking on the bright side,' said Wish Clarke, 'we're driving brand-new, rock-solid, Cleveland-built machines.'

'Turn left on the main road,' said Bell, attempting to fold the map with one hand. Failing that, he worked his arm out of the sling and stuffed it in his pocket. 'Let's go.'

He opened the stable doors.

The three red cars rumbled through the cobblestone

yard and out the driveway on to streets nearly light as day. House fires nearby and oil fields and refineries burning far off lit the sky. They turned away from the fires, west, out of the city on roads clogged with refugees riding in carriages, work wagons and rich men's autos and plodding on foot.

Isaac Bell saw that his one-day timetable to Shemaha had been wildly optimistic. They'd be lucky to make that first town in two days. Then seven or eight more towns and four hundred and eighty miles to go.

27

'Of the six longest, hottest days and freezing cold nights ever endured,' wrote Edna Matters, typing up her shorthand notes as she did every night when the autos finally stopped rolling, 'today was the longest yet, and I'm afraid it is not over.'

> This afternoon's shoot-out, our third since escaping
> Baku, ended inconclusively. Those who were shooting
> at us are still out there. Neither IB nor WC are
> ceasing their vigilance. Neither has slept more than a
> catnap. The autos are circled, as tightly as the narrow
> cliffside clearing will allow, like a latter-day wagon
> train besieged by Indians, and we are watching the
> steep slopes and the fast-falling darkness.

She looked around her. When they left the hotel stable in Baku, the Peerless autos' tires had been white as snow. They were black now, blackened by the oily streets before they were even off the Absheron Peninsula, caked with road dust and marred by the pries used to work them on and off their rims to patch punctures. Wish Clarke was fixing one now. Nellie was helping him. JDR was stretched across a backseat, sound asleep. The plutocrat was the envy of all; he could sleep through anything. Isaac was draped over the Maxim gun, as still and watchful as a cat, the bag in which he carried his rifle in easy reach, as always.

She typed.

The roads are abysmal, verging on the nonexistent, except for the occasional better-graded stretch, which IB identifies as forty-year-old Russian military roads built to subdue the region. There are fortresses and barracks, some abandoned, some occupied by soldiers disinclined to venture out. Occasionally we trundle across handsome iron bridges the Army built over rushing rivers. The road often snakes beside the railroad tracks, on which we have not seen a single train moving, though we did pass a smoldering line of blackened oil tank cars set afire.

IB, reading over EMH's shoulder, was just informed by EMH that nothing in our agreement says I cannot reveal Envoy Stone for the louse JDR is, so long as I don't reveal his true identity. Although if IB were not so exhausted from his wonderfully successful efforts to keep us alive, he might have read further to see that I gave Envoy Stone his due, albeit grudgingly, admitting that Stone actually believes, truly believes, that he and his ilk deal, in his own oft-repeated phrase, 'fairly and squarely and aboveboard.' I base this conclusion on an interview granted by sister Nellie, who's been stuck driving his Peerless all this time and arguing incessantly to no effect. Sister Nellie feels, as does this reporter, that the trouble comes by how differently we estimate the location of that board he purports to be above.

For example, in the midst of today's running gun battles – first with renegade Cossacks bent on relieving us of our vehicles, then gangs of Social Democrat revolutionaries who probably want our Maxim gun – the 'envoy' suddenly scampered into a railroad telegrapher's hut. He was not trying to hide, not running from the fight, but trying to send another business cable to America. No one denies his bravery. (He gave his borrowed pistol to sister Nellie before running a gauntlet of bullets in his abortive attempt to communicate God-knows-what.)

His elastic ethics don't trouble him at all. He bald-facedly insisted to this reporter that because he was unable to send his cable, as the wires were cut, the contents do not fall under the terms of our agreement and therefore he does not have to admit them to me. It would take a herd of expensive lawyers to get around that one. Which, of course, has always been his specialty. He said, incidentally, that before the wires were cut the telegrapher had received reports of bigger fires, continued looting, and hundreds more murdered in Baku.

Suddenly Edna heard what sounded like thunder and felt the ground shake. She stopped typing and looked up. Then she resumed typing, faster than ever, as if something was chasing her fingers.

A boulder just rolled down the hill . . .

Here comes another . . . They've started shooting again. IB can't see them. He has abandoned the Maxim gun and is running up the road with his rifle . . .

IB is shouting at EMH to close up her typewriter and take cover behind our 'rock-solid, Cleveland-built machines.' EMH keeps typing because it beats being terrified. IB appears prepared to shoot EMH if she doesn't close up her machine. But she can't stop. She just keeps typing. She is not exactly hysterical. In fact, not at all. She's typing because, against all logic, it feels like it makes her bulletproof.

Isaac is retreating from the curve in the road where he was trying to see who was shooting. He is running back to the Maxim gun. Bullets pluck his sleeve.

Isaac Bell dodged rifle fire and a blizzard of stone splinters to vault into Wish Clarke's Peerless so he could feed the belt into the Maxim gun. But Wish was pinned down under another car, from where he was shooting back with his pistol. Bell slid behind the Maxim, cocked it, and jerked the trigger, grinding out ten shots before the belt caught on the tripod.

He untangled it and fired ten more at a flicker of

movement atop the ridge that stared down at them. Three riflemen leaped up and fired back. Bell triggered the Maxim, trying to hit them before the belt caught. Eight shots, ten shots, and this time the belt did not hang up on anything. The pounding machine gun had cleared the top of the ridge before he realized why. Edna Matters had jumped in beside him and was feeding the belt as smoothly as a veteran of the Zulu Wars.

'You could get killed doing this,' he said.

'Beats getting killed doing nothing.'

She stood up, thinking the fight was over. Feeding the belt into the gun had made her even more bulletproof than typing. She did not want to listen to the low voice in the back of her mind that nothing made anyone bulletproof except no bullets.

'Look out!'

Suddenly Isaac was roaring in her ear, 'Down! Down! Get down!'

28

An immense boulder, triple the size of the others, flew at the auto.

Isaac shoved Edna down. It cleared their heads by inches and hit the guard wall that stood between the edge of the road and a sheer drop. It smashed through the wall, scattering stones, and tumbled into the ravine. Shouts of triumph from the top of the slope announced another rolling at them.

'IB was both right and wrong last night,' Edna Matters typed in the morning.

The air was bitter cold. A strong wind was blowing and the sky was full of dust clouds. Wish Clarke sat behind the Maxim gun. He was covering the ridge at the top of the slope. Isaac Bell was starting to climb it with field glasses around his neck and a revolver in his hand. He was hoping to spot Tiflis and a route on which they could make a run for the capital city.

Thanks to taking cover under an overhang of rock, WC and Envoy Stone and sister Nellie were not flattened by giant boulders. IB and I were also extremely lucky where we shivered all the long, cold night. But the last boulder that thundered down the hill before it was too dark for our enemies to aim another smashed us dead center.

We are down to two Peerlesses. We managed to rescue some of the water before the wreck fell into the ravine and was swept downstream in a furious torrent. But we could save none of the tinned food and none of the extra gasoline, which presents a serious difficulty as we very likely do not have enough gasoline left to reach Tiflis even though we believe it is close, just over the hills that we somehow got on the wrong side of when we got lost yesterday.

Looking on the bright side, as Detective WC is wont to say, the renegade Cossacks, or Social Democrat revolutionaries, appear to have been thoroughly routed. Though whether that is true, we don't really know, as the night had turned dark as a coal mine by the time the boulders stopped hurtling and the shooting had stopped. I am absolutely certain that this reporter is not the first from the civilized world to say, 'Thank God for the Maxim gun.'

Additional credit goes to IB, WC and sister Nellie, who had refused to return Envoy Stone's pistol. As we prepared to get under way in our remaining two autos, IB read over my shoulder and demanded edits. He asked me to write the following, which embarrasses me in its immodesty. He demanded I write that EMH was a dependable belt feeder who allowed him to employ our Maxim gun to great advantage.

IB then demanded I change the word 'dependable' to 'superlative'. Everyone's an editor. But to be fair, poor Isaac is reeling on his feet.

My sister Nellie has fallen in love with him.

Edna Matters stared at the page.

Who had written that? If a typewriter could blurt, the machine had blurted it out.

She glanced over her shoulder. Isaac had started up the slope. Suddenly he stopped. Something up the road had caught his attention. She raised her fingers to the keys and typed slowly.

Nellie is not the easiest person to read. In fact, she is often a cipher, a blank slate behind her smile. But in this case, I can see that she has fallen hard for IB.

Which creates quite a quandary as I have, too. Starting the night in New York he helped me through my other quandary. Which I believe means I fell first . . . However, being first on line won't help me one bit. My dear Isaac is falling for her. He doesn't know it yet. But I can tell. I wouldn't call it love. But he is fascinated and, being a man, probably doesn't know the difference –

She stopped typing and cocked her ear to listen. Someone was shouting down the slope in broken English.

'They're waving a white flag,' Isaac Bell called down to Wish Clarke.

It looked like a dirty shirt tied by its sleeve to a rifle. The man waving stepped warily into view and Isaac Bell immediately recognized the black, wavy pompadour hair. It was Josef the Georgian chauffeur he had befriended in Baku. The one that the other chauffeurs claimed was an informer for the secret police.

'What's he yelling?' asked Wish.

Isaac Bell strained his keen hearing to its utmost and heard, 'You give gun. We let go.'

He ran down the slope and joined Wish in the lead auto. 'They want our Maxim.'

'I would, too, in their position,' said Wish.

'They're welcome to it,' said Bell.

'What?'

'We'll trade it for a cease-fire and directions to Tiflis.'

'They'll kill us,' said Rockefeller.

'That thought occurred to me,' said Bell. He looked at Wish.

Wish said, 'Isaac, why don't you talk to him? I'll get the gun ready to travel.'

Bell cupped his hands and shouted very slowly and clearly, 'Tell your friends to come out where we can see them. All of them.'

Josef shouted over his shoulder.

Twelve men started down the slope. They were dressed in workmen's clothes and they looked very sure of themselves. Bell counted only three rifles. The rest carried pistols. They descended to the road and started toward the autos, fanning out and covering one another with military discipline.

'That's close enough,' Bell called, stopping them at fifty feet.

'You act suspicious,' said Josef.

'I don't like people who roll boulders at me.'

'Not us. Cossacks. We chase them.'

'So did we,' said Bell. From what he had seen, heavily armed Cossacks were not easily chased. If what the chauffeurs in the Hotel de L'Europe's stables told him was true, then an Okhrana informer could arrange for the Cossacks to be called off or driven off by loyal troops if they were renegades. How had Josef found them here in the middle of nowhere? How had he known about the machine gun?

'Who are you, Josef? Who are these men?'

'Social Democrats.'

'Aren't they illegal?'

Josef flashed his cheerful smile. 'Reason we are wanting gun.'

'Are you their leader?'

'No, no, no. They ask me translating.'

'But you just said "we".'

'Mistaking translating.'

'Translate this: Guide us to a road to Tiflis. When we see the town, the gun is yours.'

'Tiflis no safe. Much unrest.'

'Pogromy?'

'Politicals. General Prince Amilakhvari dead. Hateful

Russian. Oppressing all Caucasia. Russians bringing for priests to pray on. People protest. Social Democrats protest. Police shooting Social Democrats.'

'You want our gun to fight the police.'

Josef's smile disappeared. 'Not your business.'

'If he's a translator,' muttered John D. Rockefeller, 'I'm my old maid aunt Olymphia.'

The Social Democrat fighters led the way on foot. Wish Clarke covered them with the Maxim gun. Bell drove his Peerless. Rockefeller, Edna and Nellie trailed in the second car. The wind continued high, buffeting them and blowing dust, and the sun grew hot.

They climbed a steep road up a mountain. When they finally reached a broad plateau – an open brown steppe bare of vegetation and baked brown by the sun – their guides met up with a pair of horse-drawn phaetons. The men squeezed into the wagons and started across the flatter ground on a dusty track. After about four miles there were signs of recent roadwork, surveyors' stakes, and the cutting of streets as if the area was to be developed.

Quite suddenly the plateau ended at the rim of a cliff.

Tiflis lay below them, one thousand feet straight down.

Bell saw it was an ancient city growing large in modern times. An old town of church steeples, cathedral domes and twisted streets hugged the curves of a river.

A ruined fortress of jagged rock, abandoned walls and ramshackle outbuildings crouched on a lower cliff. In the river floated what looked like mills, each with its waterwheel.

A new city spread out from the center on a square grid of streets. Smoke drew Bell's eye a mile or so from a big open square at the center of the old city. It was the railroad station where two weeks ago they had holed up for the night on their way to Baku.

Beyond the station sprawled vast railyards with many rows of sidings. On every siding stood a train of black tank cars. Bell raked it with his field glasses. He saw no wreckage, none of the destruction they had encountered on the eastern stretches of the line. Switch engines and locomotives were expending the smoke that hung over the yard.

'Trains are running.'

'How are we getting down that cliff?'

'Good question.'

Just as suddenly as they had come upon the cliff, they saw the answer. Nellie was delighted by a perspective she would see normally only from a balloon. Her pretty face aglow, she erupted in a happy cry.

'Funicular!'

Two counterbalanced carriages, large enough to hold fifty people each and linked by a strong cable, rolled up and down a steep railroad between the top of the mountain that Bell and his people had just crossed and the city below. There was a bulge in the line halfway down the mountain, a way station where the tracks doubled to allow the two carriages to pass each other.

'Any steeper,' said Wish Clarke, 'and it would be an elevator.'

Josef jumped down from his phaeton and strode toward them, gaze locked greedily on the Maxim gun. Wish kept his finger on the trigger.

Isaac Bell said, 'Josef, order your men to place their weapons around that rock.'

Josef started to protest.

Bell cut him off. 'The Maxim is ours until they lay down their guns and we drive to the funicular.'

Wish Clarke raised a water can in his free hand and called out in a friendly voice, 'We just filled the barrel-cooling sleeve. Here's more water when you need it.' He took a swig from the can and wiped his mouth. 'You must remember to refill the sleeve every couple of hundred rounds or the heat will steam it off and you'll melt the barrel.'

'We are knowing gun.'

'I had an inkling you might.'

Wish jumped to the road, gathered the heavy weapon in his arms, heaved it off the Peerless, and laid it gently on the ground. He left the one remaining ammunition belt, then he got back behind the steering wheel and drove after Nellie's car.

Bell watched with the Savage 99 braced against his shoulder. Before they reached the funicular station,

Josef's gang had pounced on the Maxim, loaded it into a phaeton, and whipped up their horses.

'What a pleasure,' said Wish. 'The simple act of buying tickets compared to fighting across Azerbaijan and eastern Georgia while straying into stretches of Armenia.'

Isaac Bell was looking forward to buying more tickets: The train to Batum. The steamer to Constantinople. The Orient Express to Paris. And an ocean liner home.

The railway carriage from below climbed into the station. A smattering of tourists got off with curious looks for the road-weary, dust-caked travelers waiting to descend. Bell guided everyone into one of the passenger compartments and closed the door. The seats were pitched at an angle to keep them horizontal.

The carriage started rolling down the embankment.

'Isaac!' Nellie gripped his arm and pointed across the bare and rocky slope. With her sharp eye for terrain, she had spotted Josef's phaetons struggling down a steep road a half mile away.

'You'll regret giving them that gun,' said Rockefeller.

'We didn't give it,' said Wish, 'we traded it.'

It took six minutes to descend the funicular railway's nine hundred feet to the lower station.

An electric tram waited at the bottom, which they rode through the old city to the big, central Erevan Square that Bell had seen from above. He sensed the instant he alighted that despite the presence of up-to-date shops, government buildings, and an enormous Russian bank, there was a palpable tension in the air. People walked hurriedly with their heads down and avoiding eye contact. There were many police and soldiers on patrol.

'The faster we're out of here, the better,' he told Wish.

Rockefeller spotted a telegraph office. 'I must send a cable.'

'Wait until we get to the train station.'

They found another electric tram, which took them across the river and up through newer parts of the city to the Central Railroad Station.

Mobs of Georgians, Armenians and Russians milled in the concourse.

Rockefeller spotted the telegraph office and strode through them like a heavy cruiser parting the waves.

Bell said, 'Wish, keep an eye on him. We'll be at the ticket windows.'

The lines were long. Travelers shouted and gesticulated. Ticket agents shouted back and shook their fists.

'Five one-way tickets to Batum.'

'No trains.'

'What do you mean, no trains? The yard is booming.'

'No passenger trains.'

Bell already had money in his hand. He slipped it across the counter. The agent wet his lips. It equaled a month's pay. 'Go to booking office. Ask for Dmitri Ermakov. Tell him I sent you. It will cost.'

The booking office was next to the telegraph. Wish was at the door. 'He's still at it.'

'We'll be in here.'

Dmitri Ermakov made them wait twenty minutes, by which time scores of people had stormed in and out of the office. At last Bell was ushered in. He held out three times as much money as he had given the ticket agent. 'I need five tickets to Batum.'

Ermakov took the money. 'You must understand, sir, there are no passenger trains. Only oil trains.'

'There must be one or you wouldn't be talking to me.'

'When fighting was feared to break out in Baku, Baku send many oil trains.'

The result, Chief Agent Ermakov explained, was that so many oil trains had rushed out of Baku when trouble started that they were carrying more oil than the Batum refineries could cook and had to be held in Tiflis. Then revolutionaries cut the pipe line and suddenly stocks were running low in the refineries and shipping piers.

'Now every train west is oil train. But one special train tomorrow. Come back tomorrow. Show papers.'

'What papers?'

'You need special pass. Government train visas.'

'Where do I get them?'

'You get issued by my friend Feltsman, high official. Russian. You must pay him.'

'Where is Feltsman?'

'Government building. Erevan Square.'

'Where in Erevan Square? Which building?'

'Next to Russian State Bank.'

Isaac Bell stood to his full height and stared down at the Russian train official. Then he opened his coat just enough to allow a glimpse of the Bisley nestled in his shoulder holster. 'If I can't find the government building – or if I can't find Mr Feltsman – I do know where to find you . . . Is there anything else you want to tell me before I go back to Erevan Square?'

'I am remembering,' said the chief agent, reaching for his telephone, 'that it would be best if I personally telephoned Feltsman to tell him to expect you. That way he would not be out to lunch or somewhere when you arrive.'

'A wise precaution,' said Isaac Bell. He waited for the call to be completed and left somewhat surer now that the papers would be forthcoming, but considerably less certain that tomorrow's special passenger train would materialize in the chaos.

'Hold it!' said Isaac Bell.

They had just stepped down from the tram to Erevan Square and were hurrying across the busy plaza toward the government building next to the Russian State Bank when Bell saw the gleaming black pompadour that crowned the Social Democrat Josef.

'Is that who I think it is skulking at the tram stop?' asked Wish.

'Josef.'

With a furtive glance over his shoulder, revealing beyond a doubt that it was he, Josef ran to jump on the tram leaving for the railroad station.

'What's he up to?' said Wish.

Rockefeller started to make a beeline for the telegraph.

'Grab him, Wish.'

Wish snared the plutocrat.

'What? What?'

'Just wait,' said Wish. 'Something's up . . . What is it, Isaac?'

Bell had spotted three or four workmen in the crowds whom he might possibly have seen with Josef earlier on the road. Aware that he was sensing more than seeing, he looked up and scanned the tops of the two- and three-storey buildings that bordered the open space. He could feel stress in the air, almost as if every person bustling about his business was about to stop breathing.

Suddenly two enormous carriages raced into the square. Thundering alongside them, Cossack outriders brandished lances and rifles. Heavy as freight wagons yet high-wheeled and fast, they were pulled by teams of ten horses. Their coachmen, enormous three-hundred-pound men in greatcoats, hauled back on their reins and the carriages and outriders came to a banging, clashing halt in front of the elaborately decorated stone edifice that housed the Russian State Bank.

Bell motioned urgently to Wish.

Moving as one, they backed their people away.

The Cossacks looked formidable and others in the crowds retreated, too. But the men Bell had noticed a moment earlier edged closer. Others, dressed in urban working garb, converged on the carriages. Bell looked up again. Now he saw men on the roofs.

'*Isaac!*' said Wish.

'I see them,' said Bell. 'It's a bank robbery.'

29

'Expropriation,' said Wish Clarke, 'is the word favored in the revolutionary lexicon.'

'Bank robbers!' said John D. Rockefeller. 'We must inform the police . . . Officer!' He stepped into the street, waving at a Cossack.

'No,' said Isaac Bell, blocking him and forcing his arm down. 'They've got twenty men around the square and on the roofs. The cops can't stop it. They'll only make it bloodier.'

'You should not have given them that gun.'

'It would appear that way,' Wish said serenely.

'Speaking of the devil . . .' said Bell.

The tall detective drew his revolver and herded Edna, Nellie and Rockefeller toward the nearest street out of the square as Wish forged ahead, clearing a path for their retreat.

'Here he comes.'

A two-horse phaeton charged into the square.

A gunner and a belt feeder hunched over the Maxim gun. They had perched the Sokolov mount up on the high back bench where the driver ordinarily sat. The revolutionary handling the reins had shifted to the lower front bench.

The gunner triggered the weapon with an unearthly roar.

Shooting over the driver and horses' heads, he tried to aim at the bank carriage. People ran from the noise, which was amplified and echoed by the buildings, and fled the galloping horses, whose iron shoes threw sparks from the cobblestones.

The phaeton leaned into a sharp turn, tall wheels skidding. Bell hoped the weight of the machine gun would capsize the inherently unstable vehicle. But just as it seemed it would spill the attackers to the ground, the wheels slid on the cobbles and it righted itself.

A bomb sailed from a roof, trailing the smoke of a fuse. It detonated in the air with a flash and a loud bang that scattered the Cossacks on rearing mounts. A second bomb flew from a roof. It landed on the cobblestones, bounced under the team pulling the lead money carriage, and exploded, blowing open the doors of the carriage.

Men, women and animals screamed.

The revolutionaries dove into the maelstrom. Firing pistols, they ran to the carriage. One man leaped into it and threw bulging bank sacks to his partners. The Maxim gun kept firing.

The phaeton lurched and skidded and the gunner and belt feeder held on by clinging to the weapon. Bullets aimed at the bank carriage raked the rooftops instead. Then the driver got his animals under control and pulled up short. Still firing – the weapon had never ceased roaring since they entered the square – the gunner lowered his barrel. The torrent of flying lead stitched a path down the building's stone walls.

The Maxim exploded with a thunderous *Boom!* and a ball of fire.

'Darn,' smiled Wish Clarke.

Sheets of flame enveloped the gunner and the belt feeder, the driver and the phaeton itself. The horses bolted. The burning wagon raced across the square and tipped over suddenly. The traces parted. The horses galloped away.

'What happened?' shouted Rockefeller.

'Their gun blew up,' said Wish Clarke. The detective shook his head in mock dismay. 'The medicos keep telling me that demon rum plays havoc with one's powers of memory. I hate to admit they're right, but it appears that when I filled the Maxim's cooling sleeve, I must have mixed up the cans of water and gasoline.'

'Railyards,' said Isaac Bell. 'Now!'

'But there is no train until tomorrow,' Rockefeller protested.

Bell gripped his arm. 'Social Democrat revolutionaries just tried to rob a Russian State Bank. Soldiers were injured. The revolutionaries escaped. The authorities will surround the city and close the roads to capture the criminals and recover the money.'

'But there is no train –'

'We're taking a different train.'

*

299

'Never, never, never jump on the back of a moving rail-car,' said Isaac Bell. 'Always hop the front of the car.'

'Why?' asked Edna.

They laid flat on a ballast embankment beside the train tracks a mile west of the Tiflis yards, waiting for an oil train. Bell had chosen the spot for the sharp curve in the tracks that would shield them, though only briefly, from the sight of the engineer and fireman in the locomotive and the brakemen in the caboose. Behind them, a neighborhood of tenements and small factories baked in the sun. No one had ventured out to take an interest in them so far. But they could not count on that, as the police were fanning out from Erevan Square.

'If you slip and fall from the front of a car while trying to hop on,' Bell explained, 'you'll fall to the side of the train. If you fall from the back of a car, you will fall under the wheels of the next car, which will run you over.'

'A memorable thought,' said Nellie.

'Nellie and Edna, you two will go first. I'm afraid you're on your own. Wish and I will take care of the old man. If either of you can't get on, the other jumps off again. We stay together. Wish and I won't make our move until we see you're both safely on. Nellie, you've still got Wish's gun?'

'Yes.'

'Edna, you've got my derringer.'

Edna patted a pocket.

'It appears to be a well-run line, so the brakemen very likely will walk beside the train whenever they stop to inspect their trucks and air hoses. The locomotives I've seen are up-to-date Baldwin ten-wheelers with oil-burning fireboxes. They'll stretch their water stops to about every hundred miles and fuel and relief crews to two hundred. But they'll have to stop in the mountains to couple on extra pusher engines. Whenever they stop, stay out of sight.'

Wish came running from the head of the bend. 'Train coming.'

The locomotive hauling the oil train to Batum rounded the curve under a massive crown of thick black smoke. She was an oil burner, all right – no self-respecting fireman would allow such smoke from a coal furnace – a modern, ten-drive-wheeled, Pennsylvania-built 'decapod,' moving faster than Bell would have liked for the first attempt by novice hobos. But they weren't likely to get a second chance to hop a freight before the authorities started searching even oil trains for the bank robbers and the money.

The powerful Baldwin approached where they hid on the ballast slope, accelerating as it threw off the eight-hundred-ton inertia of thirty heavily laden tank cars. The locomotive passed them, trailed by its fuel-and-water tender. Then came the first car, which was comprised of a long, cylindrical, six-thousand-gallon tank laid horizontally on a flatbed. Bell pointed out the niches where the tube-shaped tank was braced on the flatbed and shouted over the thunder, 'Get inside that brace where they can't see you.'

He looked Edna in the eyes and saw a healthy mix of fear and determination. Nellie, by contrast, showed no fear. When he gauged Rockefeller's ability to take the chance, the magnate said sternly, 'I am counting on you, Mr Bell, that one day I may relate this incident to disbelieving great-grandchildren.'

The locomotive disappeared around the bend in the tracks.

'Go!' Bell said to Edna.

30

Edna Matters scrambled up the embankment. Nellie followed, overtaking her and reaching back to help her up. They clasped hands, attained the flat roadbed, and ran along the cross ties beside the moving train.

Isaac Bell took John D. Rockefeller's arm. 'Wish and I have you, sir. Just do what we tell you to.'

The Van Dorn detectives heaved the two-hundred-pound Rockefeller between them like a scarecrow stuffed with straw and sprang up the embankment.

Nellie Matters vaulted nimbly on to the flatbed of the rolling car. She grabbed a strut that braced the tank and, as Edna jumped, reached to join hands with her. Edna stumbled. For a second she dangled from Nellie's hand, her feet frantically trying to push off as she ran along the stone ballast and wooden ties. She planted one foot and tried to jump again. Bell saw his two-shot derringer fall from her pocket and bounce on a cross tie and under a wheel.

Nellie screamed with effort and lifted her aboard. The women rolled under the tank, out of sight, which was Bell and Wish's signal to hoist Rockefeller on to the next car.

Wish, with two working arms, went first.

*

The train had come down from the final mountain pass to a switching yard, where they stopped to uncouple the pusher engine, and Bell began to believe their luck would hold all the way to Batum when a lone brakeman walked slowly beside the car, shining a bull's-eye lantern at the trucks. They had, all five, shifted by then to one car, the second back from the tender. Suddenly the brakeman straightened up with a cry and began stomping at the ground. He stopped, breathing hard, and picked up a dead snake in his glove. He tossed it away and his lantern beam hit John D. Rockefeller full in the face.

Isaac Bell and Wish Clarke reached toward him with both hands. Each held a pistol in one and gold in the other.

The brakeman blinked. Then he jerked off his heavy glove, snatched the coins, and ran into the dark.

Wish held tight to his gun. 'Think he'll come back?'

'Not if he's an honest man,' Bell answered, still holding his. They waited, ears straining for the sound of the brakeman coming back with reinforcements and praying for the train to start. The locomotive whistled. Then it huffed. It was moving. The couplers clanked as the cars took up the slack. Suddenly they heard footsteps pounding, overtaking them, as the train began to roll.

The brakeman ran alongside, spotted them again. His face lit up with a triumphant grin. He was carrying something and he thrust it at them. It quivered like something alive. For a second Bell thought it was an animal or a baby. Wish Clarke recognized it for what it was and held on tight. 'Gracias, amigo!' he called to the Georgian.

He held it up for the rest to see. 'Wineskin!'

Down from the mountains at last, the oil train raced west, stopping only once for fuel and water. The day dawned bright and sunny. The air grew humid as the train descended toward the river delta from which had been carved the harbor of Batum. Wish, who had put a sizable dent in the wineskin, thrust it at Rockefeller. 'Have a snort?'

'I don't drink.'

'You'll love it,' said Wish. 'They sealed the skin with naphtha. The wine tastes like oil.'

Bell leaned out from the tank car to look ahead. He spotted the Black Sea.

The Constantinople steamer blew its whistle as Bell herded his people out of their phaetons.

'There's Father,' cried Nellie.

Bill Matters was on the dock, heading for the gangway. When he saw his daughters, his grim features melted in a smile of relief and he scooped Edna and Nellie into his big arms like they were little girls.

'How did you make out in Moscow?' Rockefeller greeted him.

Matters' expression hardened. 'I was doing fine until they suddenly clammed up. Next day, they refused to see me at all. I pressed an official I had given a lot of money to. He claimed they were angry. They told him they had been betrayed – by you, Mr Rockefeller.'

'How?'

'They wouldn't tell me. Any idea why?'

'None at all,' said Rockefeller.

'What did you do?'

'Nothing. Don't you understand? They threw dust in your eyes.'

'I don't understand.'

'You gave up. You left Moscow too soon.'

'Do you want me to go back?'

'Wait until the disturbances settle down. For now, we're going home.'

31

At Budapest, Isaac Bell surprised the party and he hoped the assassin, if he were nearby, by unexpectedly transferring everyone on to the Orient Express's new section to Berlin.

'Berlin? You're taking us the long way to Paris,' complained Rockefeller, who had insisted again on carrying his own bags to save European luggage fees when they boarded the Orient Express in Constantinople.

Bell took the heaviest from him. 'We are not going to Paris. We're joining SS *Kaiser Wilhelm II* at Bremen. There's a boat train in Berlin.'

'Much better,' said Rockefeller, happily mollified. The North German Lloyd passenger liner held the Blue Riband for the fastest time across the Atlantic Ocean.

The boat train to Bremen steamed out of the German capital on Monday night, gathered speed through the suburbs, and highballed into the dark at sixty miles an hour.

Isaac Bell, Wish Clarke, Edna and Nellie Matters, and John D. Rockefeller gathered in the dining room that occupied the front half of the observation car.

They were studying menus and discussing, longingly, the prospect of soon eating American food again when Bill Matters burst into the car. He stormed past the club chairs and stopped short at their tables. His eyes were wild, his jaw clenched.

Bell saw he had crumpled a yellow telegram in his fist.

'Father!' said Nellie. 'We wondered where you had gotten to.'

Edna asked, 'Are you quite well?'

Matters ignored them both. 'Mr Rockefeller! We must speak.' He lowered his voice. 'In private.'

'It is rather late to discuss business. Why don't you sit down and have some supper with the rest of us?'

Matters said, 'It is not too late to discuss the Peerless autos you brought for the shah.'

Rockefeller rose silently from the table and led Matters out of the dining car.

Isaac Bell watched them disappear through the vestibule door. His suspicion that Matters had not known about the bribes was proved correct. Then, according to Rockefeller, Matters had been elsewhere on 'other business' during the all-important meeting with the Persians that Bell had eavesdropped on at the Hotel Astoria. Matters had not heard Rockefeller promise to pay off the shah's loan from the czar. Shortly after Rockefeller had sent him to Moscow.

Clearly, John D. Rockefeller had gone to Baku with one purpose only: to strike a bargain to pay off the debt in exchange for a license to build Matters' pipe line across Persia. The cables he'd been so desperate to send while escaping Russia must have completed the deal and cut Matters out of it.

Bell sprang to his feet and strode to the vestibule door. He pushed through it on to the gangway, where the observation car and the sleeping car behind it were coupled. The eight-foot-wide, twelve-foot-long space was enclosed by flexible leather-and-canvas gangway connectors. While they muffled the noise of the speeding train, it was still louder than inside the cars.

Matters was shouting, gesticulating, and waving the telegram.

'You knew! You knew all along.'

Rockefeller stood still as a stork, head inclined as if straining to listen over the rumble of the wheels and the rushing wind of the boat train's passage.

'Knew what, Mr Matters?'

'You knew when you sent me to Moscow. That's why you sent me. To get me out of the way.'

'Knew what?' Rockefeller repeated more sharply now. Neither man seemed to take notice of Isaac Bell who stood by, boots balanced lightly on the swaying floor plate, his eye on Matters, who looked angry enough to strike the older man.

'You knew that you were closing a private deal for the pipe line,' Matters yelled.

'How I choose to negotiate for Standard Oil is my

affair, Mr Matters,' Rockefeller answered in a firm voice that cut through the racket. 'It was my judgment that one man speaking for the company rather than two would do a better job of cutting through heathen mendacity.'

'We had an agreement!' Matters yelled. 'The Persia pipe line was not for Standard Oil – it was for us. We would then sell it to Standard Oil.'

'I signed no such agreement.'

'You led me to believe –'

'You believed what you wanted to.'

Face contorting, Matters sucked great gulps of air. Suddenly he shouted, 'You busted up my pipes.'

Bell saw that Rockefeller knew instantly what Matters meant. 'Is that what is troubling you? You're blaming me, unfairly, for some event that occurred back in *1899*?'

'You stole the Hook.'

Rockefeller turned to Isaac Bell as if the three were golfers strolling to the next tee and explained offhandedly, 'Constable Hook. The refinery we just finished building next to Bayonne. It's our largest – the most efficient in the world.'

'You stole it from me and Spike.'

'I paid you.'

'Pennies!'

'I paid you in Standard Oil stock. I made you rich. You ride around in a fancy private car. Even I don't go to that expense.' Again he turned to Bell as if in a threesome. 'I'm quite content to charter cars when the need arises.'

'You busted up my business,' Matters shouted.

'Right there!' Rockefeller rounded on him. 'I thought you were *not* one of those who are controlled by the insane idea to destroy the Standard Oil Company. Clearly, I was wrong. You are a miserable failure who will go to your grave an unhappy man.'

Matters lunged at Rockefeller with the speed and power of a Komodo dragon.

Bell seized his wrists. But by then Matters' big hands were clamped to John D. Rockefeller's throat. He yanked Rockefeller's two hundred pounds off the platform and rammed him toward the connector curtain. Unable to break his grip, Bell let go and sank his fists into Matters' kidneys with a hard left and a harder right.

The crazed Matters gasped. His hands opened convulsively. He let go of the struggling Rockefeller. But Bell's powerhouse blows didn't stop him, only slowed him, and he shoved his back into the tall detective, smashing him with all his weight against the opposite gangway connection. Bell bounced off the springy curtain and hurled himself on Matters as Matters lunged at Rockefeller again.

Too late, he saw that Matters' explosion of rage was not as impromptu as it had seemed. Before he stormed into the diner, he had removed the vertical pins that locked the adjoining cars' gangway connectors. Then he had lured the old man on to the gangway to throw him off the train.

The connectors parted like a theater curtain. The black night thundered past at sixty miles per hour. John D. Rockefeller tumbled backward through the opening.

Isaac Bell rammed past Bill Matters and jumped.

32

Isaac Bell had a single instant to wonder whether his injured arm had the strength to save their lives. By then he was committed to the lightning move, with his good hand gripping Rockefeller's belt and the other clamped on the steel-rimmed edge of the observation car's gangway connector. He was hanging off the rear end of the car. Pain lanced from his shoulder to his fingertips. If he lost his grip, they would fall under the wheels of the sleeper behind it.

The slipstream beating the side of the train slammed them flat against the connectors. Bell tried to take advantage of the rushing air with a Herculean twist of his entire body. Combining his every muscle with the power of the slipstream, he hauled Rockefeller close and swung him back through the narrow opening into the train.

Bill Matters was waiting on the gangway.

Isaac Bell saw an instance of indecision flicker on the angry man's face. Who would he attack first? His enemy, the old man sprawled at his feet? Or his enemy's bodyguard, who was barely hanging on to the side of the car? He chose Bell, braced himself with both hands, and cocked a foot to kick the fingers Bell had clamped around the connector. Bell was already in motion.

A gunshot – a clean, sharp *Crack!* – cut through the thunder of wheels and wind. Matters fell back with an expression of astonishment that Bell had somehow managed to draw his revolver and fire. Hanging by one arm as he triggered the Bisley, Bell missed his shot. He fired again; another went wild. Matters whirled away and fled toward the back of the train.

Bill Matters raced down the first sleeping car's corridor, burst out the end door, through the gangway and into the second. Near the end of the car was his tiny stateroom. He locked the door, put on his coat, grabbed a bag, already packed with several thousand in gold, British ten-pound notes, and German marks, and his Remington pistol. Then he opened the window on the locomotive's smoke and thunder and reached high in the corner of the cabin where the emergency communication cord swayed with the train's motion and yanked its red handle.

The communication cord activated the boat train's air brakes. From the locomotive at the back, curved steel shoes slammed down hard on every wheel of every car. The effect was swift and violent.

Matters kept his feet by ramming his shoulder against his stateroom's front partition to brace for the impact. From the compartments ahead and behind his came the thud of passengers crashing into bulkheads, the clatter of flying luggage, cries of pain, and frightened screams. Steel shrieked on steel under the hurtling car as the brake shoes bit and locked wheels slid on the rails.

The train bucked like a giant animal. The cars banged couplers into couplers. The speed dropped from sixty to fifty in an instant, and dropped as quickly to forty. Matters squeezed through the window, dragged his bag after him, and tried to gauge a safe landing by the beam of the locomotive headlamp. He could see in the distance four cars ahead, the beam flickering through a forest that hugged the tracks. To jump would be to run headlong into a tree.

Suddenly the headlamp disappeared.

For a second, Matters was baffled. Then the train whistle gave a strangely hollow, muffled shriek, and he realized that the locomotive had entered a tunnel. The car he was clinging to would be next into the narrow opening after smashing him against the stonework that rimmed it. He heard a crash. His stateroom door flew open. Isaac Bell blasted through it, revolver in hand, eyes locked on the window.

In the most decisive move of his entire life, Bill Matters dropped off the train.

Isaac Bell thrust head and shoulders and gun out the stateroom window and looked behind the train. The night was black, the spill of window light negligible, and he could not see where Matters had landed.

The train whistle sounded oddly muffled. Bell started to turn his head toward it when he sensed something immense hurtling at him. He shoved back inside Matters' stateroom, and the next second saw smoke-blackened masonry inches from the window.

The boat train screeched to a stop inside a tunnel.

Bell bolted from the stateroom and out the back of the sleeper car, past shaken passengers in pajamas and dressing gowns, through the last car, and jumped off the back of the train on to the cross ties. A brakeman was running frantically with a red lantern to alert the next train that the boat train was blocking the tracks.

Bell followed him out the tunnel and along the rail-bed, searching for Matters and fully expecting to find his body smashed against a tree. Instead, one hundred yards from the tunnel portal he found a break in the forest. It looked like a meadow, but at that moment the clouds parted and he saw moonlight gleam on water.

'Good-bye,' said Edna. 'We'll see you in New York.'

'Good-bye?' asked Bell. 'We're on the same ship.'

'We're sailing Second Class. You're in First.'

'No. Stay with me. I'll pay the difference.'

'We will not sit in the same dining room as that man,' said Nellie, turning away without another word to walk briskly to the Second Class gangway.

Edna said, 'We can barely stand to be on the same ship. But it's the fastest way home. I've promised a full report to the *Sun*, and Nellie has got to take command of the New Woman's Flyover before a certain suffra*gette* tries to steal it. Apparently, Amanda Faire's husband bought her a balloon.' She lowered her voice, though her sister was far beyond earshot. 'Nellie is so distraught about Father. I've got to get her home and busy.'

Bell said, 'I hope you understand that I'm terribly sorry about your father.'

'You cannot be as sorry as we are,' said Edna. 'We've lived in fear of this day and now it has happened.'

'You *expected* him to attack Mr Rockefeller?'

'We expected him to hurt *himself*. Since the day Rockefeller broke up his business and stole the pieces. We expected him to kill himself. What you call an attack, Isaac, had exactly the same effect.'

'It is highly likely,' said Bell, 'that your father is still alive.'

The German police had dragged the pond beside the tracks and searched the forest with hunting dogs and found no body. They had visited every farm within twenty miles and canvassed doctors and hospitals. Bill Matters had thoroughly disappeared.

'Good-bye.' Edna started after her sister, then turned back and kissed him on the cheek. 'Thank you, Isaac.'

'What for?'

'Engineering my job on the *Sun*.'

'They weren't supposed to tell you.'

'No one had to tell me. I figured it out on my own. Very flattering.'

'The *Sun* was lucky to send you to Baku.'

'I meant flattering that you wanted me to come along.'

'Last stop,' said Isaac Bell.

Tugboats jetting clouds of coal smoke were working the *Kaiser Wilhelm* against North German Lloyd's Hoboken pier.

'Not precisely,' said John D. Rockefeller. 'We still have the train to Cleveland.'

'*My* last stop,' said Bell. He took a letter from his traveling suit and handed it to Rockefeller. 'Here is my resignation.'

'Resignation? I am dismayed. Why are you quitting?'

'Standards.'

'Standards? What standards?'

'You had no need to rob Bill Matters. I will not condone his crimes, but you mistreated him badly and for no purpose other than beating him.'

Rockefeller's lips tightened in a flat line. He looked away, gazing at the harbor, then he looked Bell in the eye. 'When I was a boy, my father sharped us to make us strong. He taught us how to trade by taking us again and again. Every time I was soft, he took advantage and beat me in every deal until I learned how to win. It made me sharp.'

'It made you a bully.'

'It's a habit,' said Rockefeller. 'A habit that served me well.'

Bell appeared to change the subject. 'I understand your father is still alive.'

A look of genuine affection warmed Rockefeller's cold face. 'Ninety and going strong.'

'Men live long in your family.'

'The lord has blessed us with many years.'

'Many years to break bad habits.'

'I beg your pardon?'

'You've been allotted more years than most to break habits you should break,' said Isaac Bell.

Rockefeller bridled. 'I am using my years for philanthropy – for all the good it's done me. They still think I'm a monster.'

'They think you're a bully. And they're right. But if you ask me, you've made a good start with philanthropy. I'd keep at it.'

'Would you, now? You are not familiar with business affairs, Mr Bell. You're like certain writers, theorists, socialists and anarchists – so ready to determine how best they can appropriate the possessions of others.'

'Good-bye, Mr Rockefeller.'

'You can't leave me defenseless. You took a job and signed a contract to protect me. What if Matters surfaces and tries to kill me?'

'I've assigned Wish Clarke to escort you home to Cleveland. There, your bodyguards will be provided by Van Dorn Protective Services.'

'Van Dorn? Are you going back to Van Dorn?'

'I never left.'

'What? You never left Van Dorn's employ?'

'Never.'

'You're still working up the Corporations Commission case! You tricked me.'

The trace of a smile moderated Bell's stern features. 'You are not familiar with detective affairs, Mr Rockefeller. It's my job to trick suspects. In fact . . . you could call it a habit.'

Rockefeller's eyes flickered as if he were trying to recall how much information he had given away. But when he spoke, all he said was, 'How long will these guards protect me?'

'Until you feel safe.'

'How will I ever feel safe from that murderer?'

'You will feel safe when he is hanged.'

'What makes you so sure he will be?'

'Another Van Dorn habit. We never give up.'

True to form, John D. Rockefeller did the unexpected. He laughed. 'That's a good one.' He thrust out his hand. 'I prefer friendships founded on business. I'm glad we've done business, Mr Bell.'

The grim atmosphere in the Van Dorn Detective Agency's New York field office reminded Isaac Bell of the night riots broke out in Baku. 'Himself' was back in town, Joseph Van Dorn, hulking like a bad-tempered sphinx in the back of the bull pen where Bell, who had just raced from the ferry pier, had summoned his assassin squad to bring him up to date.

Archie Abbott looked miserable and was sporting a black eye. The anxious glances he kept shooting at Van

Dorn told Bell that Archie had learned nothing about the Army deserter who won the President's Medal.

Grady Forrer, directing head of the gunsmith hunt, was watching Van Dorn as if the Boss were a rotund cobra.

Wally and Mack typically were not intimidated; the old guys had known Van Dorn too long and the self-satisfied Weber & Fields grins on their gnarly faces gave Bell hope. They looked more confident than their grasping-at-straws cable report about Spike Hopewell's so-called tricks up his sleeve. Maybe good news.

Bell glanced at Van Dorn and stepped out the door. The Boss lumbered after him.

'What's up?'

'You're spooking my boys.'

'Your boys aren't delivering.'

'Why don't you let me buy you a drink at the Normandie after I straighten them out?'

Bell returned to the bull pen alone.

'When I left for Baku, you were pursuing various leads on the Army sharpshooter, the gunsmith who improved the assassin's Savage 99, the exhumation of Averell Comstock's body, and the tricks that Spike Hopewell claimed to have up his sleeve. That no news awaited me in Constantinople or Berlin or Bremerhaven on my way home suggests unfruitful pursuits. Did the situation improve while I steamed across the Atlantic?'

Wally and Mack grinned. The rest were silent.

'Archie. How'd you make out with the general's daughter?'

'No dice.'

'Who gave you the shiner?'

'She took a swing at me.'

'Why?'

Wally Kisley laughed. 'The young lady took insult, misled that Princeton, here, was romancing her. Just when the spooning should commence, Princeton says he has business with her father.'

Archie hung his head. 'I misinterpreted her motive for inviting me to visit when he was out of the house.'

'Boom!' said Wally. 'Smack in the eye.'

'When I went back to try again, the butler said she was "not at home". So what I'm thinking, Isaac, is maybe it's time for me to get back to work in Chicago. Rosania is –'

Bell said, 'Write down her name and address for me.'

He turned to the head of Van Dorn Research. 'Grady. How did you do with Dave McCoart?'

'We've eliminated every gunsmith in the country except for two in Hartford and one in Bridgeport. But none of those fellows have panned out yet.'

'None of them ever worked on a 99?'

'None that admit it. I'm fairly convinced that the Hartford gunsmiths are in the clear. *Fairly* convinced. But the detective I sent to Bridgeport – a pretty good contract man we've used in Connecticut – was suspicious. But he could not shake the guy's story, and he was smart enough to back off before he tipped his hand. It will be worth sending a regular man.'

'I'll go,' said Bell. 'How did we do with the New York coroner?'

'He won't exhume Mr Comstock without a court order. The court refused on legalistic grounds that essentially came down to the judge's belief that an eighty-three-year-old should have been dead anyway.'

'But what about Mrs McCloud in the fire and her son in the river?'

'The judge expressed no faith in the likeliness of connections joining the Five Points Gang, the West Side Gophers, and the Standard Oil Trust.'

'Sounds like we need another judge.'

'The next judge concurred with the former's incredulity.'

Bell turned to Weber & Fields. 'Wally and Mack, you look pleased with yourselves.'

'Always, Isaac, always,' said Wally.

'It's hard not to be,' said Mack, and the two broke into Weber & Fields mode. 'A very pretty girl who was promised by refiner Reed Riggs that he . . .'

' . . . and therefore she . . .'

' . . . by extension . . .'

Bell said, 'Gents, I'm losing patience with your antics. *What did you find?*'

' . . . would be rich soon.'

'Riggs was an independent oil man,' said Bell. 'They all think they'll be rich soon.'

'Not like this. He told the girl that a certain party highly placed at Standard Oil was going to, quote, "Pungle up big". Not only would he get a bunch of money, his refinery would be bought with Standard Oil stock.'

'What certain party?' Bell asked.

'She wouldn't say.'

'Wouldn't or couldn't?'

'Wouldn't.'

'Why would this party shell out big money?'

'Blackmail. The girl said Riggs had something big on him.'

'Why would he tell a girl? Who was this girl? Where did they meet?'

'Miss Dee's on North Wichita Street, Wichita, Kansas,' said Mack.

'Arguably the finest "female boardinghouse" in the state,' said Wally.

'Which is saying a lot for a state that's home to Topeka and Kansas City,' said Mack.

'Not the sort of "ten-dollar parlor house" the likes of me and Mack could afford without Mr Van Dorn covering our expenses,' said Wally. 'But you of the silver spoon could be familiar with it.'

Grady Forrer rumbled deep and dangerously in his barrel chest, 'You are reporting that Riggs got drunk and bragged to a pretty girl in a brothel? A girl whose income depends on keeping you two happy?'

Mack Fulton returned a look of ice. 'Listen closely, young fellow, and one day you'll grow up to be a detective, too.' He turned back to Bell. 'The lady didn't think Riggs was bragging. She thought he felt guilty. Like blackmail wasn't something Riggs would do if he weren't pressed to the wall. He was having second thoughts when he fell under the train.'

'Are you sure about her?'

'Positive. She did not want to talk.'

'She was kind of sweet on Riggs,' said Mack.

'How'd you get her to talk?'

'We had to spend a full week at Miss Dee's,' said Mack.

'Never gave up,' said Wally.

Archie Abbott rolled his eyes. Grady Forrer furrowed his brow. Isaac Bell said, 'But after a week she still wouldn't tell you the name at Standard Oil?'

'That would be a job for younger men than we are,' said Mack.

'Archie,' said Bell. 'Go to Wichita.'

'Wichita? Sure you don't want to go, Isaac?'

'Get on the fastest mail train. Wire me the second you know whether Reed Riggs was blackmailing Bill Matters . . . Wally and Mack! Go find Matters' private railcar.'

'That'll take forever.'

'*Before* Matters makes it back from Europe.'

Bell put on his hat, pulled the brim low over his eyes, and headed out the door. 'Anyone needs me, I'll be at the Normandie.' It was time to tap the deep well of the Boss's experience with criminals and their crimes.

*

The Normandie Hotel's ground-floor bar at Broadway and 38th catered to out-of-town salesmen and the wholesalers whose warehouse lofts occupied the West 30s side streets off the hotel district. Joseph Van Dorn's corner table commanded the room, the long bar, and the steadily swinging saloon doors. On the table stood a bottle of whiskey and two glasses. Operating in affable-businessman mode, peering about benignly, the founder of the detective agency could be mistaken for a top salesman, a 'commission man' who paid his own expenses.

'If Riggs was blackmailing Matters, and if Spike's so-called trick up his sleeve was to blackmail Matters, does throwing John D. Rockefeller off the Orient Express make him our assassin?' he asked Bell.

'Matters was sitting in the same auto, three feet away, when the assassin shot me in Baku.'

'He could have staged it. Paid a rifleman to shoot, pretending he was the assassin.'

'That could explain why he missed an easy shot,' Bell said. 'But no, they're not the same man. Matters is the mastermind, not the assassin.'

'If I were you,' said Van Dorn, 'I would worry less about Matters than the assassin.'

'Bill Matters was gripped by a killing rage,' said Isaac Bell. 'I guarantee he will make his way home from Europe and attack again.'

Van Dorn shook his head. 'Matters is a business man on the run, not exactly his strength. The assassin is operating in a world he's chosen.' He splashed Bush-mills in both their glasses. 'Don't you find it curious we haven't caught him?'

'Yet,' said Bell.

'This killer has taken every chance in the book,' said Van Dorn. 'Shooting his victims in broad daylight. Shooting in public places. Staging elaborate scenarios – the Washington Monument monkeyshine was positively byzantine.'

'Clyde Lapham.'

'But hardly a singular event if you consider his shooting-duck trick and the killings of Reed Riggs and the poor fellow who fell in the oil vat.'

'Albert Hill.'

'Not to mention that woman who burned to death.'

'Mary McCloud.'

'And still we haven't caught him. Either he is the luckiest devil alive or we are the sorriest detectives alive.'

'There's another possibility,' said Bell.

'What's that?'

'He's not afraid of getting caught.'

'If he believes that,' said Van Dorn, 'he is crack-brained and we should have hanged him long ago. There is no "perfect crime". And certainly no string of perfect crimes. No matter how craftily they plan, things go wrong and criminals get caught.'

'This killer is not afraid. He's like the drunk who falls down but doesn't get hurt; never tightens up, just lands soft in a heap.'

'Maybe he's not afraid because he's nuts.'

Bell said, 'If he's nuts, he's a very slick nuts. Nothing fazes him. He never panics. Just changes course and slides away like mercury.'

'He would not be the first murderer without a conscience. Could it simply be that he's not afraid because he doesn't feel guilty?'

'Or can't imagine getting caught.'

'Delusions of grandeur?'

'It's almost as if he's enjoying himself.'

Van Dorn's eyes narrowed at the sight of a well-dressed gentleman who pushed through the swinging doors. He shot a glance across the busy barroom at the floor manager. The floor manager followed Van Dorn's warning nod, belatedly recognized the new arrival for the type of grifter who preyed on out-of-town customers, and guided him out to the sidewalk.

Van Dorn said, 'I want to know why the assassin takes such chances. Among others, he left his rifle – a unique weapon. Any progress tracing it?'

'I'm about to interview a gunsmith the boys found in Bridgeport.'

'Took them long enough.'

Bell leaped to his people's defense. 'They investigated eighty-four gunsmiths across the continent.'

'I was not aware there were so many. I've been stuck in Washington.'

Bell said, 'If the assassin is not afraid, maybe he *wants* to get caught.'

Van Dorn snorted like a walrus. 'Subconsciously? You've been reading that Viennese blather ... You know,' he added after a moment of reflection, 'there is such a thing as luck. Luck is real. For a while. So far, he's been lucky.'

'He's pushed his luck every kill.'

'*You*'ve been lucky. This man who had hit a dime at seven hundred yards has missed you three times. Why does he miss you?'

Isaac Bell grinned. 'Maybe he likes me.'

Van Dorn did not laugh but answered soberly, 'He won't miss if you ever manage to put his back to the wall.'

'When I do, I won't miss either.'

The underage probationary apprentice Eddie Tobin slipped quietly through the saloon doors. Van Dorn gave a brisk nod and the boy approached. 'Message from Mr Warren for Mr Bell.'

Bell slit open the sealed envelope and read quickly.

'Tell Mr Warren I said good work and thank you.'

Tobin left as unobtrusively as he had arrived.

Bell said to Van Dorn, 'Bill Matters made it back to New York.'

'What? How'd he get here as fast as you did?'

'The *Kaiser Wilhelm* holds the Blue Riband.'

'He was on your ship?'

'According to Harry Warren,' Bell answered, face grim.

'You never saw him? Where was he hiding? Steerage?'

'I had Rockefeller persuade the purser to show me the manifests. I walked the ship night and day. I checked every man in First Class, Second, and double-checked Steerage.'

'Did he stow away?'

'He did better than that, according to Harry Warren. He wrangled a job on the black gang. Sneaked across the ocean shoveling coal in the ship's boilers five decks under my nose.'

'Resourceful.'

Suspicion caromed through Bell's mind. Had Edna and Nellie brought him decent food or visited him or let him rest in their cabin? Not likely on a strictly run German liner. They allowed no mingling of the classes, much less passengers and crew.

'I gather from your expression,' said Van Dorn, 'that Harry Warren didn't arrest Mr Matters.'

'Matters brained a customs guard who spotted him sneaking off the ship. Harry Warren caught wind of it, traced him to the black gang, where he got a description from the engineers, and put two and two together.'

'So he's somewhere in New York.'

'Or boarding a train going anywhere in the country.' Bell stood from the table. 'I better warn Wish just in case he's headed to Cleveland.'

'Do you think he'll take another shot at Rockefeller?'

'He's had a week to stew while shoveling coal in a hundred-and-ten-degree stokehold. And he knows we'll catch him in the end. He'll want to wreak more damage than killing one man.'

'Wanting and doing are two different things. Like I said, Matters is a business man on the run. Even if he's a mastermind, being on the run makes him a fish out of water.'

'Until he joins up again with his personal assassin.'

33

Isaac Bell knew the great industrial city of Bridgeport well, having gone down to college in nearby New Haven. Bridgeport had provided Yale students carousing grounds beyond the long arm of the chaplain. More recently, he had bought his Locomobile at the company's Bridgeport factory.

He parked the big red auto in front of the Zimmerman & Brassard gun shop. The partners Zimmerman and Brassard had long since retired on fortunes made from the Civil War, leaving the shop to a talented apprentice with the business acumen to retain the famous name that was set above the door in gunmetal letters. He was middle-aged by now, a slight, precise man with a pencil-thin mustache and wire-rimmed spectacles.

'Mr Beitel?' asked Bell.

Beitel turned from the electric lathe, where he was working, and nodded. He was wearing arm garters to keep his shirtsleeves above his wrists and a four-in-hand necktie snugged under a shop apron. Physically, he appeared the opposite of the powerful Dave McCoart, with one exception: like McCoart, the casually able manner in which he hefted a cutoff tool said he was an artist, a man who could already see the shape of what he would fashion from the length of metal stock that was turning on his lathe.

His workshop was as neat and precise as he. It had a sturdy bench with drawers and a lip around the top to keep things from rolling off, several vises, a chest for small tools and parts, and a converted bedroom bureau with large drawers. He had just opened one, and Bell saw pistols waiting to be repaired, sandpaper, abrasive cloth, and steel wool. There was a power grinder with stones and a wire brush, a drill press, and an all-angle drilling vise for mounting telescope sights, a motor sander, and the long bench lathe where he was turning a rifle barrel.

'Good morning,' said Bell. 'I was at the Locomobile factory – ran into a little trouble on my way to Hartford – and they told me you were a particularly fine gunsmith, so I figured I'd stop on my way. My card. Jethro Smith.'

'Hartford?'

'Head office. My territory is in Oregon.'

'Who told you I was a fine gunsmith?'

'One of the mechanicians.'

'Really. Do you mind me asking which one?'

'The factory was a madhouse. They're all excited about the Number 7 auto they're entering in the Vanderbilt Cup. It's next month, coming up soon.'

'Oh, I know. Everyone in Bridgeport's planning to take the ferry over to Long Island . . . Which mechanician was it who mentioned me?'

'Let's see . . . His name's on the tip of my tongue.' It had been worth the six-hour drive through crowded towns to get his story straight at the auto factory. He snapped his fingers. 'Gary! Gary . . . Crisci. Know him?'

'Gary Crisci? I sure do. That is, I know of him. They say he'll be Number 7's mechanician. He's a top hand. I'm honored he's heard of me. What's your interest in guns, Mr Smith?'

'Rifles.'

'Are you a marksman?'

'I shoot in the occasional match,' Bell answered modestly.

'Where?'

'Out west. Oregon. My territory.'

'Are you looking to buy a rifle?'

'I need a telescope mounted.'

Bell lifted his carpetbag on to the counter and opened it. He watched the gunsmith's face as he pulled out the assassin's Savage 99 and methodically inserted the barrel into the chamber.

The gunsmith was no actor. But not even the great Edwin Booth could hide his feelings if the blood drained out of his face as it did from Beitel's, and Isaac Bell knew he had hit pay dirt at last.

'Are you all right, sir?' Bell asked solicitously. 'You look pale.'

'It's warm in here,' Beitel murmured.

'Warm subject,' said Bell.

The gunsmith took off his apron and folded it neatly on a chair. Bell extended the rifle. Beitel appeared to shrink before Bell's eyes. But he took the gun, cradled it a moment, and laid it on the counter. Then he turned around as if Bell weren't there and faced his lathe. He picked up a cutoff tool, fitted it to the tool rest, and pressed the bit to the stock turning on the machine. His hands were shaking. Sparks flew where the tool grooved the metal.

The motor whined as he adjusted a switch lever, gradually increasing the speed to two hundred revolutions per minute.

He looked up from the work and gazed slowly about the shop.

'I love this,' he said, addressing Bell over his shoulder.

Isaac Bell spoke very gently. 'I cannot promise, but it is possible that this could work out in such a way that you could keep your shop. *If* you help me find the assassin for whom you altered this weapon.'

'The assassin?'

The gunsmith bent closer to the work as if seeking refuge in a familiar task. He seemed so rattled, he didn't notice his loose necktie dangling close to the turning stock.

'Careful of your tie,' said Bell.

Beitel whispered, 'I love h –'

'What did you say?'

'*Go to hell!*'

Isaac Bell vaulted over the counter. He was twelve inches from the man when Beitel deliberately let his tie touch the rapidly turning stock. It grabbed the cloth, which wrapped around it faster than the eye could see, and jerked him down hard on the lathe. His neck broke with a loud, dry snap.

Bell switched off the machine. He hung Beitel's CLOSED sign in the window, lowered the front shades, and searched the shop thoroughly. When he was done, he telephoned the police. 'It looks like there's been an accident.'

'I've got a tough one for you, Grady,' Isaac Bell said when he telephoned Forrer long-distance from the Bridgeport train station.

'How tough?'

'The assassin's telephone number.'

Beitel's death had been no accident, and the assassin to whom Beitel had been so loyal that he had killed himself instead of betraying him had left no sign of his identity at Zimmerman & Brassard. But Beitel had not trusted his memory and had hidden on the back of a sheet of sandpaper a telephone number written so minutely that Bell needed a magnifying glass to read it.

Bell read it to Forrer. 'The Bridgeport operators don't know it. I don't want to telephone until I know who will answer and where he is.'

'It could take a while.'

336

'I'll be at the Sage Gun Company in two hours. If you don't know by then, wire me care of Washington when you do. And pass it straight to Archie, and Weber & Fields, Wish Clarke and Texas Walt.'

Bell shipped his Locomobile back to New York in a freight car and booked the first train to Grand Central. Hurrying across Manhattan to the ferry to New Jersey, he stopped at the Sage Gun Company on West 43rd, where he opened his carpetbag and handed Dave McCoart the Savage 99 and a narrow felt-lined box. McCoart removed a long, finely machined steel tube and whistled. 'Where'd you get this?'

'The assassin's gunsmith.'

'You can't buy a better telescope than Warner & Swasey.'

Bell handed him the Savage 99. 'Mount it on this, please.'

'I'll get right to it.'

'I found Beitel's notebook.'

It was bound in black leather. The pages were filled with drawings and formulas written in a precise, artistic hand.

'Turn to the end, last four pages.'

McCoart read slowly and carefully, tracing drawings with a blunt finger.

'What's he up to?' asked Bell.

'I think the guy is designing an exploding bullet.'

'Like an artillery shell?'

'In principle. But a heck of a lot smaller. I mean, this

could be chambered in a .303.' He glanced up at Bell. 'Like this Savage . . .'

'Do you think it will work?'

'If he's able to execute what he's drawn, yes. Judging by his quality work on this' – McCoart assembled the Savage's chamber and barrel with a flick of his wrist and broke it down as swiftly – 'the man is very, very good.'

He scanned the drawings again.

'Grisly imagination. A near miss with one of these would not be a miss. As for a "flesh wound", call the gravediggers.'

'More likely, the assassin's imagination.'

'Did he happen to say how far he's gotten with it?'

'He's dead. His lathe grabbed his tie. Broke his neck.'

'Damned fool wearing a tie around a lathe.'

'He meant to kill himself.'

'There's loyalty for you,' said McCoart. He handed Bell back the notebook. 'Well, at least he's not going to finish this awful thing.'

'I reckon he already has.'

'Did you find any fulminate of mercury?'

'Plenty.'

'Did you find any cartridges?'

'There are none in the shop.'

'Hopefully, he was still experimenting.'

'I'm not counting on that,' said Isaac Bell.

'Did he say anything?'

'He said he was in love.'

'In love? And he killed himself? Are you going to talk to her?'

'I couldn't hear her name.'

Like most upper-crust brothels, Miss Dee's ten-dollar parlor house on North Wichita Street was a hangout for politicians and prosperous business men. Compared to New York or Chicago, its setting was less than glamorous, on a street bordered by a lumberyard, a blacksmith, a foundry, gas storage tanks and tenements.

Wichita, thought Archie, where expectations were modest.

'Come right in,' the madam greeted him warmly. Wealthily dressed men made good customers. Handsome, wealthy customers with exquisite manners were a rare treasure. She remarked that she had not seen him before. Archie said he was not from Kansas. She said that she was not surprised and asked what in particular she could do for him.

'Would it be possible to make the acquaintance of a young lady named Jane?'

'Very possible, we have several Janes.'

Archie drew on Mack and Wally's description. 'Jane of hair as red as mine and eyes like lapis lazuli.'

'That Jane.'

'Is she still here?'

'Still here,' the madam said grimly.

'You don't sound pleased,' said Archie.

'She's tough on the business. The old geezers fall

hard for her. One of these days, fisticuffs in my parlor will end in a heart attack.'

'I hope I'll be immune,' said Archie.

'Frankly,' said the madam, 'I hope you fall so hard, you take her home with you . . .'

Archie popped the question on the train to Chicago, a city that the round and bright-eyed Jane told him she had always wanted to visit. Archie had promised a paid vacation and a shopping trip (at Van Dorn expense). If Mr Van Dorn balked, he would hit Isaac up for the dough. Any luck, Jane's gratitude would materialize as the name of her dead admirer's blackmail victim. Best of all, while in Chicago he could sink his teeth back into the Rosania case.

Archie waited until they were highballing out of St Louis before he asked about Reed Riggs. Jane's lapis lazuli eyes darkened, turning a sad, stony blue.

'Reed was a good man. A gent like you, Archie. Not fancy like you, but a gent in his heart. That's why he couldn't follow through. He was no blackmailer. It just seemed like a good idea to save his refinery, but when push came to shove he couldn't do it.'

'Did he ever actually approach the victim?'

'He told me he went to New York and talked to him.'

'At 26 Broadway?' Archie asked casually.

Jane laid a plump hand on the back of Archie's. 'Stay a gent, Archie. Don't try to trick me.'

Archie said, 'I understand that you would never

dishonor Reed Riggs' memory by betraying the name of the man he decided not to blackmail. But what if I told you that the man we think it was just tried to kill John D. Rockefeller?'

Jane said, 'Most people would think he had a pretty good idea.'

'And if I told you that we suspect he killed Mr Riggs?'

'Reed died in an accident.'

'It is possible it was not an accident.'

'Can you prove that?'

'I cannot *prove* it was murder,' Archie admitted, 'though we have a pretty good idea how the killer did it.'

Jane looked out the window. Her beautiful eyes had recovered their natural color and her spirits had risen. It was cheerfulness that the geezers fell for, Archie guessed, as much as her round shape. 'Archie, what you just said rings true. When Reed died, he left me the only thing he possessed. His decency. I hate to think of the poor man dying in fear. When they told me he fell under the train, I decided he had fainted.'

Archie said, 'If he was killed the way we believe he was, he never knew what hit him, or even saw it coming. One moment he was alive, the next he was not.'

'How can you know that?'

Archie described in detail the assassin's shooting perch that he and Isaac Bell had discovered in a Fort Scott train yard.

Jane turned from the window and touched Archie's

cheek. The conductor passing through the car noted their red hair and his stern face broke into a smile as he wondered, mother and son off to Chicago? More likely, maiden aunt and her favorite nephew.

'I will speak one name aloud,' said Archie. 'Only one. Can you please nod if he's the man Reed changed his mind about blackmailing?'

'Part of me wants to cover my ears.'

'No need,' said Archie. 'I won't say his name until you agree.'

'I still want to cover them.'

'I will say this. If it is who I think it is, then I can guarantee that Reed died just as I described and never felt a thing.'

She looked at him and believed him and Archie exulted. Jackpot!

34

'Bet you a duck I can hit four in a row.'

'Bet a duck? What are you talking about?'

'If I hit four ducks,' said the assassin, 'you give me one.'

It was too hot to stroll at the Hudson County Fair – ninety-five degrees even after dark. The midway was deserted except for ice cream stands and an enterprising kid selling chips of ice to press to sweaty foreheads. The heat made people cranky, and the owner of the shooting gallery, whose parade of moving ducks had attracted no gunfire for hours, was in no mood for jokers.

'You hit the duck, you win a prize. You win a cigar – if you're old enough to smoke 'em.' He peered dubiously at the short, slight boyish figure leaning on the counter. 'Or you get a dog.' He pointed at a plaster bulldog painted blue. 'You hit the duck four times, you win a teddy bear for your girl – if you got one. The duck's the target. You don't win the target.'

'Afraid I'll hit four?'

'You won't hit three.'

'For the duck.'

The assassin dropped a nickel on the counter for five

shots and fired three so quickly, the rifle bolt seemed to blur. Three moving ducks fell down and popped up. The owner nudged a hidden lever and the parade speeded up.

The assassin smiled, 'Faster won't save you,' fired again, and hit a fourth, then shifted slightly so that the barrel angled in the general direction of the man who owned the stand. 'Do I have any left?'

'One.'

'Give me my duck.'

A butler wearing the uniform of a United States Army orderly showed Isaac Bell into a reception room off the front foyer of the Mills mansion on Dupont Circle. Brigadier Mills' daughter, Helen, was every bit 'the looker' Archie had made her out to be – a tall, lean brunette with long arms, demanding brown eyes, and an intriguingly low voice.

Bell went straight at her. 'It is a pleasure to meet a lady with a famous left hook.'

A puzzled Helen Mills arched both her eyebrows.

'Should I duck?' asked Bell. 'I'm a friend of Archie Abbott.'

She looked Isaac Bell over, inspecting him closely. 'Only if the louse sent you to apologize.'

'I came on my own.'

'Are you on Mr Abbott's mission?'

'Mr Abbott was on *my* mission. And to be straight with you, it's your father, Brigadier Mills, I must meet.'

'What is the matter with you men from New York? Why don't you just call at my father's office? His bark is worse than his bite. He is actually quite approachable.'

'Not on this subject. It is deeply personal.'

'At least you're honest about it. Archie was misleading.'

'To be fair to my old, old friend,' said Bell, 'we must assume that when Archie laid eyes on you, he was swept off his feet and therefore not operating at his best.'

She did not appear to dislike compliments. She inspected Bell some more and smiled as if she liked what she saw. 'I'll make you a deal, Detective Bell. Stay for lunch. If you're still here when my father gets home, I'll introduce you.'

'What time does he get in?'

'We dine late.'

'You drive a hard bargain,' said Isaac Bell, 'but how can I resist?' It occurred to him that if Edna Matters wasn't whirling in his brain, and Nellie Matters not pirouetting on the edges, he might half hope that the Army would post Helen's father to Indian Territory for the weekend.

Helen's alto voice made her sound older than Archie had reported she was. Much older. She turned out to be a girl starting her second year at Bryn Mawr College. She admitted over lunch to being at loose ends about her future. But one thing for sure, she told Bell. She was determined to do more than marry and raise children.

Bell discovered that newspaperwoman E. M. Hock and suffragist Nellie Matters were heroes to Helen and her classmates; that he knew both women made him almost as heroic in her eyes. He offered advice, and before her father got home, he had convinced her to aim her studies toward a career even bolder than Edna's and Nellie's.

Brigadier General G. Tannenbaum Mills had fathered young Helen at a late age. Short, wide and stiff-necked, he looked old enough to be her grandfather but was in fact as vigorous as a longhorn, and as ornery. Helen made him a cocktail, and at her urging he invited Bell into his study. The walls were hung with swords, dueling pistols and Bowie knives.

Bell found it tough going trying to convince the old mossback that hanging a murderer was more important than shielding the Army from the embarrassment of a years-ago desertion. Mills repeated his argument in a voice trained to be heard over the thunder of a cavalry charge. 'The Army is a more fragile institution than civilians suppose. Reputation is all. To suffer a black eye and deliver that black eye to the president is —'

'Lieutenant K. K.V. Casey,' Isaac Bell interrupted.

'What?'

'Private Howard H. Gensch . . . Sergeant Clarence Orr.'

'Why are you — ?'

'They are marksmen.'

'I know that!'

'Lieutenant Casey won the President's Medal in 1903. Private Gensch won the President's Medal last year. Sergeant Orr won this year.'

'Why are you bandying their names?'

'Surely the United States Army isn't ashamed of such marksmen.'

'What do they have to do with Private Jones?'

'That's what I'm asking you, sir. Neither Lieutenant Casey, Private Gensch, nor Sergeant Orr are Private Billy Jones. Give your soldiers their due and help me hang a killer.'

'How?' Mills growled.

'Have you ever heard of a Standard Oil executive named Bill Matters?'

Mills put down his glass. 'I wondered if you would ask.'

'You know of him?'

'Oh, yes.'

Isaac Bell leaned closer, which put the veteran officer in mind of a cougar about to land on him with all four feet. 'Tell me how.'

'When we investigated Billy Jones' desertion,' Mills said, 'we discovered certain items the boy had left behind that we were able to trace – or so we thought. I went, personally, to the man that our investigation revealed was very likely Billy Jones' father. That his son had disappeared around the time that Private Jones joined the Army seemed to cinch it.'

'What "item" did he leave behind?'

'Ticket stubs from an opera house. Shakespeare shows. We traced them to Oil City, Pennsylvania.'

'Bill Matters lived in Oil City. He raised his daughters there before he moved to New York.'

'He still maintained a home in '02. For all I know, still does. Anyway, I found him in Oil City.'

'Why did you go personally?'

'I would not put the officers under me in the position of offending a powerful man who might well have had no connection with the deserter other than the fact he was grieving for a missing son who had run off back in '98 to enlist for the war.'

'Was the marksman Bill Matters' son?'

Brigadier Mills looked Isaac Bell in the eye and Bell found it easy to imagine him as a young officer leading his men into a storm of lead. 'I'm not proud of this,' he said, 'but it was my job to cover things up. I went to Matters' house. I spoke with him in private. He was alone there. I found him sitting in the dark. Mourning the boy.'

'In '02? But that was years after he disappeared.'

'He still mourned him. I promised that nothing we discussed would leave the room. I made my case. The cross-grained SOB refused to believe me. He was certain – dead certain – that the marksman was not his missing son.'

Bell said, 'Detectives run into similar denials by the parents of criminals.'

The general's answer was uncharacteristically

roundabout. 'I've led men my whole life, Bell. Gettysburg. The west. Cuba. The Philippines. I can read men. I know what they're thinking before they do. Bill Matters was telling the *truth*! The marksman Billy Jones was not his boy.'

'And yet?' Bell asked.

'And yet *what*?' Mills fired back.

'And yet I sense your, shall we say, disquiet? If not doubt?'

Angered, Mills looked away. He stared at his collection of weapons. He hesitated, face working, as if he was debating the merits of shooting Bell versus running him through. Finally, he spoke.

'Maybe you read men, too. You're right. Something was off there. I don't know what, but something was way off, out-of-kilter.'

'What?'

'Bill Matters knew that his boy was not the marksman. But he was not surprised that I had come calling.'

'What do you mean?'

'He was not surprised that I had connected him to the marksman who won the President's Medal of 1902. Even as he sat there in the dark denying the theater stubs were his.'

'Maybe they weren't.'

'I found him in a back parlor. He refused to leave the room or turn on the lights. So we talked in the dark. My eyes adjusted until I saw that the room was filled with toy theaters. You know what I mean?'

'Paper stage sets. You can buy them in New York theaters.'

'His parlor was full of them. But he sat there steadfastly denying that the theater stubs were his.'

Bell said, 'You seemed to be suggesting that Matters knows who the deserter is.'

'I am not "suggesting", I am telling you that Matters knew beyond doubt that the marksman who deserted was not his missing boy.'

'Why?' asked Bell. 'How could he know?'

'Either he knew exactly where his missing boy was in 1902 the day Billy Jones won the President's Medal or –'

'Or he knows the marksman,' said Isaac Bell.

The brigadier said, 'In my firm opinion, the deserter was not his boy. He is someone else.'

Isaac Bell was tumbling possibilities in his mind when he heard the old general say, 'And now, sir, what are your designs on my daughter?'

'Helen? I've already proposed an offer.'

'Proposed? The girl is barely eighteen. She's got college ahead of her.'

'I made every effort to convince her and she agreed to apply for an apprenticeship at the Van Dorn Detective Agency as soon as she graduates.'

'What the devil makes you think my daughter could be a detective?'

'Helen's got a mean left hook . . . Could we go back to reading men, sir? . . . I believe something is still on your mind. Something you've left unsaid about the marksman.'

Mills nodded. 'It's only speculation. I can't offer proof.'

'I'd still like to hear it.'

'I'd bet money that Matters was shielding him.'

35

'Are you sure you want to blow this all to smithereens?' asked the assassin.

'Sure as I know my name,' said Bill Matters.

They were standing out of sight of the street in a glassed widow's walk on the roof of The Hook saloon five stories above the Standard Oil Constable Hook refinery's front gate. Originally erected by a sea captain who made his fortune in whale oil, the widow's walk was festooned with wooden spires and elaborate bronze lightning rods fashioned like harpoons. Matters was safe here for a while, even with Isaac Bell closing in, for he owned the saloon lock, stock and barrel.

He could see the gut-churning proof that the refinery had prospered just as he and Spike Hopewell had dreamed it would when they built the first stage on the neck of land that thrust into New York Harbor north of Staten Island. After stealing it, the Standard had enlarged it repeatedly on the same lines they had surveyed. Orderly rows of tanks and stills covered the hilly cape. Seagoing tank steamers lined up at the oil docks. And the village had grown these last six years from a raucous boomtown into a jam-packed city of tenements and factories, shops, churches and schools – home to twenty thousand workers and their wives and children.

The assassin swept binoculars from the biggest naphtha tank across the city and up the tank-covered hill to the top of the tallest Standard Oil fire company tower, then back down the slope, over the rooftops, and back to the naphtha tank, which the red duck marked for a bull's-eye.

The heat had intensified and the humidity had thickened. Old-timers were comparing it to the deadly temperatures of '96, even the heat wave of '92 that killed thousands in the seaboard cities. It was stifling inside the widow's walk, and the heat shimmered so violently from the tanks that everything seemed to be in motion. It would take every ounce of the assassin's skill to calculate how it would bend the flight of a bullet.

'Would you consider disappearing instead?'

'I have disappeared. I don't like it.'

'What if I were to shoot Rockefeller?'

'No! Do not kill him. I want him to see this destroyed.'

'He'll build again.'

'He'll be too late. I invested in refineries at Philadelphia and Delaware and Boston and Texas. When I've blown Constable Hook off the map, I'll control seaboard production. I want him to see that, too.'

This was startling information. It was also deeply disconcerting, for to be surprised was to admit a severe lapse in the sharp awareness that made a hunter a hunter instead of prey. Bill Matters was reinventing himself. But this hadn't happened yesterday; he'd been reinventing all along.

'You're like Rockefeller,' the assassin marveled.

Bill Matters laughed. 'Master of the unexpected.'

'Then you'll disappear?'

'To Europe . . . in style.'

'May I come with you?'

'Of course,' Matters said without hesitation. 'I'll keep you busy. I'm not retiring, only starting over.'

Movement in the street below caught the assassin's eye. A strong man in overalls was rolling a wooden spool of copper cable. He disappeared below the overhang of the roof as he rolled it into the alley that led to the back of the saloon.

Matters asked, 'What the devil is that?'

'Copper wire.'

'I can see that. Where's he taking it?'

'The cellar.'

'How do you know?'

'It's for me.'

Bill Matters looked hard at his assassin. 'Now what game are you playing?'

'The unexpected. Just like Rockefeller. Or should I say, just like you.'

'*What game?*'

'Fast and loose.'

'With whom?'
'Isaac Bell.'

Heat lightning flickered repeatedly under a sullen midnight sky.

Gun in hand, Isaac Bell approached Bill Matters' private railcar on foot. It was parked on a remote Saw Mill River valley siding of the Putnam Division twenty miles from New York City and less than ten from John D. Rockefeller's Pocantico Hills estate.

Bell ignored the sweat burning his eyes and mosquitos whining around his ears. He walked on the wooden cross ties so as not to crunch on the railbed ballast. But the flashes from distant storms threatened to give him away.

Van Dorn Research had traced the telephone number Bell had found at the assassin's gunsmith to the private car platform at Pittsburgh's Union Station. The Pittsburgh field office had learned that the telephone in Bill Matters' car had been connected twice in the past six months to that platform. Wally Kisley and Mack Fulton had known which New York Central Railroad dispatchers to bribe to nail down its current location in Westchester County.

The detectives assigned to stand watch from a distance thought they had seen one figure enter the car hours ago just after dark. They had seen no one leave. Research procured Pullman Palace Car Company blueprints of the car's floor plan. Bell memorized them, ordered the detectives out of sight, and went in alone.

He saw a sliver of light shine through the curtains as he drew close. A chimney stack broke the smooth roof line silhouette marking the galley and dining room in the front of the car. Those windows were dark, as were the windows in the rear.

At fifty feet away, he heard music. At twenty, he could distinguish the words of the hit song 'Come Take a Trip in my Airship' playing on a gramophone.

The tenor Billy Murray was starting the last chorus. Bell sprinted forward to take advantage of the cover before the cylinder ran out.

> *Come take a trip in my airship.*
> *Come take a sail 'mong the stars.*
> *Come have a ride around Venus.*
> *Come have a spin around Mars.*

He climbed on to the rear platform.

> *No one to watch while we're kissing,*
> *No one to see while we spoon,*

He opened the door. The music got louder.

> *Come take a trip in my airship,*
> *And we'll visit the man in the moon.*

He was inside, back pressed to the door as he closed it quietly. This was the rear parlor, where the plush velvet seats could be converted to beds. He glided forward, toward the light, which was filtered by a curtain. The music was coming from the middle section, which the Pullman Company had configured for Matters as an office.

Suddenly a figure pushed through the curtain.

Bell slammed his arms around it in a vise grip.

36

A shriek brought Edna Matters bursting into the parlor with her .410 shotgun.

She saw Bell and lowered the gun.

'Thank God, it's you.'

It was Nellie in Bell's arms. He could feel her heart pounding fearfully. He let go. She gathered herself with repeated deep breaths.

'Hello, Isaac. We figured you'd show up. You could have knocked.'

'Our father is not here and we don't know where he is,' said Edna.

'Would you tell me if you did?'

'No, Isaac. We would not.'

Nellie said, 'Not until you understand that all he did was blow up in anger. Thanks to you, he didn't kill Rockefeller. You saved him from committing a terrible crime in a grip of rage. No damage was done. We are grateful to you for that. But does he deserve jail, considering all he suffered?'

'What happens next time when I'm not there to stop him?'

'It won't happen again.'

'Will his anger evaporate? I don't think so.'

'He'll get over it. He's not a cold-blooded killer.'

Isaac Bell said, 'He prepared a killing field. He opened the gangway connectors. He lured Rockefeller out there. He planned ahead of time how he would kill him. Any jury will call that premeditated murder.'

'It's Rockefeller's fault for cheating the poor man,' Nellie shot back.

'Father must have had a nervous breakdown,' said Edna. 'It all comes back to Rockefeller driving him mad.'

'I'm sorry, Edna, Nellie, but what he did in Germany was much worse than "blowing up in anger".'

'Would you accept him being placed in an asylum?'

'*Locked* in an asylum.'

'Where they would treat him,' Nellie said eagerly. 'With doctors. And medicine.'

'Maybe lawyers could convince a judge and jury to see it that way,' said Bell, 'particularly if he were to turn himself in. Do you know where he is?'

They shook their heads, and Nellie said, 'No. We honestly don't know.'

'Has he been here?'

'We don't think so,' said Nellie.

'What do you mean?'

'There's nothing of his in the car. We searched every closet and cabinet. Nothing.'

'How do *you* happen to be here?'

'We're using Father's car for headquarters,' said Nellie.

'Headquarters?'

'For the New Woman's Flyover. Don't you remember? I chartered a locomotive to move us to North Tarrytown in the morning.' And suddenly she was talking a mile a minute. The balloons, she said, were arriving from near and far. They were gathering in a hayfield she had rented from the owner of the Sleepy Hollow Roadhouse.

'For a dollar, Isaac, can you believe it?'

'I've met him,' said Bell. 'I can believe it.'

She barely heard him. 'Right next to Pocantico Hills! He *hates* Rockefeller. And he *loves* the idea of us soaring over his estate. He even persuaded the new village trustees to pipe gas out to the site – so we don't have to generate our own, which is wonderful, it's so much faster to inflate from mains – and he's invited the women to pitch tents, and he's opened the roadhouse baths to all of us. It's a delightfully civilized campground. Except for this infernal heat. But we'll rise above the heat, won't we?'

It was understandable, thought Bell, and a good thing, that she was hurling herself into the Flyover scheme to escape from facing her father's grim future. 'How about you, Edna? Are you ballooning, too?'

Nellie answered for her. 'Edna got a job reporting on the Flyover for the *Sun*. The editor was thrilled by her Baku story.'

'How did you happen to find the car?'

'Easy as pie,' Nellie said. 'This siding is one of Father's favorites. It's very pretty in the daylight and quiet. There's never much traffic on the Putnam Division. He calls it his cottage in the country.'

'And you found no sign at all of your father?'

'None. Poke around, if you like. But look what we did find.'

Edna asked, 'Do you remember when we were talking about my brother joining the Army?'

'Of course.'

'Look what we found,' said Nellie.

Edna said, 'I was flabbergasted when Nellie showed me.'

She took a leather pouch from a drawer and laid it on the desk.

'May I?' Bell asked.

'Go on, pick it up.'

Bell held it to his nostrils. 'Does your father smoke Cuban cigars?'

'No,' said Edna, and Nellie said, 'He prefers a two-cent stogie. Open it, Isaac. Look what's inside.'

It contained a medal, a fifty-dollar bill, and a sheet of fine linen-based stationery folded in quarters to fit the pouch. The medal was an extraordinarily heavy disk of gold engraved like a target, which hung by a red ribbon from a gold pin labeled 'Rifle Sharpshooter'. The fifty was a treasury note.

'Turn it over,' said Nellie. 'Look at the back.'

Bell saw that President Roosevelt had signed the back above the treasurer's printed signature.

'Read the letter.'

Bell unfolded it carefully, as the paper appeared weakened by being opened many times. The letterhead jumped off the page:

THE WHITE HOUSE
Washington

Bell's eye shot to the recipient's address on the bottom left of the page.

Private Billy Jones
Newark Seventh Regiment
New Jersey

He read:

My dear Private Billy Jones,

I have just been informed that you have won the President's Match for the military championship of the United States of America. I wish to congratulate you in person . . .

The president had closed:

Faithfully yours,

And signed in a bold hand:

Theodore Roosevelt

Nellie said, 'He has to be our brother, don't you think? Still alive in '02.'

'How did this end up in your father's car?'

'Billy may have hidden in the car when he first deserted. He knew the various places Father would park it.'

'He might have turned to Father for help,' said Edna.

'Would your father have "shielded" him?' asked Bell, deliberately repeating the word that Brigadier Mills had used to speculate about Bill Matters and the deserter.

'Of course,' said Edna, and Nellie nodded vigorously.

'Would your father have tried to talk him into going back?'

Nellie said, 'Father would have done whatever he thought was best for Billy's future.'

'Where do you suppose Billy is now?' Bell asked.

Edna said, 'I suspect he enlisted, again, under a different name. But if he did, maybe the reason we've heard nothing since is he died fighting the Filipino guerrillas.'

'I doubt he died in the Philippines,' said Bell. It looked to him that Brigadier Mills had read his man wrong . . . 'Could I ask you something?'

'Which one of us?' asked Nellie.

'Both. If this marksman Billy Jones is your brother, Billy Hock, could you imagine him turning his skill to murder?'

'Are you asking is our brother the assassin?'

'I am asking do you imagine he could be?'

'We haven't seen him in years,' said Edna. 'Who knows who he's become?'

'Could the boy you remember become a murderer?'

'No,' said Edna.

'Yes,' said Nellie.

'Why do you say yes, Nellie?'

'I knew him better than Edna. Isn't that true, Edna?'

Edna said, 'Yes, you two grew very close.' To Bell she added, 'So close that I was jealous sometimes.'

Bell asked again, 'Nellie, why do you say yes?'

'He was afraid. He was always afraid. So when you ask can I imagine him turning his skill to murder, I have to imagine him lashing out – first out of fear, then because lashing out banished fear, and finally . . .'

'Finally what?' asked Bell.

Edna echoed, 'Finally what, Nellie? How do you mean?'

'I don't know. I'm just speculating.'

'But you just said you knew him well,' Bell pressed, convinced she was on to something.

Nellie shrugged. 'What if finally lashing out banished fear? Then maybe lashing out could become . . . what? Pleasurable? Enjoyable? Something to aspire to.'

'We're talking about murder,' said Edna.

'We were talking about our brother,' Nellie said sharply.

'But who could find murder enjoyable?'

'A madman,' said Isaac Bell.

'We were talking about our *brother*,' Nellie repeated. 'We're *speculating* about murder . . .' When she resumed speaking, she made an effort to lighten her tone, as if asking with a hopeful smile could eliminate the worst possibility. 'What do you think, Isaac? You're the detective. Is our brother the assassin?'

'I can't sugarcoat it for you,' said Bell.

His sober tone stopped the conversation. Lost in private thoughts, they listened to the night sound of locusts singing in the heat. After a while, after mentally couching questions he knew that they could not answer, Bell rose abruptly. He found his hat and said good-bye.

'Where are you going?' asked Nellie.

'I have to catch a train.'

'Will you be back in time for my Flyover?'

'I'll do my best.'

Edna called after him. 'What do you mean by a "madman"?'

Bell stopped in the doorway. 'A person without conscience. Without fear.'

'Who "banished fear", like Nellie says?'

Bell answered, 'All any of us can really know about a madman is that he will be unpredictable.'

'If that's true, how do you catch such a person?'

'Never give up,' said Bell, but stepped into the night with his mind fixed on a deadlier device. Be unpredictable, too.

*

The houses on either side of Bill Matters' Oil City mansion looked abandoned. Their yards were overgrown, their windows blank. The garden in front of the Matterses' house was baked brown. The curtains were drawn, reminding Isaac Bell that Brigadier Mills had described Matters grieving in the dark. They could be closed against the heat. It was even hotter in western Pennsylvania than New York. The train conductor informed Isaac Bell with grim satisfaction that since weather traveled west to east, New York was soon in for 'the hinges of hell'.

No one answered when he pressed the buzzer button at the front gate. He picked the lock.

No one answered his knock on the front door and he picked that lock, too.

'Anyone home?' he called up the front stairs and down a hall.

He thought he smelled a faint aroma of cooked food and worked his way back to the kitchen. It was empty, with a single skillet of congealed bacon grease sitting on the range. He checked other rooms and found the parlor with the paper theaters that Mills had mentioned. As in the other rooms, the curtains were drawn. There was no Bill Matters sitting in the dark.

The kitchen door led into the backyard, which was as big as the gardens of a country house and concealed from the streets and neighbors behind high wooden fences and dense fir trees. It was then that Bell realized the neighboring houses on either side were empty because Matters had bought and closed them, then fenced them off and added their backyards to his. He could hear the surrounding Oil City neighborhood but not see it.

There was a ramshackle quality to the place. An abandoned wooden derrick lay on its side tangled in vines next to lengths of wooden pipe almost as if Matters was contemplating a museum of early Pennsylvania oil history. He walked around the derrick and found a pond, its water thick with algae. Beside it was a marble gravestone. No name was chiseled on the stone, only an epitaph, which Isaac Bell recognized as William Shakespeare's.

GOOD FREND FOR JESVS SAKE FORBEARE,
TO DIGG THE DVST ENCLOASED HEARE.
BLESE BE YE MAN YT SPARES THES STONES,
AND CVRST BE HE YT MOVES MY BONES.

From behind him, Bell heard, 'Shakespeare's not really buried here. The girls surprised me for my fortieth birthday. Raise your hands before you turn around.'

37

Isaac Bell raised his hands and turned around.

Matters was pointing his old Remington at him, and he was not alone. Rivers, the fit and remarkably unscarred old prizefighter, was holding a Smith & Wesson like a mechanical extension of his fist.

Bell addressed Matters. 'They say no man is a hero to his butler. You must be the exception if Rivers gave up a cushy job in Gramercy Park to join you on the lam.'

'Mr Matters gave me the cushy job when *I* was on the lam,' said Rivers. 'Fair is fair.'

'Are you a murderer, too?'

'The jury thought so.'

'I'll cover him,' said Matters. 'He's got a revolver in his shoulder holster. And if I'm not wrong, I think you'll find a derringer in his hat.'

'Reach higher and stand very still,' said Rivers. He pocketed his gun and took the Bisley from Bell's shoulder holster. 'Fine pistol!'

'Keep it,' said Matters. 'Detective Bell doesn't need it.'

Rivers stuck it in his belt with a grin.

Bell said, 'If you like that, wait 'til you see my derringer.'

Rivers knocked Bell's hat off his head. He snatched it from the grass, dipped into the crown, and removed the miniature, custom-built single-shot derringer Dave McCoart had lent him while he built him a replacement for the two-shot Bell had lost in Russia.

'Wow! You're a high-class walking arsenal. Look at this –'

Rivers had made two mistakes. In picking up the tall detective's hat, he had placed himself partly between Bell and Matters. And he had already let Bell distract him. In the split second before Matters could move to clear his field of fire, Bell kicked with all his might, rocketing his left boot deep into the prizefighter's groin. Then he dropped to the grass and reached into his right boot, drawing and casting his throwing knife in a single motion.

Bill Matters cried out in shock and pain. The heavy Remington six-shooter fell from his convulsing fingers and he stared in horrified disbelief at the razor-sharp blade that had passed between the bones of his wrist. The flat metal shaft quivered from the front of his arm and a full inch of the point protruded red and glistening from the skin on the back.

Bell picked up the Remington and brought it down like a sledgehammer on Rivers' skull as the gasping butler tried to straighten up. Then he whirled back at Matters and landed a blow with the old pistol that knocked the oil man flat.

He had one pair of handcuffs. He secured Matters to

an iron ring in the oil rig, took the guns from the unconscious Rivers, removed his whiskey flask and his bootlaces, dragged him forty feet away, and tied him to the rig by his thumbs. He returned to Matters.

'What are you going to do?' asked Matters.

'Take my knife back, to start,' said Bell. He yanked it out of his wrist, wiped the blood off on Matters' shirt, and sheathed it back in his boot.

'I'll bleed to death.'

'Not before you answer a heap of questions.' He screwed the cap off Rivers' flask and poured whiskey into the wound the knife had slit. Matters sucked air. 'Beats infection. Now, Bill, let's talk.'

The rage that Bell had seen explode on the Bremen boat train flared red-hot in Matters' eyes. Bell said, 'It's over. I've got you dead to rights. There is no escape. It's time to talk. Where is your assassin?'

Slowly, the fire faded.

'Where? Where is the assassin?'

'You're looking at him.'

'*You* shot your old partner Spike Hopewell? What about Albert Hill and Reed Riggs, and C. C. Gustafson in Texas?'

'Them, too.'

'Where'd you learn to shoot like that?'

'Hunting in the woods. I was a natural. Good thing, too. Bloodsucking bank foreclosed when Father died. The sheriff drove off our pigs and cows and turned my mother and me out of the home. We lived on the game I shot. Later, I ran away to the circus and a Wild West Show.'

Isaac Bell reminded Bill Matters that they had been sitting together in the Peerless with Rockefeller when the assassin fired at them in Baku.

'I paid a Cossack a thousand rubles to throw off suspicion.'

'Did you pay him to wound me or kill me?'

Matters looked Bell in the face. 'Wound. My girls were sweet on you. I reckoned it might turn out well for one of them.'

'No one ever denied you were a loving father. Did you arm the Cossack with one of your Savages?'

'I didn't have any with me. He used his own rifle.'

'Really?' said Bell. 'The 1891 Russian Army Mosin is about as accurate as a pocket pistol. The short-barrel Cossack version is worse – You were never the assassin. Why are you trying to protect a hired hand with your own life?'

'What hired hand?'

'It's not in your character to protect the assassin. You are not an honorable man. Will you look me in the eye and tell me you're an honorable man?'

'Honorable never put game on the table.'

'Then why are you protecting your hired killer?'

'There is no hired killer. I did my own killing.'

'And poisoned Averell Comstock and threw Lapham off the monument?'

'I did what I had to do to advance in the company.'

'You're trying, and failing, to protect a hired killer.'

'Why would I bother?' asked Matters.

'Only one answer makes sense.'

'Yeah, what's that?'

'The assassin is your stepson.'

'My *stepson*?'

'Billy Hock.'

'You could not be more wrong.'

'Your stepson who ran away and joined the Army.'

'I never thought of Billy as my stepson. He was my son. Just as both my daughters are my daughters.'

'Call him what you will,' said Bell, 'he became the finest sharpshooter in the Army. You made him a murderer.'

Matters' expression turned bleak. There was no more anger in him. 'My son is dead.'

'No, your son is your own personal murderer.'

'I *know* he is dead.'

'Your daughters don't know. The Army doesn't know. How do you know?'

'I found his body.'

38

The tall detective, who was leaning close to interrogate the handcuffed criminal, rocked back on his heels. He stared, eyes cold, mind racing. He paced a tight circle, cast an eye on the still-unconscious Rivers, gazed across the pond, and down at Matters. The man was as skilled a liar as Bell had ever encountered. And yet . . .

'If Billy was dead, why would Edna and Nellie tell me that he ran away from home and joined the Army?'

'That was my story. I told them that. It was better to let the girls think he died a soldier.'

'How did he die?'

'He drowned in that pond.'

'Here? In your backyard? But you never reported his death.'

'I buried him myself.'

'Why?'

'To protect the girls.'

'From what?'

'He committed suicide. The poor kid tied a rope around his neck. He tied the other end to a concrete block. Then he picked up the block and waded into the pond until the mud got him and the block dragged his head under. I saw his foot. His trouser leg had trapped air and it floated. Don't you understand, Bell? The girls loved him. The idea that he was so unhappy that he would commit suicide would destroy them. I know, because I still ask myself every day what did I do wrong? What could I have done better?'

'Spike said you were never the same after that.'

'Spike was right.'

'Why did you have Spike shot?'

'Spike wasn't as dumb as I thought. Or as "honorable". He figured out what I was up to, and when the Standard started breathing down his neck in Kansas, he threatened to tell Rockefeller that I was out to destroy him. He thought I could help him, that I could stop the Standard from busting up his business . . . Before you start blaming some other innocent, I repeat, I didn't "have Spike shot". I shot him myself.'

'No you didn't,' said Bell. 'You were a thousand miles away at Constable Hook at your regularly scheduled meeting with Averell Comstock.'

'I was not at Constable Hook. I was in Kansas.'

'Van Dorn detectives read it in Comstock's diary,' said Bell. 'You were not in Kansas the day Spike was shot. And before you cook up a new lie, Comstock's secretary confirmed that indeed you did show up for that meeting, on time, as always . . .'

Matters tugged at the handcuffs. In a bitter voice he asked, 'When did you start checking up on me?'

'We checked up on all the new men who were in a position to attack Standard Oil from within the

374

company. After you tried to kill Mr Rockefeller, we naturally focused full attention on you. Where did you bury Billy?'

'Right here.' Matters pointed at the headstone. 'Shakespeare's grave.'

Bell peered at the stone, imagining the sequence of events. The boy was dead. The headstone was already there. Matters dug a hole. The stone marked an unmarked grave.

Matters said, 'Funny thing is, he never wanted to come to the theater. Hated it. Poor kid never could fit in. Fidgeted the whole play.'

'You buried him right here when he drowned himself?'

'Like I just told you. You can dig up the poor kid's bones if you don't believe me.'

'I believe that you buried him. But I don't believe that he drowned himself.'

'He drowned,' Matters repeated doggedly.

'Drowning was the least likely method Billy would have chosen to kill himself. If he drowned, he was not a suicide.'

'He drowned.'

'Then someone murdered him.'

'I would never hurt him.'

'I believe you. But you found his body.'

'I told you.'

'Did the girls mention that I knew Billy slightly at college?'

'They told me you stood up for him.'

'As bullies will, they found his worst fear and used it against him. Do you remember what that was?'

'What do you mean?' Matters asked warily.

'The crew boys were throwing him in the river. Billy was rigid with fear. Absolutely petrified – he looked like his skull was popping through his skin – screaming he couldn't swim. They'd have pulled him out in a second, but he was so terrified of water, he couldn't see it was just college hijinks. *There is no way on God's earth that boy would have killed himself by drowning . . .*'

But even as he spoke, Bell remembered Billy's courageous attempt to conquer his fear by asking the crew to let him train to be coxswain. Could he have tried again and triumphed in a final deranged act?

Isaac Bell found himself staring intently at the Shakespeare gravestone.

'Did you say that Billy didn't like the theater?'

'Hated it.'

Bell could hear old Brigadier Mills thundering in his mind. *Ticket stubs from an opera house . . . Shakespeare shows . . . We traced them to Oil City, Pennsylvania.* The thunder shaped a bolt of lightning. Why would the boy keep ticket stubs to plays he hated?

'I asked why you didn't report Billy's death.'

'I told you. To protect the girls.'

'Which one?'

39

Which one?" Bill Matters echoed Isaac Bell.

'You're protecting *one* of your daughters. Which one?'

'What do you mean, which one?'

'Edna? Or Nellie? The one who killed Billy.'

'*Killed him?* You're insane.'

Not insane, thought Bell. Not even surprised, looking back. He himself had remarked on the New York Limited, *Strange how the three of us keep turning up together where crimes have occurred.* And when he engineered Edna's job covering Baku for the *Evening Sun* and the editor asked *Mind me asking which sister you're sweet on?* some sixth or seventh sense had already made him a sharper detective than he knew: *Let's just say that with this arrangement, I can keep my eye on both of them.*

Not insane. Not surprised. Only sad. Deeply, deeply sad.

Bill Matters was shouting, 'They loved him. Why would one of them kill Billy?'

'Because she's a "natural", to use your word.'

'Natural what?'

'Assassin.'

'She snapped,' Matters said quietly. 'That was the first thought in my mind when I saw them. She snapped.'

'Who?' Isaac Bell asked. 'Was it Nellie? Or Edna?'

Matters shifted his eyes from Bell's burning gaze and stared at the pond.

'Who?' Bell asked, again. 'Nellie? Or Edna?'

Matters shook his head.

'Who did you see?'

'She was out there. In the water. I thought she was floating on a log. 'Til I saw his leg. I leaped in, grabbed her, tore her off him. Pulled him out, dragged him on to the grass. He was incredibly heavy. Such a little guy. Deadweight.'

'Dead?'

'I held him in my arms. She climbed out and stood behind me. I kept asking her why. Why did you do it? She didn't deny it.'

'She admitted that she drowned him?'

'She said it was Billy's fault. He was a coward. Wasted his opportunity.'

'What opportunity?'

'Of being a man. Men are allowed to do anything.'

Bell realized he did not fully believe Matters. Or didn't want to. 'No one saw? No one in those houses?'

'Night.'

'You saw them.'

'Full moon. Lunatic moon.'

'Who? Was it Nellie? Or Edna?'

Matters shook his head.

'Which of your girls is innocent?' Isaac Bell demanded.

'Both,' Matters said sullenly.

'One is guilty. Is it Nellie, your blood daughter? Or Edna, your stepdaughter?'

'I love them equally, with all my heart.'

'I don't doubt that you do. Which is the assassin?'

'I can only say neither,' said Matters. 'Even if they hang me.'

'Oh, they will hang you, I promise,' said Bell.

'Your question will hang with me.'

Isaac Bell realized that if somehow the assassin were to stop killing and commit no more crimes, then he could spend the rest of his life wondering and never truly knowing which of them was the woman she seemed to be and which had been a murderer. But why would she ever stop? How many more would die before he caught her?

He was struck suddenly by a terrible insight. He saw a way, a way as cruel as it would be effective, to force Bill Matters to confess.

'There is no question you will hang, Bill.'

'I don't care.'

'The only question is, will the girl who hangs beside you be the right one?'

'What do you mean?' asked Matters. But Bell saw that he knew exactly what he meant. The blood had drained from his face. His jaw was rigid. His hands were shaking so hard, they rattled the cuffs.

'The only truth you've ever told is that you love both your daughters.'

'I do. I do.'

'Your assassin covered her tracks so cleverly that she could be either of them. Either Edna. Or Nellie. But justice must be done.'

'Hanging the wrong one won't be justice.'

'Sadly, justice makes mistakes. In this case, the better liar – the natural – will go free.'

40

Grim-faced Van Dorns in dark coats and derbies flanked Isaac Bell as he strode the grassy field across the road from the Sleepy Hollow Roadhouse. The ancient tavern was still surrounded by mud. The hayfield was a verdant, boot-pounded carpet under a multicolored fleet of gas balloons in various stages of inflation.

Nellie Matters' yellow balloon was the tallest, its bulbous top rising higher than the trees at the edge of the Pocantico estate. It was fully inflated, and she was ready to soar under a gigantic billboard for equal enfranchisement.

To VOTES FOR WOMEN she had added NELLIE MATTERS' NEW WOMAN'S FLYOVER almost as if to ask *When you get the vote, will you vote for Nellie?*

Other balloons were almost filled or half-filled, hanging odd rumpled shapes in the still air. The suffragists who had brought them had added the names of their states to VOTES FOR WOMEN and phrases aimed at Rockefeller in hopes of persuading the Standard Oil titan to put his influence behind their push to amend the Constitution to give women the right to vote.

Newspapermen and-women wandered among them, invited under the rope that held at bay the public, for whom a tiered fairground grandstand was provided. Typewriters pounded away on picnic tables in an open tent. Photographers swarmed, lugging glass-plate cameras on tripods and waving smaller Kodak instruments that allowed snaps on the run.

Bell spotted Edna Matters darting about in a white cotton dress and made a beeline for her. She had perched a *New York Sun* press card at a jaunty angle in the hatband of her straw boater and was jotting notes in a pocket diary. Seen from behind, the wisps of chestnut hair trailing her graceful neck could have belonged to a boy until she turned toward him and a smile lit her beautiful face.

'Hello, Isaac! What a day Nellie's made! Everyone came. Even the dread Amanda, in a scarlet balloon.'

Bell took her arm. Edna saw the Van Dorns. 'Hello, Mack, Wally. Lovely to see you again. You're just in time. They're about to soar. Nellie's going first, then the rest will follow.'

Bell said, 'The boys will escort you to New York.'

'What's wrong?'

'I am terribly, terribly sorry, Edna, but we have your father at our office.'

'Is he —'

'A doctor's patched him up. He's all right. I will hold off turning him over to the police until you have a moment with him.'

'I better get Nellie.'

'I'll get Nellie.'

He saw Nellie watch him coming.

She gave him a warm smile and a big wave, as if inviting him to join her.

It had been years since Bell's one ride in a balloon, but he recognized the working parts from her exuberant stories: the ten-foot-diameter wicker basket of tightly woven rattan; her bank of 'emergency gas' steel cylinders containing hydrogen under pressure that she could pipe into the narrow mouth of the envelope; the 'load ring', the strong circle that rimmed the mouth, holding the fabric open and anchoring the basket that hung from it; and the giant rope net that encased the towering gasbag.

The controls were simple: three levers on the edge of the basket were linked by wires to drop sand ballast to ascend or release gas to descend. The dragline to reduce weight and stop descent was coiled in the bottom of the basket. A fourth, red-handled lever was connected to the bank of cylinders of emergency gas.

Nellie was smiling in a shaft of sunlight that shined down through the fabric dome eighty feet overhead. She reminded Bell of a sea captain about to set sail – in command, confident, and alert. She stood with one hand inside her vest in the classic pose of Admiral Lord Nelson. Or Napoleon, he thought grimly. And he thought, too, that he had never seen her more beautiful.

She had high color in her cheeks and excitement blazing in her eyes.

Bell vaulted into the basket. The bask ropes – the shrouds that suspended the basket from the load ring – were quivering, vibrating from the power of the gas straining to lift it.

'Hello, Achilles' heel,' she greeted him cheerfully.

'What?'

'You're my Achilles' heel. Every time I try to shoot you, I miss.'

'If you want to be mythological, Nellie, say hello to your Nemesis.'

'Her, too. But if you weren't my Achilles' heel, you would be dead already. Somehow I could never bring myself to kill you.'

'Too late to change your mind,' said Bell.

Nellie drew her hand from her vest. Her pearl-handled derringer was already cocked. She aimed at Bell's heart. 'Don't get close.'

'It's over,' said Bell.

'Get out of the basket before I shoot you. You know I will.'

Bell moved toward her.

Nellie said, 'I will pull the trigger this second if you do not sit on the floor. Now! You will die and it won't change a thing and I'll still get away.'

'How far do you think you'll get in a balloon?'

'Last chance, Isaac. You're bigger and stronger. I can't let you close.'

He crossed his ankles and lowered himself into a cross-legged sitting position, poised to spring the instant she looked away. She loved to talk. It would not be hard to keep her talking.

'The wind is dead calm,' he said, 'you'll go straight up. When the gas dissipates, you'll come down within a couple of miles from here.'

'I will go higher and higher until I find the wind. The troposphere. The stratosphere. The exosphere! As high as I have to to catch the wind.'

'You can't breathe up there. You'll die.'

'The wind always swings west. My body will be blown out to sea.'

'Do you want to die?'

'How would you like to die in prison or hang, Isaac? Tell me.'

'First tell me something.'

'Anything, Isaac.' She actually seemed on the edge of laughing. 'What can I tell you?'

'Whose idea was it to kill for your father? His? Or yours?'

'I volunteered.'

Bell shook his head. He had tried to convince himself that her father had somehow coerced her. 'Why did he accept? His own daughter?'

'He knew I could deliver. He'd seen me in action.'

'When you murdered your brother?'

'Stop asking silly questions, Isaac. Ask something important.'

'How did you learn to shoot?'

Nellie answered as if telling a story she had read in a book. 'I ran away from home when I was fourteen. Like you. I joined a circus. Like you.'

'Your father told me the same story. The sheriff drove off his mother's pigs and cows. What's your excuse?'

She ignored the question. 'By the time Father found me, the trick shootist had taught me everything she knew. I had a talent for guns – steady hands and a keen eye. I can see farther than any human being. And I can concentrate; most people can't.'

'A natural?'

'As natural as breathing.'

'And lashing out to banish fear?'

'I'm never afraid,' said Nellie. 'By the way, I see you gathering your legs to jump . . . Don't!'

Bell made a show of relaxing his legs. 'Is that your rifle in the bag?'

'I'm at my absolute best with the rifle.'

'Loaded with explosive bullets?'

'Stop showing off, Isaac. Everyone knows you're a crack detective.'

'Who's it for?'

'Who do you think it's for?'

'Rockefeller.'

'For what he has done to my father, John D. Rocke-feller will pay with much, much more than his life.'

'What could be more than life, Nellie?'

'What Rockefeller loves most. Do you have any other questions, Isaac?'

He had to keep her talking. 'A young soldier was commended by the President of the United States for winning the highest shooting metal in the nation. Why would he desert the Army?'

'*She* saw no future in the Army.'

'There is a long, brave history of women serving their country disguised as men.'

Suddenly she was bitter, her cheeks taut, her voice harsh. 'I had no choice. How else could a girl win the President's Medal? I knew I was the best shot, better than any man. How else could I prove it?'

'But how hard it must have been fooling men in their barracks. How did you do it, Nellie?'

She was all too ready to boast and the bitterness dissolved. But she never took her eyes from him. Nor did her derringer waver as she demonstrated planting her legs apart, lowering her voice to mock him and the people she fooled: 'Manly tones; theater tricks like skullcap and wig, trousers, boots. A detective must know that men believe what they assume is true.'

'But why did this young sharpshooter desert?'

'She won the medal. Why stay? It was time to move on. I always move on.'

'Or was she afraid they would find her out? Just as she feared she would be found out when her brother was murdered and she joined the Army disguised as a boy?'

'She was never afraid.'

'After she learned that her father loved her so much, he would forgive her of anything . . . ?'

'Or refuse to believe his worst fear,' Nellie replied coldly. 'Even when he saw it with his own eyes, all he could say was how much he loved my mother.'

The derringer remained rock-steady as she hiked herself up to sit on the rounded edge of the wicker basket while clutching her carpetbag under her arm. 'Billy was only Father's stepson.'

'And your half brother, your own mother's child.'

'I never knew my "own mother". She died when I was a baby.'

'But why did you kill Billy?'

Nellie's eyes bored into Bell's. 'Lots of reasons, Isaac. He was such a coward. I was trying to get rid of his silly drowning fear. I made the mistake of confiding in him. I told him I was running away to join the Army . . . I loved him, Isaac. I loved him very much. But he would have ruined everything if he told. And I couldn't stand him being afraid.'

'How did you kill him?' Bell kept waiting for her to look away, but her eyes were fixed on his.

Suddenly the women in the nearest balloon called, 'Nellie! We're almost ready.'

She waved to them, the gun tucked to her side, neither turning her head nor taking her eyes from Bell.

'How could a girl drown a boy as big as she? Didn't he fight back?'

'He was groggy.'

'You poisoned him.'

'I didn't poison him,' Nellie said indignantly, 'I gave him a little chloral hydrate.'

'Chloral hydrate? That's knockout drops.'

'Just to calm him down. Not poison.'

'Calm him to kill him?'

'I was helping him beat his fear. I knew if he swam once, he could swim forever. But it didn't work. He was a hopeless coward.'

'Did he pass out? Is that how he drowned?'

'Aren't you listening, Isaac? He was groggy. He didn't pass out.'

'You drowned him.'

'He was a hopeless coward.'

'You drowned him.'

'Let's just say the chloral hydrate created an opportunity.'

'Was that how you drugged the old man who fell from the Washington Monument? Slipped him knockout drops?'

'Chloroform.'

'What did you feed Comstock?'

'Arsenic.'

'Where did you learn – ?'

'I worked as a pharmacist once. I've done lots of things, Isaac. I love different things. I was an actress for a bit. Every time I ran away, I found a fascinating job. I went back to the circus and became an acrobat.

For a while. I was a medical student, one of the first girls at Johns Hopkins. I didn't stay long.'

'Long enough to know your poisons.'

'And anatomy,' she smiled, reaching to touch the back of her neck.

Bell's hat flew from his head. Before it touched his shoulder his derringer filled his right hand, the barrel aimed at her face. He saw shock in Nellie's eyes but no fear even though she knew he would fire before she could. Still, she was lightning fast.

There was a part of Isaac Bell, the part that beat deepest in his soul, that held innocents sacred. Until this moment, that part could never have imagined triggering a gun at a woman. He knew full well that Nellie Matters was no innocent but a cold-blooded murderer trying to kill him. He pulled the trigger. He was not entirely surprised when his bullet missed her head by a full inch and broke a control wire that parted with a musical twang.

The close call caused Nellie to flinch and her shot whizzed past Bell's ear.

For a microsecond that stretched like an eternity, they stared at each other. His gun was empty. Her two-shot had one bullet left. He gathered himself to charge, reasoning that a wild shot would more likely wound than kill him. Nellie aimed the derringer directly at his face. Then she gave him a big 'Nellie smile'.

'I guess you missed because Van Dorn detectives

bring their suspects in alive? Or are you just a lousy shot?'

'You missed, too,' said Bell. 'Again. So if you can't shoot me and I'm not about to swallow poison for you, how will you stop me from taking that gun away from you?'

'*Gas!*'

She jerked the red emergency lever and held tight. The tanks spewed their compressed loads of hydrogen. The gas roared up the mouth of the already full envelope and the balloon lurched like a rogue elephant breaking its chains. Then Nellie pulled the ballast lever, releasing the total weight of the sand all at once, and somersaulted backward to the grass.

Isaac Bell sprang to his feet. Halfway out of the basket, he saw the ground vanish beneath him as if he were suddenly peering down the wrong end of a telescope.

The balloon was fifty feet in the air, five stories high, too high to jump, and soaring toward the clouds.

BOOK FOUR
Thunderbolt

October 1905
Constable Hook

The runaway shoots for the stratosphere

VOTES FOR WOMEN

41

Nellie Matters' runaway gas balloon shot skyward, lofting Isaac Bell toward the stratosphere where the air was too thin to breathe. The other colorful Flyover balloons, so enormous an instant ago, suddenly looked tiny, dotting the Sleepy Hollow field like a game of marbles. A white circle in the green grass marked the spot Nellie had dumped the sand.

Bell thought he saw her running to another partially inflated balloon. But with no ballast left to counteract the urgent lift of the lighter-than-air gas, he was too high up in another second to distinguish individual figures, so high he could see Rockefeller's estate spread to the Hudson River. He heard a locomotive and realized that the only noises were from the ground; after the initial roar of extra gas, the balloon was ascending silently. A New York–bound passenger train, the crack Lakeshore Limited, was heading for the North Tarrytown railroad station towing two black cars. They would be chartered by Rockefeller, who was returning from Cleveland with his entire family, and Isaac Bell had the momentary satisfaction of knowing that whether or not he got out of this fix, he had at least stopped Nellie Matters from shooting the old man this morning.

The only way to stop his wild ascent was to release gas.

Bell traced the control lever wires. The ballast wire that went down through the bottom of the basket was useless, as Nellie had already dumped every grain of sand. Of the two that went up into the mouth of the giant gasbag, one connected to a 'rip panel' at the top of the balloon. Nellie had explained more than once, while spinning her balloon tales, that pulling that lever would tear the fabric envelope wide open and release all the gas at once. It was an emergency device for instantly emptying the balloon when it was on the ground to keep high winds from dragging it into the trees or telegraph wires. To pull the rip panel lever at this height would be to fall like an anvil.

The wire broken by the bullet that had missed Nellie turned out to be the gas control. It had snapped inches above the lever. Looking up eighty feet, Bell could see the business end was still attached to the release flap in the dome at the top of the balloon. Parting while under tension, it had sprung up into the mouth. He could see it swinging inside the empty gasbag, tantalizingly near but infinitely far out of reach. There was no framework to climb inside the balloon – the gas pressing against the fabric envelope gave it shape – but even if it had a frame that he could improvise for a ladder, the gas would asphyxiate him before he climbed ten feet.

He jumped on to the rim of the rattan basket and shinnied up a bask rope to the steel load ring. Hanging by one hand, he caught ahold of the ropes that were woven into the enormous net that encased the bulging envelope like a giant spiderweb. Then he reached down for the knife snugged in his boot. He touched the blade to the straining fabric to slash an opening to vent gas.

He felt a breath of cool air for the first time in a week. The balloon had carried him above the heat wave into a cold current in the upper atmosphere, and he saw he hadn't a moment to lose. The patchwork of farm fields far below appeared to be moving. The blue line of the Hudson River was receding behind him. Wind that Nellie had predicted was carrying him east over Connecticut.

But just as he braced to press down on the blade, it struck him forcibly that there were vital aeronautical reasons why both the regular gas release and the emergency rip panel were situated at the top of the balloon. He drove his hand between that rope and the fabric to overcome the pressure inside it and pulled himself higher up by the netting ropes until he could brace his feet on the load ring.

Like a celestial giant climbing from the earth's South Pole to the North Pole, he worked his way up and out, hanging almost horizontally from the web, as the bulge of the globe-shaped balloon spread from the narrow mouth at the bottom toward the Equator.

He climbed some forty feet as it swelled wider and

wider. Then he climbed gradually into a vertical stance as he crossed the Equator at the widest part of the balloon.

When he glanced down, he saw the silvery waters of the Long Island Sound riddled with white sails and streaked by steamer smoke. He glimpsed the sand bluffs of the North Shore of Long Island and realized that the balloon had risen up into a more powerful air current. In its grip, he was traveling rapidly. And the balloon was still climbing. The farms appeared smaller and smaller, and the clusters of towns gave the illusion of growing closer to one another as it gained altitude.

Past the equatorial bulge, he was able to move faster, scrambling to get to the top, tiring from the effort, but driven by an arresting sight: the balloon was now so high that he could see the green back of the twenty-mile-wide Long Island and, beyond it, the deep blue waters of the Atlantic Ocean. If he didn't suffocate in the stratosphere, the ocean would be waiting below.

He reached the dome, the top of the gas envelope, drew his throwing knife from his boot, and plunged it into the fabric. In the strange silence, the hiss of gas escaping under enormous pressure was deafening. It blasted from the small slit he had cut. But he felt no effect, no indication that the balloon had ceased to climb, much less begun to sink. He dragged the sharp blade through more fabric, skipping over the netting, lengthening the slit, hunting the ideal size to reduce the lift of gas so the balloon would descend quickly but still float.

He felt light-headed. His foot slipped from the rope web. His hands were losing their grip. The knife started to slide from his fingers. The gas! He suddenly realized the gas was jetting past his face and he was inhaling it, breathing it into his lungs, slipping under the edge of consciousness. He ducked his face below the slit and held on with all his fading strength. It was getting worse. His head was spinning. He gathered his will and dropped down a row of rope netting and sucked in fresh air. When he could see straight again, he reached overhead with the knife and slashed more holes in the fabric.

There were thousands of cubic feet of lighter-than-air gas lifting the balloon. How much did he have to let out to make it sink? He recalled Nellie describing a fine line to calculate the balance between the weight to be lifted and the volume of gas. He heard a ripping sound and looked up. The fabric between the two slits he had cut was tearing, joining the slits, and suddenly the gas was rushing from the united fissure.

Bell's stomach lurched. He thought for a moment that the gas was making him sick. Then he realized the balloon had lost all buoyancy and was plummeting back to earth.

With no way to control the release, Isaac Bell's only hope was to climb down to the basket and throw everything over the side to reduce the weight dragging the balloon back to earth before it collapsed. Retracing his ascent, hand under hand, boot under boot, he slipped from cross rope to cross rope, down toward the middle bulge as fast as he could.

Was the bag less taut? No doubt about that. The fabric had ceased to press so hard against the net. He looked down. He saw the farms. He saw the silver Sound and Long Island shore. But the balloon had fallen so far that he was no longer high enough to see the ocean.

He lowered himself around the Equator and started the long horizontal climb down under the overhead curve of the globe-shaped envelope, hanging from the net, swinging hand over head, working his way into the vertical wall of the lowest part of the balloon, until he finally reached the load ring and slid down the bask ropes into the basket.

A farm spread under him, green fields speckled with black cows, a big sprawling house sheltered by shade trees, red barns, a pond, and round silos poking up at the sky like pencils standing on end. At the edge of the fields stood the darker green of trees, the wood lot. The Sound was no longer in sight.

Bell ripped the hoses from the steel hydrogen tanks and wrestled the heavy cylinders over the side, one after another, until they were gone. There wasn't much else to throw, but he was still falling. He hurled the dragline out of the basket.

For a moment, he entertained the fantasy of landing in the woods, where springy treetops might slow him down. But the balloon was aiming at the farmhouse. The shade trees might slow him down, but it was soon apparent he was not on course for the shade trees either. Quite suddenly he was directly over a barn. In another instant, he was close enough to distinguish roof shingles. The weather vane on the peak was shaped like a rooster. The dragline touched. Did it slow him slightly? He grabbed the basket ropes and braced for the crash.

The basket hit the roof, splintering shingles, and blasted through them into the hayloft. Bales of hay had no effect on the impact. The loft floor collapsed. The basket hung up in the rafters and stopped, abruptly. In the still air, the near-empty gasbag settled down over the barn.

Isaac Bell dropped from the bottom of the basket to the floor.

He was reeling to his feet when a red-faced farmer burst into the barn.

Bell took out his wallet. 'I will pay for your roof. May I use your telephone?'

'I don't want women voting!' the farmer yelled.

'What?'

'My whole damned barn says Votes for Women.'

'Do you have a telephone?'

'No.'

'Rent me a horse that can make it to the nearest railroad station.'

Bell wired the New York field office:

FIND NELLIE MATTERS?
GUARD ROCKEFELLER.

He caught a local train to New Haven and called the office on a Southern New England Company long-distance public telephone while he waited for an express. Nellie Matters, Grady Forrer reported, had escaped in another balloon.

'She can't hide in a balloon.'

'Night is falling,' said Grady. 'She can hide all night.'

'Guard Rockefeller,' Bell repeated.

'Rockefeller is safe. We've got an army around him.'

'I'll be there soon as I can.'

Long before the express pulled into Grand Central, Isaac Bell had a very clear idea of what Nellie Matters believed John D. Rockefeller valued more than life. When he got to Manhattan, he rounded up every Van Dorn detective in the city and chartered steam launches to ferry them across the harbor to Constable Hook.

42

'Hey, you!'

Nellie Matters closed her hand around the derringer in her pocket. She had almost made it home free to The Hook saloon.

'You! Stop right there!'

I belong here, she reminded herself. In the persona of her disguise, she had every right to be hurrying along this street that paralleled the chain-link refinery fence. But the man who shouted at her was sweating in the heavy blue, brass-buttoned uniform of a Constable Hook cop. She pitched her alto voice down to a range between a raspy tenor and a thin baritone.

'What's up?'

The cop cast a sharp eye on her workman's duds. Her wig, the finest money could buy, was a thick mop of curly brown hair barely contained by a flat cap. A narrow horsehide tool bag hung from her shoulder strap. A pair of nickel-plated side-cutting pliers protruding from an end pocket was supposed to be the finishing varnish coat on a portrait of a journeyman electrician. No one in the refinery city had challenged it until now.

'How old are you?'

I belong here! 'How old am I?' she shot back. 'Twenty-four next month. How old are you?'

The cop looked confused. She let go of the gun in her pocket and drew his attention to her tool bag by shifting it from her left shoulder to her right.

'Jeez. From behind, youse looked like a kid cutting school.'

'That's a good one,' Nellie laughed. 'I ain't played hooky since they kicked me out of eighth grade.'

The cop laughed, too. 'Sorry, bud. They stuck me on truant patrol.'

'Tell you what, pal. If your sergeant set a quota, I'm short enough to go in with you. But I can't stay long. Gotta go to work.'

The cop laughed again. 'You're OK.'

'I surely am,' she said to herself as the cop wandered off and she hurried to The Hook saloon. 'I am OK as OK can be . . . And how are you, Isaac?'

Isaac Bell sealed off the Constable Hook oil refinery with armed Protective Services operators commanded by Van Dorn detectives. He put white-haired Kansas City Eddie Edwards in charge because Edwards specialized in locking out the slum gang train robbers who plagued many a city's railroad yards. The company cops, whom the Van Dorns regarded as strikebreaking thugs in dirty uniforms, resented the invasion and resisted mightily until word from the Eleventh Floor of

26 Broadway reverberated across the harbor like a naval broadside.

'Mr Rockefeller expects every refinery police officer to do his duty by assisting the Van Dorn Detective Agency to protect Standard Oil property.'

Even before Rockefeller knocked the refinery cops in line, Eddie Edwards was glad-handing the chiefs of the Constable Hook Police Department, the refinery's private fire department, and the city's volunteer fire department. These savvy, by-the-book moves bore immediate fruit. Cops were assigned to guard every high point in the city where a sniper might set up shop. Standard Oil transferred battalions of extra firemen from other refineries. The ranks of the Constable Hook volunteers were swelled by volunteers from every town in New Jersey. Standard Oil tugboats from its Brooklyn and Long Island City yards arrived equipped with fire nozzles and were soon joined by Pennsylvania Railroad and New Jersey Central Railroad tugs and the Baltimore & Ohio Railroad's fleet from St George. Then a beat cop assigned to the high school truant squad reported encountering a short, slight, youthful electrician who fit one of the Van Dorn Agency descriptions of how the assassin might look disguised as a man.

'In the city,' Eddie Edwards told Isaac Bell. 'So short and skinny, the cop thought he was a kid. Near the fence. Not inside.'

'Yet,' said Bell.

Bell questioned the cop personally and came away fairly certain he had seen Nellie. Her breakdown 99 would fit easily in the electrician's horsehide tool bag the cop described. He wondered for the twentieth time whether she had gotten her hands on any of Beitel's exploding bullets. A few well-placed shots would set six hundred acres ablaze. Her presence confirmed exactly what she had told him. She was out to avenge her father by destroying what Rockefeller loved most. More than life, more than money, the magnate loved what he had built, and the Constable Hook refinery was the biggest thing he had ever built.

'Isaac!' It was Wally Kisley, out of breath. 'Found a duck.'

The cops exchanged baffled looks.

Bell and Wally headed into the refinery on the run. The Van Dorns blanketing the place under explosives expert Wally's guidance had discovered the shooting gallery target on a twenty-thousand-gallon naphtha tank.

'She's here,' said Isaac Bell. 'This nails it.'

'With her sense of humor intact,' said Wally.

The duck was high up on the huge tank, near the top. This one was painted red and stuck to the metal wall with a magnet. Electrical wire attached to its rail bracket ran down the tank. Nellie had concealed the wire artfully by snugging it against the heavy copper cable that grounded the tank's lightning rod.

'Can you disarm it without blowing us up?'

'I'll answer that after I find what she hooked to the other end of this wire.'

The two detectives traced it down the side of the tank to its concrete footing. Wally said, 'Nice job hiding the wire. Doubt our guys would have noticed if the duck weren't bright red.'

'She's showing off.'

The wire snaked halfway around the bottom of the tank, hugging its edges, and still paralleling the lightning rod ground wire until it veered across the oil-soaked ground and disappeared down a storm drain. Bell snapped his fingers. A husky Van Dorn Protective Services operative lumbered over with a toolbox.

'Lift the grate. Don't disturb the wire.'

The P. S. man inserted a crowbar in a drain slot and pried the cast-iron grate out of its seat. It was very heavy. Bell gave him a hand tipping it out of the way while Wally held the wire.

Bell wrinkled his nose. 'What's that smell?' he asked.

'Oil fumes.' The blistering-hot weather caused oil, kerosene and naphtha to vaporize. The air reeked of flammable gases.

'No, it's worse.'

'You're right. Like something's rotting.'

Bell said, 'I wonder how a hundred-pound woman picked up this grate. Wally, give that wire a tug.'

'I don't know what it's attached to yet.'

'I do. And it won't explode.'

'Then you tug it.' He stepped away and made a show of covering his ears.

Bell hauled on the wire. It pulled easily from the storm drain. 'There's what stinks.'

The wire was wrapped around a raw chicken leg that was putrefying in the heat. Pinned to the meat was a sheet of paper. Nellie had written, 'Hello, Wally. Give my regards to Isaac.'

'The lunatic is taunting you, Isaac.'

Bell looked up at the sky and pondered Wally's remark. Dark, anvil-topped thunderheads were marching out of the west, as they had every afternoon of the heat wave. 'Nellie is a lunatic,' he agreed, 'but she is one smart lunatic. If she's taunting me, she has a plan. I just don't know what it is yet.' Eyes still on the sky, Bell recalled Edna asking what he meant by a 'madman,' never realizing the assassin was a 'madwoman.' His answer to her was his answer to Wally now.

'Unpredictable.'

How to catch her? Be unpredictable, too? But there was the rub. What did Nellie Matters expect?

The infernal heat was finally her friend.

Nellie Matters was stymied by the combined presence of the Van Dorns, the Standard Oil cops, and the city police. Isaac – of course he rallied them, who else? – had robbed her of the high ground, every tower, every cupola, every hilltop she could use for a shooting blind. Her first choice, the remote fire department watchtower on top of the highest hill on Constable Hook, had cops guarding the ladder. So much for climbing with a pretty smile and a bullet for the lone fireman on duty.

Her alternate choice, the widow's walk on The Hook saloon, offered short-range shots at storage tanks above the city and the oil docks below. Close shots were doubly tempting with the heat cooking crazy, flight-bending thermals. But the widow's walk would be suicide. With a score of cops and detectives congregating at the nearby refinery gates, she could not escape.

The heat was her friend. Hot weather caused oil to vaporize. It charged the air with volatile gases. So what if Isaac Bell had stolen her high ground? Nellie Matters would play fast and loose. Get ready for the unexpected, Isaac. A surprise is lurking under you. Flamboyant, theatrical, showy Nellie Matters will take the *low* ground.

The heat boiled thunderstorms. Thunderstorms hurled lightning.

Lightning ignited the volatile gases that collected in the tops of oil tanks. Every tank at Constable Hook bristled with lightning rods because Rockefeller's ultra-modern enterprise obeyed the laws of physics that stated that lightning blew unprotected oil tanks to Kingdom Come. Those who challenged the law were directed next door to Bayonne, where lightning strikes a few years back had ignited fires that burned for three days and left the operation a shadow of its former self.

Nellie walked down wooden stairs deep into The Hook saloon's cellar. The walls were rough-hewn stone. Round tree trunks formed the beams that had supported the upper floors for two hundred years. The original brick sewer, disused now except to carry rainwater from the building's gutters, led under Constable Street into the storm drains that riddled the refinery hillside.

She was not prone to reflection, much less self-examination, but she knew that something different resided in her makeup that refused to be afraid. Which wasn't to say there weren't things she disliked, primary among them any threat of being restrained. To crawl into a three-foot-diameter drainpipe was to be restrained in the extreme. But she had no choice.

She climbed into it with her nickel-plated side-cutting pliers and the end of the cable she had had delivered on a spool. It unrolled freely as she dragged it through the sewer. She knew she was inside the refinery fence when the brick-walled sewer connected with the modern concrete drainpipe.

Dull light poured down from a drain. She had to pass another. The third was her goal, beside the twenty-thousand-gallon naphtha tank where she had left Isaac a target duck and a rotten chicken leg. The cable grew heavy as it got longer and dragged on the concrete. As she crawled under the second drain she heard thunder. There were two things she did not want to imagine: a sudden rainstorm that would drown her or a bolt of lightning striking the cable. She reminded herself that being electrocuted by lightning was much less likely than being drowned by rain because she had wisely waited to attach the cable to a lightning rod – four lightning rods, in fact – until the end was aimed at the tank and she was out of the drainpipe. The third grate appeared. Almost there. She heard another peal of thunder, closer this time. She crawled directly under the grate. Raindrops wet her face. She lifted the end of the cable to the grate and used the pliers to fasten it to the cast iron with a twist of wire.

Then she turned around in the cramped space and started crawling back to the saloon as fast as she could. The last thing she wanted was to be wiring the other end of the copper cable to The Hook saloon's ground wire when a thunderbolt struck the harpoon lightning rods on the roof of the widow's walk.

Isaac Bell was making the rounds of his men guarding the oil docks – the huge piers on the Kill Van Kull where the refinery was loading tank ships with kerosene, gasoline and naphtha – when a puff of icy air announced another squall sizzling in from the Upper Bay. In the middle of the tight little storm he saw one of his chartered steam launches heading for the dock. Its bow was weighted down by Grady Forrer, who stood gripping a coiled line and ignoring the rain.

Bell stepped forward, Forrer threw the line skillfully, and in a moment they were conversing in the partial shelter of a loading shed. 'One of my boys was rereading the assassin reports,' Forrer bellowed over the wind, the falling rain, and the huffing of several steam engines. 'He reminded me that we learned that Bill Matters was moving up the ladder when he was invited to join a Standard Oil Gang private venture.'

Thunder echoed down the tank-covered hills. A bolt of lightning lit the rooftops of the city. Another bolt blazed over the tanks above the city and landed harmlessly on a lightning rod.

'It made him one of the boys to partner up with Averell Comstock and Clyde Lapham, even though it was a sort of joke subsidiary.'

'What kind of joke?'

'Shares in a Constable Hook saloon.'

'Here?'

'Across from the front gate. They named it The Hook.'

Bell bolted into the storm.

Forrer raced alongside him, slipping and sliding on the oily path. 'Comstock and Lapham are dead. Matters is in jail.'

'Leaving Nellie to "inherit".'

Nellie Matters was finishing connecting the copper cable she had strung from the naphtha tank to the heavy wire that grounded the saloon's lightning rod. The thunderstorm raging outside was the biggest in days. The sooner she could let go of the highly conductive cable, the better.

'Hey, what are you doing?'

One of the bartenders had come down the stairs they'd been specifically ordered not to.

'What does it look like I'm doing?'

'What are you, an electrician?'

Her bag was open. The Savage and its telescope were in the bottom, still wrapped in their horse blanket. But tools were out. She said, 'You're not supposed to be down here.'

He finally recognized her as 'Eddie,' the nephew of the new owner.

'Sorry, Eddie. Where's your uncle? Haven't seen him around.'

'Went to Atlantic City to get away from this heat.'

'What are you doing?'

'My uncle wants this wired here.'

'What for?'

'Why don't you ask him when he gets back?'

'Something fishy's going on.'

'What are you talking about?'

'I had a job as an electrician's helper. That's a ground wire you're messing with.'

He grabbed her arm. 'Man, you're skinny.'

Isaac Bell left Grady Forrer far behind as he ran full tilt up the refinery hill, through the front gates, and across Constable Street. He had noticed The Hook saloon. It looked like an old sea captain's house with a widow's walk on the roof. He shoved through the swinging doors.

The barroom was empty except for a floor manager, who shouted from behind the bar, 'We're closed!'

'Where are the cops watching the widow's walk?'

'Home,' said the floor manager. 'We don't pay off cops to hang around – Hey, where you going?'

Bell paused at the foot of the stairs only long enough to turn the full force of his eyes on the man. 'Stay there, you won't get hurt.'

He bounded up three full stories, then into a sweltering attic, and up steep stairs on to the widow's walk fully expecting to find the assassin aiming her rifle. But the room was empty. Nellie was not in it. Thunder pealed. He stalked to the windows and glared out at the refinery. He knew with every fiber in his being that he was close. But she was not here.

A derringer slug in the shoulder had knocked the fight and the curiosity out of the nosy bartender. Nellie pointed the gun in his face, fished steel handcuffs from the bottom of her tool bag, and tossed them to him. 'Put one on your wrist.'

Stunned and disbelieving, he did as he was told.

'The other on the cable. Above, there, where it's nailed to the wall.'

'Hey, wait. It's lightning outside! It'll electrocute me.'

'Better odds than this bullet,' she said. 'Who knows if lightning will strike?'

'It hit yesterday. Twice last week.'

Nellie laughed. 'Didn't anybody ever tell you? Lightning can't strike twice.'

'It's the highest building on the street, higher than the tanks. It gets hit all the time. Why do you think they have four separate rods?'

'Bullet?'

He gave a terrified groan and clicked the manacle around the cable.

Isaac Bell racked his brain, trying to figure out what Nellie was up to now. Having the house right next to the refinery was a powerful opportunity. How would she use it if not to shoot from this brilliantly situated observatory?

Leaning a hand on the window frame as he gazed upon the storm, he felt a thick, rounded ridge on the sash. It looked and felt like it had been painted over and over for decades. But it was not made of wood like the rest of the room. Rope? No, cable. Metal cable. Still trying to winkle out Nellie's deranged thoughts, he picked at it idly with his boot knife and saw a gleam of brass or copper. He traced it up to the ceiling, out the wall, under the gutter, and on to the roof. He flung open the window, thrust head and torso into the rain, and swung gracefully on to the sill. There he stood to his full height with his back to the four-storey drop and traced the cable on to the flat roof, where it split into four separate strands. The strands went to the four corners. On each corner was a full-size bronze replica of a whaler's harpoon.

'Nellie,' he whispered, 'I underestimated you.'

Thunder pealed. Bell looked down and, as if he had conjured her with his voice, saw a slight figure hurry across Constable Street. It was her, carrying a tool bag long enough for her gun. Lightning flashed. Nellie stopped and looked up at the widow's walk. Their eyes met.

Bell shouted with all the power in his lungs to the Van Dorns at the gate, 'Get her!' A thunderclap drowned out his voice. Nellie blew him a kiss, and a bolt of lightning wider than a man plunged from the heart of the sky.

43

Ten million volts of electricity stormed down the ground wire, electrocuted the bartender manacled to it, and raged out the sewer and under Constable Street. Fumes from spilled oil were trapped in the refinery storm drains. These the lightning ignited. Fireballs shot from the drain grates. At the far end of the cable Nellie Matters had strung, the electricity jumped through the air and drilled a hole in the steel wall of a naphtha tank.

Isaac Bell heard the Standard Oil fire whistles chorus ghostly screams.

He staggered to his feet, vaguely aware that a thunderbolt had slammed him back through the windows. He had landed on the widow's walk floor. He knew he hadn't taken a direct hit; neither his skin nor his clothing was burned. But his heart was pounding, as if the immense surge of electricity passing so near had almost stopped it. His lungs felt half-paralyzed, hardly able to pump air, until he collected his spirit and demanded they get back on the job.

His vision cleared. He saw columns of flame fringed with black smoke.

In the refinery yard, fireballs danced jigs among the tanks.

Bell scanned the chaos below for signs of Nellie and quickly realized that what looked like chaos was orderly chaos. Thanks to the Van Dorn advance warning, the men running up and down Constable Street and dashing in and out of the refinery gates were moving with purpose. The company's firemen hurried through the yards, ringing bells and dragging hose. Blazing oil overflowed from a burning tank. Workmen moved swiftly to pump oil from tanks near the fire to distant empty tanks and into barges on the waterfront. Others dug trenches to divert burning oil from vulnerable tanks.

Nellie was gone. But Bell was convinced that she would not run from the fires she had set. She would stay and finish what she had started. She would not find it easy. Prepared for the battle, the Constable Hook refinery she was trying to destroy was the best defended in the world. It was fighting for its life but not yet desperate.

If Bell knew Nellie, that would not discourage her. The question was how would one woman alone continue to attack? He stayed on his widow's walk vantage point to find the answer.

A tank roof blew. Thick crude oil bubbled out. The side walls collapsed and a river of crude rushed down the hill. The black torrent split where the slope flattened. Some of it collected, forming a half-acre black lake. Shimmering in the heat, it roared spontaneously into flames. Globs of flaming tar flew in the air and landed on tank roofs. Firemen climbed the tanks with shovels and hoses. They extinguished the fires on all but one. It ignited with a roar and gushed smoke that the flames sucked in and flung at the sky.

The crude that continued to rush down the hill was flowing toward the waterfront. The river split again suddenly and the main branch rampaged on to the docks, caught fire, and ignited stacks of case oil. Mooring lines and tug hawsers were set alight, and as the flames consumed them, they parted, sending ships and workboats adrift on a tide of burning oil. The ships caught fire and burned swiftly. Flames leaped up rigging faster than sailors could climb. Tugboats raced to the rescue and batted flames down with torrents from their fire nozzles.

The second stream of oil veered below the docks and splashed against a three-storey hotel and restaurant on a pier in the Kill with a roof board that read:

GOOD NEWS CAFÉ

ROW, FISH, EAT DINNER, AND DRINK A SOCIAL GLASS

The oil ignited. Flame flashed up the restaurant's wooden walls. A man and woman in cook whites ran out lugging a cash register and a glass case of cigars. The burning oil encircled the building and closed in on the couple from both sides. They ran toward the water on a path swiftly narrowing. The fire chased them on to the dock to the water's edge, where they teetered, clutching their rescued treasures.

If I hadn't missed my shot at Nellie Matters, Bell thought, these people would be safe.

A B&O railroad tugboat swooped against the dock. Deckhands pulled them aboard. But the burning oil chasing them splashed off the dock on to the water. Floating, still burning, it surrounded the tugboat with a ring of fire. Six tugs steamed to its aid, fire nozzles pumping water to confine the burning oil while their stricken sister steamed away and wetting down one another's wheelhouses to cool paint bubbling in the heat. The tugs formed a cordon, spraying to prevent the fire from spreading on the water to nearby ships and piers.

After Isaac Bell saw the burning oil encircle the restaurant, and then the couple, and then the tug, he suddenly realized how Nellie Matters would attack next. He turned around and looked up the hill. The slope was a shallow incline and The Hook saloon was tall. He climbed out the window again and on to the roof of the widow's walk. From that vantage he could see over the city's tenement roofs. The swiftly expanding oil refinery had continued building higher up the hill. Tank yards and kerosene and gasoline stills were everywhere, below, around, and up behind the city.

Now he saw Constable Hook as Nellie saw it. He had

dubbed her 'heiress' to The Hook saloon, but, in fact, she was also heiress to her father's dream of building on a hilly cape an ultramodern gravity-fed refinery with access to the sea. The refinery that her father had envisioned and the boomtown that sprang up with it were one in her mind. If Bill Matters couldn't have the refinery, having lost it to Rockefeller, he would destroy it. Since he was locked in a jail cell, Nellie Matters would destroy it for him. By their way of thinking, the city it had nurtured and ultimately surrounded did not exist.

He swung back in the window and raced down the stairs and across the street to the gates. Wally Kisley was there. 'Did you see Nellie?' Bell asked.

'No. I was just looking for you. You OK?'

'We forced her hand,' Bell said. 'This wasn't her first choice, setting it off down here.'

'It's gonna be a record breaker anyway. Good thing the company doubled up on firemen.'

'If we hadn't blocked the high ground, she'd have attacked from up there. You can't see from here, but I saw it from the roof. A mammoth crude oil tank above the city.'

Wally nodded. 'Number 14. The first of the new crude storage tanks to feed the stills below. One hundred thousand gallons.'

'That's her goal – a Johnstown Flood of burning oil.'

Wally Kisley was incredulous. 'Why attack the city?'

'There is a deranged logic to her scheme,' said Bell.

'While everyone's trying to protect the city, she can concentrate on the refinery.'

He borrowed a police sergeant and a squad of local cops from Eddie Edwards' headquarters at the refinery gates. The cops led him and Wally on a shortcut past twisted ruins of burned-out tanks and through tank yards and stills. Firemen were deluging them with hose water to cool them. They entered the city streets, passing a school from which the children had been sent home and a hospital into which injured firefighters were stumbling.

Bell spotted Edna Matters, somber in black. She had an *Evening Sun* press card in her hatband and was taking down in shorthand the words of the rail-thin, harried-looking chief of Constable Hook's volunteer firefighters. 'Gossip that we refused to fight Standard Oil's fire is bunk. We are protecting twenty thousand people in our city – families, friends and neighbors.'

'Can you speak to the rumor that water is running so low that you won't have enough pressure to fill your hoses?'

'Bunk! We get our water direct from the Hackensack River and the Hackensack is wet yet.'

Three fire horses galloped past pulling a steamer pump engine and the chief jumped on the back. Edna closed her notebook. 'Hello, Isaac. Thank you for letting me see my father the other day.'

'Have you seen Nellie?'

'Of course not. If I had, I would have turned her in.

What could make her do . . .' Her voice trailed off. 'Whatever made Father do it, I suppose.'

Bell said, 'Be careful here, Edna. Don't let the fire get above you.'

The city streets ended abruptly at a shiny new chain-link fence. It had a gate manned by two cops. On the slope above the gate loomed Tank 14, which was painted white to reflect the heat of the sun.

'How could she miss?' said Wally. 'Big as the battleship *Maine* and twice as explosive.'

Freshly poured concrete footings were laid on both sides of the tank. Sheets of steel were stacked next to them, awaiting assembly.

'I need twenty strong men,' Bell told the sergeant.

'There ain't a man in The Hook not fighting the fire.'

'OK. Take four armed men, empty the jail, bring the prisoners here.'

'I don't think I'm allowed –'

Bell cut him. 'A champion sniper with a gun that fires exploding bullets is going to blast a hole in that tank by hitting it repeatedly in the same spot until one of them ignites a crude oil fire that will drown your city in flames. I need your prisoners to erect a barricade. Now!'

The sergeant took off at a dead run. Bell removed his coat and said to the others, 'Let's get to work.'

Wally asked him quietly, 'You're just guessing about those bullets, aren't you? Who knows if the smith actually made them.'

'*I* know,' said Bell. 'I found one in his shop. It looked like he had set up to run a batch of them. My only *guess* is that Nellie got the first batch. Knowing her, she probably did.'

'You *found* one? Where is it?'

'In my rifle.'

When night fell, the fires lighted Constable Hook bright as day, from Tank 14 on its highest hill to the Kill Van Kull waterfront, where flames were eating through the piers, consuming the sheds, and burning the pilings down to the waterline. An entire warehouse of case oil was fueling a pillar of flames visible from every point of New York Harbor, and a burning barge of oil barrels glared at Staten Island like vaudeville limelights.

Isaac Bell had still not seen a trace of Nellie Matters. But Tank 14 was shielded on all four sides by a hastily erected barrier of sheet steel. 'Now she can't pierce the tank by hitting it repeatedly in the same spot,' Bell told Joseph Van Dorn. 'And since it's on the top of the hill, there is no vantage point on the Hook – no hill, no building, no tree – high enough to shoot through the roof.'

'She'll shoot other tanks,' said Van Dorn.

'She'll start fires. We'll put them out. Eventually, she'll run out of ammunition and strength.'

44

Amanda Faire was bitterly disappointed.

The redheaded keynote speaker for the Staten Island Suffragette Convocation at the Cunard estate on Grymes Hill had expected her usual packed house rapturously chanting her catchy watchword 'Women's votes are only Faire.' But despite her appearance being advertised in all the New York newspapers, and her arrival heralded by a magnificent scarlet balloon tethered on the lawn, half the chairs in the lecture tent were empty.

'I'm afraid we lost some of our gentlemen to the firebug tourists,' apologized her mortified hostess. She gestured helplessly at the smoke-stained western sky. 'New York, Jersey City, Newark and the Oranges are all flocking to see the conflagration.'

'Well,' Amanda said, bravely, 'those who took the trouble to come deserve to hear me.'

'I'll introduce you.'

'I'll make my own introduction, thank you.' That was all she needed, a windbag driving the rest of the audience to the fire.

Amanda, who had positioned her podium so that her balloon created a striking backdrop directly behind her, stood to thin applause. As she opened her mouth to begin her speech, she could not help but notice a restive stir in the seats. Now what?

They were staring at her. Past her. Mouths were dropping open.

A woman cried, 'There goes your balloon.'

Nellie Matters never doubted the wind would be in her favor. Things always worked out that way. Just when she needed it, it had shifted south, blowing the red balloon north the short two miles from the Grymes Hill estate to Tank 14. From a thousand feet in the air, she could see what had burned in Constable Hook and what remained to burn. She was dismayed. The fires were going out. There was so much left untouched.

On the bright side, the Savage's magazine indicator read '5.' Five of Beitel's exploding bullets. *Her* exploding bullets. She had thought them up. She was their creator. The gunsmith had only made them.

Tank 14 would finish the job.

She spotted it easily, a huge white circle on the top of the highest hill on Constable Hook at the point where the cape met the mainland, smack in the middle of Isaac Bell's shield. Clever Isaac. But the thin roof of the tank was hers. She aimed dead center, adjusted for the balloon's swaying, and fired. Through the telescope she saw the bullet explode in a red flash. It didn't pierce the roof, but it must have weakened it. One or two more shots striking that precise spot should do the trick, and the little red flash would detonate the flammable gas in the top of the tank, which would ignite the ocean of oil below.

She fired again.

Bull's-eye! It hit the scar from her first shot. The powerful telescope showed a crack emanating from the scar. The next would do it. Isaac, where are you?

She looked about.

There you are!

He was leaning on the shield and pointing a rifle at her. Poor Isaac. I can't shoot you. But you can't shoot me either. What a pair we make. You better get away from the tank because it is about to explode.

As if he had heard her thoughts, he suddenly ran, crouched low, clutching his rifle. No, he hadn't heard her. The balloon was moving and he had to shift his field of fire.

'What's the use?' she whispered as she lined up her final shot. 'We could never shoot each other.'

Isaac Bell had one exploding bullet. He doubted that the impact of striking the balloon's thin fabric skin would detonate the gas. Nor would passing through the gas and the fabric as it flew out. If the shell could be set off that lightly, what would have kept it from exploding in his fingers when he loaded the rifle?

The only solid object on the balloon was the steel load ring at its mouth.

He found it in the telescope. It was almost too easy.

The telescope was so powerful and the rifle was so finely balanced and the balloon so steady in the light breeze. He could not miss even if he wanted to.

He saw a red flash where the bullet exploded. In the next instant, thousands of cubic feet of gas billowed into flames above Nellie's head. The balloon's skin melted, but it did not fall, as if the heat of the burning gas somehow pinned it to the sky.

Nellie looked up. Bell saw her whole body stiffen with terror.

The burning gas snaked tentacles of flame down into the basket.

He would not let her die that way.

He found her beautiful face in the telescope. He exhaled lightly to steady his hand.

He caressed the trigger.

45

One Month Later
The Empire State Express

Archie Abbott barely made the train, running like crazy to answer a last-minute invitation from Isaac Bell:

'I'll buy you breakfast on the Empire.'

When he entered the diner, Bell was already seated next to an exquisitely dressed gent about their age. Bell jumped up and intercepted him before he reached the table. 'Thanks for coming.'

'Of course I came. I've been worried. It's been a while. Since . . . well, you know what since. How are you, Isaac?'

'Keeping busy,' said Bell. 'Best thing when you have a lot on your mind.'

'Where've you been all month?'

'Back and forth to Chicago. Practically living on the 20th Century. Would you do me a favor?'

'Sure.'

'I'm stopping at Croton – appointment at Pocantico

Hills. Would you help that gentleman on to the Ossining train?'

'What's wrong with him? He looks fit.'

Bell handed Archie a key. 'You'll have to unlock him from the table.'

'Oh. Ossining. Sing Sing. Who are you taking to jail?'

'Laurence Rosania.'

'*Rosania?*'

Upon hearing his name shouted the length of the car, the Chicago jewel thief tossed Archie Abbott an elegant salute.

'Come on,' said Bell, 'I'll introduce you. High time you met.'

'Isaac! He was mine. I almost had him.'

'I just couldn't think of a better way to keep busy than to catch a jewel thief.'

'Of all the terrible accusations voiced against you,' Isaac Bell told John D. Rockefeller, 'I have never heard it said that you don't pay your debts.'

'You're implying I owe you something?' the old man said coldly.

'You owe me your life. Twice. Bill Matters in Germany and his daughter in Westchester. Not to mention most of your refinery.'

'I am disappointed in you,' said Rockefeller. 'You never struck me as the sort of man who would try to cash in on saving my life.'

'I'm saving another life.'

'What will this "debt" cost me?'

'You will pay me in full by granting Edna Matters an exclusive interview.'

'I never submit to interviews.'

'Speak to her openly and freely for as long as it takes and you and I will be even.'

Rockefeller sat silently for a time.

When he spoke he said, 'I'm told Miss Matters is in bad shape.'

'Very bad shape,' said Bell. 'She lost her father and she lost her sister. She loved them both.'

'A bitter man and a lunatic.'

'But still her father and still her sister. She is beside herself with grief and guilt and confusion.'

'Is interviewing me supposed to be some sort of rest cure?'

'It is my last hope.'

'That's all you ask?'

'That's all I demand.'

'I never submit to interviews,' Rockefeller repeated. 'You are demanding a lot.'

'She is worth it,' said Isaac Bell.

Isaac Bell drove Edna Matters to Rockefeller's Westchester estate.

They were building a fence around Pocantico. The man at the gatehouse said that a six-foot-high iron barrier twenty miles long would surround the entire property. There was talk of moving the railroad.

Gunfire echoed in the woods. The gamekeepers had orders to shoot stray dogs.

The fence caught Edna's attention. 'What happened?' she asked Bell. 'Has JDR gone mad?'

'He's afraid.'

'He should be afraid. He should hide in terror. He drove my poor father mad.'

The house where Rockefeller was living while work continued on the main mansion came into view.

'Stop your auto!' Edna cried.

Bell stopped the Locomobile. She was deeply upset.

'I don't know if I can do this,' Edna said. 'In fact, I know I can't. Take me back to New York.'

Bell held her hands in his and looked her in the eye. 'Why not?'

'I never suspected my father. I never suspected my sister. My own blood. Some "woman newspaperman" I am. How can I trust my judgment?'

'The richest, most powerful business man in the history of the world is offering a unique opportunity to a wonderful writer. No one else can do it but you. You owe it to history.'

'How did you talk him into it?'

Isaac Bell took Edna in his arms. He held her close for a long time. Then he whispered, 'I told Mr Rockefeller that he would never get a better chance to leave an honest account of himself.'

Epilogue

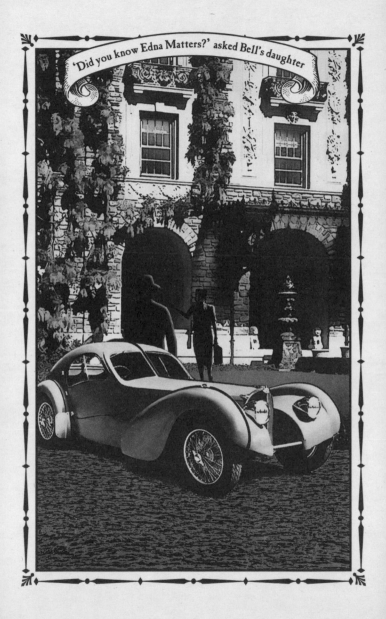

'Did you know Edna Matters?' asked Bell's daughter

Thirty-Five Years Later, 1940
Pocantico Hills, Westchester

Isaac Bell swept through the front gates of Pocantico Hills in a midnight-blue Bugatti Type 57C drophead coupe and raced up the long driveway. Silvered hair lent dignity to his natural elegance, but he still looked too rugged to be diminished by his years. If that threat hovered on time's horizon, it did not seem to trouble him.

The Bugatti, a roadster with sculpted lines as smooth as oil, rounded the final bend, holding the road as tightly as if on rails, and Bell stopped in front of a mansion. Well-proportioned and solidly built, the house looked like it had stood overlooking the Hudson River forever, although he recalled passing by in his Locomobile when the stone masons were laying its foundations.

'Daddy!'

A flaxen-haired co-ed bounded out the door, juggling a portable typewriter, a bulging briefcase and an overnight bag. The estate librarian followed with an armload of books. 'Come back anytime, Amber.'

'How did it go?' Bell asked in the car. 'Still want to be a newspaperwoman?'

'More than ever. The interview was amazing. I can't thank you enough for getting me in. I read every day and stayed awake half the nights typing up my shorthand notes. Rockefeller told E. M. Hock stories no one's ever read anywhere. No wonder they locked it up until he died.'

'Edna could get a rhinoceros to confess its life history,' said Bell. 'She'd have made a great detective . . . As would you.'

'I don't want to be a detective. I want to be a reporter like her. Did you know that when JDR was almost seventy years old, he personally negotiated a right-of-way for a pipe line across Persia right under the nose of the Czar of Russia?'

'I always wondered,' said Bell. 'Very little of it made the papers at the time. They were all worried about a revolution.'

'Did you know that he traveled to Baku with Van Dorn detectives for bodyguards?'

'That's an old Van Dorn legend . . . Did he happen to mention which detectives?'

'He told E. M. Hock he could not reveal their names in case they had to operate clandestinely on another case . . . Daddy, do you think Rockefeller deserved to be the most hated man in America?'

'What do the interviews tell you?' Bell countered.

'E. M. Hock wrote in her introduction that she had a personal prejudice because of JDR's business dealings with her father. Having admitted that, she then said that she thought he deserved to be the most hated man in America. But *he* kept saying everything he did was right. And he really seemed to believe it. What do you think?'

Bell said, 'He brought kerosene light to ordinary people, which allowed them to read and learn at night after work. He did it by imposing order on chaos. He thought he was smarter than most people, which he was. But he was not smart enough to know when to stop.'

'. . . Dad?'

'What?'

'Did you actually know Edna Matters?'

'Miss Matters and I were friends.'

'Friends?' His daughter's inquiring eyebrow arched as sharply as a miniature Matterhorn.

He ran up and down the Bugatti's gears while he pondered his reply. She would make a good reporter or a good detective; she was not afraid to ask hard questions.

'Before I met your mother.'

His fierce blue eyes took on a tinge of violet as he recalled trying to 'save' Edna from blaming herself for not seeing something that would have somehow given her the power to stop her father and her sister from becoming monsters.

Bell downshifted to pass a New York State Police car.

After the siren faded behind him, he let go of the

shifter to take his daughter's hand and answered with the authority of a man who had known since the 1906 San Francisco Earthquake for whom his heart was spoken.

'I think you know how I feel about your mother.'

'You're nuts for her.'

'From the day we met.'

He just wanted a decent book to read ...

Not too much to ask, is it? It was in 1935 when Allen Lane, Managing Director of Bodley Head Publishers, stood on a platform at Exeter railway station looking for something good to read on his journey back to London. His choice was limited to popular magazines and poor-quality paperbacks – the same choice faced every day by the vast majority of readers, few of whom could afford hardbacks. Lane's disappointment and subsequent anger at the range of books generally available led him to found a company – and change the world.

'We believed in the existence in this country of a vast reading public for intelligent books at a low price, and staked everything on it'
Sir Allen Lane, 1902–1970, founder of Penguin Books

The quality paperback had arrived – and not just in bookshops. Lane was adamant that his Penguins should appear in chain stores and tobacconists, and should cost no more than a packet of cigarettes.

Reading habits (and cigarette prices) have changed since 1935, but Penguin still believes in publishing the best books for everybody to enjoy. We still believe that good design costs no more than bad design, and we still believe that quality books published passionately and responsibly make the world a better place.

So wherever you see the little bird – whether it's on a piece of prize-winning literary fiction or a celebrity autobiography, political tour de force or historical masterpiece, a serial-killer thriller, reference book, world classic or a piece of pure escapism – you can bet that it represents the very best that the genre has to offer.

Whatever you like to read – trust Penguin.